BATHTUB

ADMIRALS

REVIEWS

Jack Hogan and Buzz Rucci are a couple of buddies in the modern U.S. Navy. They signed up to risk their lives defending their country, but instead they're risking their sanity playing at war in a series of military maneuvers and preparedness exercises. They are "bathtub admirals," performing meaningless excercises in the name of global peace . . . or something like that. In the spirit of Phillip Jennings' recent Nam-A-Rama (2005), or Joseph Heller's classic Catch-22 (to which Huber makes a brief reference, acknowledging his novel's pedigree), this is a witty, wacky, wildly outrageous novel that skewers just about anything you'd care to name, from military budgets to political machinations to America's success as the self-appointed guardian of the world. Considering the author, a career Navy man, has mostly written for military publications and Web sites (although he has turned out some short satirical pieces), and especially considering this is his first novel, it is a remarkably accomplished book, striking just the right balance between ridicule and insight.

—David Pitt, *Booklist*

Retired navy commander Huber's debut novel is a profane and hilarious parody of the post–Cold War navy. Huber's hero is Jack Hogan, a straight arrow trying to keep his sanity in a bureaucratic culture where connections and politics trump competence. Hogan's career appears bright during the waning days of the Cold War, but when the iron curtain crumbles, the "sandbox generals and bathtub admirals" are reduced to playing war, and Hogan's stock sinks while that of careerists like his friend Buzz Rucci rises. Huber is funniest when satirizing the bureaucratic infighting and petty rules ingrained in naval culture, but he also scores direct hits on feminism, politicians and the military's policy toward homosexuals. Populated by outrageous characters and fueled with pompous outrage, Huber's irreverent broadside will pummel the funny bone of anyone who's served.

—*Publishers Weekly*

BATHTUB ADMIRALS

A NOVEL

JEFF HUBER

KÜNATI

LARGO, USA

BATHTUB ADMIRALS

For information, contact Kunati Inc., Book Publishers in both USA and Canada.
In USA: 6901 Bryan Dairy Road, Suite 150, Largo, FL 33777 USA
In Canada: 75 First Street, Suite 128, Orangeville, ON L9W 5B6 CANADA,
or e-mail to info@kunati.com.

FIRST EDITION

Designed by Kam Wai Yu
Persona Corp. | www.personaco.com

ISBN-13: 978-1-60164-019-2   EAN 9781601640192
FIC000000 FICTION/General

Published by Kunati Inc. (USA) and Kunati Inc. (Canada).
Provocative. Bold. Controversial.™

http://www.kunati.com

TM—Kunati and Kunati Trailer are trademarks
owned by Kunati Inc. Persona is a trademark owned by Persona Corp.
All other trademarks are the property of their respective owners.

Library of Congress Cataloging-in-Publication Data

Huber, Jeff.
  Bathtub admirals : a novel / Jeff Huber.
    p. cm.
  Summary: "A fictionalized real-life tragi-comic take on America's rise to global
dominance based on an actual commander's experience with the U.S. Navy and his
often satirical or comic view of the politics of the bathtub admirals in charge"--
Provided by publisher.
  ISBN 978-1-60164-019-2 (alk. paper)
  1. United States. Navy--Fiction. I. Title.
  PS3608.U239B38 2008
  813'.6--dc22
                        2008000911

Dedication

For Tua, Denise, Carolyn and R.J.

FORECASTLE

★ ★ ★ ★ ★

During my time in the aircraft carrier Navy, "Fo'c's'le Follies" were a series of comedy sketches the air wing squadrons put on in the cavernous anchor room at the bow of the ship at the end of an at-sea period to make fun of each other and blow off steam. *Bathtub Admirals* is intended to be the Fo'c's'le Folly version of the U.S. Navy during the 1980s and '90s and is, to a certain extent, a chronicle of America's rise to the status of sole superpower.

Bathtub Admirals is not a tell-all book. Most of the major events described actually happened, but not the way I describe them. Names, places and identifying scars were changed to protect the author. Some things I remembered wrong, some things I remembered wrong on purpose. Some things I forgot entirely and was too lazy to do any research, so I remembered something new.

You "insiders" may or may not agree that this book fairly describes how America became, for better or worse, what it is today. If not, try and take a joke, all right?

ACT I
The Cold War

And Aweigh We Go

Monday morning, over coffee, Jack Hogan's lovely wife told him she'd filed for divorce.

"You're never at home," Liz said. "And when you are at home, you're always at work."

Jack shrugged. "It's my job to be at work."

"I'm not happy."

"What else is new? You weren't happy when I met you."

Liz pouted. "Then why did you marry me?"

Jack took a sip of coffee. "Could I have an easier question, please?"

Liz threw her prune pastry in Jack's face and stormed out of the house.

★　★　★　★　★

Tuesday morning, Jack's mom called. Doctors had found a tumor the size of a racquetball in his stepfather's head. They couldn't do shit for him, Mom said. That's not how she said it, but you get the idea.

She'd brought Joe home from the hospital, planned to take care of him to the end, like she'd done with Jack's real dad. "Can you and Liz fly out to Charleston and visit for a few days?" she said.

This sucked.

Jack had some important Navy stuff to do that he couldn't talk about with Mom. "If I manage to fence off some free time in, say, two months, will that be, uh, soon enough?"

"Do what you have to do," Mom said. "Come visit when you can."

★ ★ ★ ★ ★

Wednesday morning, Grandma called. Grandma must not have heard the good news about Joe yet, because she sounded chirpy as ever, glad to be out of the nursing home for a change, wanting to know how the big project to give her a great grandson was coming along. "You're the last boy to carry the family name," she said, "and I won't last forever, you know."

"Working on it every chance we get," Jack said. "And you have my personal assurance, Grandma; we'll stay on the job till we get it done right, to your exact specifications, one hundred percent guaranteed."

"Or my money back?"

"No, Grandma. We pissed away your wedding present money on a big party. You should have been there. The cops came by, lots of people went to jail—"

"Oh, stop it," Grandma said.

"Besides, you're already a great grandma. In fact, you're a tremendous grandma."

Halfway across the universe, in a small town in Illinois, Grandma laughed. Her Jackie. A regular comedian, just like his dad had been.

★ ★ ★ ★ ★

Wednesday night, Jack did what he'd done Monday and Tuesday night. He sat in front of the stereo he'd bought in the Philippines, listened to jazz, and made empty space out of the inside of a large bottle of cheap white wine.

★ ★ ★ ★ ★

Thursday morning, Jack woke up thirty minutes later than he needed to with a cheap wine hangover and hurled mighty oaths at the alarm clock he'd forgotten to remember to set. He shit, showered and shaved in three minutes. He'd done it faster. He dragged a comb across his hair, which he wore slightly longer than Navy regulations allowed, and squirted Visine in his eyes. He threw on jeans, running shoes, his old college football jersey, and a leather flight jacket. Standard civilian attire—for Jack, that is. Don't judge everybody by him.

In the kitchen, he took four Motrins and washed them down with a quart of Gatorade.

☆ ☆ ☆ ☆ ☆

The Ensignmobile—the 1980 Trans Am he'd bought new when he got commissioned—growled as he backed it out of the driveway. He still took good care of that car. Nine years old now, it looked much the same as it had when he bought it, except now there was a SICK EM BABY sticker on the back bumper. The sticker showed a muscle-bound cartoon cat with two tails, representing an F-14 Tomcat fighter jet, getting ready to jump off the wing of a smiling E-2 Hawkeye, the Navy's mini-AWACS. The Tomcat was the sexiest airplane in naval aviation those days. The Hawkeye—with its clunky, shoulder-mounted radar dome and turboprop engines—was not sexy at all.

Jack hated that sticker. The second he'd stuck it on the bumper after he got assigned to the E-2 training squadron out of primary flight school he wanted to take it right off again. But he was afraid he might pull some paint off the bumper if he did that, so he left it there.

Once on Interstate 15, he gunned the Trans Am south toward Naval Air Station North Island in Coronado, his head on a swivel, scanning for the California Highway Patrol.

You might think it impossible that Jack could drive that fast and turn his head like that with a force ten hangover. Keep in mind, though, that since days of Homeric legend, sailors have been known to drink a Cyclops under the table and still be able to haul ass.

The rent-a-cop at the main gate kept his seat and saluted the officer's sticker on Jack's windshield. Jack found a spot in the last row of the long-term parking lot. He snagged his gym bag—stuffed with books and extra underwear—from the passenger seat and locked the car. Bag in hand he jogged the quarter mile to the pier that berthed his ship, the aircraft carrier USS *Constellation*.

☆ ☆ ☆ ☆ ☆

On *Connie's* quarterdeck, five-feet-nine-inch-tall Lieutenant Robert "Buzz" Rucci flexed his bulging quadriceps and lifted his flattop uniform cap from his head. With the other hand, he massaged his flattop crew cut, his body builder's arm straining against the polyester short sleeve of his summer white uniform.

Standing these in-port watches sucked. Everything about being ship's company sucked. You were part of the crew, not part of the air wing. At sea, you didn't fly; you stood watches. Ashore, you were part of the ship's duty section, which was why Buzz was standing watch on the quarterdeck right now, instead of out on the pier, doing airline bottle shooters with the air wing guys. He'd give a gonad to be doing what he'd joined the Navy to do—flying as a radar intercept officer in the back seat of an F-14 Tomcat, staring at the back of some dip-shit fighter pilot's head.

Back in Aviation Officer Candidate School, where Buzz and Jack Hogan had been roommates, everything had been about the glory and glamour of naval aviation. They hadn't said anything about doing tours as part of ship's company, or standing quarterdeck watches. And they hadn't whispered a hint about how pissed off a young wife from a good family could get, once she got used to the easy life in a fighter squadron, when her husband became part of a ship's duty section and had to spend every fourth night on his ship when it was in port.

Which wasn't very often on this ship. This ship was usually at sea.

This was supposed to be a "career enhancing" tour of duty for Buzz. That's what his detailer at the Bureau of Personnel had told him. A chance to excel and break out of the pack.

Yeah, right, Buzz had told him.

No, no, the slime-ball detailer had said. Administrative assistant to a carrier's operations officer was one of the best billets he could get.

Well, okay. Buzz had qualified as a tactical action officer, in control of the ship's weapons from down in the bowels of the ship's combat direction center.

Just like what you do in the back of an F-14, the shit-stain detailer had said.

Yeah, right. Sitting in the dark in the ship's combat direction center, staring at radar displays. Like it must have been for Jack, flying in back of an E-2 Hawkeye. Not horrible, exactly, but not something you'd brag about to a girl you just met in a bar, either. Good thing for Jack he was a good-looking guy—in a kicked in the face kind of way—or he'd still be looking to round first base.

You'll regret it if you don't take this job, the douche-bag detailer had said. It's as good for your career as the assistant navigator job your old running mate Jack Hogan scored.

Yeah.

The quarterdeck phone rang. The navigator up on the bridge howled, "Where the fuck is Jack?" for the umpteenth time that morning. "If your buddy isn't here in five minutes, he'll be on report for missing ship's movement."

"I'll have him call you the second he comes up the brow, sir."

"You damn well better."

Fuck this, Buzz thought. Nothing more fun than being around to get bitched at about somebody who wasn't, then getting a phone slammed in your ear. The gator. What a prick. It must suck for Jack, having to work for that asshole.

But where the hell was Jack anyway? He'd taken a week's worth of leave prior to getting underway to spend some time at home with his babe wife. Jack and Buzz lived in the same neighborhood, up by Naval Air Station Miramar. They'd both bought houses there when they'd been assigned to Fightertown USA, home of TOP GUN, after their primary flight school tours. Jack's place was just up the street from his, but Buzz hadn't seen him in days. Did Jack decide to lock the front door and have a marathon fuck fest with Liz, and let this paltry shit about getting underway slip his mind?

Buzz coiffed his flattop again, wiping beads of perspiration from his scalp. Indian summer could get hot in San Diego. That's why they didn't switch over to winter blue uniforms out here until late October. But the weather would change soon enough, where they were going.

Buzz despised going to sea. He should have stuck with baseball. He could have had a great career in baseball, except he couldn't hit a curve ball. He couldn't pitch a curve ball either, or a slider, or a knuckleball. You needed big hands to pitch junk like that. You needed an arm to pitch a fastball, and Buzz didn't have one of those either. That's why his biceps were so big.

The only thing Buzz could pitch was bullshit, and he could pitch more of that than anybody knew how to catch. Except for one guy.

A big guy, six feet something with comic book shoulders, wearing a flight jacket over civvies like he didn't give a shit you weren't supposed to do that, coming yup-yup-yo across the parking lot and up the officers' brow.

"Reporting my return aboard, sir."

Buzz saluted him. "Jesus, Jack, could you have cut it any closer? The gator's been living in my ass all morning, asking where you were. He said for you to call him the second you got aboard."

"Thanks. I'll blow him off right away."

"How was leave?" Buzz said. "You let that babe wife of yours have her way with you?"

Jack winked. "That's about the size of it."

Buzz laughed.

Up the Rabbit Hole

Jack double-timed it across the empty hangar bay—the air wing wouldn't fly aboard until that afternoon—trying not to gag on the smell of metal and jet fuel that stank up every corner of the ship.

He slipped through a hatch on the port side. They called it a hatch; it was just a big door with a watertight fitting. He started climbing ladders. They weren't ladders, really. They were more like stairs. They went up at an angle like stairs, and had handrails like stairs, and had steps instead of rungs. They probably called them ladders because that's what they'd really been on old Navy ships, and when they switched over to stairs, they forgot to change the name. Or something like that.

He'd taken this route to his stateroom so many times that his head didn't have to think about where it was going, because his feet knew their way by heart. Pretty soon, though, his legs started bitching at the rest of him that the rest of him was making them work too hard.

Jack realized he'd gone up three flights-of-stairs-you-called-ladders too many. He slammed his gym bag against the wall you called a bulkhead, looked up at the ceiling you called an overhead, and begged God to spare him this shit right now. He turned around and started back down ladders. He tried not to think about why you called them ladders so he wouldn't go past the O3 level again (where his stateroom was), and keep on going until he was going down decks instead of levels.

Levels turned into decks when you got to the first deck, which was the hangar deck, also known as the hangar bay. Deck numbers got bigger as you went down—second deck, third deck, and so on. Level numbers got bigger as you went up from the hangar deck, except that as you went up levels, you used different kinds of numbers to count them: O1 level, O2 level, et cetera.

It was an easy system to keep straight in your head because it was all very consistent. Except that the flight deck was up on the O4 level. And you always called the floor a deck, regardless of whether you were standing on a deck or a level.

Jack didn't have a clue who had come up with the Navy's system for naming and numbering things. But he'd like to meet the bastard someday and put a boot in his ass because with all this interior monologue about why you called things what you called them on a Navy ship, he'd gotten himself all the way down to the hangar deck again.

This was just the sort of thing that happened when you drank like a whale for three days to get ready to go to sea.

He should be grateful, thinking about it. Being underway for two months would do him good. You couldn't drink alcohol on a U.S. Navy ship, so he'd get a good detox thing going. But he didn't want to think about his drinking too much either, because he didn't want to climb past the O3 level again.

Up at the O3 level, Jack got off the ladder and turned left, which, when you were on the port side, was forward. Port and starboard were easy to keep straight too. Port was left and starboard was right, unless you turned aft and faced the ass-end of the ship. Then everything turned ass-backwards, and port was right and starboard was left.

Right?

Jack made his way forward, reflecting that as ass-backwards as things on a Navy ship were, he understood them a damn sight better than he understood anything in the real world, where you called things by their right names.

In his stateroom, he threw his civvies and flight jacket on the lower bed, which you also called a berth, and sometimes a bunk, but that you normally called a rack. From a metal closet welded to the bulkhead, he pulled a fresh set of brutally starched khakis. He put them on the way he'd learned to from the Marine drill instructors at Aviation Officer Candidate School: the shirt (that nobody called a blouse anymore) first, then trousers (which real people called pants). The shirt tucked in neater that way. He slipped on tan socks and aviator's brown shoes, and looked in the mirror over the stateroom's metal sink.

Shit. He'd forgotten to pin his shirt shit on his shirt.

Come on Jack, he thought. Focus.

He draped the shirt that wasn't a blouse anymore over the back of his metal chair and jerked open the metal dresser drawer where he kept his shirt shit. Lieutenant bars went on the collar points. Nametag over the right breast pocket, dual-anchored naval flight officer (NFO) wings over the left. On the button flap of his left pocket, Jack attached his surface warfare pin.

He'd been all shot up about qualifying as a surface warfare officer when he'd wrangled his way into this assistant navigator job. You could count on one hand the number of Navy pilots and NFOs of his rank who were also qualified to drive ships. That might mean something to the ship drivers on his captain and admiral selection boards—if he made it that far before he pissed off the entire known universe.

He'd paid a price to earn the surface pin, though. Thousands of extra hours aboard the ship when it was home, studying engineering ⁀d weapon systems. Hours that Liz had loudly complained he ⁀ be spending with her.

⁀. Jack had been a naval officer for six years when he met ⁀ar Officers' Club. First thing out of her mouth when ⁀ anchored NFO wings was that cheesy crack about "non-flying officer." What a crack she turned out to be. He'd told her on their first date that he was a career man, and that the Navy would always come first. Maybe he shouldn't have told her that. Let her figure it out for herself. What he should have done was tell her to go take a non-flying fuck at a rolling donut from the get-go.

He buttoned the shirt, jammed its tails into the waistband of his trousers, and grabbed his flight jacket from his rack and his sunglasses and *Connie* ball cap from his metal nightstand. Sixty-two seconds later, up on the O-9 level, he breezed onto the navigation bridge, which you sometimes called the pilothouse, and flipped a two fingered salute at the Officer of the Deck.

"OOD, request permission to enter the bridge."

Under Way

The Officer of the Deck, Jack's roommate, Lieutenant (junior grade) Gary Constantine, flipped an equally half-assed salute back at him. Gary had the short, bald, flabby-ass look of a classic surface warfare officer. "Permission granted. Good of you to join us, Jackie. Better late than never, huh? You mind going over to the starboard side and getting that boss of yours off my back before he has an embolism?"

Jack looked to his right and caught the eye of the navigator, a squat, salt-and-pepper haired commander with a set of pilot wings on his chest and a sourpuss on his puss. The gator, sitting in his elevated, barbershop-style chair just aft of the navigation table, said, loudly enough for everyone on the bridge to hear, "Jack, glad you could make it. You know, they have these new things called alarm clocks. You should invest in one. They don't cost much."

Jack made his way starboard, twisting his shoulders through the swarm of watch standers, safety observers, and lookie-loos that always overpopulated the bridge when *Connie* got underway.

"I'll put one on my shopping list, Gator. What do they look like?"

That got a guffaw from all the enlisted men. Funny guy, that Mister Hogan. Frosted the gator's ass with that one, didn't he?

Jack took station at the navigation table next to wiry, mustachioed Chief Petty Officer Kirk, the senior enlisted quartermaster in the navigation department, who reeked of cheap pipe tobacco he'd no doubt just consumed in the small office behind the bridge that he and Jack shared.

"You ready to do this, Mister H?"

"I was born ready, Chief. The Compass Kids all set?"

The Compass Kids were junior enlisted men assigned to shoot visual navigation bearings as the ship transited the channel on its way out to sea.

Chief Kirk nodded. "Everybody's on station, sir, all compass repeaters check four-oh." In Jack's ear, he whispered, "About that alarm clock crack, sir. I don't recommend pitching the gator too much shit this morning. He ain't the happiest camper in the trailer park right now. The captain's been whipping him like a stepchild all morning."

Jack took the sunglasses from the map pocket of his flight jacket and slid them over his face. "At least the morning fog has burned off, Chief. The Kids should see all their landmarks." He pointed out the bridge windscreen. "Look, up in the sky…"

Across the channel, a Boeing 707 with UNITED AIRLINES smeared all over it skimmed the skyscrapers as it made its final approach to San Diego International.

"Couldn't ask for a prettier day to go to sea," Chief Kirk said.

"No," Jack said, and, making sure the gator wasn't listening, he whispered, "Don't worry about the captain and the gator and the rest of the elephants, Chief. Just stay out of their way so they don't step on you. We'll hose their shit over the side once we're out to sea."

"Roger that," Chief Kirk said. "Hey, speaking of which ..." He looked at his watch, tapped it, held it to his ear and looked at it again. "It's about that time, and I don't see nobody moving in that direction." He tapped the watch again, like that would do a shit bit of good if the watch had anything wrong with it. It was a digital plastic Jap job, like everybody else's watch was.

Jack looked across the bridge at Gary, who stood next to the captain's chair. "Officer of the Deck, are we ready to get under way?"

Over on the port side, Gary cocked his head a quarter turn in the direction of the captain and shrugged. Captain Julius "Zach" Taylor, slim, steely eyed and closely shorn, sat in a raised chair identical to the gator's, his legs crossed at the knees, his back twisted, his left elbow on an armrest, the forefinger and thumb of his left hand covering his mouth.

On the starboard side, Jack turned to the gator. "What's up with the captain?"

The gator leaned forward. "He's had a cork up his blow hole for three days. I figure his wife must have cut him off, or he didn't pick up admiral this time around. Or both."

"Is he going to snap out of it so we can get under way?"

"I'll get this turd rolling." The gator swiveled his chair toward the port side and sang out, "Captain, all checklists for getting under way are complete, the ship is ready for sea."

On the port side, Gary saluted Zach Taylor. "Captain, request permission to cast off all lines."

Zach Taylor started, glanced at his Jap job, and spun on Gary. "Christ yes, cast off all lines. How the hell else are we going to get under way?"

Gary passed the word via walkie-talkie. From the starboard side, sailors drew in mooring lines from the pier. Four tugboats eased the ship toward the turning basin. On the bridge, the duty bosun mate sounded one prolonged, throaty blast of the ship's whistle, shattering picture windows halfway across Coronado Island, which the Department of the Navy would pay to have replaced.

The tugs pointed *Connie*'s bow toward the channel. The conning officer, a skinny ensign fresh out of Surface Warfare Officer School, blurted in a cracked alto voice, "All engines ahead one third."

Jack donned a headset that put him in communication with the Compass Kids, who were stationed on the open-air signal bridge just above the pilothouse. "Here we go, guys," he said. "We'll start taking one-minute fixes in thirty seconds. Everybody have your landmark?"

"Port, aye."

"Starboard, aye."

"Aft, aye."

"Fifteen seconds. Ten. Five. Standby. Mark."

Jack wrote the reported bearings in a logbook and repeated them to the chief. Faster than the unpracticed eye could follow, Chief Kirk's hands manipulated a compass arm, a spacer and a pencil across the chart taped to the top of the navigation table. "On track, excellent fix."

Jack, hovering over the chief to double-check his accuracy, said, "Concur. In fact, it's a tremendous fix, Chief." He announced, "Conning Officer, based on a tremendous fix, navigation holds the ship on track."

Officially, there was no such thing as a "tremendous fix," but Jack pulled non-standard crap like that all the time, so nobody noticed.

"Very well," Stick Boy the conning officer croaked.

Zach Taylor, standing next to Stick Boy in front of the helm console in the middle of the bridge now, turned to the harbor pilot. "I think we're a foot right of course."

The harbor pilot, an ancient, heavy civilian in a wrinkled blue blazer said, "We're okay for now."

Stick Boy, uncomfortable at being under Zach Taylor's close

scrutiny, said, "What should I do, Captain?"

Zach grimaced. "Hold what you got for now. What little you got."

"Aye, aye, sir." Stick Boy didn't get the dig about "hold what little you got." It implied that you had a small penis and your balls hadn't dropped yet. Which in Stick Boy's case was true.

Jack saw a smirk growing on the face of Petty Officer Johnson, the enlisted helmsman who actually controlled the wheel that controlled the rudders that steered the ship while the officers stood around and decided where he should steer it. Johnson glanced over at Jack. Jack touched a forefinger to his lips then turned his attention back to the navigation table where he got ready to help Chief Kirk with the next fix.

Pleasure craft blared their stadium horns and scrambled to make way for the thousand-foot-long warship as she steamed around the arc of the Coronado Channel. Thirty minutes after she left her pier, *Connie* steamed past Buoy 1SD and entered international waters. With the gator's concurrence, Jack secured the navigation detail and went to the office aft of the bridge. He shut the door, locked it, sat at his desk, and booted up his Smiley Macintosh computer.

A two-key macro brought up his favorite screen saver, a series of white concentric squares that chased each other across a black background as they caromed off the edges of the computer's tiny built-in monitor. Jack reached over and turned off the overhead lights. In the seat of his pants, he felt the slight roll of the ship you could sense this high, a hundred feet above the waterline. He breathed stale memories of the chief's pipe tobacco, which made him want a cigarette, a habit he'd given up in deference to Mom's wishes when Dad had died.

You don't want to hear about that sob scene just now.

Jack rolled his head and sighed. The vertebrae in his neck popped. He shifted in his chair to relieve the pressure in his lower back, which he'd sprained in a body surfing accident during his first sea tour. His eyes tracked the bouncing squares across the computer screen, and then they closed.

☆ ☆ ☆ ☆ ☆

Fighting with Liz. Telling Mom he couldn't come out to Charleston because he had to go to sea. Keeping the truth about Liz and Joe from Grandma. That was a lot of baggage to be carrying around, even for a big strong boy like Jack.

He let himself wonder if standing late night Officer of the Deck watches on the bridge, in charge of the safety of the ship and the five thousand sorry slobs in her crew and air wing while Zach Taylor and the gator slept, was such a good idea. But the ship only had four qualified OODs. If Jack crapped out, Gary and the other two dip shits would have to miss sleep to pick up the slack.

And what would Jack do? Walk up to the gator and say, "Boss, I need to share something. I have issues right now, and I'd like to take a little time off, make some space, find my center?"

No. He wasn't going to do that. Way too vaginal. Plus, that would be taking an axe to his naval career, and his naval career was all he had going for him at the moment.

Two soft taps at the door.

"Mister H, you okay in there?"

"Yeah, Chief. I'm fine. Just sitting here playing with myself. I'll be done in a minute."

Chief Kirk chuckled. "Ain't no rush, sir. Take your time. Just don't get none on my desk, okay?"

"Roger that."

Feeling the hangover again now that the rush of getting underway had worn off, Jack reached into his desk drawer, took out a bottle of eight-hundred-pound Motrins, and swallowed one dry. He shut off the computer, turned the lights back on, went out to the bridge and relieved Gary as Officer of the Deck. After consulting with the gator, he ordered Stick Boy to set a northerly course for the Aleutian Islands.

Action in the North Pacific

Jack leaned against the navigation table to take pressure off his lower back. He could still out-run most nineteen-year-old sailors on the physical readiness test. But he wasn't getting much exercise on this Northern Pacific (NORPAC) gig, and having his feet planted on a metal deck eighteen hours a day wasn't exactly a Swedish massage.

Connie hurled herself ahead at thirty knots, the mountains growing larger and larger in the Plexiglas windscreen. Chief Kirk looked up from the navigation plot. "Holy shit, Mister H, how close is Captain Zach going to cut it this time?"

Jack checked the time on his Jap job and sidled over to the helm console, where Stick Boy had the conn. "How soon do we turn?"

"Thirty seconds, sir."

"Keep an eye where you're going, Stick Boy. This is a bigger car than you're used to driving."

Jack skulked over to the port side where Gary, on watch as OOD, stood by Zach Taylor's chair. "Time to turn," he whispered in Gary's ear.

"I know," Gary whispered back. "But I need the captain's permission. He told me yesterday not to do anything what-so-fucking-ever unless I checked with him first, and I can't get his attention."

Jack raised his voice. "Captain, I show time to turn as right now."

Zach Taylor looked up from the paperwork in his lap and peered at the mountains, taking a fine measurement with his superior eye. "Bullshit. We have a good thirty seconds to go."

Two seconds later, he waved the back of his hand at Gary, Jack, and Stick Boy. "All right, goddammit, turn us around and bring us into the wind."

☆　☆　☆　☆　☆

The Northern Latitude Area was a fiord-like body of water in Alaska's Aleutian Island chain. Sheer mountain cliffs surrounded three sides of the NOLA. The mountains protected the carrier and her escorts from attack by Soviet cruise missiles, whose radars couldn't sort out the ships from the mountains. A barrier reef covered the entrance to the NOLA. The single break in the reef was barely wide and deep enough for a super carrier like the *Connie* to transit, and was relatively easy to protect from penetration by Soviet attack submarines.

Officially, the NORPAC exercise's purpose was to demonstrate that U.S. carrier battle groups could operate with impunity within striking distance of the Soviet ballistic missile submarine pens in the Kamchatka Peninsula. If you asked Jack Hogan, NORPAC's real purpose was to justify the Cold War Navy's budget and burn off excess testosterone.

The Joint Chiefs of Staff had two choices for taking out the Kamchatka ballistic missile submarine pens. They could send the dozen ships and ten thousand men in a carrier battle group to the NOLA, let them operate to the point of exhaustion, then launch a squadron of A-6 Intruder bombers on a one-way mission and hope one or two of the jets made it through the Soviet air defenses and dropped a nuke on the sub pens …

Or …

They could order some matinee idol Air Force major—sitting in an air-conditioned missile silo in Bumfuck, Nebraska—to push a button and fling a fistful of nuclear tipped intercontinental ballistic missiles in the general direction of Kamchatka. Hell, they had enough ICBMs to barbecue the whole planet five or six times over. Fencing off a handful of them for Kamchatka wouldn't make a shit bit of difference.

But if we threatened the sub pens with our fleet, then the Soviets would have to build and train and maintain a fleet of their own to deal with it, and spend all those rubles, and look one way while we went another, and wheels-within-wheels, and hocus pocus, and blah, blah, blah. And here Jack and 9,999 other sorry bastards were, breaking their balls trying to make this red-ass NOLA bullshit work.

Carrier aircraft operations required 25 knots of wind down the deck. In open ocean, you turned into the natural wind and cranked up the ship's speed until the combination added up to 25, and you stayed there for the half hour or so it took to launch and land everybody. In the NOLA, you had to work wind and distances precisely enough to launch and recover everybody before you rammed the carrier into the reef or the mountains.

Jack, near the end of his assistant navigator tour and the *Connie's* most experienced OOD, spent most of his time on the bridge. Partly because it was his job to be there, but partly because Zach Taylor had shit-canned the other two OOD dip shits, and it was just the Jack-and-Gary show now. Gary needed all the help he could get in dealing with Zach Taylor.

In "normal times," Zach Taylor was a man of many moods, few of them good. On NORPAC, the guy went totally Queeg on everybody. The gator theorized that Zach just wanted to get this final underway deployment of his major command tour over with before somebody else fucked the dog for him and knocked up his chances of making admiral.

You couldn't blame Zach for shit-canning the other two OOD dip shits, though. They'd asked for it, mostly.

The first dip shit was a surface warfare lieutenant commander who'd been shit-canned from every other ship in the surface Navy—

the Navy of destroyers and cruisers and amphibious ships—because he'd been such a dip shit his whole career. The dip-shit thing that he'd done on this ship was let the battle group's supply ship, the *Mars*, pass down the *Connie's* starboard side within two hundred yards in the middle of the night. Standing orders on the *Connie* required OODs to notify the captain if any ship got closer than five thousand yards, day or night.

Zach Taylor had been asleep in his at-sea cabin when the *Mars* passed within two hundred yards, and the dip-shit lieutenant commander hadn't bothered to tell him about it when it happened. He hadn't bothered to tell Zach about it when Zach came out on the bridge in the morning, either, or when the dip shit reported he was going below at the end of his watch.

Zach never would have found out about it at all except that the captain of the *Mars*, Commander Winifred "Bull" Palsy, *Connie's* old executive officer from the West Pacific cruise the year before, called Zach on the bridge-to-bridge circuit that afternoon.

"Hope you're having a fine Navy day," Bull said over the radio. "Just wanted to call and say thanks for letting us pass close down your side."

Zach must have thought he was losing his other marble. "When did that happen?"

"Last night," Bull said.

Zach Taylor about shit. The dip-shit lieutenant commander was about to have a real fine Navy day.

Zach ordered the enlisted duty messenger to go down to the dip shit's stateroom to shake his ass out of his rack. When the dip shit finally hauled himself up to the bridge, still half asleep, his shirt tail half out and his shoes untied, Zach ripped him open a couple new assholes and shit-canned the dip shit right there on the spot.

It was kind of the same thing with the second dip shit, except the second dip shit was just a jay gee, like Gary. All the jay gee did was put his eyes over the night hood of the port side radar repeater in the middle of a midnight watch. The night hood was a semi-rigid rubber cone that fit over the radarscope so the glow from it didn't light up the whole bridge and ruin everybody's night vision. At the top of the cone was a visor piece that you could peer through to see the radar picture. All the jay gee had meant to do, when he leaned over and looked down the hood, was to check on the surface picture and make sure none of the ships in the vicinity were on course to collide with *Connie*. Really, that's all he'd meant to do. But once he looked down the hood, those bright green blips against the dark green background hypnotized him, looking like little neon dolphins swimming across the ocean, having such a jolly good time and asking him to dive down the night hood and join them. The jay gee's jaw went slack and his legs soon followed, and the next thing he knew, he'd dozed off, gone face-first down the night hood, and broken his nose on the radarscope.

Zach picked that minute to wake up and walk out to the bridge, where he saw the jay gee tits-up on the deck, his nose bleeding all over his blouse. Zach had the jay gee flown off the ship and transferred to civilian command the next day.

Jack and Gary and Buzz thought Zach wasn't being quite fair when he shit-canned the jay gee. The jay gee hadn't been nearly as big a dip shit as the lieutenant commander dip shit had been. The jay gee sure wasn't the first OOD of a Navy ship who ever dozed off for a second on a late night watch. And the lieutenant commander dip shit's career had been over anyway, while the jay gee's career had been nipped in the bud.

But, oh well. Those were the breaks.

Sea Stories

Zach Taylor wasn't getting along with Admiral Felon either.

"They're like oil and magnesium," the gator said from his barber chair on the starboard side, late one night, after flight operations had secured and Zach had gone off the bridge. "Or vinegar and water. Or whatever."

The only reason the gator was still up was because Gary had the watch, and Zach didn't trust Gary on the bridge at night unless he or the gator was around to keep an eye on him. Jack had stayed up to make sure Gary didn't doze off and fall down the night hood, and wake up tits-up on the deck with blood on his blouse, and get shit-canned.

"Admiral Felon is on the phone with Zach every ten minutes, bitching at him about one thing or another," the gator said, starting a sea story to keep everybody awake.

Rear Admiral Phillip "Fix" Felon commanded the *Constellation* battle group, and was living on *Connie* (and in Zach Taylor's ass) for the duration of the NORPAC deployment.

"Plus," the gator said, "whatever the hell's up with Zach and his wife? Guy's been married to her thirty years. You'd think they'd have learned to get along by now. I just thank God my wife had the good grace to walk out on me before I married her. Easier that way. Cheaper. Faster. Funnier too."

✯ ✯ ✯ ✯ ✯

Jack nudges Gary. "Never got married to his wife?" he whispers. "Don't you just wonder what that's all about?"

"I bet we can get him to tell us," Gary whispers back. "Careful, though, let's not spook him. He's probably so tired he doesn't realize he blurted that one out. Let's get him talking about something else and then pull a switch on him."

Jack grins and nods.

Buzz walks onto the bridge.

"Oh, good," Jack says. "Buzz is here. What's the buzz, Buzz

buddy? What brings you all the way up here to the nosebleed level? Why aren't you racked out in your stateroom? They fumigating it or something?"

Gary chimes in:

Buddy Buzz, he had no hair.

Buddy Buzzy, was he there?

He might be white. He might be black.

He might be sleeping in his rack.

"Stow it," Buzz says. "I just got off watch in combat, so I came up from my dark hole to take a look out at your dark hole. So pipe down on the Buddy Buzzy bullshit, okay?"

"Roger that, Buddy Buzzy," Jack says. "Hey, come over here a second."

Gary keeps the gator occupied while Jack conspires with Buzz over by the helm console. "We're trying to milk some good shit out of the gator about his ex-non-wife," Jack says, "so we can pitch him shit about it forever later. But we don't want to spook him, and we're afraid he'll know we're up to something if we say anything. So you get him ranting about Fix Felon, like you did last time, and we'll see if we can change the subject on him."

☆ ☆ ☆ ☆ ☆

"Fuck Fix Felon," the gator says. "I flew with that asshole in my first squadron. An NFO who started out as an intelligence weenie and then became a ship driver and then became an NFO and then became a pilot."

"How did he pull off a stunt like that?" Gary says.

The gator says he'll tell them the whole story, but it's convoluted, so if they want to hear it, they'll have to shut their pie holes and listen and not interrupt him. But he promises that this is one of the top ten sea stories of all time. What's more, when he gets to the end of it, if they don't agree it's one of the top ten sea stories of all time, he'll kiss all their asses on the corner of First Street and Orange Avenue in Coronado and give them half an hour to draw a crowd.

"Sounds like a deal to me," Gary says.

The gator begins:

The gator's at this party in a hotel suite in Thailand with his buddies from his first EA-6 Prowler squadron, and they're all shit-faced.

"Yeah, Gary," Buzz says. "The EA-6 Prowler, that's the jet with the bent dick—looking thing on its nose for air-to-air refueling. The gator used to fly it before his non-ex-wife bent his dick for him."

"Who's telling the story?" the gator says. "You or me?"

"Sorry, Gator," Buzz says.

"Buzz is right, though," the gator says. "The EA-6 Prowler is like an A-6 Intruder that drops bombs, except the Prowler doesn't drop bombs, and it has room in the cockpit for three assholes instead of one asshole, like the Intruder has room for—"

"By 'assholes' he means NFOs, Gary," Buzz says. "Naval flight officers, like Jack and me, with two anchors on our wings, who don't actually fly the airplane. As opposed to asshole pilots with only one anchor on their wings, like the gator has on."

"Again with the interruptions?" the gator says.

"Sorry, Gator."

"Give me fifty pushups later," the gator tells Buzz. "When you can get around to it. Yeah, Gary, the EA-6 Prowler is an airborne radar jammer. Except it was a butt jammer when Fix Felon flew in the seat behind mine. Except he never did go flying, actually, but that part of the story comes later ..."

The gator didn't take the non-ex-wife bait this time, but that's okay, Buzz and Gary and Jack think. This new Fix Felon story might be good enough that the gator won't have to kiss everybody's ass on the corner of First and Orange. And if it isn't, that's okay too, right?

Anyway, the gator's saying, they're all shit-faced in this hotel suite in Thailand, and in walks this tall, Abraham Lincoln–looking lieutenant commander with pilot wings on his chest who nobody's ever seen before. Ugly as a wet poodle with AIDS, this guy is, but that's all right. The world needs character actors too, the gator says.

The squadron's skipper, who's as shit-faced as the rest of them, tries to stand up and say, "Who the fuck are you, Boris Karloff, crashing into our party like *The Curse of the Mummy* or something?" But what he does instead is stumble off the couch and spill his drink and the rest of him tits-down on the carpet. The squadron XO, a little short guy, grabs the skipper's tits and the rest of him up off the floor and hauls him off to a bedroom.

The Mummy lurks around the room with a drink in his hand, looking like he expects everybody to recognize him and shake his hand and kiss his ass. But nobody does that because they're all too shit-faced.

The short XO comes back from the bedroom, troops over to *The Mummy* and stands under him. "Just who the fuck do you think you are?" he says.

The Mummy looks down at the little XO and says, "I'm Phil Felon, your new operations officer. Who the fuck are you, little man?"

The little XO goes ballistic, jumping up and down and cussing up a blue streak. *The Mummy* crooks a finger at him and leads him into the kitchen. Thirty seconds later, he comes out of the kitchen with his arm around the little XO, who has a Colgate smile smeared on his face, and who says, "Hey, guys, meet our new operations officer."

Gary asks if that's all there is to the story. The gator tells him to keep his pants on, the story gets better from here.

Go back a few years, the gator says. This is all second-, third-hand. The gator doesn't know how much of it's really true. He heard it from a good buddy of his, a Filipino pimp, who's not the most reliable. But it sounds good, so here goes, the gator says.

This *Young Abe Lincoln*–looking lieutenant checks in off transfer leave at the A-7 Corsair light bomber training squadron and says he's there to get checked out in the airplane. But Young Abe has to take emergency leave first. His grandma just died or something. So he checks back out of the squadron. Nobody sees him again until six months later when he shows back up in the ready room. This stash ensign has the duty, and *Young Abe Lincoln* tries to get the ensign to sign his papers saying he's completed the A-7 flight training, but …

The A-7 squadron skipper walks in just then, sees what *The Mummy's* trying to pull, and says, "Not so fast."

The skipper crooks a finger at *Young Frankenstein* and takes him back to his office. Two men go in, one man comes out—*Young Frankenstein*, and he makes the ensign sign his papers and walks out. The ensign goes to look for the skipper in his office, and there's nobody there!

"What happened to the skipper?" Gary says.

"Nobody knows," the gator says. "*The Mummy* just disappeared him, like in *Catch-22*."

"OOOOOOOOOOOH!" everybody says.

Except Gary, who says, "*Catch-22*? What's that?"

"Famous novel," says the gator.

"By whom?" Gary says.

"Joseph Heller," says the gator.

"Who's he?" Gary says.

"Famous author," says the gator.

"What did he write?" Gary says.

"*Catch* … Hey, you look like you might be a little retarded, SWO Boy. You're not, are you?"

Gary, the surface warfare officer hereafter also known as SWO Boy, says, "No, sir. I'm very smart. I'm just pulling your chain. I know what *Catch-22* is. I read it in grade school. My mother taught me to read when I was four, so I'd learn things and be smart, because she knew I wouldn't be the matinee idol type."

"Yeah, well, like I said before," the gator tells Gary, "the world needs character actors too. Now, do you want to hear the rest of the story or not? If so, keep your pie hole buttoned, or I'll send you to bed without any milk and cookies to put in it, which from the looks of you, you don't need any more of anyway."

"I promise to keep my pie hole buttoned," Gary AKA SWO Boy says. "Please tell the rest of the story, Navigation Man."

The gator, now also known as Navigation Man, says, "And don't call me Navigation Man. Not while the captain's around, anyway."

"Aye, aye," says SWO Boy.

Navigation Man looks at Buzz and Jack to make sure they're still awake, still paying attention, and notices his audience has gotten bigger. The duty bosun mate and the quartermaster have crept over by his chair to listen, and a couple of lookouts who got off watch an hour ago. The lookouts shouldn't still be up here, but it's okay because Chief Kirk—who got up at 0430 like he always does—is keeping an eye on them. And they know they'll get a chief-sized boot up their scrawny young asses if they pop their pie holes open while the gator's talking and the chief's around, so they'll keep them buttoned.

Navigation Man continues:

Fix Felon, in various personae, roams the earth in search of phony warfare qualifications. To this day, nobody knows how he got them put into his official service record without ever having flown an airplane, or been an NFO in the passenger seat of one, or jumped out of one with a parachute, or driven a ship or a submarine. And yet here he is, on our ship, in our battle group, in command of our entire known universe.

"Scary!" Everybody shudders.

"Of course," Navigation Man says, "like I told you, I heard all that from a lawyer who used to be a Navy JAG officer, so most of it probably isn't true. And however he got all those warfare pins, Fix Felon just wears his pilot wings now. Ask Buzz, NFO Man. Buzz sees Felon lurking around in combat all the time, right?"

"Some nights," says Buzz, now sometimes called NFO Man, "he likes to come in and spy on us, see if he can catch us sleeping when we're supposed to be jacking off. But he only does it after midnight, and he always wears a disguise. Sometimes he's a Catholic chaplain and shakes holy water on us. Sometimes he dresses up like a master chief mess specialist and brings us cookies. Sometimes he pretends to be a visiting politician acting like he's drumming up votes so he can figure out if any of us aren't Republicans. Not that it matters what he dresses up like. We'd recognize that Boris Karloff–looking bastard if he dressed up like a ballerina. Which he did, back on WESTPAC, come to think of it. Several times."

Everybody laughs.

"Keep it down," Navigation Man says. "We don't want to wake up the captain and have him come out here and catch us all jacking off."

Everybody tries to keep it down, but they all have the late night/ early morning giggles now.

"That's the end of the story," Navigation Man says. "Is it safe for me to take Orange Avenue home when we get back, or do I have to find an alternate route?"

"You're safe," Gary the SWO Boy says. "You never have to kiss our ass ever again, Navigation Man."

"Damn your impertinence, SWO Boy."

They never find out about the deal with Navigation Man's ex-non-wife, or about when he was a roadie for the Grateful Dead one summer in college. Before Jack and Buzz and Gary can steer him back in that direction, somebody brings up Bull Palsy, the *Connie's* old XO from WESTPAC, and everybody has some shit to pitch at that son of a bitch. What he did to whom, how he did it, how far up he did it, how long it took for the bleeding to stop after he did it, how many tampons it took to stop the bleeding ...

And the next thing everybody knows, the sun's coming up, and it's time for them to turn into their racks—which is a Navy way of saying "go to bed." (Except for Gary, who has two more hours on watch.)

But before everybody but Gary turns into their racks, they take one last look at the mountains as the sun climbs up to light their universe, and think about how much fun they've had, on the bridge, telling sea stories; and they feel for just a moment, that maybe, just maybe, life doesn't suck a thousand dicks after all.

☆　☆　☆　☆　☆

Zach Taylor had been a single-seat A-7 Corsair pilot in Vietnam. He had infinite confidence in himself and little confidence in anybody else, especially the "black shoe" surface warfare types who ran his engineering plant and manned his bridge teams.

As an aviator, Jack was the only OOD left on board who had any sway with Zach, but that influence was mitigated by the fact that Jack was an NFO, and not a pilot—and an E-2 NFO at that, which put him only slightly higher on the Navy pecking order than black shoes like Gary. Gary, as we have seen, couldn't do anything on the bridge what-so-fucking-ever unless he checked with Zach or the gator first. Gary was actually a pretty competent ship driver, and a good officer all around. But he was a black shoe. And the other two black shoe OOD dip shits had no influence with Zach whatsoever, because Zach shit-canned them, remember?

Yakkety Yak Zach.
Wake up, crawl out of your rack.
When the clock strikes one,
He'll take his gun,
And jam it
Right up your crack!

✮   ✮   ✮   ✮   ✮

Needless to say, the old Vietnam A-7 pilot's eyes were the sharpest navigation tools on the bridge. Zach's highly developed sense of space, time, and distance was far superior to anything lesser beings could calculate with radars and maneuvering boards. And an A-7 Corsair pilot's eye was a damn sight better than an EA-6 Prowler pilot's eye. Just ask the gator.

"Yeah," Navigation Man said, after Zach had left the bridge for the night, and everybody gathered around to hear another sea story.

The Horse He Rode In On

Jack slept in two-or three-hour squirts. Not sleep, really. More like the kind of thing you do when your third-grader reads you the poem she wrote in school today.

For the first two weeks of NORPAC, as he lay in his rack, Jack listened to the daughter he didn't have read him stories about the bridge, watching from the navigation table as the mountains grew bigger and bigger. Chief Kirk cried like a girl, tugging at Jack's sleeve, saying, Make him turn us, sir, make him turn us, oh my GOD! Jack flew across the bridge like Bizarro Superman, and slapped Bizarro Zach Taylor upside the head, screaming, How about dropping your Bizarro cock for a minute and letting us turn the ship around?

A month into the NORPAC, what had at first seemed like common terror punctuated by fill-your-pants terror became routine. At rest, Jack's mind began visiting compartments it had stayed out of since the deployment began.

✮   ✮   ✮   ✮   ✮

Liz was a beautiful woman, but not a pretty one to live with. She loved horses and not much else. She didn't like Jack being in the

Navy, didn't like Jack's music, didn't like Jack's friends, and didn't like his habits—especially his drinking habits. Which, in reality, weren't all that bad compared to a lot of naval aviators Jack knew.

Hell, Jack didn't think she liked herself all that much. They argued constantly while they were dating. He'd somehow convinced himself they'd get along better once they were married. What the hell had he been thinking?

Silly question. He wasn't thinking. Not with the head on his shoulders and neck, anyway.

Like she'd rehearsed it a hundred times in front of her mirror, Liz had explained over coffee what her lawyer had told her. California was a common-property state, and she was entitled to half the marital property accumulated over their two-year marriage. Moneywise, those had been two good years for Jack. His Scripps ranch house had almost doubled in value. He'd socked away his career bonus pay in mutual funds that had done well. In all, this short, miserable marriage would cost him over a hundred grand.

Why was divorce so expensive?

Because it was worth it.

☆ ☆ ☆ ☆ ☆

Mom's husband Joe had landed in the first wave at Normandy Beach, to hear him tell it. Jack sat down one day and figured out that Joe had been nine years old when the allies invaded France. The guy must have lied to his recruiter about his age, Jack reckoned.

A chess aficionado, Joe was. Talked all the time about the time he played Bobby Fisher to a stalemate. One time too many, he talked about it. The last time he talked about it was two seconds before Jack put him in checkmate in three moves.

Jack and Joe couldn't spend two days together without a fight breaking out, Mom getting upset, Jack leaving, going back to wherever his duty station happened to be at the time.

Joe's only redeeming value was that he'd made Mom happy after seven years of widowhood, and he'd gooned that away by growing a tumor in his head, and now Mom would have to suffer through the lingering death of another husband.

Why couldn't the bullshit bastard have been a man and stepped in front of a bus or something?

First Watch

Jack had the first watch—0400 to 0800—the last night of NORPAC. The last morning of it, rather. Keeping track of time got hard doing two-section duty with Gary, four hours on, four hours off.

Flight ops had secured at midnight. This would be a slack watch, nothing to do but avoid grounding and collision. Tame stuff, after two months of non-stop pucker party.

At 0430, Navigation Man strolled onto the bridge in his bathrobe and handed Jack an envelope. "I'll be in my at-sea cabin," he said, and he yawned as he went by the duty quartermaster's station on his way out. The duty quartermaster saluted him back.

The gator. He could almost convince you from time to time that he was a real human being. Then he'd turn around and do something to remind you he really wasn't. Like this yawning in his bathrobe, in front of the bridge team, and making a big deal that he was going back to his rack, when he had to know everybody on watch wanted to hit their racks so bad they ached, but had to stay on their feet for several more hours.

And this "be in my at-sea cabin" bullshit of his, like he was important enough to have a second cabin on the ship. Only the captain rated two cabins—at-sea and in-port. Yeah, the gator deserved a second cabin all right. Made out of logs, up in the mountains. And he could go there right now. Take along a pair of snowshoes with him, go for a nice walk some night in the middle of a blizzard.

Jack walked over to the captain's chair where there was enough light to read by and opened the envelope. It was an AMCROSS, an American Red Cross message.

SUBJECT NAVAL OFFICER'S SISTER MICHELLE REGRETS TO REPORT DEATH OF GRANDMOTHER MARY HOGAN. FUNERAL SERVICES WILL BE HELD ON 21 DECEMBER AT SAINTS PETER AND PAUL CATHOLIC CHURCH IN ALTON, ILLINOIS. FAMILY UNDERSTANDS THAT SUBJECT NAVAL OFFICER WILL BE UNABLE TO ATTEND OR COMMUNICATE DUE TO MILITARY DUTIES.

21 December was tomorrow. No, today. That's right, this was the four-to-eight watch. Today was already tomorrow. Or was it the other way around?

Not that it mattered. If the funeral were a week from now, Jack couldn't leave the ship to attend it. You only got to go home if a parent or spouse died. And Jack couldn't send a reply to the AMCROSS message because this NORPAC mission was classified. Nobody was supposed to know the *Connie* and her battle group were up here. Except for the Soviets. If the Soviets didn't see them demonstrating they were operating in the NOLA, it wouldn't be much of a demonstration, would it? A classic Cold War operation, this was. They had to make sure the enemy knew about it, but that their friends and families didn't.

Jack looked out the bridge windscreen. All he saw was the white stern light on Bull Palsy's *Mars*. Then all he saw was Grandma's kitchen table, a stainless steel Formica deal, and a Frigidaire standing behind it. Grandma, still hale and healthy, opening the Frigidaire, taking out the blue Shirley Temple Pitcher she and Grandpa had bought on their honeymoon at the Chicago World's Fair, saying, "Fresh squeezed lemonade, Jackie. Your favorite!"

Jack crumpled the message in his fist and dropped it in the shit can next to the port side radar repeater. He wanted to rest his eyes on the night hood, and fall into it. But there was no time to cry about Grandma now.

He looked out the windscreen again, and once again saw the white stern light of *Mars*. Commanded by *Connie*'s old executive officer, Bull Palsy, still. "Bull" Palsy, so nicknamed he'd tell you, because of his thick manly torso. Jack, Buzz, Gary, and the rest of the crew who'd known him on WESTPAC would tell you Bull's call sign was more of a testament to his temperament and I.Q. This guy thought red at a stoplight meant "charge."

Bull was Zach Taylor's protégé. They'd flown in the same A-7 squadron in Vietnam. During last year's West Pacific cruise, when Bull was still *Connie*'s XO, Zach would leave him alone on the bridge during flight ops, training him for promotion to command of his own aircraft carrier. Like Zach, Bull had little regard for the nautical rules of the road that mere mortals adhered to. "I'm the flagship," he'd say. "Let the rest of the battle group get the fuck out of my way."

Jack turned to his Junior Officer of the Deck, a tall ensign with a cheesy moustache and plastic framed, Navy issue eyeglasses. "Groucho, keep an eye on *Mars*. Make sure she stays in her own orbit."

"Keep an eye on *Mars*, aye," Groucho said.

Jack walked to the helm console and saluted Petty Officer Johnson. "Request permission to take the helm under instruction."

"You have the helm under instruction, sir."

Jack took the wheel. "What are you going to teach me tonight, Johnson?"

"I thought we'd work on maintaining a steady course, sir."

Muffled guffaws from the other enlisted men occupying odd

corners of the darkened bridge. Jack said, "Hey, fuck you guys." That brought more guffaws, which prompted Jack to say, "Fuck you guys again," which prompted still more guffaws, and comments like:

See? I told you Mister Hogan was an okay guy. Likes a good joke, takes one and gives it back. Just watch out you don't mess with him when he's not messing around.

The helm compass repeater drifted a gnat's ass right of two-three-zero degrees, the ship's ordered heading. "What do you think, Johnson? Bring the rudders five degrees left?"

"That's what I'd do, sir."

Jack turned the wheel left, and the ship's heading crept back toward two-three-zero.

"So, Johnson," Jack said, "what did you think of all this jumping through grommets up here in Frozen Alaska?"

"Frozen Alaska? You mean like the dessert? That's a good joke, sir."

"Yeah, maybe. Thanks for not laughing at it. So what did you think about all this?"

Johnson scratched his chin. "Be honest with you, sir, it all seemed dumber than dirt to me. But I'm just a stupid bosun mate, what do I know?"

"Don't give me that 'stupid bosun mate' crap. You bosuns are the only real sailors left in the Navy. Everybody else is a technical fag."

Johnson coughed and shrugged. "Guess I never looked at it that way, sir."

Jack kept the helm another ten minutes, then turned it back over to Johnson. "You're getting pretty good, sir," Johnson said. "For an officer, I mean."

"Thanks for the backhanded compliment, Johnson. I'll give you the back of my hand sometime, I will."

Johnson did a shitty job of trying not to grin. "Sorry, sir. That didn't come out the way I meant. I meant, you know, you're the only officer who practices handling the helm. You and Mister Constantine, that is. The other officers, it's like they're—"

"Too good to practice doing an enlisted man's job? Is that what you're saying, Johnson?"

"Sorry, sir. That didn't come out right either."

"Don't worry about it, Johnson. I'll keep your impertinence under my hat."

"Thank you, sir."

"You're welcome. Now shut up and steer the ship."

Johnson took the helm and corrected the ship's course by a tenth of a degree.

Yeah, that Mister Hogan was an okay guy, he thought.

☆　☆　☆　☆　☆

The sun cracked the horizon as Gary's team filed onto the bridge. Gary took the night hood off the port-side radar repeater and tapped the track that represented the *Mars*. "I take it Commander Palsy and the Lost Planet Seamen behaved themselves last night?"

"More or less," Jack said. "Considering."

"Considering the lunatic who runs her? Just don't let your guard down, Jackie. We're not home yet, and Bull Pup is overdue to pull a disaster out of his hat."

"Roger that."

The last of Jack's watch-standers to report off duty was Johnson. "Properly relieved, sir. Sorry about my shitty shave. I overslept, didn't have time to give myself a good one before I came on watch. Appreciate you not jacking me up about it."

Johnson was barely old enough to shave. Even with the Arctic sun illuminating the bridge now, Jack could barely see a trace of peach fuzz on Johnson's upper lip. Jack rubbed his own chin and realized he hadn't shaved himself in two days. "Tell you what, Johnson. I won't say anything about your shitty shave if you don't say anything about mine."

"Deal, sir."

"Good man. Strike below and get some sleep."

★ ★ ★ ★ ★

As Jack left the bridge he crossed paths with Navigation Man, freshly scrubbed and shaved, coming the other way. "Hey, Jack, that message about your grandma. I guess handing it to you while you were on watch was a little rough. I was tired, I guess. You knew she was dying, right? I mean, she was pretty old, wasn't she? That's what grandmas do, isn't it? Run out of gas and cough out on you?"

"Yes, sir. She's been failing for years. No big deal."

What else was Jack going to say?

"Good. Hey, grab yourself a shave before you come back up to the bridge. You don't want to set a bad example for the enlisted men."

"Aye, aye, sir."

Yep. The gator. Still an asshole.

★ ★ ★ ★ ★

On his rack, Jack found a handwritten note from Gary.

It's laundry day, Dog Fart. Please put your putrid clothes out for the coop cleaner to haul away. The room is starting to smell like a backed up head.

G.

P.S. Heard about your grandma while you were on watch. Sorry.

Jack pulled the shirt shit off his shirt, stripped off his khakis and underwear, wadded them in a ball, stuffed them in his bulging nylon mesh laundry bag, and set the bag in the passageway outside the door.

The fresh sheets rasped against his clammy skin. He considered grabbing his jab slaps and bathrobe and going down the passageway to the officers' shower. A jet of hot water on his lower back would feel real good right now, he was thinking, when his eyelids collided with each other.

✯　✯　✯　✯　✯

With a cane in one hand and a bag of goodies in the other, Grandma walked up the sidewalk. Jack's dog Miltie, a collie, rushed out the front door and sat at her feet.

"Hello, Miltie girl! I'm so glad to see you again!"

Miltie scraped her tail against the sidewalk and lifted a forepaw for Grandma to shake. "I'm happy to see you too, Grandma. So happy! So happy!"

What a dip-shit dream, Jack thought as he was dreaming it.

What a bunch of Lassie bullshit.

Through the Rainbow

Connie left the NOLA that afternoon. A squall line rolled through as she approached the break in the barrier reef, and blew over as quickly as it had come. Chief Kirk, working the navigation plot, tapped Jack's arm and pointed forward. A rainbow had formed over the reef. The ship passed under it.

"A sign of luck, Mister H."

Jack grunted. "Which kind, Chief?"

"Maybe your grandma sent it to us as an omen, one way or another," Chief Kirk said.

Jack hadn't realized that Chief Kirk had known about the deal with his grandma. Jack had to blink a couple times. That was a fine thing for his chief to have said to him, and being a proper naval officer, Jack should have said a fine thing back to him about it. But just then, Jack couldn't think of a fine thing to say, so he didn't say anything. He figured that Chief Kirk, being the proper chief petty officer of the United States Navy that he was, would understand.

"Ten seconds to mark the next fix," Jack said to The Compass Kids through his sound-powered headset.

Twelve seconds later, Chief Kirk drew a tight fix on the navigation chart, and Jack announced, "Conning Officer, based on an unbelievably perfect fix, navigation holds the ship on course."

"Very well," Stick Boy croaked.

Zach Taylor, standing over Stick Boy's left shoulder, arched his right eyebrow and curled his upper lip.

☆ ☆ ☆ ☆ ☆

Jack had the midwatch that night—midnight to 0400. Gary was down at midrats—midnight rations—packing away enough energy to go to sleep.

The battle group steamed south in a line formation at thirteen knots. First, in the guide position, was Bull Palsy's *Mars*. *Connie* steamed four thousand yards—two nautical miles—behind the guide. The missile cruiser *Farragut* held station four thousand yards behind *Connie*. After *Farragut*, at two thousand yard intervals, came the other small boys: *Fox*, *Adams*, *Spruance*, *Knox*, *Flatley*, and *Mitscher*. Visibility was disappearing. The winds were swelling up. The seas were blowing down.

But conditions weren't that bad, Jack thought, compared to what they'd seen. This watch ought to be a milk run. Avoid colliding with the guide. That's the ticket. Avoid it like a German U-Boat. Ignore the pain in your back and your legs and your feet and the rest of you, including, and especially, your head.

And stay awake.

Run emergency scenarios through the old noggin, that's what you'll do. What if you lose a boiler? What if you lose steering? What if you lose your mind before the end of this fucking watch?

Don't get too caught up in your interior monologue now. Look out the windscreen. Put the binoculars on the guide. Nothing there but a single white stern light, like there should be. But it's the stern light on the *Mars*, you have to remember, and like Gary said, the Bull Pup's been way too quiet the whole deployment. And just because the NORPAC's behind us doesn't mean you can let your guard down.

Jack let his binoculars hang from the strap around his neck. They weighed a ton. "Junior Officer of the Deck, give me the range to *Mars*."

Groucho peered into the night hood of the port-side radar repeater. "Four thousand yards."

"Very well," Jack said.

Four thousand yards sounded like a lot of distance until you stopped to consider that it took almost six thousand yards to bring a super-carrier like Connie from thirteen knots to dead in the water, even with all engines back full emergency.

The OOD phone rang. It was Buzz. "Jack, I'm on watch down here in combat, and I'm so tired and so bored. I'm about to fall out of my chair."

One advantage of standing watch in combat, Jack thought, as he bent his knees and stretched his back. You didn't have much of a view down there, surrounded by radar displays, but at least you got to sit. You had to keep tabs on Buzz, though. He could sleep sitting up with his eyes open with the best of them. He'd logged over a thousand hours in the back of an F-14 Tomcat doing just that.

But Jack was bored and sleepy too, so he and Buzz fell into the familiar pattern of old shipmates keeping each other amused on a slack watch.

How was Buddy Buzz tonight? A little fuzzy, was he? What was that? How did the formation look from the bridge?

Jack glanced ahead at *Mars*. Something looked different. He couldn't say what, exactly. The night might have gotten darker. He took the phone from his ear. "Groucho, range to *Mars* again?"

"Three thousand, nine hundred, ninety two yards."

Creeping up on her. "Very well. Report the range every thirty seconds."

"Thirty seconds, aye."

Kind of demanding of Jack, to make Groucho check the range that often. Every minute or two would have been enough. But Groucho didn't have anything better to do, so fuck him.

Jack put the phone back to his ear. "You still there, Buzz?"

"Yeah. Something going on up there?"

"Just keeping an eye on *Mars*."

"Too bad there isn't a way to keep an eye on the head Martian," Buzz said, which thoroughly cracked Jack up.

"Range to *Mars* three thousand, eight hundred, seventy yards," Groucho said.

"Very well," Jack said. Still creeping up.

Over the phone, Buzz said, "Remember the day Bull made that enlisted mess crank do fifty pushups because the coffee was cold?"

Jack said, "Remember the time he walked around the ship all day with his fly open and nobody said boo to him about it?"

Groucho said, "Three thousand, six hundred yards."

Jack frowned. What the hell was going on? Was the radar not working right, or was dip-shit Groucho taking sloppy range measurements, or was *Connie* really closing on *Mars?* You couldn't tell, just looking at a white stern light in the dark.

"Buzz, how does the formation look on radar down in combat?"

"Looks fine down here. Except … Holy shit, what's up with *Mars?*"

"Holy shit!" Groucho said. "I show *Mars* dead in the water."

"That's not good," Jack said.

"What's not good?" Buzz said.

"This is going to be a train wreck," Groucho screeched. "The whole battle group's going to slam into the ass end of *Mars*."

"Got to run, Buzz," Jack said. "We're about to collide with *Mars*." He dropped the phone. "In the pilot house, this is Mister Hogan, I have the conn. Helmsman, right ten degrees rudder."

"Right ten degrees rudder, aye," Petty Officer Johnson said.

"Steady on course two-two-zero."

"Two-two-zero aye, sir."

Jack reached forward and grabbed the handset to the fleet tactical radio circuit off the bulkhead. "Safeguard, safeguard, safeguard. This is *Constellation*. My rudders are right, coming to course two-two-zero. *Mars* is dead in the water. *Farragut*, *Adams*, *Knox*, and *Mitscher*, turn left to one-four-zero. *Fox*, *Spruance*, and *Flatley*, come right to two-two-zero."

He hung up the handset. "Bosun, sound emergency five."

The duty bosun mate released five short blasts of the ship's whistle into the Arctic night. Over the fleet tactical circuit, the battle group acknowledged the Safeguard call:

"*Farragut*, coming left."

"*Fox*, coming right."

"*Adams*, coming left …"

Jack marched over to the captain's chair and picked up the phone that connected to Zach Taylor's at-sea cabin.

"Captain," Zach said over the tinny sound-powered circuit.

"Lieutenant Hogan, Officer of the Deck, sir. *Mars* went dead in the water. I've brought us right and fanned out the battle group."

"Holy shit!" Zach said. "I'll be right out."

Jack rang the gator's room and repeated what he'd told the captain.

"Holy shit!" the gator said.

The OOD phone rang again. "Holy shit," Buzz said. "The entire known universe just pitched a tent down here in combat wanting to know what the hell is going on."

"Would one of those happy campers be Admiral Felon?" Jack whispered.

"I think that's him lurking over my shoulder," Buzz whispered back.

"What's he dressed up like tonight?"

"Hard to say. He's wearing a fake beard and a wig. I can't tell if he's supposed to be Abe Lincoln or *The Wolf Man.*"

"Scary. Put him on."

Jack told Admiral Felon what he'd told Zach and the gator. Admiral Felon howled and hung up.

Zach and the gator burst onto the bridge in bathrobes and slippers. Zach looked at Jack with bloodshot eyes. "Has the admiral heard?"

"I just briefed him, sir."

Jack walked across the bridge with Zach and the gator, surveying the scattered battle group: white stern lights, white masthead lights, green starboard running lights, red port running lights—running all over the goddamn ocean like hook-and-ladder trucks in a Chinese fire drill.

Zach Taylor shook his head. "I wonder who Admiral Felon's going to rip a new asshole over this?"

The phone at the captain's chair rang. Zach got it. "Yes, Admiral. Yes, Admiral. Yes, Admiral." He slammed the phone down, and looked at Jack, the corners of his mouth turned down. "The admiral says to tell you that you did a nice job." Zach stuffed his hands in his bathrobe pockets and left the bridge. The gator followed him.

The OOD phone rang. "Jack, it's Buzz. Check this out. Admiral Felon just got off the battle group command net, the one all the ships' skippers listen in on, and gave Bull Palsy the most incredible public ass-reaming I ever heard."

"You're kidding."

"I kid you not. Turns out the dip-shit chief engineer on *Mars* decides he wants to do a bottom blow on one of his boilers. So he tells his dip-shit OOD to go dead in the water, and the dip-shit OOD does it."

"What a dip shit," Jack said. "He ordered all stop in the middle of the night, leading the formation, without telling the rest of the battle group?"

"Without telling anybody," Buzz said. "When Felon called over there and told the OOD he wanted to talk to Palsy ASAP, the OOD said, 'It'll be just a minute, Admiral. We'll have to wake him up.'"

"Holy shit!" Jack said. "What a bunch of dip shits."

"What a ship of fools," Buzz said.

Jack laughed.

Word Got Around

The Dirty Shirt Wardroom, where air wing guys could eat wearing their flight suits, was forward on the 03 level. Ship's company Airedales like Jack and Buzz ate there too, partly because it was convenient, and partly to remind themselves that they were still aviators, and this ship's company purgatory wouldn't last forever. Black shoes—surface warfare types like Gary—could eat there too, but they seldom did. That's because when they did eat there, all the Airedales pitched them shit about being black shoes, and the black shoes didn't have any shit to pitch back at them. Which was just as well. Like the gator put it, black shoes wouldn't know how to pitch shit if they had any shit to pitch.

So all the black shoes ate in the formal wardroom down on the second deck, where they had to wear khakis.

Except for Gary, who ate in the Dirty Shirt with Buzz and Jack all the time.

As a career fat boy, Gary had caught shit all his life, so the shit he caught in the Dirty Shirt rolled off his roly-poly back. And it gave him a chance to pitch shit at Buzz and Jack and the rest of the ship's company Airedales about being NFOs.

"Pilot wannabes," he'd call them. "Like precocious puppies who think they'll grow up to be real people, but no matter how hard they try, they'll never be anything but dogs."

Almost all of the ship's company Airedales were NFOs on their second sea tours. That's because all the pilots got out and went to work for the airlines before they had to do any of that second sea tour ship's company bullshit. Except for hard-core types like Zach Taylor and Navigation Man, who stayed in for the long haul. Which explained why those two were so fucked up, according to Gary.

Since NFOs didn't have airline jobs waiting for them on the outside, the Navy had more second sea tour NFOs than it knew what to do with. That's why the Bureau of Personnel assigned so many of them to ship's company on aircraft carriers. "To make you miserable enough to get out and sign up for the management training program at Burger King," Gary told them.

As far as Gary was concerned, the only ship's company NFO who had a real job was Jack, the assistant navigator, who'd had to learn to become a black shoe. Most of the ship's company NFOs worked in combat, liked Buzz did. The *Connie* had so many NFOs working in combat that Buzz only had to stand—sit—one watch a day. Sometimes zero watches a day.

This worried Gary. Poor idle Buzz. So much time on his hands, and so few hands to hold his crew sock with while he jacked off into it in the privacy of his stateroom. Such small hands, Buzz had, so delicate. But Buzz's hands were plenty big enough to handle what little they needed to handle.

So fuck him.

☆　☆　☆　☆　☆

By noon, after the morning of the night of The Almost Great

Big Train Wreck between *Mars* and the rest of the battle group, everybody had heard how Bull Palsy almost poked the pooch, and how Jack had pulled everybody's fat out of the fryer.

Gary and Buzz sat in a corner table in the Dirty Shirt, eating Nairobi Trail Markers (which is what they called Salisbury steaks) and drinking bug juice (Kool-Aid widely suspected to contain minimum adult required amounts of jet fuel).

"I swear to God," Buzz told Gary, "when Jack said 'I'm about to collide with *Mars*' I damn near shit my pants."

Gary wiped a dribble of gravy from his chin with his thumb. "Glad I was asleep for once. I've had enough excitement for one underway period. You heard the rumors?"

"About Fix Felon relieving Bull Pup from command of *Mars* when we get home? No way. Bull won a Silver Star in Vietnam. To get himself relieved of command, he'd have to knock up Fix Felon's wife and daughter both."

"A felony not outside the realm of possibility," Gary said, and reached for his glass of orange-flavored petroleum. "To hear Bull talk on WESTPAC last year, he's tagged half the loose bimbage from here to eternity."

"Yeah, right," Buzz said. "Fat-ass Bull would be lucky to score with his own mother. Speaking of fat, have you gained more weight since we left on NORPAC?"

"A pound or two."

"A pound or two? You look like you're growing a water bed over that belt of yours, SWO Boy." Buzz slid his blueberry pie closer to him where Gary couldn't reach it. "No, I don't think Bull will get relieved of command. This might knock him out of the running for his own aircraft carrier, though."

"Don't bet on that," Gary said. "It's a small Navy, Buzz. AOCS types like you and Jack forget that." Gary was a graduate of the United States Naval Academy. Having lived in the poke-and-stroke your pal culture since the age of seventeen, he knew how good old boy connections worked. "This story gets out and Bull will be on the horn with all his asshole buddies, putting his own spin on it, telling everybody how The Almost Great Big Train Wreck was Jack's fault."

Buzz just realized something. "Where is Jack, anyway? Doesn't he always eat with us?"

"He's on watch, Buzz. Remember? Six weeks ago, Zach shitcanned the other two OOD dip shits, and Jackie and I went down to two sections."

"No, I don't remember. I must have been taking a nap when that happened. No wonder it seems like I haven't seen him in a month and a half. Do you see him at all?"

"Only when we turn over the watch, Buzz. That's what two section duty means. Either he's on watch or I am."

"The horror," Buzz said. "Jack can't say I didn't warn him, though. I told him when he took this assistant navigator job that it might involve actual work."

"He's good at driving the ship," Gary said. "I'll give him that."

"I'm sure he took to it like a duck takes to an oil spill," Buzz said. "Jackie likes to work hard, the dip shit. Work. Shudder. The only reward for hard work is more hard work. I'll have to tell him that next time I see him, rub it in his face."

"Don't pitch him too much shit," Gary said. "I don't think he's been having an easy time of it since he heard his grandma died."

"His grandma died? Why didn't I know about that?"

"You were probably asleep."

Buzz nodded. "I probably was. I usually am. It's a survival thing, you know. Being at sea sucks the life out of me. When you're awake at sea, it's like being at sea. When you're asleep at sea, it's like being asleep anywhere else. And I'd rather be anywhere else than at sea, so when I don't absolutely, positively have to be awake at sea, I'm asleep."

"With all that sleeping, Buzz, I don't see how you get your paperwork done. I mean, you must have quite a bit of it, being the operations officer's administrative assistant."

"Oh, sure. But my chief does most of it. What paperwork my chief can't do, I take up to Jackie's office while he's on watch and stick it in his inbox. He's always got so much paperwork to do he never notices the difference. Then I swing by his office the next day and fish my paperwork from his outbox."

Gary smirked. "And it's complete, and it's immaculate, and you turn it in to your boss and he thinks you're the greatest thing since sliced bread."

Buzz frowned. "You've heard this story?"

"Not this one. I just know Jackie doesn't do anything half-assed. Must be nice to have a friend who does all your work for you."

"It is," Buzz said. "That's why I let him hang around with me and be my sidekick."

"You're a wonderful human being, Buzz."

"Thanks, Gary. That's nice of you to say." Buzz dug into his blueberry pie, and took a sip of his powdered milk. "Too bad about Jackie's grandma. But he's a big strong boy. He'll manage. Besides, he's got a babe wife waiting at home for him who isn't knocked up like my wife is, so fuck him."

Gary almost said something about Jack's wife Liz, but didn't. Gary wasn't supposed to know about that situation, even though he did. And if Buzz didn't know, it meant Jack hadn't told him, so Gary wasn't going to tell him either. "I'll take your word for it about him being okay. You've known him a lot longer than I have."

"Since he was a something or other in his dear mother's eye," Buzz said. "AOCS then NFO basic flight school in Pensacola. We flew in CAG Six together, our first sea tour; me in an F-14 Tomcat staring at the back of a fighter pilot's head, Jack in back of an E-2 Hawkeye, totally in the dark, looking at a radarscope with his windows closed.

Toss-up who had a worse view."

"He as good in the air as he is driving the ship?"

"The best air tactician alive, in his opinion. Made his name a household word—in his household, anyway—when he intercepted a whole regiment of Soviet bombers out on a practice raid in the middle of the night against the *Ranger*, the carrier we were on. Jackie planned and ran the whole air battle himself, and he was just a jay gee at the time."

"He did? He was?"

"You mean you haven't heard the story about The Great Big Backfire Raid? It's a Cold War legend. I wonder why it is I haven't told it to you yet."

"Maybe because it's a story about Jackie, and not about you?"

"But it is about me," Buzz said. "I was there, playing a supporting but significant role. I stole the show, actually."

"How glorious for you, NFO Man."

"And how fortunate for you, SWO Boy, that I was there and can tell you the story of the legend of The Great Big Backfire Raid."

"In the convoluted way that only you can tell it."

Buzz sat back in his chair and crossed his manly arms over his manly chest. "Do you want to hear the story or not?"

Gary burped and looked at his Jap job. He had to relieve Jack on the bridge in an hour. He had a ton of other crap to do. But he had so much other crap to do he'd never get it all done. And even if he ever did get it all done, somebody would just come along and give him more crap to do. He dabbed his napkin at a fresh gravy stain on his shirt, and burped again.

"Oh, all right," he said.

The Great Big Backfire Raid

The way Buzz tells it, he and Jack are on their first WESTPAC cruise, steaming west toward the Philippines. Word comes down from the intelligence weenies that the Soviet Naval Air Force has managed to get a whole regiment of their TU-22 Backfire bombers in shape to fly for once in their sorry existence. The Soviet Navy's head cheese, Admiral Gorschkov, decides as long as he has a whole regiment of full-up Backfires, he might as well have fun and be a prick about it. So he orders them to run a practice strike on an actual American carrier group in the actual Pacific Ocean.

"Which at the time," Buzz said, "was actually us on the *Ranger*."

"Actually, I don't care how big a prick Admiral Gorschkov was," Gary said, and made circles in the air with his forefinger. "Faster. Funnier. Cut to the chase. Save the rest for the book you're writing for your kid. Unlike some people, I have actual work to do. So get on with it."

Buzz got on with it. "So some elephant back at the Pentagon shits a decision to press *Ranger* north toward Kamchatka like we'd do if this was World War Three for real. Word comes down from CAG—CAG is the air wing commander, for you black shoe types, and please don't ask me why they call him CAG right now because that's an interesting story in itself, and I don't want to spoil this one by going off on a tangent."

"You're already off on a tangent, brain death. Can we get back to the Great Big Bomber story?"

"Sure. Word comes down from CAG that he wants the squadron J.O.s—that's 'junior officers' to you black shoe jack-offs—"

"Focus?" Gary said.

"Okay, okay ..."

CAG cancels flight ops so the air wing J.O.s have time to come up with a kick-ass plan to catch the Backfires by surprise, and fire a million pretend missiles at them, and fly through their formation and drop flares, and send them back to Kamchatka with their tails between their legs. The squadron skippers, who always climb all over each other to see who can kiss CAG's ass the most, order their J.O.s to spend all the extra time they have since they aren't flying—which they are not happy about—coming up with a kick-ass plan.

"Why did the skippers care?" Gary said. "CAG told the J.O.s to do the planning, not the skippers."

"Yeah, but every skipper wanted to be the skipper whose J.O. came up with the best plan, and take it to CAG and kiss his ass the most with it, and pretend like they helped the J.O. come up with the kick-ass plan. You know, like a Cub Scout project. The dumb kid did all the work himself; dad just looked over his shoulder and supervised, wink, wink."

"I see," Gary said. "Invasion of the Corn Hole Dads."

"Invasion of the Corn Hole Dads, that's good," Buzz said. "That's rich. I'll put it in the book I'm writing for my kid."

"Do it later," Gary said. "So, back to the story. The J.O.s all go to work?"

"Fuck no," Buzz said. "The J.O.s all go to bed. We're not black shoe morons like you. Our skippers give us extra work to do, we blow it off."

"Except for Jackie."

"Of course, except for Jackie."

Dip-shit Jackie pulls three all-nighters in a row in the *Ranger's* Dirty Shirt, shits reams of paper coming up with this convoluted plan he calls "Thunder Dome."

"He calls it Thunder Dome, I'm sure," Buzz said, "because he has an inferiority complex about being an E-2 guy, and he wants to make sure everybody knows an E-2 guy came up with the kick-ass plan, and not some fighter puke."

"Skip the psychology, get back to the Backfires."

"All right, all right …"

Jack works his ass off, and Buzz and the rest of the air wing J.O.s pitch him tons of shit about it as they roam through the Dirty Shirt for sodas and bug juice, in between naps.

"And you're all horrified and jealous," Gary said, "when it turns out Jackie's skipper loves his plan, and kisses CAG's ass the most with it, and the rest of you have to shake your asses out of your racks and go fly it."

Buzz frowned again. "I thought you said you hadn't heard this story."

"I haven't, Buzz, but you take so long to tell it, I could have come up with twenty different endings by now."

"You don't want to hear the end of the story, then?"

"Yes. Please, Mister NFO Man, please tell me the end of your Dip-Shit Backfire story."

Buzz coiffed his flattop. "There's not much else to tell. We go out, we kick Backfire butt, they go back to Kamchatka with their tails between their legs."

Gary smirked. "That's it?"

That was "it" all right, at least as much of it as Buzz wanted to tell Gary. Buzz was, after all, trying to keep this story about Jack a story about himself, and he couldn't do that if he explained to Gary that Jack's air defense plan was so innovative and so effective that it had literally put the fear of God into the Godless Commies, and that some elephants in the Pentagon already considered The Great Big Backfire Raid to be the beginning of the end of the Cold War, and that Jack, as a very junior officer, had already established himself in certain circles as one of the greatest tacticians of the airpower age.

At least, that's how Jack would tell the story of the Great Big Backfire Raid, if he every actually talked about it. Jack's great big stroke of genius hadn't been all that brilliant, really, as far as Buzz was concerned. His battle plan opened with an operational deception gambit. An attack submarine, steaming hundreds of miles ahead of the battle group, popped an antenna to the surface and broadcast a series of radar and radio signals that simulated the activities of a carrier battle group. When that goaded Admiral Gorshkov to launch his Backfires prematurely, Jack's plan had a trio of E-2s spaced well out in front of the actual carrier group that used their passive electronic detection systems to localize the Backfires as they took off from their base in Kamchatka.

After that, it was just a matter of launching every airplane in the air wing that could shoot an air-to-air missile and vectoring them in the general direction of the Backfire gaggle, and after that launching every other airplane that could refuel the shooters and make sure they all got home before they ran out of gas.

Anybody who'd really cared to could have come up with a plan like that, if they'd bothered to put in a few all-nighters in the Dirty Shirt coming up with it like Jack had, but nobody except Jack had cared to do that. That Jack's scheme proved a single carrier air wing could wipe out Admiral Gorschkov's entire Pacific Fleet Naval Air Force the second they left Soviet airspace had made his reputation in high circles as a world-class tactician and strategist was total bullshit as far as Buzz was concerned. What was the point of achieving success if you had to work hard to achieve it? That was Buzz's motto.

"That's it," he said. "Of course, there's a postscript, a coda, if you will, a brief passage of falling action."

"I'm falling asleep here. What?"

A week later, the *Ranger's* admiral gathers the whole air wing up in the fo'c's'le—he makes everybody take off their flight suits and wear khakis, the dick—and they all fumble around trying to make a formation around the big-ass anchor chains, and those big shiny things the anchor chains wrap around that pull the anchors up and down—

"Windlasses," Gary said.

"Whatever."

The admiral gets up on a platform by the bow, where the ship comes to a point like a black shoe's head, and announces that the intelligence weenies say that because of Jack's kick-ass plan, Admiral Gorschkov has decided it's impossible to defeat a U.S. carrier group with bombers, and has ordered the entire Soviet Naval Air Force to disband.

"Holy shit," Gary said.

The admiral calls Jackie up to the platform and shakes his hand and sticks a Navy Commendation Medal on his chest. Jackie's all red in the face and aw shucks about it, and is crawling over one of the big-ass anchor chains on his way back to the formation when the admiral says:

"Not so fast."

Jackie stops in his tracks.

"I just remembered," the admiral says. "You're only a jay gee. You're not senior enough to have a Navy Commendation Medal. Haul your big young carcass back up here."

Jackie turns white, and everybody thinks he's going to cry like a girl.

"It was awful to look at, but fun," Buzz said.

Jackie hauls his big young carcass back over to the platform, like some French faggot going to the guillotine, and he trips on a step, and the admiral says, "C'mon, c'mon."

Jackie stands in front of the admiral. The admiral takes hold of the medal he just pinned above Jackie's pocket, like he's about to rip it off, and says, "Nope, you can't wear this ..." and he moves his hands to the silver jay gee bars on Jackie's collar and says, "... while you're still wearing these."

He rips the jay gee bars off Jackie's collar and slaps a set of lieutenant railroad tracks where they used to be.

"Holy shit," Gary said. "Did Jackie faint like a girl?"

"Nah," Buzz said. "He let us down on that score. We all expected him to. It was a setup. Everybody knew what was going to happen except Jackie, the clueless dip shit. He did cut a nice loud fart, though."

"Droll," Gary said.

"I laughed till I shit," Buzz said, "then I cried like a girl."

They all get home to Fightertown months later and everybody is talking about how some E-2 NFO homo kicked the Backfires' butts, and the fighter guys just tagged along like a flock of wet poodles. How this E-2 fag might get command of the fighter wing someday— the horror—because he might be the next E-2 guy to make admiral, which is a big deal, because E-2 admirals are rare.

"About as rare as me and my old lady doing the deed is these days," Buzz said.

"Re-droll," Gary said.

Jackie's reputation from The Great Big Backfire Raid gets him a job teaching tactics at the air power training base in Purgatory, Nevada, and then his assistant navigator job, where he earns all his ship driver quals.

"So from now on," Buzz said, "all the senior dip shits who sit on promotion boards will go gaga over Jackie's service record till the day he dies or shits the bed, whichever comes first."

Gary crossed his flabby arms over his waterbed. "All that hoopla over a little thing like defeating the whole Soviet Naval Air Force without firing a single shot."

"Over a little thing like that," Buzz agreed.

"How very Sun Tzu. I guess that sort of thing might impress some people."

"Sickening, isn't it?" Buzz said. "So many people get taken in by that razzle-dazzle show-off shit. Besides, Jackie didn't do it all by himself. I, NFO Man, was there. I'm the one who shot the first pretend missile."

"So, really, Buzz, Jackie just took all the credit for your hard work."

"I'm so glad someone else sees it that way. Finally."

His story finished, Buzz looked around the Dirty Shirt for somebody more important to talk to than Gary, which was normally anybody else there. Unfortunately for Buzz, his recital of The Great Big Backfire Raid had gone on well past lunchtime, and the only guys left in the Dirty Shirt were a pair of ensign intelligence weenies who were playing with a deck of Tarot cards as part of their training to someday become senior intelligence weenies. Junior intelligence weenies, as a rule, aren't all that intelligent, but these two were intelligent enough to know what would happen if Buzz Rucci came over to their table and started bending their ears. So the second they saw him looking over at them, they got up and hauled ass out of the Dirty Shirt.

Buzz turned back to Gary just in time to see him dabbing his napkin against a new trail marker stain on the crotch of his khaki pants. "Hey, Gravy Groin. I just had a thought."

Gary rolled his eyes. Even they were getting fat. "Remarkable, Buzz. Call the bridge and have them make an official log entry."

"Be that way, then," Buzz said and moped.

"Oh, grow up," Gary said through his last forkful of trail marker. "So you were saying, everybody thinks Jackie will make admiral?"

"Won't help himself, he keeps pissing off bastards like Bull Palsy."

"No," Gary said, wiping his face with his napkin. "But like you said, Jackie's a big strong boy. I'm sure he'll do all right. I won't be around to see it though."

"You're getting out of the Navy?"

"Unlike our pal Jackie, I have no interest in being an admiral. 'Navy. Aim Low.' That's my motto."

"And you're hitting the mark so far, SWO Boy. Don't you want to stick around, have command of your own little ship someday, a frigate or a destroyer of a tuna boat or something?"

Gary wadded his napkin and threw it at the table, and missed.

SWO Boy Blue

Up on the bridge, Jack bent his knees and tried to ignore the pain in his feet and his back and the rest of him. His Jap job said Gary would be along to relieve him in thirty minutes. Unless, of course, the chief engineer decided to call away a no-notice General Quarters drill. In that case, Gary would have to report to his damage control locker and stop an imaginary flood or put out an imaginary fire. That could take hours.

Jack asked God to please spare him that shit.

☆ ☆ ☆ ☆ ☆

Down in the Dirty Shirt, Gary looked at his napkin lying on the deck. He thought about picking it up, but decided to complain to Buzz about his lot as a surface warfare officer instead.

"My four year commitment from the academy is up in six months. I'll turn down promotion to lieutenant and go back to school and get a master's degree in business."

Buzz shook his head. "You don't want to stick around long enough to become Skipper Fatty?"

"In another ten years? I won't last that long. You don't get it, Buzz, what it's like to be a black shoe. You Airedales think the Navy is just one big party. You get drunk, blown, and laid from day one in flight school. Dumb ass NFOs like you and Jack don't have airline jobs waiting for you on the outside like the pilots do, so you take these bonuses to stay in till you're old enough for a euthanasia board, but you don't care because you're still getting drunk, blown, and laid, so you don't ask questions."

"Was there a point to all that you just said?" Buzz asked.

"The point is, we don't get no stinking drunk blown and laid. All we get is the bone up the butt from day one."

"But I thought you black shoes liked the bone up the butt from day one."

"Aw, stow it." Gary, on a roll now, railed about how little black shoe ensigns got three months of Surface Warfare Officer School then got shoved out to the fleet, where they were expected to become master ship handlers before they knew how to find the officers' head. If they were lucky, they got assigned an enlisted chief who showed them the ropes. But most of them got a chief who didn't show them anything except how to fuck up, which they didn't need because they already knew how to fuck up.

And you'd never excel at anything. The second it looked like you might have a clue what you were doing, they piled more and more crap on you until you were just as burned out as the rest of the dip shits.

Gary'd been on two-watch bills before he and Jack went down to two sections on the bridge, when either Jack was the OOD or Gary was. The only reason he got off the engineering watch bill was because the gator threatened to rip the chief engineer's dick out of his pants and throw it over the side if he didn't cut Gary a break. Gary thought he might start getting a little sleep, only standing twelve hours of watch a day, but then that new ensign who looked like Michael Jackson hurled himself off the flight deck four weeks into the NORPAC, and the chief engineer made Gary take over the sorry dead asshole's division, and his damage control locker.

"No, sir," Gary said. "No life of a SWO Daddy for me. It's not about who can do the best job. It's about who can do the most mediocre job."

"But you're the most mediocre job they have, Gary. You have to stay in. Your Navy needs you."

"Fuck the Navy. I stick around much longer, I'll hurl myself off the flight deck too."

"So?" Buzz said. "What's the harm in that? You're so fat you'd never drown."

"That's another thing—"

Buzz glanced at his Jap job and got up from the table. "I'd love to hear it, but I'm late for my nap. I need to rest up so I can hit the gym in time to be all manly and pumped up for my watch in combat."

"You have an actual watch today?"

"Yeah," Buzz said, all gloomy. "I drew the short straw. Oh, well. Life's a bitch, and then you have kids with one."

Gary shook his head, wondering if the bitch he might never have kids with might bitch at him too much. He reached for his still half-full glass of orange sludge, and his hand froze an inch away from the glass. "Wait."

"What?" Buzz said, and stopped, and turned back around to face Gary. "Put your hand down and ask your question."

Gary put his hand down. "What you said about the Great Big Backfire Raid. If Admiral Gorschkov stood down his naval air force after that, how come we still come up to frozen Alaska and practice fighting his naval air force?"

"How the fuck would I know?" Buzz said. "Why worry your pretty little head about it? Tell you what, SWO Boy, do something nice for yourself to get all these troubling questions out of your mind. Treat yourself to a piece of pie from the dessert cart, maybe with some whipped cream, and a scoop of ice cream, or two scoops of ice cream. Why not? You only live once. And don't worry about having to buy new uniforms when that waterbed of yours gets even bigger. Bellbottom shirts will come back in style any day now."

And Buzz disappeared to his stateroom.

Gary watched him leave, muttered "asshole," patted his waterbed, and tried not to think about that piece of pie. He looked at his napkin, still sitting on the deck. Then he glanced furtively over at the dessert cart. He got up. He went over to it. He hesitated.

He decided.

He acted.

He got himself the biggest piece of pie left in the pan, and that part that broke off from that other piece too, and slapped a dollop of whipped cream on top of it, and two scoops of ice cream, and some chocolate sauce. And some of the caramel sauce too. And some of the candy sprinkles, in all the nice colors, and a little of the shredded coconut, and a handful of those mixed nuts.

Eating all that shit he didn't need depressed him even worse than he was depressed before. To make himself feel better, he thought about what he hadn't told Buzz about what he knew about Jack.

Before he and Jack had gone port and starboard on the bridge, when they still occasionally spent time in their stateroom together, he'd heard plenty of Jack tossing and turning and talking in his sleep about Liz and Joe and the rest of it. Sometimes, if you didn't know the guy any better, you'd think he was crying. Whatever success Jack might achieve in the Navy, he was paying too high a price for it.

But then again, Gary thought, Jack's not a totally heinous fat piece of shit like I am. So he's got that going for him.

So fuck him.

Gary picked the last candy sprinkle off his dessert plate, one of the pretty green ones, and held it on the tip of his finger, and looked at it, and threw it back on the plate, and pushed himself away from the table, and looked at his Jap job.

Fifteen minutes until he had to relieve Jack on the bridge. Not enough time to take a nap, or get any of his other crap done. Not even time enough to take a healthy crap. Might as well sit here a few more minutes.

He reached to his dessert plate to snag that last candy sprinkle, and almost had it to his mouth when from out of the 1MC ship-wide announcement system came:

"Bong! Bong! Bong! Bong! This is a drill, this is a drill, General Quarters, General Quarters, all hands man your battle stations."

"Fuck me in the heart," Gary cried, instantly hoping nobody had heard him say it, because they'd pitch him shit forever about it later.

General Quarters

"Fuck me in the heart," Jack said up on the bridge, instantly hoping the gator hadn't heard him say it. The gator would pitch him shit forever about setting a bad example for the enlisted men.

✮   ✮   ✮   ✮   ✮

Down in the Dirty Shirt, Gary hauled himself out of his chair. His feet slogged his waterbed and his narrow shoulders and his wide hips and the rest of him down to his damage-control locker on the second deck. He put on a yellow rain slicker and a helmet and a breathing apparatus that weighed forty pounds. Then he picked up a fire hose and lurched six decks deeper into number four main machinery room, leading a four-man hose team of enlisted men who didn't like playing fire putter-outers in four main machinery room any more than Gary did.

✮   ✮   ✮   ✮   ✮

An hour into the General Quarters drill, Jack's back and right leg went numb. He schlepped over to the starboard side, hoping nobody noticed him limping, and propped himself against the navigation table.

"You okay, Mister H?" Chief Kirk said.

"Yeah, Chief. Do me a favor, though. Go back in the office and bring me a fistful of those eight-hundred-pound Motrins in my desk drawer."

"Sure, sir. Just be careful how many of those things you take."

"Nothing to worry about, Chief. They're sugar free, right?"

✮   ✮   ✮   ✮   ✮

Two hours later, down on the sixth deck, Gary and the rest of the sailors on his damage control team finally didn't really put out the fire that wasn't really there.

On the bridge, the duty bosun mate announced, "Secure from General Quarters" over the 1MC.

Gary and his enlisted firemen put away their hose, and Gary put away his fireman gear, and tromped what was left of his bloat up more decks and levels of ladders than he cared to count so he could relieve Jack on the bridge.

When he got to the O3 level, he stopped by the officers' head just off the admiral's blue tile area and crapped out all the crap he'd eaten for lunch.

Up on the bridge, Chief Kirk said, "Wonder what's taking Mister Constantine so long to get up here and relieve you?"

Jack lifted his binoculars off his neck and laid them face-down on the navigation table.

"No doubt he's in an officers' head, relieving himself of a few thousand candy sprinkles."

Chief Kirk laughed.

$$\star \quad \star \quad \star \quad \star \quad \star$$

On the O2 level, just under the Dirty Shirt, Buzz rolled over in his rack and said, "What the fuck?" when the duty bosun announced the end of General Quarters. He'd disconnected his stateroom's 1MC speaker when General Quarters went down. The electrician's mates must have snuck in while he was asleep and re-connected it, the sneaky little shits.

Oh well. No sense getting worked up over it. He checked his Jap job. His watch in combat didn't start for hours yet. He put his head back on his pillow.

The door was still locked. His phone was still off the hook. Life was still good.

A Perfect Cluster Fuck

Christmas Day, four days south of the NOLA, Admiral Felon decided he wanted to conduct flight operations, even though the NORPAC had been successfully completed. The air wing still had a little gas money left, and Fix wanted them to burn it up before the end of the fiscal quarter, or some bullshit like that. The battle group was out of range of any suitable divert air field, and the weather officer had warned that a storm front approaching from Kamchatka could close in on them at any time.

Jack had the deck when *Connie* prepared to launch the first go at noon, and was standing by the captain's chair when he overheard Zach Taylor tell the gator, "I told Fix this morning that we could get cloud clobbered in a heartbeat, and there's nowhere to send the air wing if they can't land back here. But he said, 'We call ourselves an all-weather, blue-water air force. Let's prove we really are one.'"

Zach crossed his legs, and waved the back of his hand at the world in general. "Prove it, shit. All we're going to prove is that we know how to crush our heels into our dicks. This is goddamn dangerous."

That got Jack's attention. If Zach Taylor thought something was dangerous enough to admit out loud it was dangerous—*goddamn dangerous*, at that—then it was mighty goddamn dangerous.

Conditions were getting worse as aircrew manned their jets. The weather officer came up to the bridge and showed Zach Taylor a cartoon he'd drawn depicting a frightened aircraft carrier rolling up the face of a giant wave, an oil slick trailing from its stern.

Zach picked up a phone and rang Fix Felon. "Admiral, the latest forecast looks bad. Do you want to hold the launch and see how things develop?"

He listened and scowled. "Aye, aye, Admiral. Launch as scheduled." He waited for Felon to hang up and slammed the phone down.

The weather officer went below to the weather office and hid under his coffee mug.

Jack ordered the conning officer, Stick Boy, to bring the ship into the wind as the first jets taxied to the catapults.

The rescue helicopter launched, then the fixed wing aircraft. As the last jet launched off the bow, Mother Nature shit a ton of bricks. Winds kicked up to fifty knots and swells rose to forty feet. Green water broke over the carrier's bow.

Zach's phone rang. "No, Admiral. Like I said this morning, we don't have a divert field. Yes sir, I'll order an immediate recovery."

"We'll have to do a radar approach," the gator said.

"No shit," Zach said. "You think I'm blind?"

The gator called air traffic control, down on the second deck behind combat, and told them to start working out a precision approach.

Jack did some calculations of his own. At fifty knots, the natural winds were such that the ship could only make bare steerage—a couple, three knots, maybe—without exceeding wind restrictions. Too little wind, planes crashed. Too much wind, they couldn't get down to catch a wire. Steaming at bare steerage meant the ship's rudders would have little effect on the ship's heading, and holding course to keep the wind down centerline of the landing area would be a bitch to pull off. The sea swells the storm front had kicked up came from thirty degrees left of where the wind blew from, which made things suck even worse.

As *Connie* slowed her turn and came back into the wind, a swell that must have been a hundred feet high, looking like a special effect in a movie because nothing in real life could look like that, slammed into *Connie's* port bow. It sounded like a bomb cooking off, and slammed the ship out of the wind, forcing the first jet coming down the glide slope to wave off.

Zach Taylor started badgering Stick Boy about staying on course. When the second jet had to wave off too, Zach lost patience and barked rudder orders directly at Petty Officer Johnson on the helm, which confused the hell out of Johnson and Stick Boy both. Strict naval procedure demands that only the conning officer can give orders to the helmsman, and forbids the helmsman to take orders from anyone but the conning officer.

Jack stepped in. "Captain, do you want to take the conn?"

Zach ignored him, and continued to shout at Stick Boy and Johnson as a third plane waved off, then a fourth.

The gator, standing behind Zach's chair, said, "Uh oh."

Zach screamed another order at the helm. Stick Boy looked at Jack, his mouth open and nothing coming out of it.

A fifth plane waved off.

The gator turned white. "They're going to run out of gas before we can get them aboard."

"Shit! Shit! Shit!" Zach screamed. His phone rang. He ignored it, and shouted another steering order, something incoherent that sounded like "Swing your partner before I split your engines."

Petty Officer Johnson looked at Jack. "Sir, what do I do?"

Jack said, "In the pilot house, this is Mister Hogan, I have the conn. Helmsman, belay that last order. Right thirty degrees rudder."

That didn't make sense to Johnson either. Thirty degrees was too much rudder to use during a recovery. "Orders to the helm, sir?"

"Just do it. Now."

"Right thirty degrees rudder, aye."

★　★　★　★　★

Like all carrier helmsmen, Johnson had been trained not to "oversteer" during a recovery. If you used too much rudder, you'd rock the boat and create a Dutch roll at the ass end of the ship while jets were trying to land on it. But these weren't normal circumstances. Johnson had never seen anything like this before. Best to follow Mister Hogan's orders to the letter, he figured.

He sure hoped Mister Hogan knew what he was doing.

★　★　★　★　★

Jack didn't have a clue what he was doing. He'd never seen anything like this before either. You heard about conditions like these from old timers, but you always figured they were bullshitting you. Jack knew you normally didn't want to oversteer during a recovery, but normal procedures weren't working. Might as well try something radical, like using full rudder throw.

He looked aft from the port bridge wing. The next jet, an A-7, was on final. He glanced forward to see the ship's bow knifing into the next swell. "Left thirty degrees rudder."

Johnson snapped the wheel to port, which held the ship in the wind long enough for the A-7 to catch the one-wire, the first of four arresting wires on the flight deck.

Jack turned to look aft again, and caught a glimpse of Zach Taylor. Zach was curled in his chair, staring at something a thousand yards away. Sweat stains under his eyes and dark circles under his armpits. And a smell coming from him: something you hardly ever noticed, somebody else's body odor, that far into an at-sea period, unless it was an unusual odor, something like …

Holy shit, Jack thought. He's afraid.

Zach focused for a moment and met Jack's eyes. Then he turned away and stared at the low visibility.

Jack looked aft, then forward again, and gave another rudder order. He was barking rudder orders out his ass, now: left rudder, right rudder, shift them, and amidships; ease them, increase them, and steady as you go.

Picture that, all those rudder orders flying out of Jack's ass, crashing around the bridge like bats in a belfry.

Imagine how it looked to Petty Officer Johnson!

The Rocky Horror Recovery went on for over an hour. They had to launch three extra tankers to keep everybody in the air until they could bring them all aboard.

Jack was about out of gas himself when the E-2 Hawkeye, recovering "dead last" as it always did, reached final. Over the radio, its pilot called "Hawkeye ball, low fuel light."

They'd recovered the tankers by then, but that didn't matter. The E-2 was the only aircraft on the carrier that couldn't refuel in the air. Jack knew all five guys in the airplane. One of them had been Jack's instructor in flight school. The other four guys Jack liked. He knew their wives and kids too. They wouldn't have enough gas to come around for a second try. Jack said a quick prayer.

Connie's bow met the base of the next swell.

"Left thirty degrees rudder," Jack ordered.

Johnson cranked the rudders left.

The Hawkeye caught the four-wire.

The rescue helicopter came aboard.

The swells ebbed and a heavy rain began to pound the flight deck as enlisted men in yellow slickers scrambled to chain the aircraft down to the pad eyes embedded in the flight deck.

Jack's hands began to shake as he ordered Johnson to bring the ship out of the wind. "Somebody else want to take the conn for a while?"

One of Gary's watch-standers walked up to him and snapped him a salute. "Sir, request permission to take the conn, coming to course—"

"Belay your reports," Jack said. "Just take it."

He looked at the ensign taking the conn and realized she was a girl. He hadn't seen her before. She had, in fact, just flown aboard the day before on the COD—the Carrier Onboard Delivery aircraft, a C-2 Greyhound. This ensign was the first woman ever assigned to a fleet aircraft carrier.

Jack didn't know that, or how important it made her, so he said,

"And grab yourself a shave before you come up on the bridge again. You don't want to set a bad example for the troops."

A glance at his Jap job told him the recovery had gone on forty minutes past watch turnover time. He limped over to Gary, who stood by the captain's chair. "Can't give you much of a pass down, SWO Boy. I got a little distracted."

"So I saw. Fair piece of ship driving, Dog Fart. Let's get your watch team relieved and send them to chow."

The last of Jack's team to report off was Petty Officer Johnson. "Sorry I let you down, sir. You shouldn't have had to step in and give me rudder orders like that."

"Fuck that 'sorry sir' shit," Jack said. "If you hadn't followed those rudder orders to the letter, a lot of guys in dry flight suits would be in wet flight suits right now."

"Thanks, sir. And pardon me for saying so, but you did pretty good for an officer."

"Damn your impertinence, Johnson. Strike below and get some chow."

"Strike below and get some chow and damn my impertinence, aye, sir."

Gary and Jack reported to Zach Taylor, still in his barber chair, watching rain pellets splatter against the wind screen, his legs and arms crossed, a couple hairs on his crewcut out of place.

"I have the deck, sir," Gary said.

Zach sighed. "Okay."

$$\star \quad \star \quad \star \quad \star \quad \star$$

Jack was alone at a corner table in the Dirty Shirt, halfway through a plate of mystery stew, when eight guys in flight suits from the A-6 Intruder squadron walked over. The squadron's skipper, a blonde guy Jack knew vaguely from his CAG 6 days, said, "Word on the street is Captain Zach lost it on the bridge and you stepped in and saved everybody's bacon again."

Jack blinked and put down his fork. "It wasn't that dramatic, Skipper. Just a little more weather than we expected. The captain was more comfortable with me taking the conn from the ensign, that's all."

"Yeah, right," the skipper said. "That was a little more weather than Dorothy and Toto were expecting too. Whatever. We all owe you one."

The skipper held out his hand, and Jack stood and shook it. The rest of the A-6 guys shook Jack's hand as well. Then all the guys in the Dirty Shirt who'd landed in the Rocky Horror Recovery got up, and stood in line to shake his hand.

"And an E-2 pussy," one F-14 pilot said as he walked away. "Who would have thought he had it in him?"

★ ★ ★ ★ ★

Lying in his rack, Jack thought how proud his dad would have been to see what a bold, competent naval officer his son had become.

Then he felt ashamed of himself for being such a sentimental dip shit.

Off His Rocker

They weren't home yet.

The morning before *Connie* pulled back into San Diego, she was scheduled to transfer two thousand pallets of ammunition to *Mars* for further transfer to the carrier *Kitty Hawk*, which was to sortie for a WESTPAC deployment later in the month.

The shitty weather had followed *Connie* all the way down the west coast of North America. The entire naval operating area off Southern California was smothered in fog like the whipped cream on Gary's blueberry pie. From the bridge, you could barely see the red and white striped lines that marked the landing area on the angle deck.

Gary, on watch as OOD, used radar to bring *Connie* to waiting station, a nautical mile astern of *Mars*. (Zach Taylor might not have thought too much of Gary's skills, but as Jack and the gator would tell you, that chubby little SWO Boy knew how to drive a ship.) Jack, filling in for Gary's Junior Officer of the Deck, who was in sickbay with a nervous colon, manned the port-side radar repeater. "Holding steady at two thousand yards," he reported.

The gator sat in the captain's chair. Since shitting his pants in the middle of the Rocky Horror Recovery, Zach Taylor had spent most of his time in his at-sea cabin. Jack had only seen him once in passing, and Zach had seemed to go out of his way to avoid eye contact.

"I can't see *Mars*' stern light," the gator said. "Can either of you?"

"Negative," Jack said.

Gary shook his head. "Double negative."

The gator clucked his tongue. "I'm going to tell the captain we need to cancel this. Let *Kitty Hawk* go fish."

As the gator reached for the phone, Zach Taylor swept onto the bridge, scrubbed and shaved, wearing crisp khakis.

"We on station?"

"Yes, sir," the gator said.

Zach looked out the windscreen. "Oh, yeah, there's *Mars*."

Gary, Jack, and the gator stole sideways glances at each other. Zach's eyes couldn't be good enough to see through fog, could they?

Zach walked to the conning officer's station, elbowed Stick Boy out of the way, and picked up the microphone to the bridge-to-bridge radio. "*Mars, Constellation* actual, let me talk to your captain."

Seconds later, Bull Palsy answered. "*Mars* actual here, Captain. It's a great Navy day, isn't it? I can see your bow just fine from here."

"Yeah, right," the gator mumbled.

"You're slightly obscured from here," Zach said. "Nothing we can't work with, though. I'll bring us a little closer."

Zach grabbed a pair of walkie-talkies from the console next to his chair and handed one to the gator. "Stay here. I'm going to the bow," he said, and whisked off the bridge.

A minute later, the gator's walkie-talkie crackled.

"Gator, Captain, how do you read me?"

"Loud and clear, sir."

"Put on two more turns."

Jack looked up from the radar repeater. "You want me to take the conn, Gator?"

"You've had enough fun for one bad acid trip," the gator said. "Stay on the radar. Let somebody else share the adventure." He turned his head to starboard and announced, "This is the navigator, I have the conn. Lee helmsman, order two more turns."

"Turns for zero seven two RMP aye," the lee helmsman said.

The captain's phone rang. The gator tapped Gary's shoulder. "Get that for me, huh? If it's the admiral, tell him all the grownups are busy right now."

Gary reached behind the gator and took the phone. "Yes, Admiral. Have we commenced our approach? I think so, sir... Sir? No, they're all busy. The captain's off the bridge, sir."

"He's off his fucking rocker," the gator muttered. "That's what he's off of."

Admiral Felon growled in Gary's ear and hung up.

"Range one thousand, eight hundred yards," Jack reported.

A collision at sea can ruin your whole day, he thought, that's how the shopworn Navy saying went. It could ruin your career too. If *Connie* so much as swapped a molecule of paint with *Mars*, Zach Taylor would be relieved of command, and an 80,000-ton aircraft carrier slamming into its supply ship was likely to do a lot more than minor damage. If Zach managed to kill somebody pulling a stunt like this in zero visibility, he'd almost certainly do some hard jail time, and a lot of his bridge watch-standers—namely the gator,

Gary and Jack—might have to tag along to the big house and keep him company.

The gator tapped his walkie-talkie against his thigh. "Anybody see *Mars'* stern light yet?"

Gary lifted his binoculars. "I can't even see the captain on the bow."

"Me neither," the gator said. "How about that, guys? Did you ever dream you'd see a day when you couldn't see the captain and wished you could?"

"What's the captain doing?" Gary said.

Just loud enough for Jack and Gary to hear, the gator said, "Looks to me like Zach and Bull are trying to one-up Fix Felon."

"One thousand yards," Jack said.

"Will the admiral stop them?" Gary said.

"I bet not," the gator said. "He's still embarrassed about making us fly the other day against Zach's advice, when we almost lost half the air wing. I think Zach's daring Felon to step in now, and I don't think Felon will do it. Hell of a way to escalate a pissing contest, huh?"

"Yes, sir," Gary said.

Jack wasn't sure who was more embarrassed—Fix Felon for having ordered the air wing to fly despite the weather advisory, or Zach Taylor for having fallen apart in the middle of the recovery. He wasn't sure if Taylor was trying to prove something to Felon, or to himself, or to everybody else, or some combination of people, or if, as the gator had said, Zach had just gone off his rocker.

Over the walkie-talkie, Zach said, "I can see her now. Four more turns."

The gator relayed the order, and the lee helmsman dialed in zero seven six RPM on the engine order telegraph, which sent a signal to the control rooms in each of the four main machinery rooms down on the sixth deck. Teenaged machinist mates, none of whom had a clue what was going on up on the bridge or the bow, or between Zach

Taylor and Bull Palsy and Fix Felon, turned their throttle wheels the exact correct amount to allow four more revolutions worth of 1,200 pounds-per-square-inch superheated steam into their giant main turbine engines. (To give you an idea how much power that is, a pinhole leak in a 1,200-pound steam line could slice a sailor's fingers off faster than it takes to sneeze.)

Up on the bridge, Gary, Jack, and the gator didn't see *Mars* until *Connie*'s bow had already glided down the port edge of her stern.

On the starboard side of the flight deck, the gunner's mates' rifle launchers popped, and shot lines went over from *Connie*. Messenger lines came back from *Mars*, and transfer rigs played out between the two ships. Two pallets of ammo—of the thousand pallets scheduled—had transferred over to *Mars* when Zach Taylor marched triumphantly back onto *Connie*'s bridge. "That's enough," he said. "I have the conn. Signal for breakaway."

The duty bosun mate sounded six short blasts on the ship's whistle. *Mars* reeled in the transfer rigs. Zach eased *Connie* left until she was clear of *Mars*, and gave the conn back to Stick Boy.

Zach's phone rang and the gator picked it up. "Captain, for you. Admiral Felon."

Zach sauntered to the port side and took the phone.

"Yes, Admiral. That's right, we only sent across two pallets. But we proved we could do it, didn't we? Just like we proved we could do blue-water flight ops in shitty weather the other day. Yes, Admiral, I'll write the whole thing up in my after-action report to Naval Air Force Pacific. I'm sure AIRPAC will want to hear about the whole thing, every little detail, especially the part where, in front of several witnesses, I advised you against launching the air wing that day. Yes, I will write that in the report, Admiral. All right then, sir, you have a great Navy day too, Admiral."

Zach hung up, rubbed his hands together, and strutted back and forth across the bridge. The watch-standers, officer and enlisted alike, stayed out of his way. As he passed the port-side radar repeater, Zach tapped Jack on the shoulder, looked him in the eye, and leaned in close enough that Jack could smell his Old Spice aftershave.

Zach whispered, "How about that shit, hot shot?"

Back on Dry Land

They broke out of the fog twelve thousand yards before Buoy 1SD, just like the weather officer had said they would. One second, nothing out the windscreen but Egyptian cotton, the next, boom, there it all was. Point Loma on the left, Coronado on the right, and the entrance to the channel in between, dead on the bow, right where Chief Kirk had said it would be. And above it all sat a sky as blue as a blond baby's eyes.

The channel guard helicopter rushed the harbor pilot aboard, and by the time the duty messenger had hustled him up from the flight deck to the bridge, the big wrinkled bastard was red as a tomato and sounded like he'd punctured a lung.

Chief Kirk, leaning against the navigation table between fixes, nudged Jack. "We going to have to call away a medical emergency for the sloppy old fart? I'd hate to see any more delays in getting home."

The harbor pilot wiped his face with his handkerchief and walked up to Zach Taylor. In between wheezes, he said, "How was your trip, Captain?"

Zach smiled brilliantly. "Stimulating."

☆ ☆ ☆ ☆ ☆

A rap on the office door, and Chief Kirk came in. "Damn, Mister H., liberty call went down twenty minutes ago. Everybody else done got off and went."

"Just proofreading one last piece of paperwork, Chief. Then I'm out of here too."

"Must be one important piece of paperwork, keep you from running home to that wife of yours. Where'd you meet her, anyway? Miramar Officers' Club."

"Nah. V.D. clinic."

"Yeah, right." The chief chuckled and looked over Jack's shoulder to see what he was working on. "Oh, no. Don't tell me the gator made you write his officer's fitness report for him."

Theoretically, senior officers wrote their subordinate officers' fitness reports, but the gator didn't trust Zach Taylor to write his FITREP, and he knew better than to try to write his own. The gator could barely write a check.

"The man knows his limits," Jack said. "And he knows how to delegate."

The chief plopped in his chair and slapped his ball cap on his desk. "You giving him a sterling endorsement?"

"The guy parted the Red Sea according to this," Jack said. "Paragon of virtue, best ship-handler since Jason of the Argonauts, greatest military leader since Alexander the Great, blah, blah, blah. You know. Standard lies you put in every officer's FITREP."

"He'll owe you big-time for that. That's what I love about you, Mister H. Most times, when an elephant tells somebody he wants something bad, he gets it bad. Somebody wants something bad from you, they get it back with candy sprinkles on top."

"Yeah, well," Jack said as he put the gator's FITREP in a blue administrative routing folder, "I did slip the term 'pole smoker' in halfway through the third paragraph. Maybe the captain's secretary will catch it before it goes out the door. Maybe he won't."

The chief tapped some of that putrid shit he called pipe tobacco into the bowl of his hand-carved meerschaum. "He doesn't, that's how the gator's FITREP will go to his captain selection board."

"Who knows, Chief? It might help him get promoted."

Chief Kirk lit a kitchen match on his thumbnail and drew the flame into his pipe. It smelled God-awful.

"Where the hell do you buy that pipe tobacco, Chief?"

"Don't buy it, sir," the chief said out a corner of his mouth, the pipe's stem clenched between his teeth while he cupped both hands over the bowl to get a good alpha-class fire going. "We grow it down in the jet shop. Couple other chiefs and me, we fixed us up a whole hydroponic tobacco farm down there, got ultraviolet lights set up in it and everything."

"You ever heard of these things called tobacco shops, Chief?"

"Don't believe in them, sir. Hell, kick the door open if the smoke's bothering you. Nobody left up here to give a shit except you and me."

Jack got up and opened the door. "Okay, Chief, your little ruse to get me out of here worked. As usual, great doing business with you. Let's not do it again real soon."

"Roger, that, sir. Oh, wait."

"What?" Jack stopped in the doorway.

"I almost forgot." The chief put his fuming pipe in his ashtray and stood. He pulled an oblong package from the map pocket of his flight jacket, the one he only wore when nobody else was around, because a surface warfare chief like him wasn't supposed to have a flight jacket. He'd gotten it in some dope deal he'd made with a chief buddy of his in the ship's supply department. He probably traded one of the ship's ten thousand dollar chronometers for it.

"This being your last at-sea period with us and all, Lieutenant, I wanted to give you a little something to remember us by."

Jack took the package. "Should I open it now?"

"Shit, yeah, sir. What's the fun of giving it to you in person if I can't see the look on your face when you open it?"

It was a stadimeter, an old fashioned range finding instrument, like the one Chief Kirk and Jack had used on WESTPAC, when they had time, to calculate the distance to other ships. They'd done it partly to double check the radar's accuracy. But mostly they'd done it because it was fun to do things the way sailors had done things in the days of wooden ships and sails. This stadimeter was a work of art, with chrome plating and ornate engraving on the range scale.

"Chief, I don't know what to say. I can't take this. It must have cost—"

"Shit, sir, cost ain't no problem. I been hanging out with the chief bosun mate. He taught me how to shoplift, heh, heh, heh."

"No, Chief, really—"

The chief snapped his fingers. "I just remembered something else, sir. Damn. I forgot to throw the hasp on the rain gear locker on the signal bridge. I better go take care of it, or I'll be forever trying to steal it back."

Jack blinked, and Chief Kirk was gone.

"Hey, Chief! You want to come back here and put your goddamn pipe out?"

Drunken Sailors

Buzz was sitting at the bottom step of the ladder to the officers' brow.

"Jackie. How about a ride home?"

"Something happen to your Porsche?"

"Don't know. Haven't checked. Too drunk to drive it anyway."

"That was fast."

"Yeah. Fast. My dip-shit chief had ten cases of beer and a butt load of airline bottles waiting on the pier for all the troops in combat, and they challenged me to a chugging contest. You can guess the rest."

"Your guys got you drunk and just left you here?"

"Nah. They offered me a ride. I told them I'd wait for you. I knew you'd stick around and finish up some last minute paperwork. Dip shit."

"Come, on, dumb ass, let's go home."

Buzz got up without help, but it was a close thing.

Buzz put the passenger seat back and passed out. He snored most of the way home.

Jack drove out the back gate, up First Street, then right at the corner of First and Orange Avenue, where Navigation Man didn't have to kiss anybody's ass, and where MEXPAC was. MEXPAC was the Mexican bar and grill where you went to get drunk and then stumble back to your ship the night before it pulled out, so you woke up in your rack on the ship, and not in your bed at home, and miss ship's movement, like Jack almost had.

Left on Fourth Street, across the Coronado Bay Bridge, south on I-5 for a few miles, then north on I-15 for a half hour.

Buzz came to as they passed Naval Air Station Miramar, yawned, stretched and looked through the open T-Top.

"Check it out," he said.

Jack took his eyes off the road and looked left. A fistful of Tomcats and an E-2 circled the field, squeezing in some day landing practice before the sun went down.

"Home sweet home," Buzz said. He pulled his seat back up and rubbed his eyes. "When are you going to get rid of this Trans Am, Jack? You've had it long enough. Sell it to some Marine, get yourself a real car, a Beamer or a Mercedes."

"I'll dump it when I transfer to shore duty, I guess."

"You got orders yet?"

"Yeah. I'm going to the E-2 RAG here at Miramar. Get qualified as an advanced flight instructor before I go to my department head tour."

"Small world," Buzz said. "I'm going to the Miramar Tomcat RAG. Same deal. Get my instructor patch, then back to a fleet fighter squadron."

RAG—Replacement Air Group—was what they called advanced

flight training commands in World War II, where they checked out newly winged naval aviators in fleet aircraft so they could hustle off to a Carrier Air Group—CAG—to replace the guys who'd been killed by the Germans and the Japs. They changed the official name of what they called fleet replacement training squadrons every few years, whenever some rear echelon motherfucker needed an "accomplishment" to put on his fitness report, but in practice, everyone still referred to them as RAGs. And they still called the Carrier Air Wing—and the senior captain who commanded it— CAG.

"We'll still be neighbors," Jack said.

"Just like old times," Buzz said. "You can drive me home from the Miramar O' Club on Wednesday nights. Those two years of ship shit on Connie will seem like a fucked up wet dream."

Jack pulled off on Mira Mesa Road, turned up Scripps Ranch Hill Drive, and stopped in front of the Rucci residence. Buzz's three-year-old son and very pregnant wife stood waiting on the porch. Jack wondered how long they'd been standing there, waiting. Buzz took one of those breath spray squirt bottles from his flight jacket and shot some down his mouth. Like that was going to do a shit bit of good. He reeked.

"Bone the eyes out of Liz for me," Buzz said as he fumbled out the passenger door. "Doesn't look like I'll be getting any tonight."

☆　☆　☆　☆　☆

Their houses were on the hill leading up to Scripps Lake, split level jobs with views of Mira Mesa. When the Blue Angels came to Fightertown, you could watch their show from your back deck. With vaulted ceilings and lots of open space, the interiors were a mishmash of a dozen architectural styles—if you could apply the term "style" to anything built in Southern California.

From the garage you went through a door that took you to the entrance foyer. The stairs to your right took you down to the "luxury" master bedroom suite. Jack took the stairs to his left that led up to the main living space, a multi-level arrangement of rooms: the living room with a fireplace, then two steps up to the dining room and kitchen, a den off to the left of that, and tiny spare bedrooms tucked behind the den. Jack reached the top of the stairs and dropped his gym bag on the floor.

The fireplace was still there.

And the view of Mira Mesa.

And his stereo, in its walnut cabinet, sat against the wall opposite the fireplace.

And a single chair from the six-place dining set he'd bought when Liz moved in with him sat in front of the stereo. She'd insisted they get an extra chair to go with that set in case one broke or got scratched. This must be the seventh chair, sitting in front of the stereo.

His records were stacked by the stereo. Looked like all of them, four piles of fifty or so. When Liz came along, he'd quit sorting and cataloging them like he had when he first became a collector. The den and the dining room were clean as a whistle. The back bedrooms too. No dressers or tables down in the master bedroom, and nothing but carpet where the bed ought to be. Wouldn't that do his back a world of good?

Except—holy shit—she forgot the mirror on the wall above the vanity. How about that?

Back upstairs for another look. Hey, the curtains were still on the windows. The kitchen cabinets and drawers were wiped slicker than snot on a doornob, but the big appliances hadn't walked off. Things weren't so bad. All he needed was a frying pan and a roll of toilet paper and the place would be downright cozy again.

Nothing left in the fridge but the half-gallon jug of cheap wine he'd left himself as a homecoming present. Damn considerate of her to have left that.

He hooked a finger into the handle of the wine jug, took it out, and shut the refrigerator door.

He went over to the kitchen sink to wash his face and saw the answering machine on the breakfast bar, its light blinking. She must have left the answering machine so she could leave a message on it. Tell him it was all a joke; all the house stuff was up in the attic. Early April Fools!

Yeah, right. Wishing shit was chocolate ice cream wouldn't make it cold.

It wasn't Liz. It was Mom.

Mom wasn't sure when he'd be home to get this message. She figured Liz must be visiting friends, that's why she hadn't answered any of Mom's calls.

Mom had meant to have his sister Michelle send him one of those AMWAY messages about Joe like she had about Grandma, but with one thing and another, and Mom was sorry, she was sorry, sorry, sorry, but she just wasn't herself, what with one thing and another, but she would be soon, don't worry about her.

She had to go. She and Michelle had to get back to the church, and take Joe to the cemetery, and pay the priest. Call her as soon as he got home. Bring Liz out for a visit. He had vacation time coming, didn't he? Did they call it "vacation" in the Navy, or did they call it something else? She could never keep straight what they called things in the Navy.

She loved him.

Jack leaned on the kitchen wall and tapped his forehead against it, the wine jug dangling from his left forefinger.

On his way back to the living room, he flicked on the thermostat. It got chilly in San Diego in January when the sun went down. He'd like a fire in the fireplace. But what would he make one out of, the dirty underwear in his gym bag? That would reek worse than Chief Kirk's pipe.

Jack lifted the turntable's dust cover. He took an album from the top of one of the piles. Miles Davis. He'd work.

Jack placed the disc washer against the turning record, just the right amount of pressure to pick up the dust without creating static. He had to do it by sound and feel, with the sun winking out in the windows behind him. There weren't any light fixtures in the ceiling, and the floor lamps were all gone, of course.

He lowered the tone arm. If he'd done everything right, the first thing he heard wouldn't be a pop or a hiss. It would be the sound of Miles playing nothing that wasn't what he heard in his head.

And there it was.

Jack sat in the seventh chair and picked the wine jug up from the floor. He twisted the top off, threw it in the empty fireplace, and drank.

ACT II

A Kinder, Gentler Nation

A Total Quality Experience

Jack didn't recall there being so many steps on the ladder leading up to the second deck of Hangar 6 at Naval Air Station Miramar, the home of his new duty station, the E-2 RAG. Two years of standing bridge watches couldn't have done that much damage to his back and knees, could it? Nah. It was probably just the hangover.

Another knuckle in the Navy's cockamamie scheme for naming and numbering things, he thought. In a Navy building, you went up a ladder from the first deck to get to the second deck. On a Navy ship, you went down. The only time negotiating ladders on a ship was easier than negotiating ladders in a building. Otherwise, the latter beat the pants off the former, heh-heh.

They'd changed the passageway on the second deck since he'd been a student here: different tile, different paint, new pictures and plaques on the wall. The crowd in the ready room looked familiar enough, though: a class of NFO students in one corner studying their training manuals, a class of pilot students in another corner, pretending to. Two instructors playing ace/deuce, three others up front by the big-screen TV reading *The Wall Street Journal*, four more over by the coffee mess arguing over who got the last of the double-chocolate donuts. The rest of them were just sitting around, looking like they'd rather be hanging from a crucifix than hanging around here.

Jack couldn't think of the name of the guy who said he could tell a winning team from a losing team just by walking into the locker room, but whoever that guy was, these guys were a busload of

Chicago Cubs.

The ensign at the duty desk had mousy bangs she must have trimmed herself that spilled over puppy brown eyes. She hadn't quite outgrown her complexion, but she was being brave about it. You put a dab of lipstick on her nose and she could entertain at kids' parties. Only a mother could love a face like that, and only if you paid her enough.

"Hi. I'm Jack Hogan, a new instructor, checking in off transfer leave."

"Good morning, sir. I'm Ensign Simon."

Her voice went with the rest of her. She was the depressed kid sister you wanted to grab up off the couch and throw out the front door, and hope she stumbled across a life out there.

"Nice to meet you, Ensign Simon. What's your call sign? 'Carly?'"

"Yes, sir. How did you guess?"

"Easy. Famous singer."

"Who is?"

"Carly Simon."

"Who's she?"

"Famous singer."

"Who is?"

"Carly … Hey, you look like you might be a little retarded. You're not, are you?"

"No, sir. I'm very smart. I know who Carly Simon is. I'm just pulling your chain. Pretty good for an ensign, huh?"

"Yeah, real good. You do any other tricks?"

"Not yet, but I'm working on a whole bunch. I stand the duty a lot, and I need things to keep myself entertained. That's one of my jobs here: semi-permanent duty officer."

"Semi-permanent duty officer? Who gave you that job?"

"The senior watch officer."

"Oh, nice guy."

"He's not so bad. Here he is now, walking in the other door."

Jack knew the guy from someplace, couldn't remember his name. NFO lieutenant, prematurely gray, always wore that big-ass academy ring of his, actually knocked it against a table every time he sat down at one. Married to a gal from someplace back east where they manufacture politicians. And something else about the guy Jack couldn't recall just that second.

The guy saw him. "Jack Hogan, you old sea dog, I heard you were getting assigned here, good to see you, tell me everything you've been up to."

He came over and shook Jack's hand. That's right, Flip Wilson, Jack could see on the guy's nametag now. "How you been, Flip?"

"Just fine, and I've heard all sorts of big things about you. Hey, guys, anybody who hasn't met him yet, this is the world-famous Jack Hogan, just back from NORPAC. He's the guy who flew with me in The Great Big Backfire Raid."

That's right; that was the other thing Jack couldn't remember about Flip Wilson. The guy was a total asshole. Six months after The Great Big Backfire Raid, you could find five hundred or more guys who'd flown in it, or planned it, or run the whole show by themselves without having suffered the inconvenience of actually having been there. Flip was one of those guys. Flip was like that about everything. A great listener, Flip. Always wanted to hear everything you'd been up to so he could global-replace your name with his and rebroadcast it. A Promethean bullshit artist, Flip was. He hadn't been to literally thousands of fabulous places, and he hadn't done a million fascinating things or met anybody famous there.

Remarkably, half the stiffs in the mausoleum came back to life and lurched over to shake Jack's hand. They'd all heard about The Great Big Backfire Raid. All the tactics schools taught it now, yeah they did. What had it really been like?

Jack was sick and tired of the Great Big Backfire story, sick of hearing it and tired of telling it. And the truth be told, Jack himself wasn't sure how much of it was true anymore. It had happened five years ago. Not that long, in the context of the entire history of human conflict, but by now, *The Iliad* was more historically accurate than anybody's version of The Great Big Backfire Raid.

"It was no big deal," Jack said. "We set a trap and scared the hell out of them. Probably took their commie mommies a week to scrub the shit stains out of their pants."

Hoo-hoo-hoo! Hee-hee-eee! "Commie mommies," that was rich. A regular comedian, this Jack Hogan guy was.

The stiffs wanted to hear about NORPAC too. Tell us about The Almost Great Big Train Wreck, they begged, and The Rocky Horror Recovery, and The Off His Rocker Rendezvous.

Jack was running out of ways to fend off all the requests when Carly stood all five feet of her up from behind the duty desk and announced: "FIVE MINUTES TO SQUADRON QUARTERS! ALL OFFICERS FALL OUT IN THE PARKING LOT."

Jack let the herd clear out and went to the coffee mess to grab a drink of water, and wound up grabbing three of them. Why was he so thirsty? He'd had plenty to drink last night, heh-heh.

☆ ☆ ☆ ☆ ☆

Jack snuck into the last row of the officers' formation as the skipper walked up to the podium. Captain Otis was a good old boy from Georgia or some shit-kick place like that. He was a big ex-athlete-going-to-pot kind of guy, with a perpetual sunburn, a skinhead haircut, and a set of ears like an elephant's. Jack had never met Captain Otis, but he'd heard plenty about him. Yeah, you could see from the ears on the guy how he'd picked up a convoluted call sign like "Mister Potato Head." As soon as Potato Head opened his mouth, you also understood how he got his official unofficial secondary call sign, which was "Goober."

"How y'all doin'?" Otis-Goober-Potato Head said, once Carly—who was also the public affairs officer, it looked like—figured out how to throw the squelch switch on the cheap-o amplifier to the public announcement system, and minced back into the officers' formation.

"Can y'all hear me now? How bout y'all in the back yonder of the enlisted gaggle? Gimme a big ole thumbs-up if y'all can here me back there."

No thumbs.

"How bout if I talk a little louder, haw-haw?"

Still no thumbs.

Thump, thump, thump. Phew, phew.

Ibid on the thumbs.

"Carly, hon, how bout y'all skedaddle back up here and fiddle with the doodads on this here gadget some more?"

Carly skedaddled back to the cheap-o amplifier. She put her knees together, and leaned over and put her hands on them. She squinted through her bangs, and studied the three knobs on the amplifier's control panel like she was trying to figure out how to defuse an atom bomb.

"Go on, touch it, Carly," Goober said. "It ain't gonna bite. Little house current never hurt nobody no how, haw-haw."

Carly reached for the knob in the middle, stopped her hand just shy of it and held it there for a second. She breathed through her mouth, closed her eyes, and put her hand on the knob. When nothing happened, she opened her eyes again and looked over at Potato Head.

Goober shook his head and circled his finger. "Go on, hon, turn her clockwise a little now."

She turned it clockwise a little.

"How bout now?" Goober said. "How bout now? How bout now? How bout now?"

Two thumbs-up in the last row of the enlisted formation.

"Think we're getting there Carly. Keep her coming. How bout now? How bout now?"

All the sailors in the back row of the enlisted formation stuck their thumbs up. Maybe they could hear Goober now, maybe they couldn't. Maybe they just wanted Skipper Potato Head to get on with it. Or maybe they'd heard Otis all along and were just fucking with him the whole time.

Goober beamed. "Nice job, Carly. Didn't Ensign Simon do a fine Navy job, y'all? How bout y'all give her a nice round of applause?"

If the sound of two hands clapping is twice as loud as the sound of one hand clapping, the sound of all hands clapping as Carly traipsed back to the officers' formation was deafening.

Goober got on with it.

"I hope y'all are having a fine Navy day, cause I'm having a fine Navy day, and I'm glad to have the chance to share this fine Navy day with y'all. Now, I hope y'all have had a chance to think about what we jabber-jawed about last week …"

Oh, man. It was a hot day, like it could get in April in San Diego, and it sounded like Goober was just getting warmed up. A lot of sailors standing at parade rest were going to dive nose first into the pavement if this kept up. Jack hoped he wouldn't be one of them. His back wasn't a bit fond of this parade rest shit, and you only got one chance to make a bad first impression.

"… I want to read y'all a quote from a very wise man," Goober said. "Now, when I say this man is a very wise man, what I mean to say is that this man is a very, very, very, very, very wise man. But I don't want to go on too long about how very, very, very, very wise he is because I want to keep this very, very, very, very, very short …"

The muscle in Jack's Achilles lumbar started to twitch.

"Now this very wise man, Doctor Deming, he wrote this here book for a big bunch of them little Japanese business fellahs 'cause they didn't have a pot to piss in. Some of my best friends is little Japanese business fellahs, now, so I can say that about them …"

The horror. Doctor W. Edwards Deming. Jack had heard about him on the *Connie*. Deming was the guy who'd sold the Navy brass on his Total Quality Leadership program they were shoving down everybody's throat now. And it looked like Goober was a true believer. Setting himself up for a Total Quality retirement career, no doubt.

Jack closed his eyes and thought about those dancing squares on his Smiley Mac, and the muscles in his back loosened up a little.

"Now, Doctor Deming says—and whenever Doctor Deming says something you want to listen very, very close, because like I already said, Doctor Deming is a very, very, very wise man …"

Jack looked up from the surface of a Bavarian mountain lake. The hills were like white elephants. The sky was as high as his grandmother's eye. And so was this Goober motherfucker. What the hell was he saying now?

"… and notice how I said Doctor *is* a very wise man, not *was* a very wise man. That's cause Doctor Deming is alive today. I would have said *was* if he wasn't."

Pull in case of emergency. Think about your baby spoon, the silver one Mom still has. She mail-ordered it from someplace in Germany, the city where they made all those porcelain dolls before the allies fire-bombed the shit out of it in World War II. Kurt what's-his-name wrote a novel about it. What was the name of the city? What was the name of the novel? What was what's-his-name's last name?

You wish the prick next to you would let you think a minute, so you could remember …

"Hogan. That's you, right?"

"Leave me alone."

"He's calling your name. Up front."

Fuck me in the heart.

☆ ☆ ☆ ☆ ☆

"Now Lieu-tenant Hogan here is our newest in-structor. He just checked aboard this morning, which is why he's so new."

Somebody give this prick a bazooka and let him shoot me with it.

"And the secretary of the Navy is proud to present him with this here Meritorious Service Medal for all them meritorious things he done out there on that there NORPAC."

How about that? The gator must have written up the citation in Jack's office while Jack was on watch. Probably used Jack's forty-pound dictionary from college to look up all those big words like *the*. Still, he'd gone to the trouble to look them up. Looked like Navigation Man wasn't such a pole smoker after all.

Carly smiled at Jack from the front row of the officers' formation as he made his way back to the back row—if that was really a smile. Real people couldn't twist their faces like that, so it was hard to tell what Carly was actually trying to do with hers.

Jack was almost back in his place when Goober said, "Not so fast there, Lieu-tenant. I just thunk me of something. Skedaddle back on up here."

Not this happy horseshit again.

Well now, y'all had to be a lieu-tenant commander to merit one of them there Meritorious Service Medals. And Jack had gone and merited one of them there medals, so they had to go and promote him early, didn't they?

"Want y'all to come see me in my office after I get done inspecting the troops," Goober pissed in his ear as he pinned gold lieutenant commander's oak leaves on Jack's collar points.

Jack went back to the formation, hid behind three enormous ensigns who'd been football linemen at the academy, and snuck away before Goober started the inspection.

He found the doggone officers' head in the same place they done had it before when he was an ensign flight student. He sat in a stall, locked the door, and leaned his head against the wall.

Just for a minute.

This is a Drill?

Not a soul left in the ready room except this thing at the duty desk that looked like a cross between a field mouse and a wet poodle, which was Carly.

"Where is everybody?" Jack said.

"They're not here, sir."

"I got eyes, Carly. Where did they go?"

"Drinking, probably. That's what they usually do when they don't have to be here, which is most of the time. They were only here this morning because they didn't have a choice. That's a big rule with Captain Otis. Everybody has to show up for quarters and listen to him talk. He likes to talk."

"No!"

"Yes, he likes to talk, and he almost never has anybody to talk to because everybody is almost always anyplace but here, because nobody wants to talk to Captain Otis, because they don't like him. I think he gets lonesome."

"Lonesome? He's got you here. On a semi-permanent basis."

"I know. I think he wants to adopt me."

"Lots of skippers feel that way about their ensigns, Carly."

"No. I mean legally adopt me."

"Then why don't you let him? You have anything better to do?"

"I can't let him adopt me because I'm already adopted."

"Oh." Jack didn't mean to be a dick. It just occurred naturally sometimes. "Sorry."

"Don't be," Carly smiled, or whatever it was she was doing with her face. "I set you up for that. I was just pulling your chain. Like I said, I have to think up lots of things to amuse myself, in my function as semi-permanent duty officer."

"I guess."

"I really am adopted, though, and I hope to find my real parents someday. I'm very interested in the field of genealogy. It's one of the things I research to fill the time while I'm on semi-permanent duty. I'd like to find my real parents, if they're anywhere to be found. I want to discover what makes me tick."

"It's your ticker, Carly, your heart. Research some anatomy while you're at it."

"I know it's my ticker that makes me tick. I'm very smart."

"I know you're smart. You said that already. I'm sorry to hear it. I hope it gets better soon. Anything else wrong with you I ought to know about?"

"My ticker. I have a broke-dick heart. Like all the broke-dick planes we have in the squadron, which is all of them, in spite of Captain Otis's Total Quality Initiatives to fix them."

"What about the flight simulators over in the training building?"

"They're all broke-dick too."

"Then how does the squadron do flight training?"

"It doesn't. That's the other reason nobody's here. I think that's the reason Captain Otis wants to talk to you—"

"How do you know he wants to talk to me?"

"Because he tells me everything. I deduce that's because he doesn't have anybody else to talk to, even his wife, probably. Anyway, I think he thinks you're smart, what with your brilliant service record and everything, and he wants you to come up with a Total Quality way to do flight training without airplanes or flight simulators."

"That'll take a Total Quality Miracle," Jack said.

"I know. That's another reason nobody's here, because Captain Otis is so totally full of shit."

This not-bad-looking petty officer who must have been Otis's secretary was half in and half out of the door to Potato Head's office, looking in at what had to be Goober himself. She had a Colgate smile pasted on her face, nodding at whatever happy-ass thing he was saying in there.

"Yes, sir. Yes, sir. Yes, sir," she said, three times in a row like that, and pulled herself out of the doorway like she was breaking free from a Romulan tractor beam. The second she was out of Goober's line of sight, she opened her mouth, stuck her finger halfway down it and made gag noises. She cut that crap out right away when she saw Jack standing there.

"Oh, hello, sir. Congratulations on the medal and the promotion. Welcome aboard. Have you met anybody else in the squadron yet?"

"Just Ensign Simon."

"Oh. Her. She's nice. I guess. Just don't feed her anything. She'll start following you wherever you go."

Yeah. "Is the skipper in?"

"Yes. Is he expecting you?"

"He is."

"Well. You don't have a choice then. You might want to tape the backs of your ears to your head so he can't talk them off of it."

☆   ☆   ☆   ☆   ☆

A beat-up wooden tennis racket with a head on it the size of the top of a soda can leaned against Goober's desk. On top of the desk was a garish wooden nameplate made in the Philippines with CAPTAIN OTIS printed on it in white letters, no first name, no middle initial. On one wall was a black and white photograph of a football player. It might have been Potato Head's grandson, except the helmet under his arm sported the first facemask ever made, so it had to be Otis.

Gimcracks, doodads, curios all over the place ... Was that

supposed to be a statue of Elvis? Goober's kid must have made it in first grade.

Potato Head himself, on the couch, on the phone, on hold, waiting for somebody, letting Jack stand there and wait for him. Goober had on a BanLon shirt that might have fit when they took that picture of him with the first facemask. You could probably tell what color the shirt was supposed to be back then too. The shorts from Goober's seventh grade gym class were supposed to be white. You knew that because a spot by the hem on the left leg still was. Black stretch socks (droll). But what in the wide world of sports were those things on the toes of his tennis shoes? Strips of rawhide? They couldn't be. But they were. Not sewn on, not glued on, not stapled on, but riveted on, with actual rivets.

Otis hung up the phone. "Damn, done got me disconnected again."

They must have gotten tired of blowing him off again.

"How y'all doing then, there, Jack?"

Goober's cracker act had to be a put-on, right?

"I notice y'all looking at my tennis shoes, Jack. Let me tell y'all about that. Like lots of old farts like me who like to play tennis, I'm a toe dragger. I drag my toes; that's why they call it that."

Yeah?

"I done went through lots of tennis shoes in my day, and tennis shoes ain't as cheap as they once was, which you'd know, if you'd have took up tennis back when I did, which you should have. Except you couldn't have took it up back then, cause you wasn't even born yet, was you now?"

Huh?

"Course, mind you, I don't pay no retail for no tennis shoes, hell no. I ain't paid retail for nothing since my daddy done bought me my first piece of pussy, but I don't want to go off on that tangent right now cause I want to go off on a different tangent."

What. The. Fuck?

"Reason I brung up my shoes, Jack, is cause that's one Total Quality way I use to save money. It's good as making money, saving money is, Jack. That's what Doctor Deming teaches us. I'm talking about Total Quality Management, which is the civilian counterpart of Total Quality Leadership, which is the Navy counterpart of Total Quality Management. Y'all following what I'm getting at here?"

Totally.

"The Cold War's over, Jack. Just got over yesterday. Mister Gorbachev done brought that there wall down. You must have heard about it on TV."

Jack had read about it on the radio. He still hadn't replaced the TV Liz had taken when she cleared out the house.

"It's a kinder, gentler Navy now, Jack. There won't be no more Big Ole Backfire Raids, nor no more NORPACS neither."

Goober's cracker act had to be real, then. Nobody manufactured something like "nor no more NORPACS neither" unless that was how he really done talked.

"Y'all need to find you something else to make yourself important about, Jack. That's why I brung up management just now, cause I got a little situation I want you to take over and manage for me."

Here it comes …

"Got me a training officer now, well he's a Brit exchange officer, a left-tenant commander, if you know what I mean …"

No.

"What I mean is, he's all fucked up."

Ah.

"I keep trying to get him to figure out ways to do flight training without no airplanes nor no simulators, and he just won't play ball. I give him one idea after another, and he won't do nothing with them. Says they're no good, the no good."

You don't say?

"So, what I want you to do is go over to the training department and be in charge. Not officially in charge, but really in charge, you know what I'm saying?"

Not really.

"I can't fire him 'cause that might hurt his self-esteem, which wouldn't be a Total Quality way of doing things. And you two are the same rank now, but he's senior to you, so I can't put you officially in charge over him. But you're gonna know, and he's gonna know, and I'm gonna know that you're the one who's really in charge. It just won't be official. It'll be ..."

Superficial?

"... a tacit understanding among officers and gentlemen."

Goober went on about his ideas to replace training flights and simulators with arcade games, board games, card games, parlor games and the like. The students could play charades, for example, to act out in-flight emergency procedures.

Jack might have stood there listening until his lower back crushed like a stick of chalk if the fire alarm hadn't gone off.

And he might have gotten in trouble eventually with The Not-Bad-Looking Petty Officer if she'd still been there when he and Potato Head came hauling ass out of Goober's office. Officers and enlisted personnel of opposite sexes were strictly forbidden from fraternizing with each other unless they had their clothes on, unless the officer and enlisted person in question were in the Medical or Dental Corps, in which case fraternization was required and clothes were optional.

Jack wondered why The Not-Bad-Looking Petty Officer wasn't still there. She couldn't have been there when the alarm went off, or Jack and Goober would have seen her as they came out of the office, because they were really hauling ass. Jack thought she might have been the one who set off the alarm, but she wasn't. She went somewhere else, which we'll find out about later.

Goober went clopping like a Clydesdale past the ready room toward the ladder in his leather-toed tennis shoes, probably hoping it was a false alarm, because if the hangar done burnt down, he wouldn't have no command to command no more, nor no pot to piss in, neither. And the accident reports—all that Total Quality Paperwork!

Jack kind of hoped it was a real fire, so he could get his detailer at the Bureau of Personnel to cut him a set of orders out of this Total Quality Quagmire. Assuming it wasn't a drill, Jack ducked his head in the ready room to see if any of the drunks had come back and passed out in there, and hadn't heard the alarm.

Carly wasn't passed out. She was still semi-alert at her semi-permanent duty station.

"Come on, Carly! Are you deaf? Can't you hear the fire alarm?"

"What, sir? I can't hear you over the fire alarm."

"Quit pulling my chain, Carly. There might be a real fire."

"There isn't. It's a practical joke. Somebody pulled the fire alarm to get you out of Captain Otis's office before he talked your ears off."

"How do you know it's just a practical joke?"

"Because I know who pulled it."

Carly did that thing with her face that might look like a smile if you saw it on the face of a real person or a puppy. Neither of which she was, exactly.

Jack rubbed his back and sighed. "Why don't you escort me over to the trainer building before we both get in trouble?"

I Know

They climbed the stairway you called a ladder of the trainer building that housed all the broke-dick flight simulators.

"You know, sir," Carly said, "when you climb up a ladder on a

Navy ship, the deck numbers get smaller instead of bigger like they do in a Navy building, until you get to the first deck, when the decks become levels and—"

"I've been on a Navy ship, Carly. I know all about that ship shit."

"Well, sir, I haven't been on a ship, but I know all about that ship shit too, because I researched it. That's how I learn new things, through research and observation."

"I know. You told me. You're very smart."

"Thank you. That's very nice of you to say."

"Shut up."

"Yes, sir. Aye, aye, sir."

"And cut the 'sir' shit, Carly. We don't do that 'sir' shit in the aviation Navy. This isn't a destroyer."

"I know. It's a building, because the deck numbers get bigger as you go up—"

"That's not what I meant."

"Then what did you mean, sir? I'm very smart, but I can't read minds. You'll have to express yourself more clearly, choose your words more carefully, instead of just coughing them out of your ass."

"Where the fuck did you pick up language like that?"

"I observed it, sir, in the ready room, while standing semi-permanent duty, sir."

"Okay, Carly, really. The 'sir' thing. This is a squadron. Junior officers don't call each other 'sir.'"

"Even in a destroyer squadron?"

"Destroyer squadrons are different from aircraft squadrons."

"How?"

"Well, now, they don't have destroyers in aircraft squadrons, and they don't have aircraft in destroyer squadrons, do they?"

"But destroyers carry helicopters. Aren't they aircraft?"

"Oh, please." Jack stopped at the landing to the fifth deck and took a break, wondering if the vise grips in his back were going to choke the living shit out of his lumbars before he choked the living shit out of Carly with his bare hands. "You know, Carly, Captain Otis's secretary tried to warn me what would happen if I gave you food. What was I thinking when I offered you half of that Snickers bar?"

"You weren't thinking, sir."

"I guess that's pretty obvious."

"Yes, sir, it is."

Jack started back up the ladder. Carly followed.

"I've never observed a helicopter in person," she said, "but my research indicates that they're called rotary-wing aircraft, as opposed to fixed-wing aircraft, like the E-2 Hawkeyes and F-14 Tomcats we have here at Naval Air Station Miramar, Fightertown USA, master jet base, home of Top Gun—"

"Yeah, your semi-mother raised a smart kid all right. I bet she took you everywhere with her. I bet she tried to lose you there too."

"Yes, my semi-mother took me everywhere with her. She showed me to everyone she met, she was so proud of me, and how smart I was. She told everyone I'd be a great scientist some day, like Madame Curie."

"You picked yourself a funny path to becoming a great scientist. I don't think Madame Curie started out as a semi-permanent duty officer."

"Oh, the life of a research scientist never interested me. I yearned for a world of action and adventure. That's why I became a naval officer."

Jack stopped for another break at the ninth deck. "Action and adventure, huh? Then when are you going to get away from your semi-permanent duty desk and go to flight school?"

"I'm never going to flight school, sir. Remember? I have a broke-dick heart. I can't pass a flight physical, sir."

"Again with the 'sir' thing, Carly. In a squadron—an aircraft squadron—ensigns don't call lieutenants 'sir.'"

"But you're not a lieutenant anymore, sir. Remember, at quarters, when Captain Otis promoted you to lieutenant commander?"

Oh, yeah. That. "In all the excitement, I guess I forgot."

"How could you forget? It was only an hour ago."

"Okay. Uncle. You can call me 'sir' all you want."

"Goody. Thank you, sir."

"You're welcome, ma'am."

"You're not supposed to call me 'ma'am,' sir. My research indicates 'sir' and 'ma'am' are things junior officers call senior officers as a sign of respect. Senior officers aren't required to show respect for junior officers, and in my observation, they never do."

"Shut up," Jack said, and started up the ladder again, breathing a little heavy now.

"You've gotten out of shape, sir. You need to start going to the gym."

"Yes, ma'am."

"Quit calling me 'ma'am.'"

"Then quit calling me 'sir.'"

"But you just said I can call you 'sir' all I want. Remember?"

"Whatever."

They kept on going to the 13th floor, where the training office was. The door to the office was locked. Taped to it was a sign that read:

THE TRAINING OFFICER IS AWAY ON SEMI-PERMANENT TEMPORARY ASSIGNMENT. RETURN DATE TO BE DETERMINED.

CHEERS!

"Oh, well," Jack said, and he and Carly headed back down the ladder.

☆ ☆ ☆ ☆ ☆

It became their routine. Jack met Carly in the morning at her semi-permanent duty desk at the hangar, and they walked over to the trainer building, and up thirteen flights of ladders, where they found the training office locked. They went back to Hangar 6, where Jack kept Carly company till after lunch. Then he went to the gym, then he went to the beach or ran errands till happy hour, then he went home and made empty space out of the inside of a bottle of cheap white wine.

Except on Wednesdays. Wednesdays, Jack had to stay sober enough to drive Buzz Rucci to the Wednesday Night Live experience at the Miramar Officers' Club.

Wednesday Night Live

This woman was running all over the place, naked as a jaybird, and nobody was paying attention to her. Not because she was a hag. She wasn't. She was a professional harlot, and she had a regular gig at the world famous phenomenon known as Wednesday Night Live at the Miramar O' Club.

All kinds of crazy shit went on at Wednesday Night Live. Shit so crazy you wouldn't believe it if somebody who was there told you about it. And maybe you shouldn't believe them, because nobody there was a reliable eyewitness, because everybody who was there was shit-faced.

Except Jack.

A lot of guys stationed at Miramar only got drunk on Wednesday nights. Wednesday night was the only night Jack *didn't* get drunk because that was the night he had to stay sober enough to be Buzz Rucci's designated driver. So on this particular Wednesday night, Jack was the only guy in the place paying any attention to the naked professional harlot. But it's not like he started hitting on her or anything. Oh, no. He didn't hit on her, or any of the other women who haunted Wednesday Night Live.

Not all of the women who hung out at the O' Club on Wednesday night were professional harlots. Some of them were rank amateurs. Some guys actually brought their wives to Wednesday Night Live. Don't ask me what that was about—a stroll down memory lane, maybe.

Buzz kept telling Jack, as they arm-wrestled over a pitcher of beer, that he ought to find himself a nice girl. But not too nice, if Jack knew what Buzz meant. Nice in some ways, but not nice in others, if Jack caught his drift.

Buzz already had himself a nice girl. She was at home, with two kids and a tank full of fish.

Jack wouldn't mind meeting a nice girl, but he wasn't going to meet one at Wednesday Night Live. After the Liz fiasco, every time he got a good look at a good-looking woman at Wednesday Night Live, all he saw was an eighteen-wheel truck stuffed with Samsonite luggage. And he had no interest in looking for nice girls anywhere else. As far as he was concerned, for now, he needed a woman like dogs need power tools.

Because he was relatively sober on Wednesday nights, and everybody else was blind drunk, Jack saw a lot of things that nobody else there saw.

One week, he saw this mummy-looking bastard lurking around, looking like he expected everybody to walk up to him and kiss his ass. Jack thought he must be Fix Felon. Jack had never actually seen Fix Felon. He'd only talked to him on the phone the night of The Almost Great Big Train Wreck.

"Is that him?" he asked Buzz.

Buzz, who was buzzed, said, "Is whom whom?"

Jack left the table and twisted his shoulders through the crowd to get a good look at *The Mummy*, but before he could get close enough,

The Mummy disappeared.

The Mummy showed up every Wednesday night after that, but always vanished into thin air before Jack could reach him, and he always wore a different costume. One week, *The Mummy* wore a surface warfare pin. The next, he was a submariner. The week after that, he was a Navy SEAL (as a SEAL, *The Mummy* looked like *The Creature From the Black Lagoon*).

The following week, as Jack was getting ready to leave for the club, Buzz called.

"I can't make it tonight. Jenny's about to pop another kid and I have to take her to the hospital. Go ahead without me. If she passes out from the painkillers before last call, I'll grab a cab and catch up with you."

☆ ☆ ☆ ☆ ☆

"What's wrong?" Carly said. "It's Wednesday night. Why aren't you at the O' Club with Buzz? Did he have an accident or something?"

"Sort of," Jack said. "His wife's having another kid. Why don't you let go of your death grip on the semi-permanent duty desk and come to the club with me?"

"I can't."

"Oh, come on. Nobody's going to care if you blow off the duty for an hour or two. You can bring your pager."

"That's not it. I can't go to the club because I'm not old enough to go anyplace they serve liquor."

Stunned, Jack said, "You're not twenty-one? How did you get commissioned as an officer?"

"Like I told you, I'm very smart. I graduated from college at the head of my class when I was eighteen. I spent a year after that sitting on the couch at home, until my semi-mom threw me out and made me go to Officer Candidate School, hoping I'd stumble across a life."

★　★　★　★　★

Jack was halfway down the ladder, headed back to the parking lot, when a voice behind him said, "Talk about déjà vu all over again. Is that you Mister Hogan? I ain't seen you in a month of Chinese New Years."

Jack turned. "Chief Dangerfield! I haven't seen you since The Great Big Backfire cruise!"

The next thing Jack knows, he's at the Miramar Chiefs' Club, sitting on a bar stool next to Chief Dangerfield's. Chief Dangerfield has an old score to settle. Jack drank him under the table on liberty in the Philippines six years ago, and Chief Dangerfield is out for revenge.

Chief Dangerfield, he's a talkative guy. Gets a few beers in him and you better strap on your laugh belt, because once he gets going, there's no stopping him. His eyes bulge, and his knee starts shaking, and he starts tugging at the knot of a tie that's not really there. Jack and Chief Dangerfield start talking about great chief petty officers of the Navy they have known, and Chief Kirk's name comes up.

"I worked with him on *Connie*," Jack says.

"I've known him since he was just a sty in his father's eye," Chief Dangerfield says. "We went to boot camp together. A great guy, Chief Kirk. Ran into him about a year ago, right here."

Seems after *Connie* got back from NORPAC, Chief Kirk shows up at this very Chiefs' Club, wearing the flight jacket he wasn't supposed to have and smoking the pipe he shouldn't have brought with him, because they won't let him in the Chiefs' Club with the thing going like a class alpha fire.

Which was total bullshit, as far as Chief Dangerfield was concerned. Chief Kirk's been at sea for the last twenty years, he doesn't know anything about this politically correct "no pipe smoking in the club" bullshit.

But Chief Kirk's okay about it. He goes out on the back balcony, figures nobody will mind if he smokes out there.

Brother, has he been out to sea too long.

Forty feet away from where he's smoking his pipe is this table full of stiffs, hanging half out of their chairs, like they're waiting for some nice Roman boy to come along and nail them back up.

This old battle-axe with them—some crack officer's wife, out slumming at the Chiefs' Club, looking for somebody who wants to mingle with one of the upper crust, and believe you me, this old broad has enough crust on her to go around in a joint like this, both upper and lower, if you know what I mean. Anyway, she gets a whiff of Chief Kirk's pipe, and her nose starts twitching like a rabbit's, and her mouth starts moving like a carp's.

"Young man. Young man. Young man."

Chief Kirk goes over to the far, far corner of the deck and sits by himself: just a boy and his pipe. "Fuck 'em if they can't take a smoke," he says.

This hot babe who tends bar at the Miramar Chiefs' Club could have made her living working at the Officers' Club, except she was too classy. But not too, too, classy, you know? That type. Actually, she only works at the Chiefs' Club because the chiefs tip better than the officers do.

Anyway, she gets a whiff of Chief Kirk's pipe smoke wafting through the window, and something primal stirs in her. She throws her apron on the bar and goes out back to see if she can sniff out some pipe.

Chief Kirk sees her coming a mile away. Well, parts of her he sees from a mile away. Some parts of her are closer than a mile away. This broad, she's got parts galore. Good parts, great parts, incredible parts. But Chief Kirk, he's mostly interested in the first two parties of the rest of the parts, if you know what I mean.

He sees her walking his way, figures he's about to catch a pitcher of shit about his pipe. But that's not what happens.

This bar babe, she walks up to him, she says, "Hey, Chief, nice pipe. Mind if I join you?"

"Not at all, ma'am." Chief Kirk says. Nice boy, Chief Kirk. Has a nice set of manners on him. Plays a nice straight man too.

The bar babe says, "Ooh, did you carve that pipe all by yourself?"

"Yes, ma'am, with my trusty knife." Chief Kirk whips out his knife and shows it to her.

"Ooh," she says again, admiring the knife. "Is that scrimshaw on the handle?"

"Yes, ma'am. Made out of whale bone."

"I like bone," she says. "Whale or otherwise. Whalebone's nice."

"Well," Chief Kirk says, "it took me a year to carve this mermaid on the pipe."

"That's a nice mermaid you got there," she says. "I bet she keeps you good company on those cold nights in the North Atlantic, while you're trying to run away from all those U-Boats. I bet you have to be careful not to catch a torpedo in the shower stall."

"The mermaid's okay," Chief Kirk says. "This was my first try at carving a pipe. It's a little rough."

"I like it a little rough," she says. "Is this your first pipe ever?"

"No," he says. "My dad gave me my first pipe."

"Small world," she says. "Me too! That's how I got hooked on pipe. I come from a long line of pipe. My great, great, great grandfather was Sir Walter Raleigh."

"You don't say?"

"Oh yeah," she says. "Women in my family have been pipe aficionados for years. It's a tradition. All the girls get their first pipe from their fathers. Either that, or their uncles."

Chief Kirk's not sure what to make of that last remark.

"Looks like you take good care of that pipe," she says. "Do you keep it in your pocket when you're not smoking it, or do you shove it in a box every chance you get?"

Something starts to flicker in Chief Kirk's lighthouse. "So you like pipe?" he says.

"Like pipe?" she says. "I love pipe. I adore pipe. I can't live without it. A night without pipe is like a day without sunshine."

"Tell you what then," he says, "how soon can you get off?"

"Are you kidding?" she says. "I just got off ten minutes ago, and I'm ready to do it again. Let's go!"

I tell you, she could take a pipe all right. Very experienced. Suck pipe, blow pipe, lay pipe, thread pipe. She knew the whole repertory. A regular Sarah Bernhardt of pipe, she was.

Chief Kirk and the bar babe would have been perfect for each other, but things didn't work out. Come morning, they wake up, and she asks him if her butt looks big. Chief Kirk throws on his flight jacket and hauls ass back to his ship. He doesn't want to see a woman for another twenty years after he's had a pipe load of that "Does my butt look big" bullshit.

Unfortunately for Chief Kirk, by the time he gets back to his ship, a hundred female sailors have reported aboard for duty.

☆　☆　☆　☆　☆

Jack's trashed and thinking Chief Dangerfield is starting to sound like Buzz Rucci with his cockamamie story. In fact, Chief Dangerfield has turned into Buzz.

"What are you doing here?" Jack says. "What happened to Chief Dangerfield?"

"He got too snockered and they threw him out," Buzz says. "Your poodle Carly told me you were over here and might need help."

"Jenny have her baby?"

"Yeah."

"Boy or girl?"

"I didn't look that close. C'mon, give me your keys, we'll hit the O' Club and celebrate."

★ ★ ★ ★ ★

Wednesday Night Live was getting old, as was the professional harlot who led Jack and Buzz to their table. She brought them a pitcher of beer. "Out late tonight, boys?"

"It's my fault," Buzz said. "My wife just had a kid. I wanted a puppy, but my wife said if we got a puppy, I'd have to take care of it. So I compromised."

"Poor baby," the harlot said and disappeared.

Jack, drunk as a skunk, wondered where she'd disappeared to.

Buzz had a funny look on his face.

Jack tried to prop his elbow up to arm wrestle with Buzz, but his face hit the table instead.

★ ★ ★ ★ ★

Carly was curled up on a cot in the ready room, next to her semi-permanent duty desk.

★ ★ ★ ★ ★

Goober sat at home in his underwear, watching a rerun of The Porter Wagner Show. (Featuring Dolly Parton!)

Sons of the Desert

Jack woke up on his living room floor, next to the seventh chair, wondering how he got there. Buzz must have driven him home. Or maybe Carly had. He went to the kitchen and drank a quart of water directly from the tap in the sink.

The phone rang. It was Buzz.

"Jack, are you watching TV?"

"Still don't have one."

"Jesus, Jack, you're missing everything. They're showing it on all the news channels. Iraq just invaded Kuwait."

"Why?"

"Who cares? A Great Big Butt Kick's about to start, and we have to get in on it."

"How?"

"I pulled a Fix Felony for us."

"A what?"

"A Fix Felony," Buzz said. "You know, an underhanded maneuver to get what you want through the unwarranted influence of the shadowy underpinnings in the network of power."

"How did you do that?"

"I have asshole buddies in the Bureau of Personnel now. I traded my mother for them. It was a career move. I can have us on a horse to camel-land before you can say, 'bite my ugly bumper sticker.' What do you say? Are you up for it?"

"Don't you have a wife and a new baby coming home from the hospital tomorrow, Buzz?"

"That's why I want to leave today. You ever listen to a baby cry all night? Come on, Jackie. Please. I could go by myself, but that wouldn't be any fun."

Jack took a deep breath and released it slowly.

"Oh, all right."

★　★　★　★　★

Buzz, asleep in the right seat of the Trans Am. Jack, his head on a swivel, scanning to see if any cops are going to come along and fix this broke-dick traffic light on Mira Mesa Boulevard that's stuck on red.

Buzz opens his eyes, looks around, says, "No cops, nobody's coming, let's go," and goes back to sleep.

Jack pops the clutch and guns it, but not fast enough.

Some dip-shit Marine flying up Mira Mesa Boulevard behind

them in a '78 Mustang forgets to remember to watch where the fuck he's going. He finally sees Jack's Trans Am and the broke-dick traffic light, and slams on the brakes, but not soon enough. The dip-shit Marine clips the shit out of Jack's rear bumper, right on the "ouch, my fucking bumper sticker."

Jack presses the gas pedal and keeps going, because he and Buzz have a plane to catch. He's concentrating on the road out ahead of him, because he doesn't want to get into another accident. But it's hard to concentrate out ahead, because something in the rearview mirror is distracting him: the flashing bubblegum machine on the top of a cop car.

Jack pulls over, reaches across the sleeping Buzz, and grabs his registration out of the glove compartment. The Marine drives past and gets away Scot-free. Jack gets two tickets, one for running a red light and one for leaving the scene of an accident, which combined will cost him even more that fixing the shit-canned fucking bumper.

☆ ☆ ☆ ☆ ☆

"We there yet?" Buzz says as Jack pulls into the parking lot at Hangar 6.

"Go back to sleep," Jack says.

"Wilco."

☆ ☆ ☆ ☆ ☆

"Nice of you to come by and see me at the semi-permanent duty desk before you go," Carly said. "I'm ever so humbled and grateful."

"Cut the semi-pathetic bullshit and give me a hug."

Carly jumped up and kissed him on the cheek, and hugged his neck as hard as she could.

OOOOOOOOOH!

Smooch noises from every corner of the ready room. Looked like the Cubs were in town for a home stand. How had Jack not noticed all the losers hanging out there before he let Carly kiss him like that? He must be headed off to war or something.

The ready room stiffs turned back to the war news on the big-screen TV. They could have watched the game at home, but their wives wanted to watch a chick flick on the Lifetime channel.

Everybody was involved with the war coverage again, except Flip Wilson, who had three NFO students pinned against a corner, saying, "There I was, the Backfires diving out of thirty-five thousand feet, and Jackie's shaking like a girl, tugging at my sleeve, saying, 'What do I do, Flip, what do I do?'"

Douche bag.

"Will you bring me something back?" Carly said.

"How about a medal?" Jack said.

"Sure. Can I have a red one?"

"You want candy sprinkles on it?"

"I'm not particular. I just want something to put on my chest, over my left uniform pocket. I don't have anything to put there yet." She unzipped the flight jacket somebody must have given her to make her feel better, and showed him nothing over her pocket. "See?"

"Tell you what, Carly. I'll bring you something to put on your chest if you grow a chest to put it on."

"Whatever you can find," Carly said. "A SEAL badge. A Joint Chiefs of Staff Insignia, if that's the best you can do. I'll even settle for a set of NFO wings."

Frosted his ass with that one, didn't she?

But she didn't mean anything by it. She was just pulling his chain.

In Harm's Way

"I'm telling you," Buzz told him, wide awake now in the right seat of the Trans Am. "You can dump this car as is. A Marine looks at that crunched up bumper, he'll think it's a custom job."

Jack found a spot in the last row of the long-term parking lot at San Diego International, and Jack and Buzz went yup-yup-yo to the terminal.

They climbed into an airplane with BUMFUCK AIRLINES smeared all over it and took off. The pilot took off, that is. Jack and Buzz were just along for the ride. But being NFOs, they were used to that, so it was okay.

They went hard and heavy at the airline bottles, and Buzz started talking. Buzz must have been getting better at telling stories, because after all the Potato Head jabber, Buzz Rucci stories were starting to sound to Jack like knock-knock jokes. In fact, they were knock-knock jokes.

"Hey Pontius Pilate!"

"Hey Pontius Pilate who?"

"Hey, punch this pile o' trash in the ass and let's make some time here, okay?"

☆ ☆ ☆ ☆ ☆

The BUMFUCK AIRLINES pile of trash sets down in Bahrain, and two drunken sailors spill out of it.

A United States Marine meets them at the bottom of the boarding ladder. A huge Marine in a T-shirt and camouflage pants, with an M-16 rifle in one hand and a case of Foster's Lager in the other one. He wears a big-ass beard, like he doesn't give a shit Marines aren't supposed to do that. He hands Buzz and Jack a Foster's, plops the rest of the case down on the tarmac, and plops his big ass down on top of that.

"Major Turbo Sims, gents, pleasure to meet you. Nice of you to join us, but you're a little late. They just announced the ceasefire. War's closed."

Buzz collapses on the tarmac and cries like a girl. "We were late for Clobberin' Time," he wails.

Turbo looks at Buzz in disgust. "Isn't that just like a swab?"

"I can't go on," Buzz says.

"Take it easy," Turbo says.

"I can't go on. I can't."

The clock strikes one.

"Go on with you," Turbo says. "The war's closed, but the bar's still open. Happy hour's just getting started around these parts."

"I'll go on," Buzz says, and stands.

"Then let's go," Turbo says. "So we get there before closing time."

Turbo and Swab-o and Jack-o jump in a cab and head for downtown.

★ ★ ★ ★ ★

A Royal Navy Left-tenant Commander meets them at the door of the Private British Expatriates' Club. The Left-tenant Commander has a full beard like Turbo's and curious three-tone eyes—black toward the center, brown in the middle, and red around the edges. His breath smells like a coyote's ass probably does. He's about to tell them they can't come in because they're not members of the private club when he recognizes Jack.

"I know you," The Left-tenant Commander says. "You work for me. I'm your boss, the training officer. I trust you've met our commanding officer, Captain Potato Head. He's quite the Total Quality Quack Job, isn't he?"

"Nice to meet you finally," Jack says. "How come we haven't met before?"

"Because I charmed The Not-Bad-Looking Petty Officer into typing me semi-permanent orders over here so I could get away from that Total Quality Crack Head. I've been over here, drinking heavily, for almost two years now. Potato Head doesn't even know I'm gone."

"A brilliant maneuver," Jack says. "Very Sun Tzu."

"How nice of you to say, old man," The Left-tenant Commander says. "Come in, come in, to our den of sin, and bring your friends in too."

★ ★ ★ ★ ★

A Brit BUMFUCK AIRLINES stewardess who moonlights as a semi-professional harlot flashes Turbo a smile full of bad teeth. "Hello, handsome and brutish. Just back from blowing up the entire known universe?"

"No, ma'am," Turbo says. "I'd never blow up the entire universe. If I did that, there wouldn't be anything left for me to blow up, would there?"

"What's it like?" the crooked smile says, "killing all those babies?"

"I don't kill babies, ma'am," Turbo says. "I let somebody else kill them then I eat them for breakfast."

"You CREATURE," the crooked smile says, and slaps Turbo upside the head. "Take that!"

"Aw, go take yourself a flying fuck at the moon," Turbo says, unfazed.

"The moon," the crooked smile says. "It's lovely tonight, don't you think?"

"Yes, ma'am," Turbo says. "You couldn't ask for a nicer night to make babies to replace the ones you just ate."

"Then what are we waiting for?" the crooked smile says. "Let's go!"

Turbo and the crooked smile disappear out the front door.

★ ★ ★ ★ ★

A second crooked smile crooks a finger at Jack and Buzz and leads them to a table. She disappears and comes back with a pitcher of beer. She sets it on the table and disappears again.

Jack thinks he may have an idea where she disappeared to.

Jack and Buzz start arm-wrestling.

"The ride in the big airplane must have tired you out, Buzz. You're not putting up much of a fight this evening, with that twenty inch bicep of yours."

"We must have flown over China while you were talking my ears off," Buzz says. "I must have caught a touch of the Hong Kong Flu."

Buzz coughs.

"No, that's not it," Jack says. "You seem distracted, like there's something going on with you besides drinking beer and arm-wrestling right now."

Buzz smiles.

"We should order another pitcher of beer, in case we knock this one over," Jack says. "Where did our waitress go? She couldn't have disappeared under the table, could she? If she did, I can't imagine what she might be doing down there, because she sure as hell doesn't have her mouth wrapped around my dick."

Buzz spits up a mouthful of beer. Before Jack can slam Buzz's wrist against the table, a bugle blares. The Left-tenant Commander comes by and says, "Tap's out. Bar's closed. Time for all drunk little American Navy boys to go home."

Buzz and Jack get into a cab that turns into the airport, and they fumble out of it. They stumble up the stairs of the ladder that leads to a big airplane that has DRUNK IDIOTS IN UNIFORM GET FREE UPGRADES TO FIRST CLASS smeared all over it.

☆ ☆ ☆ ☆ ☆

Whatever Wednesday Night it was the Wednesday night they got home, The Wednesday Night Harlot had saved their table for them. She smiled. She had semi-permanent teeth now. She sat them down and brought them a pitcher of beer and disappeared.

Jack and Buzz arm-wrestled.

"Try not to smile so much this time," Jack said.

Buzz smiled.

✯ ✯ ✯ ✯ ✯

Jack dropped Buzz off in front of his house shortly after midnight. Buzz's wife Jenny and his four-year-old son, and his one-year-old son, and his infant son were waiting for him on the front porch.

Tailhook

"In Las Vegas in September 1991, many naval aviators were returning from life-or-death missions in Desert Storm. That—and the usual free-flowing alcohol—gave the nightlife its special kick. Hundreds of single women were drawn to the three-day event—some for the second or third consecutive year—and freely participated in wild party activities, ranging from sexual suggestiveness to gross indecency.

"While Navy men saw careers sunk over being at the wrong party at the wrong time, some Navy women walked away from more serious offenses without a scratch ... [One male lieutenant], who shaved women's legs in public, was prosecuted for 'conduct unbecoming an officer,' but three female officers whose legs he shaved were not disciplined on an equal basis ... [T]he Navy ... is rushing to spend millions to alter combat ships for the accommodation of women. Why? ... This is the new Navy: a man's career depends on having the "correct" view on women, as defined by feminists who know how to exploit sexual politics to get their way."

Elaine Donnelly, *National Review*, March 7, 1994

✯ ✯ ✯ ✯ ✯

"For many of the naval aviators and sailors who attended the 1991 Tailhook convention, the events that have so humiliated the Navy are nothing but an alcohol-stained blur. But for many of the women who found themselves at Tailhook, especially the 83 women who were molested or otherwise assaulted, the memories are as clear as the warm desert air over Las Vegas."

Philip Shenon, the *New York Times*, May 20, 1996

☆ ☆ ☆ ☆ ☆

"The United States military is facing the gravest accusations of sexual misconduct in years, with dozens of servicewomen in the Persian Gulf area and elsewhere saying they were sexually assaulted or raped by fellow troops ... The latest accusations are the most extensive set of sexual misconduct charges since the Navy's Tailhook incident of 1991."

Eric Schmitt, the *New York Times*, February 26, 2004

1991

That Friday, desperate to get away from his family, Buzz jumped on a big airplane with DRUNK IDIOTS HEADED FOR VEGAS smeared all over it, and went to the infamous Tailhook Convention.

The Tailhook Association was, in theory, the "professional organization" of U.S. Navy carrier aviators, who at that point in history were the only aviators left in the world who landed on a flight deck by sinking a Tailhook into an arresting gear wire. But as far as Jack could tell, the only "professional" function the association served was to throw its annual drunk, blown and laid bacchanal in Vegas.

Jack had been to one Tailhook blowout, in his lieutenant days, and he'd seen enough. It made everything he'd seen at Wednesday Night Live at the Miramar O' Club or on liberty in the Pacific look like something your Grandma might cater. Too many naval aviators. Too much testosterone. Too much alcohol. Too many Top Gun groupie girls. And the only senior admirals in attendance were naval aviators themselves, which meant there was no adult supervision. It's not so much that the aviator admirals were immature—well, yeah, they were immature all right, but that wasn't the main problem. The main problem was that a lot of these old guys thought the world was still the same place it had been during their anything-goes, Vietnam-era junior officer days, and had no idea that the behavior norms they displayed toward women in their halcyon days were no longer acceptable, at least not within the confines of the continental United States.

To Jack, the cherished naval aviation Tailhook convention tradition was on an irreversible collision course with the reality of American sexual politics, so come that Friday in 1991 when Buzz climbed aboard the big plane headed for Vegas, Jack waved goodbye from the tarmac, went home, and got a good night's sleep.

Saturday morning, Jack drove Carly to her soccer game. She was in a ladies' league now, the hottest number on her team. She needed a ride because her Dodge Neon had a semi-perpetual flat tire.

He picked her up at the Bachelor Officers' Quarters. She had a semi-permanent room there, right across the street from the O' Club. Too bad she was too young to drink, Jack thought. Imagine all the money she'd save in cab fare that she could piss away on booze at the Club.

Carly asked Jack on the way over to the soccer field if he wanted to stay and watch the game.

"I prefer to do my girl-watching at the beach, Carly. Watching you and your ladies' league pals run around a soccer field is like grinding glass in your eyes."

"I understand," Carly said. "We have to take care of our eyes, don't we?"

She leaned over, put her mouth against Jack's ear, and said …

"HAWKEYE MAN!"

Jack swerved and almost hit a dog taking a piss against a fire hydrant. He stopped the car.

"Don't you ever, ever repeat that 'Hawkeye Man' crap again. You blurt that out in the ready room and I'll be branded for life."

"Don't you want a call sign, sir? Everybody else has one."

"Everybody else needs one. Call signs—they're a self-help personality transplant, like sewing cool squadron patches all over your flight jacket. Yeah, I know, I could use some help in the personality department myself, but not that kind of crap. That kind of crap is for cub scouts and fighter pilots."

And if Jack ever wanted to have a call sign, he sure as hell wouldn't want a totally gay one like "Hawkeye Man." Christ, something like "Jack Off" or "Butt Plug" or even "Sue" would be better than "Hawkeye Man." Did anybody ever hear of a fighter ace with a call sign like "Tomcat Man?" Hell no. Anybody with a Mickey Mouse nickname like that would get laughed out of the Miramar O' Club.

Carly sat back in the passenger seat and twiddled her thumbs. "So what's in it for me, if I promise never to say Hawk—"

"What do you want?"

"Well, if you don't have anything specific planned for the next several hours …"

Jack sighed. "Oh, all right."

☆　☆　☆　☆　☆

Coming back from the soccer game, Carly said, "But that's why they call it 'football' everyplace except America, where we call it 'soccer.'"

"Yeah," Jack said. "It's a lovely game if you lost both your hands in World War I or something."

"But in American football, you hardly ever use your feet."

"Sure you do. You run on them, you step on them, you trip over them, you crush your dicks with them. If that's not using your feet, I don't know what is."

"It's certainly not using your head," Carly said, smugly.

"Whatever."

As they drove through the front gate, Carly said, "If you love football so much, why didn't you play professionally after you got out of college?"

"Because I wasn't big enough or fast enough or good enough. Any other questions?"

"Lots," Carly said, delighted at the invitation to intrude into Jack's past. "Like, how did you wind up flying E-2 Hawkeyes? It isn't a very sexy airplane."

Jack shook his head. "Well, see, I wasn't very confident around girls when I was in high school, and one thing led to another, and the next thing I knew, I was flying in the back of E-2s."

"That's another thing," she said. "How come you didn't become a pilot?"

"My eyes weren't good enough."

"But you don't wear glasses."

"My eyes aren't bad enough to wear glasses. I'm twenty–twenty-five distant in my left eye."

"But they give waivers for that."

"They didn't when I went through flight school. When I went through flight school, you had to have perfect vision to be a pilot."

"But they give waivers now."

"It's too late now. I'm an NFO. It's what I know how to do, what I'm good at."

"But—"

"Shut up."

☆　☆　☆　☆　☆

Jack pulled up in front of the Bachelor Officers' Quarters.

"I'm thinking of putting in for Surface Warfare Officer School," Carly said.

"I thought you had a broke-dick heart."

"I do. It's too broke-dick to fly a Navy airplane, or even be an

NFO in the back of one, but it's not too broke-dick to drive ships. They give waivers for that now if all you want to do is drive a ship."

Jack scowled. "You don't want to drive a ship. Serve your four years as a semi-permanent duty officer and get out and go be Madame Curie someplace, like your semi-mom wants you to be."

Carly jumped out of the Trans Am and slammed the passenger door behind her and ran into the BOQ.

★ ★ ★ ★ ★

Monday morning in the ready room, Goober said, "Carly, hon, why don't y'all take a semi-permanent break and go outside a couple minutes. Us men folk, we got some man stuff to jabber-jaw about."

Later, it would take steam from a teakettle to unglue Carly's ear from the outside of the door.

Alone with the men folk, Goober said, "Now, what y'all done let the fighter guys do at that there Tailhook Convention in that there Las Vegas weren't no big deal, in my personal opinion, nor nothing to get no negative publicity about, neither. Pushin' and shovin' gals around, droppin' water balloons on 'em, rippin' their blouses off … Shoot, back in my day, that's how y'all let a purty gal know y'all liked her."

To this day, a lot of people still agree with Goober's assessment of the Tailhook fiasco. What the hell, it was just a little consensual sex and juvenile highjinks among adults. Nobody really got hurt, and the boys paid for everything they broke. No harm, no foul, right?

Heh, heh, heh. *Wrong!!!*

Poor Goober

Tuesday afternoon in the Fightertown Auditorium, all the Tomcat slugs sat on one side of the aisle, all the E-2 stiffs sat on the other.

AIRPAC, the three-star admiral who commanded Naval Air

Force Pacific, stood on the stage behind a big screen made out of chicken wire, in case everybody started throwing beer bottles at him.

He glared at the fighter guys. "How could you be so stupid, getting caught having fun like that?"

"We're sorry," the fighter guys said, hanging their heads.

" 'Sorry' isn't good enough," AIRPAC said. "The bad news is, somebody has to be sacrificed for your sins."

"SHUDDER," the fighter guys said.

"The good news," AIRPAC said, "is I think I can get away with making a sacrificial lamb out of an E-2 guy."

"HOORAY!" the fighter guys said.

In the E-2 guy section, somebody cut a nice loud fart. It was Jack.

"I respect your opinion," AIRPAC said. "But I'm sorry. I have no choice but to crucify Captain Otis."

Jack stood. "But Potato Head wasn't even there!"

AIRPAC smiled. "You have to see things from my perspective. Somebody has to be sacrificed, and it can't be a fighter guy, so it has to be an E-2 guy. And since it has to be an E-2 guy, it might as well be one nobody likes."

AIRPAC had a good point there. Even Jack couldn't argue against that kind of logic.

★　　★　　★　　★　　★

A curtain on the stage behind AIRPAC opens to reveal a crucifix. The fighter guys converge on Goober and rip his blouse off and flog him with cut-up sections of fire hose and carry him up to the stage. Somebody hands AIRPAC a spear, and AIRPAC poises to jab Potato Head up the ass with it.

An enlisted Navy journalist's mate snaps a picture of the tableau for the Fightertown Family Newsletter. Later, Mel Gibson will make a movie of the whole thing.

AIRPAC pauses. A single tear rolls down his cheek. He throws the spear down on the stage. "I can't do this. It's too slimy. Even for me."

"NO!" the fighter guys cry in horror. "Say it ain't so, AIRPAC. Nothing's too slimy for you."

AIRPAC weeps like a girl. "There must be another way."

His face lights up.

"I know!"

"What?" the fighter guys ask.

"Let's just go over to the club and leave him hanging there. What do you say? First round's on me."

"HOORAY!" everyone cheers. AIRPAC washes his hands, and E-2 and fighter guys alike file out of the auditorium behind him.

Except for Jackie, of course, and Carly.

They take Goober down from the cross and drive him back to Hangar 6 and help him up to his office. They put him on his couch, prop his head so he can see his daughter's statue of Elvis on his desk, and throw a blanket over him.

"Get some rest, Skipper," Jack says.

"Thank you very much," Goober says as he dozes off. "And y'all have a fine Navy night."

Fighter Follies

Leaving Goober hanging there would have satisfied the ranking member of the Senate Armed Services Committee—hereafter known as Senator Tailhook and sometimes as Auntie Tailhook— if it hadn't been for the comedy skit the fighter guys put on at the Miramar O' Club the next Wednesday night.

Buzz and Jack are out on the patio by the pool, in the back row, Buzz already half in the bag.

On stage, some fighter squadron jack-offs—junior officers to you civilian types—are putting on a skit.

Skit Senator Tailhook is on the phone to Skit Chief of Naval Operations, saying:

"BITCH, BITCH, BITCH, BITCH, BOOM, BOOM, BOOM!"

(She's bitching up a storm at him.)

"BLOB, BLOB, BLOB, BLOB, BLOB, BLOB, BLOB!"

(She's threatening to sic *The Blob* on him.)

A jack-off in a wig playing Skit Lieutenant Tailhook runs on stage.

"Auntie Tailhook, are you talking to that mean old man?"

"Yes, dear," Auntie Tailhook says. "I'm telling him how angry I am over what those mean boys did to you at Tailhook. Do you want to talk to him?"

"No, I don't want to talk about it again, ever. I'll save it for the book I'm writing for Buzz Rucci's kid, the one that will make me millions of dollars."

Skit Lieutenant Tailhook looks out longingly at Buzz, who's still sitting in the back row next to Jack.

Jack nudges Buzz. "Wake up. You're in the skit."

"Huh? I'm in the skit? I thought I was here in the back row with you."

"There now," Auntie Tailhook says. "All will be well soon. If you ever have any trouble with those mean boys again, just click your heels three times and give your Auntie Tailhook a call."

"There's no aunt like you. There's no aunt like you. There's no aunt like you."

The jack-off playing Lieutenant Tailhook exits, stage left, and receives a standing ovation. Sarah Bernhardt never had it so good.

Auntie Tailhook gets back on the phone with the Chief of Naval Operations.

"GLUB, GLUB, GLUB, GLUB, GLUB, GLUB, GLUB."

(She's carping at him.)

She stops that all of a sudden, puts down the phone, makes orgasm noise, and sings, "Ah, sweet mystery of life, at last I've found you."

The jack-off playing Skit AIRPAC comes out from under the desk, puts his finger in his mouth and makes gag noises. He looks at the audience and says, "That sucked."

APPLAUSE! ADORATION!

"You want to know how much that sucked?"

HOW SUCKED WAS IT?

"That sucked worse than being an E-2 guy."

Pandemonium.

☆　☆　☆　☆　☆

Not bad, Jack thought. Not Noel Coward, exactly, but not bad for a bunch of fighter guy jack-offs.

☆　☆　☆　☆　☆

Everything would have been taken in the light of good fun and high spirits, except this bull dyke JAG Corps admiral was in town, out from D.C., in the Miramar O' Club dining room, snorting down half a side of prime rib roast, when she heard all the commotion out on the patio. She thought it was her mate calling, so she went out to the patio and saw the skit.

She ran to the lobby and used the pay phone to call her sidebar bi-lesbo squeeze and told her about the skit. Bi-lesbo squeeze called her Aunt, the real Senator Tailhook, and told her about it.

The real Senator Tailhook called the real Chief of Naval Operations and told him.

Nothing was ever the same again.

The Great Escape

Jack's doorbell rang. It was Buzz.

"I'm your new neighbor," he said. "Just moved in nine years ago. I meant to stop by sooner, but time just got away from me."

"Get in here," Jack said. The door just missed Buzz's ass as Jack shut it behind him. Jack sat on the carpet. Buzz took the seventh chair.

"Your place looks nice, Jack. The 'uncluttered' look suits you. I like those curtains. They come with the place? I seem to remember that stereo from that day before that night in the Philippines. When are you going to break down and get yourself a television?"

"When I get around to it. What brings you by?"

Buzz shifted in the seventh chair uncomfortably. "Thought I'd stop in and get your advice on some big trouble I'm in. I tell you, Jack, the fallout from the jack-off Senator Tailhook skit is bad."

"How bad is it?" Jack said, always ready to play straight man for Buzz.

"It's so bad, Jack, this time they won't settle for crucifying an E-2 Guy. This time they want to disappear a fighter guy."

"The horror, Buzz."

"They looked around the fighter wing to see who they wanted to disappear the most, and guess what?"

"Tag, you're it?"

"I'm it."

"So there was something to that business in the skit about you and Lieutenant Tailhook?"

"There might have been."

"You behaved badly in Vegas, Buzz?"

"A bit."

"A bit? How bad were you?"

"I was so bad …"

★ ★ ★ ★ ★

Friday night, Buzz is in this Vegas hotel suite with a bunch of his fighter buddies, and they're all shit-faced. This girl lieutenant with freshly shaved legs and a nametag that says LIEUTENANT GIRL over one tit and a set of pilot wings over the other tit walks up to Buzz, looks at his NFO wings and says, "Nice wings. You get an extra dick to go with that extra anchor?"

"I'm an NFO," Buzz says.

Lieutenant Girl makes the cheesy crack about "non-flying officer," and Buzz tells her to go take a non-flying fuck at the moon.

"The moon," Lieutenant Girl says. "It looks lovely tonight, doesn't it?"

"Sure does," Buzz says. "Let's go."

Lieutenant Girl disappears the both of them to a hot tub filled with mud on the balcony of her hotel room.

★ ★ ★ ★ ★

"Uh, huh," Jack said. "And Lieutenant Girl turns out to be the same girl lieutenant who gets shoved around the next night on the thirteenth floor and turns into Lieutenant Tailhook."

"Kind of," Buzz said, all morose.

"So you're alone in the mud on the balcony with Lieutenant Tailhook—"

"Not alone, exactly. There's another couple with us. The other girl was that Not- Bad-Looking Petty Officer you almost got in trouble with."

"I wondered where she disappeared to when the fire alarm went off," Jack said. "The first time I saw her, she was making gag noises."

"Small world," Buzz said. "The last time I saw her, she was still making gag noises."

"Who was the other guy?"

"Not sure," Buzz said. "I wasn't seeing too straight just then. He was a big mummy-looking mother fucker with gray hair."

"You think it was Fix Felon?"

"I think so, but I couldn't tell for certain. He was naked. I couldn't identify him for sure unless I saw him in some sort of disguise."

☆ ☆ ☆ ☆ ☆

Buzz and the alleged Fix Felon play tag team in the mud with Lieutenant Girl and The Not-Bad-Looking Petty Officer until dawn on Saturday morning, then they all take a shower together and go off to their separate rooms and sleep.

Saturday night, the mob scene on the thirteenth floor familiar to all aficionados of Navy scandals goes down, and everybody disappears to their rooms and tries to pretend they weren't there.

Sunday afternoon, Buzz flies back to Fightertown USA, in a big airplane with GUILT-RIDDEN DRUNKS RETURN HOME smeared all over it. Agents of the Naval Investigative Service meet Buzz at the bottom of the boarding ladder and whisk him off to a secret room in a secret building on the outskirts of Fightertown and interrogate him.

"These NIS agents, Jack, they're tough."

"How tough are they?" Jack said.

"Almost as tough as the Keystone Kops, and twice as smart."

The NIS agents wave a rubber hose in front of Buzz's face and threaten to tell Buzz's wife what he did in Vegas if he doesn't tell them what he did in Vegas.

So Buzz tells them what he did in Vegas.

"Buzz, you dip shit!" Jack said. "If you hadn't told them anything, they wouldn't have had anything to tell your wife."

Buzz made the sound of one jaw dropping. "You're right. Oh, my God, I'm an idiot."

"Hardly front-page news, Buzz. Let's get back to The Great Big

Balcony story. You told them you were in the mud with Lieutenant Tailhook and Petty Officer Gag Noise and a mummy-looking mother fucker."

"Yeah, and they got real serious when I mentioned the mummy-looking mother fucker and asked if I thought he was Fix Felon."

Jack frowned. "And you said?"

"I told them what I told you. I couldn't identify the guy for sure because I was drunk and he was naked. They smiled after that and let me go. I'm still not sure why."

Jack got up and paced on the living room carpet. "They let you go because the only reason they grilled you in the first place was to make sure you couldn't point a finger at Fix Felon."

Buzz nodded.

Jack kept pacing. "But I can see why they want to disappear you out of town—in case you change your mind and decide you remember for sure that it was Fix Felon."

Buzz nodded again.

"The only thing I'm not clear on," Jack said, "is how the jack-offs who put on the Senator Tailhook skit found out about you and her niece in the mud. You didn't tell anybody about it, did you?"

Buzz shook his head. "Just Flip Wilson."

Jack almost jumped through the vaulted ceiling. "You told Flip fucking Wilson?"

"Bad idea?" Buzz said, tearing up.

"Hell yes, bad idea, you dip shit. You might as well have taken out an ad in the *San Diego Union!*"

Buzz slumped in the seventh chair and sobbed into his tiny hands. "I'm a fuck-up."

Jack looked out the patio door window at Mira Mesa. "What am I going to do with you, Buzz? I can't let you go anywhere or do anything or say anything unless I'm personally there to supervise you."

Buzz brightened. "I'm glad you see things that way."

Jack turned from the window and looked at Buzz. "Huh?"

Buzz ran a hand through his flattop. "When they told me they were sending me to sea until this Tailhook shit blows over, I told them they had to send you with me to personally supervise everything I do and say wherever I go. And they agreed. So I called my buddies at the Bureau of Personnel and traded my grandparents for a set of orders for both of us to the USS *Ernie King*, which deploys to the Arabian Gulf very soon."

Jack slumped. "How soon is very soon?"

"Tomorrow afternoon," Buzz said. "Can you handle that?"

Jack walked over to the living room wall and banged his forehead against it.

☆　☆　☆　☆　☆

The next morning, Jack scrambled to get packed for sea.

"When will you be back?" Carly said.

"I don't know." Jack threw a handful of books into his gym bag.

"What do you want me to do here while you're gone?"

"I don't care. Vacuum. Polish the chair. Howl at the moon off the back balcony. Have your soccer girlfriends over for a pajama party. Whatever you do—"

"I know. Don't let the front door hit me in the ass on my way out."

Jack threw some semi-clean underwear into his gym bag. "Thanks for washing this stuff."

"You're welcome."

Jack looked around the place. "Anything else?"

"I'll be gone when you get back."

"How come?"

"I got accepted to Surface Warfare Officer School," she said, almost trembling. "I report in two weeks."

Jack threw his gym bag on the floor. "What did I tell you about that?"

"I know," Carly said. "Surface Warfare School is for fags and Filipino pimps."

"That's right, and I don't want you hanging around those kinds of people."

"You're not my semi-dad, Jack. You can't control my life."

Jack sighed and sat in the seventh chair. "I know."

Carly sat in his lap. "I have to do something to make use of all my military observation and research."

"But SWO School?" Jack said. "You know the first thing they do to you at SWO School, they rip your dick out. Or in your case, they'll hack your tits off."

Carly looked at him with her puppy brown eyes. "So what do I have to lose?"

Jack rubbed his neck, and rested his forehead on her shoulder. "Okay."

"I have your blessing?"

"You have my semi-blessing."

"Thank you, sir."

"You're welcome, ma'am."

Carly hugged his shoulders. "I love you, Jack."

"Yeah," Jack said. "I have to go."

Buzz's three boys and pregnant wife waved goodbye as Jack eased out the clutch and steered the Trans Am toward I-5.

The fat rent-a-cop kept his seat and waved them through the main gate of Naval Air Station North Island. Jack found a spot in the last row of the long-term parking lot. Jack and Buzz went yup-yup-yo across the parking lot, and up the officers' brow of the aircraft carrier USS *Ernest J. King*.

ACT III

Beadwindow

"BEADWINDOW" is a simple, rapid procedure for use to police the security of insecure networks. It brings to the immediate attention of operators the fact that an Essential Element of Friendly Information (EEFI) has been disclosed on the circuit.

EEFI List:

Friendly or enemy position, movement or intended movement.
Friendly or enemy capabilities or limitations.
Friendly or enemy operation—intentions progress, or results.
Friendly or enemy electronic warfare/electronic emissions.
Friendly or enemy communications security breaches.
Linkage of codes or codewords with plain language.
Inappropriate transmission.

From *Allied Communications Publication 124*

The Tall Thai Girl

Cruise on the *King* had totally sucked. Five solid months of patrolling the no-fly zone over southern Iraq, risking life, limb and career every time you stepped into an airplane. You never quite knew what the hell you were supposed to be doing. In theory, you were protecting the Iraqi population on the ground from attack by the Iraqi Bad Guy's air force, but once America and its allies began flying over Iraqi airspace, their airplanes became Bad Guy's real targets, and nobody really gave a shit about the Iraqis on the ground any more.

At that point, Operation Southern Watch became a manhood measuring contest. "Operation Thou Shalt not Fly," Jack and Buzz called it. We can fly in your sovereign airspace and you can't, we were telling Bad Guy, and if you try to fly in your own sovereign airspace, we'll blow you out of the sky. U.S. airmen who let Bad Guy's air force fly in their own sovereign airspace without blowing them out of it generally got a one-way ticket home and a set of permanent orders to civilian command, but worse things could happen to you in the Thou Shalt Not Fly Zone.

You could become *The Birdman of Alcatraz* if you accidentally shot down a friendly aircraft, or God help you, if you shot down an airliner full of civilians. And if you let yourself get shot down by Bad Guy's air force or air defense artillery, brother, you better hope they killed you because death was nothing compared to the kind of hell you'd catch when high command got its talons on you. Then there was the infighting among the post-menopausal Air Force generals and Navy admirals that nobody could keep track of from moment to moment, not even the post-menopausal generals and admirals.

When you weren't flying, there was always some kind of meeting or lecture to attend, or mission to be planned, or pointless paperwork to be done, or ass-chewing to be endured. You were lucky if you got four hours of uninterrupted sleep, and frankly, you were considered a slacker if you needed any more sleep than that.

On its way home, the *King* pulled in for a liberty call at Pattya Beach, Thailand. It was the first time her crew and air wing had set foot on dry land since leaving San Diego almost six months earlier.

Jack sat on a barstool. Buzz sat on a stool to his right. Red and gold dragons covered the walls. It was a hats and hooters kind of night. B.B. King and Led Zeppelin blared from the loudspeakers, but you could barely hear them over the din of sailors and Thai bargirls chatting each other up. A short Thai girl squeezed Buzz's right bicep.

"You got big muscle, sailor man," she said. "You marry?"

Buzz sipped his beer and leered. "Not this side of the international date line I'm not."

Buzz, Buzz, Buzz, Jack thought. All those dope deals you made with God about this sort of thing after the Tailhook fiasco.

Another Thai Girl took a seat to the left of Jack, at the end of the bar. She was tall—for a Thai Girl, that is. She was semi-tall by U.S. Department of Agriculture standards. She wore a short dress with a cracker-jack collar, like an enlisted sailor's winter dress uniform. Jack saw her first and said nothing. Buzz saw her second and opened his mouth.

"Nice dress, Sweetheart. You buy that at K-Mart or did your mother make it for you?"

"Glad you like," The Tall Thai Girl said. "I have two dress like this, one white, one blue, like sailor boys have." She had on the blue one, but it was eggshell blue, not black, like sailors' blues are.

"How soon do you get off work?" Buzz said. "Maybe we can take in a museum or a Broadway show or something."

"I get off as soon as you pay bar fine," The Tall Thai Girl said.

The short Thai girl, who'd been trying to get Buzz to pay her bar fine for over an hour, tugged at his sleeve. "You flex muscle too many time around here. You make up mind."

"Mind?" Buzz said. "What mind? My pal Jack is the only one with a mind around here. I'll have to ask him."

Jack was bombed out of his mind, more buzzed than Buzz was. He shrugged and waved his hand at the scene in the bar. Officers and chiefs, Jack's age and older, running around with two or three of these Thai girls on their arms, like they thought they were Hugh Hefner or somebody.

"Okay, okay," Buzz said. "I know I swore off this kind of thing after Tailhook. And I really meant it then. But that was then and this is now."

Buzz paid the short Thai girl's bar fine and they disappeared into the night.

Jack tugged at the medallion on the silver chain around his neck. He'd never worn a neck chain before, but this one had been a gift from Carly. He could still feel the engraving on the medallion, so he must not be too drunk. One more beer, he decided, then he'd hit the road.

"Sorry," the Thai barman said, "last call ten minutes ago. Bar closed."

That couldn't be. Jack's Jap job said it was only …

LATE.

Holy shit. Jack was a lot drunker than he thought. He'd never find his way back to his hotel, and there was nobody left in the bar to take him there except—

The Tall Thai Girl, who still sat at the end of the bar.

She smiled at him with perfect teeth.

Five deployments to the Pacific Rim and Indian Ocean, and Jack had never taken a bargirl home with him. These kids, working at hooker joints their uncles and fathers and grandfathers owned. But he'd never been stupid enough to be snot-slinging drunk alone at a hooker bar at closing time either.

"Can you get me to my hotel?" he asked The Tall Thai Girl.

"Which one you stay?"

"I forget the name. The one on the beach that looks like an ocean liner from the front."

"Royal Thai Hotel," she said. "I know that one. Pay bar fine, I take you there."

They took a wild ride through the Pattya Beach night in a motorcycle cab, The Tall Thai Girl sitting on Jack's lap in the sidecar."

The bellman in the lobby stopped The Tall Thai Girl. "You have paper?"

She reached into her purse and showed the bellman her paper that said she didn't have any sex diseases, signed by a Thai doctor who made a living signing papers that said Thai bargirls didn't have any sex diseases. Thai girls who didn't have sex disease papers from Thai doctors couldn't work in Thai bars, and Thai bellmen wouldn't let them bring their clients into Thai hotels.

"This look okay," the bellman said, and smiled at Jack, who leaned against the front desk. "Have nice night, sir."

The Tall Thai Girl got Jack into the elevator and up to his room. She fished the key from his pocket, opened the door, and helped him in. Jack fell into his bed with his clothes on.

"You want me stay?" she said.

"Why not?"

"Can I take shower?"

"Sure," Jack slurred. "Take one for me while you're at it."

The Tall Thai Girl hummed a song in the shower. Jack's eyes closed. The hum turned into a drone, like the drone of an E-2 Hawkeye's propellers.

Sons of the Desert, Part II

The drone of propellers rattling in his flight helmet wakes Jack up. How long has he been asleep? Not long, he hopes.

Things look normal on his radarscope. The sweep passes clockwise through the north, over the no-fly zone. Buzz is out there, in his F-14 Tomcat, in the center fighter lane, staring at the back of his fighter pilot's head.

Over to the east, not in their assigned fighter lane, two French F-1 Mirage single-seat fighter jets circle over Al-Have-Another-Look. Over the clear, non-encrypted radio circuit that everyone can hear—including the bad guys—one Mirage pilot says, "Look, Henri, she is waving at me."

"No, Pierre, she is waving at me," the other Mirage pilot says.

Jack tries to key his microphone footswitch to say, "Beadwindow, inappropriate transmission," but his leg is asleep, and he can't move his foot.

"I tell you, Pierre, she is waving at me."

"*Alors*, I think you are seeing things in this desert, Henri. Let us go down for a closer look, to determine which one of us she is waving at."

They shouldn't do that, the dip shits. The bad guys have a surface to air missile site in Al-Have-Another-Look, disguised as a milk truck. That's what the intelligence weenies say. If the Mirages fly too low, a SAM can reach up and grab them out of the sky. Jack tries to key his footswitch again, and warn them not to descend, but his leg's still asleep.

Oh, well. There's no danger, probably. If the intelligence weenies say there's a SAM site at Al-Have-Another-Look, it's a pretty sure thing there really isn't. Jack shifts in his seat to relieve pressure from his lower back, and blood flows down his leg. His foot starts to tingle.

☆ ☆ ☆ ☆ ☆

"You no want sleep in you clothes," The Tall Thai Girl said. Jack's eyes snapped open. The Tall Thai Girl was pulling off his socks and shoes. Where the hell had he gone?

He'd heard this sort of thing before, or read about it or seen a lecture about it. Something or other stress syndrome. Guys having lucid, hallucinatory flashbacks to traumatic incidents they'd experienced, often triggered by large doses of alcohol or drugs. Jack might have panicked that something like that might be happening to him, except he was way too drunk and way too tired to give a shit just then.

The Tall Thai Girl put his socks and shoes on the chair by the dresser, and stood at the edge of the bed, wrapped, Jack now saw, from knees to shoulders in a white beach towel.

"What you think?" she said, turning for him like a fashion model.

"You're beautiful, Sweetheart."

"Glad you like." She loosened the towel and dropped it to the floor. "How you like this?"

"Magnificent," Jack said, and passed out again.

★ ★ ★ ★ ★

"*Magnifique*," says Henri.

"*Ooh, la la*," says Pierre.

They continue to descend.

The Muslim Babe has been sunbathing naked on the roof of the tallest building in Al-Have-Another-Look for months. That's how the intelligence weenies determined there was a SAM site there.

An alert young intelligence ensign on the *King* first spotted her on the roof while poring over satellite imagery. He studied it privately in the Male Officer's Head, then turned it over to the *King*'s senior intelligence officer, who transmitted it to Intelligence Central back in Washington after saving a copy for himself and a select group of close friends.

A senior analyst at Intelligence Central ordered changes to all the spy satellites' orbits so they could maintain round-the-clock surveillance of The Naked Muslim Babe. After a week of solid satellite coverage, the senior brain trust at Intelligence Central discovered a milk truck parked next to the building on the roof of which The Naked Muslim Babe was being naked.

"It has to be a SAMBUSH!" the head of Intelligence Central cried.

The milk truck had to be a camouflaged SAM battery, and The Naked Muslim Babe had to be a ruse to sucker coalition fighter pilots into flying low enough to take a good look at her, luring them into SAM range.

There was no other logical explanation.

Double Emergency Flash Immediate messages went out to all

coalition forces operating in the no-fly zone:

STAY AWAY FROM THE NAKED MUSLIM BABE AT AL-HAVE-ANOTHER-LOOK.

Which explains why the French Mirage pilots are flying over her now.

★ ★ ★ ★ ★

Jack came to again in the hotel. Naked, The Tall Thai Girl danced at the foot of the bed in front of him. Jack was starting to feel like that time traveler character—Billy Something—in that World War II book by Kurt Somebody. That book about how the Allies had firebombed the snot out of that German city where Jack's mom had ordered his baby spoon from. That Billy Something guy would be in the middle of World War II one second, on his honeymoon the next, and locked in a cage with a movie star on an alien planet the second after that. Creepy. But what the hell, Jack thought, it pretty much seems like my whole life has been like that time travel guy's, so I might as well play along.

"Put up your hair," he told The Tall Thai Girl. "It covers too much."

Her hair, so black it was blue, fell to the back of her knees. She tilted slightly and tied her hair in a series of knots, then piled it on top of her head, like she might have done that once or twice before.

She turned for him again. Like Venus with arms, marble stained with tea.

She crawled onto the bed and continued undressing him. "Let see what in here," she said as she pulled off his shorts. "Ooh. Look like you wide awake now."

She straddled him and leaned forward. "Kiss my breast."

Breasts like hers couldn't be real, like they just fell off the back of a grapefruit truck. But they couldn't be fake, could they? How could a Thai bargirl afford fake tits?

She reached behind herself and grabbed him between the legs. "You so hard," she said.

She kissed him and stared into his eyes. Eyes like a blonde baby's she had, only hers were brown, like a puppy's. The room started to spin. In the corner of The Tall Thai Girl's right eye something flashed, looking like the letter "M."

Here we go again, Jack thought.

☆   ☆   ☆   ☆   ☆

Flashing M!

Flashing M!

Flashing M on the edge of his radarscope.

M is for "missile."

How long has Jack been staring at and not seeing it?

The line of bearing goes through Al-Have-Another-Look.

The data readout says "SPOONFEED," the radar that goes with the SA-22 surface to air missile.

This can't be. The intelligence weenies couldn't possibly have been right about a SAM site being at Al-Have-Another-Look, could they?

On Jack's scope, the Mirages descend below ten thousand feet. Jack's leg is awake now. He puts his foot on his microphone switch and crushes it to the floorboard.

"SAMBUSH, SAMBUSH, SAMBUSH! SAMBUSH at Al-Have-Another-Look! Lafayette flight, scram south."

"*Merde!*" cries Henri.

"Holy shit!" cries Pierre.

Pierre and Henri turn south, accelerate and climb.

In the back seat of his F-14, half asleep, Buzz hears Jack call SAMBUSH on the non-encrypted circuit, rouses himself, keys his microphone, and whispers, "Jack, Beadwindow."

Jack rolls his eyes, and keys his mike switch, and whispers back, "for God's sake, Buzz, why are you whispering over the radio?"

"I didn't want everybody to hear that you just committed a Beadwindow," Buzz whispers, "identifying an enemy SAM site over an unencrypted circuit."

"How many times do I have to explain to you, Buzz?" Jack whispers over the unencrypted circuit. "Whispering over an unencrypted radio circuit isn't like whispering across a table or whispering over the phone. When you talk on an unencrypted radio circuit, everybody listening in can hear you just fine whether you're whispering or not."

"Then how come you're whispering on an unencrypted circuit too?" Buzz says.

Jack slaps himself on the helmet.

☆　☆　☆　☆　☆

In the passenger seat of the milk truck by the building where The Naked Muslim Babe basks on the roof, Sergeant Muhammad listens to all the whisper talk over the unencrypted radio circuit and flicks a switch that turns off the Radio Shack transmitter on top of the truck that's tuned to sound like an SA-22's SPOONFEED radar. He nudges his driver. "Mission accomplished, Ahmed."

"Indeed," Corporal Ahmed says. "We have defiled with their heads once again."

☆　☆　☆　☆　☆

The M on the edge of Jack's radarscope stops flashing.

☆　☆　☆　☆　☆

In King Kong Kamp in Saudi Arabia, Lieutenant General Small, the Air Force three-star in charge of the air show in the Gulf region who has been listening in to the entire exchange on the unencrypted radio circuit, keys his microphone. "King Kong actual copies

'Beadwindow,' out." General Small leans back in his huge, leather upholstered command chair, crosses his arms, and giggles. Then, with a predatory leer, he reaches for the handset of the encrypted circuit that connected him directly to the two-star admiral who commands the *King* battle group.

On the Carpet

Jack stands at attention on the carpet in the middle of CAG's office on the *Ernie King,* his back not liking this "stand at attention when I talk to you" business one bit.

"I'm ready to send this clown home right now," Captain Roy George says. Captain George—"Boy George" you called him behind his back—sits in a stuffed chair against the bulkhead to Jack's right. Boy George is the chief of staff to the *King* battle group commander, Rear Admiral Zach Taylor. George is old and tubby and bald, and wears the homely looking standard issue black-framed eyeglasses typically referred to as "birth control devices." He's a surface warfare officer who spent his entire career driving amphibious ships, hauling Marines all over the world and showing them the finer things in life. What Boy George knows about combat aviation you couldn't wipe a lapdog's butt with.

"What I don't understand," Boy George says to CAG, "is why he gave the SAMBUSH warning over an unencrypted circuit."

"That was the only circuit I could warn them on," Jack says.

"Why?" Boy George blubbers.

"We can't use an encrypted net when the French fly because we don't trust the French with our crypto codes."

Boy George grimaces and looks at CAG. "Is that true, Pro?"

CAG, Captain Joe "Pro" Bono, sitting behind his desk, shrugs. Tall and swarthy, Pro doesn't talk much these days. Like Buzz and a lot of other guys, Pro behaved badly at Tailhook. He wasn't in the mud on the balcony with Buzz. He was at a hot oil massage orgy on another balcony. Rear echelon types at the Pentagon are still trying to figure out who to tell the new Chief of Naval Operations to crucify over Tailhook so he can get Senator Tailhook off his back, and Pro is still on the short list. And Pro Bono has himself a high-dollar lawyer, who advised him to keep his mouth shut, so Pro has pretty much turned into a fifth amendment poster boy.

From the couch against the bulkhead to Jack's left, Captain Xavier "Deuce" Macintosh, the air wing's deputy commander, who guys like Jack normally address as "Deputy," takes his dime store cheaters from his nose and lets them dangle from the black cord around his neck. With those cheaters and that gray mop on top of his head, you'd think the Deputy was just some nice old man, like your grandpa, or your Uncle Sam. You'd never guess, just from looking at him, that he was a shit-hot F/A-18 Hornet pilot, and some other things as well.

"That's true, Chief of Staff," Deputy tells Boy George. "We don't trust the French with our crypto."

Boy George crosses his womanly arms atop the waterbed growing over his belt. "But aren't the French our friends?"

"For now," Deputy says. "But they might not be our friends tomorrow."

"Some friends," Boy George says.

"We've had worse," Deputy says. "The Iraqis used to be our friends too."

"Oh, yeah," Boy George says. "I forgot about that."

Jack gets a word in edgewise. "I don't see what the big deal is. I didn't reveal anything over the unencrypted circuit about what the bad guys were doing that the bad guys didn't already know. I mean, they were the ones doing it, right?"

Boy George blows a gasket.

Bitch! Bitch! Boom! Boom!

Smartass fucking Airedale.

Piss! Piss! Moan! Moan!

Pain in my goddamn ass.

Jack pictures the bouncing squares on his old Smiley Mac, and an Asian girl takes his baby spoon out of his head and puts it in her mouth.

★　★　★　★　★

"You so big," The Tall Thai Girl said. "Good thing me have tonsil take out."

She took Jack's hand and wet his fingers in her mouth, then guided them between her legs. Jack's fingers looked around for something to play with, but it wasn't there.

The Tall Thai Girl doesn't have enough words of English to tell him what happened to it, but one thing's for sure:

Something Happened.

★　★　★　★　★

"And it better not happen again," Boy George shouts, "or you'll be on the next big airplane home. You know what that would mean?"

It would mean serious shit, the end of Jack's naval career.

"It won't happen again," Jack says, and does a smart about-face, and marches out CAG's office door. He turns right, which on the starboard side is forward, and heads up the passageway toward his squadron's ready room.

CAG's officer door opens behind him. "Wait up, Jackie," Deputy calls out. Deputy catches up with Jack, grabs him by the ear, hustles him ten frames forward, and pulls him into the Male Officers' Head off the starboard passageway.

Deputy checks under the doors of the stalls. "Just to make sure Fix Felon isn't in here listening. You never know with that guy. It's all I can do to keep anything secret from him."

So Deputy Macintosh has Fix Felon connections, Jack thinks.

"All clear," Deuce says as he checks under the last stall. He walks up to Jack, a grandfatherly smile pasted on his face, and slaps Jack upside the head.

★ ★ ★ ★ ★

"You don't have to slap me, I'm awake."

"Just love tap," The Tall Thai Girl said. "Stop feel me there. I don't got one no more. They take when I was little girl, I no remember it."

She hugged Jack's neck and cried.

Jack stroked her hair that was so black it was blue. "It's all right. It's okay."

★ ★ ★ ★ ★

"Don't be a baby, you're okay," Deputy says. "I didn't hit you that hard. Just a love tap." He helps Jack up from the floor of the Male Officers' Head.

"What was that for, sir"

"Don't ever, ever, mouth off to Boy George again."

"Sorry, Deputy. But what's the deal with Boy George? Doesn't everybody hate him?"

"Beware the Chief of Staff, my son. Yes, everybody hates him, but everybody fears him too. He has connections. He went to high school with Senator Tailhook."

"But doesn't everybody hate her too?"

"Yes. And everybody also fears her."

"Everybody?" Jack says. "Even Fix Felon?"

"Especially Fix Felon. Senator Tailhook is the only person alive who can keep Fix Felon from taking over the entire known universe. If she ever places him in the mud in the balcony at Tailhook with your buddy Buzz, she'll flail Fix Felon alive."

"I see."

"I hope you do," the Deputy says. "That's why Zach Taylor has

Boy George as his chief of staff."

While Zach Taylor hates Boy George as much as everybody else, Deputy explains, he hates Fix Felon even worse. So Zach has allied himself with Boy George in order to ally himself with Senator Tailhook in an attempt to cock block Fix Felon and maybe take over the entire known universe himself.

Jack shakes his head. "What does all that have to do with me, and the no-fly zone, and this stupid Beadwindow business? From the way Boy George went on about it, leaking information on the insecure radio was a bigger deal than letting the French get shot down would have been."

"You think that milk truck was really a SAM site?" Deputy says.

"That's what the intelligence weenies told us."

The Deputy laughs. "The intelligence weenies tell us what we want them to tell us."

Jack scratches his head. "Why would we want them to tell us a milk truck is a SAM site if it's really just a milk truck?"

"So we have an excuse to be here," the Deputy says. "So we can play war."

"Play war?"

"Sure. If we can't have real war, we need play war, so the sandbox generals and bathtub admirals can fight among themselves over who gets to control the toy soldiers and ships and airplanes, and see who can kiss the ass of the bedroom politicians the most, and get themselves put in charge of the entire known universe."

Something flickers at the top of Jack's lighthouse. "So that's why King Kong—General Small—hates Zach Taylor so much?"

"Bada-bing," the Deputy says, shooting Jack with his thumb and forefinger. "Anything that makes the Navy look bad makes the Air Force look good, and anything that makes Admiral Taylor look small makes General Small look big."

Deputy smiles again, and puts an arm around Jack's shoulders.

"A Jesuit priest who taught at my high school once told me that the right thing to do and the smart thing to do and the thing you can live with aren't always the same thing."

"I don't get it," Jack says.

The Deputy's smile disappears. "I was afraid you wouldn't. Sorry to have to do this to you, Jackie, but ..."

Deputy pulls out the crucifix hanging under his T-shirt from a chain around his neck and places it on Jack's forehead. "Thou shalt not remember a word I've just said," he intones, and knees Jack in the groin.

✮ ✮ ✮ ✮ ✮

Sweat shot from Jack's pores, his body working overtime to pump out the alcohol.

He reeked.

This wild dream of his was taking a bizarre turn. Jack remembered talking to the Deputy in the head off the O3 passageway, but none of that other stuff: the smack in the head, the lecture about play war, the kick in the groin. Where had he made that up from?

He disentangled himself from The Tall Thai Girl and went to the bathroom.

The spray from the showerhead stung like needles, the towel felt like sandpaper against his skin. The sheets were dry when he crawled back into bed. He'd have sworn they were damp when he got up. Had he been dreaming that too?

The Tall Thai Girl stirred. "You smell nice. You take shower for me?"

"Yes, I took shower for you."

She rolled over and straddled him. "Make love now," she said.

She lifter her hips to lower herself on him, and stopped. The medallion on the chain around Jack's neck caught her eye. She reached out and felt it and ran her finger across the inscription.

"What this say?"

"Pull me."

So you can pull your own chain since I'm not there to pull it for you, Carly had written in the letter Jack had received on the *King*.

"What happen you class alpha hard-on?" The Tall Thai Girl asked.

"I'm just tired."

"You still pretty drunk, too."

"And that," Jack said.

"You lie back, get sleep." The Tall Thai Girl curled against him. Jack looked up at the ceiling fan.

☆ ☆ ☆ ☆ ☆

The next letter from Carly said she'd reported to her ship, a brand new *Arleigh Burke* class missile destroyer. She had qualified as officer of the deck in only a month, and expected to earn her Surface Warfare Officer pin in record time. "I intend to become the Madame Curie of the Navy," she'd written, and drawn a smiley face next to that.

The next morning, Jack went to the ship's store and bought an eighteen-karat gold surface warfare pin to give her when he got back from cruise. That afternoon, reading the official message traffic, he saw the safety bulletin that announced Carly's ship had collided with a supertanker in a freak accident just off the coast of Virginia. Her ship had sunk within thirty seconds, and Carly and all her shipmates had gone to a damn sight better place than a United States Navy destroyer.

Jack wrote Carly's semi-mom to tell her how sorry he was. Carly's semi-mom never wrote back.

☆ ☆ ☆ ☆ ☆

The Tall Thai Girl said, "No cry. Sleep."

Dumb Soldiers

Jack watches the sweep on his scope pass through Buzz and the back of his pilot's head as they track south in the center fighter lane on their last watch over the no-fly zone.

They're back on the unencrypted radio circuit because the French Mirages have shown up, more or less on time, according to the master air plan put out by King Kong. The Mirages are out of their lane again, circling over The Muslim Babe, now that everybody knows the milk truck was just a milk truck after all.

An Air Force AWACS and a pair of F-15 Beagle fighters take off from King Kong Kamp in Saudi Arabia to relieve Jack and Buzz on station. Thirty more minutes, and Jack and Buzz and the rest of the sorry slobs on the *Ernest J. King* can kiss this play war goodbye and go home.

The AWACS and the Beagles track north from the south.

Twenty-five minutes to go.

A new contact pops up on Jack's radarscope, north of the no-fly line, and tracks south. It's low and slow, so it can't be a fighter. It has to be a helicopter, and it almost certainly has to be one of ours. Bad Guy never flies in the no-fly zone any more. Why should he bother? All he has to do is sit back and watch us fly it, and wait for us to stomp on our dicks and embarrass ourselves.

The helicopter crosses the no-fly line as Buzz and his pilot's head reach the southern end of their fighter lane and turn north for one last time.

To the south, AWACS and the Beagles are fifteen minutes out.

Jack's back hurts and his foot's numb again, but he manages to key his footswitch and say, "Ghost has new contact. Bullseye, three-one-zero, forty-five, low and slow."

This tells Buzz the contact is a helicopter forty-five miles northwest of Al-Have-Another-Look.

"Declare," Buzz says, wanting to hear if Jack knows whether this contact is good, bad, or otherwise.

"Bogey, negative squawk," Jack says, telling Buzz he doesn't know for sure if the helicopter is a friend or foe because the helicopter's pilot has his electronic identification turned off. U.S. Army helicopter pilots do that all the time, oblivious to the fighters flying above them, trip-wired to shoot down anything that flies in the no-fly zone.

"Investigate, get a VID," Jacks says, telling Buzz to visually identify the bogey.

AWACS and the Beagles are five minutes out. Buzz and his pilot circle over the helicopter. "Tally ho," Buzz calls over the unencrypted circuit, then he whispers, "Contact is a Dumb Soldier."

Jack moans. Again with the whispering over the radio. Everybody can hear you, Buzz, you dip shit, and you just used an unauthorized code word. "Dumb Soldier" is a private joke between Buzz and Jack, something they call the dip-shit Army pilots who hover around the no-fly zone with their identification gear shut off.

"Ghost copies, Dumb Soldier," Jack says, figuring the damage has already been done, and hopefully, that nobody cares about an unauthorized code word getting used on the radios once in a while.

Actually, nobody does care at this point about unauthorized code words, or about much of anything else going on in this no-fly zone play war. Except for one guy. Unfortunately for Jack, that one guy— General Small, King Kong actual—is listening in on the unencrypted circuit, sitting in back of the AWACS as it approaches station. He's getting in his monthly flight hours so he can qualify for flight pay.

King Kong hears Jack and Buzz say "Dumb Soldier" and cries for joy. One last chance to fuck with the Navy—and Zach Taylor—before the *King* leaves the theater of operations. He keys the unencrypted circuit and blares, "Beadwindow! Unauthorized Code Word!"

"Oh, fuck," Jack says, recognizing King Kong's voice. "Fuck, fuck, fuck." He hangs his head, and looking down, sees that his still numb foot is still pressed against his microphone switch.

Buzz keys his mike and whispers, "Jack, you just said 'fuck' over the unencrypted circuit."

"Oh, shit," Jack says, his foot still on his mike switch.

King Kong thinks he's died and gone to heaven. "Beadwindow! Beadwindow! Beadwindow! Inappropriate transmission!"

King Kong grabs the handset to the encrypted circuit next to his command console on the AWACS. A signal goes up into space, bounces off a satellite, comes back to earth, and lands in the phone on the desk of Rear Admiral Zach Taylor onboard the USS *Ernest J. King*. The phone rings. Zach Taylor picks it up and puts it to his ear. The signal crawls out of the earpiece, down Zach's back, into his trousers, up the crack of his ass and goes:

Bitch! Bitch! Boom! Boom!

The image of Captain Roy "Boy" George appears in Jack's radarscope, and crooks a finger at Jack. Jack leans forward. Boy George reaches out, grabs Jack by the neck of his flight suit, and pulls him through the scope. Jack shoots out his Hawkeye's radar antenna, and he flies over the desert, and over the Gulf, until he reaches the *King*. Then he falls, and falls, and falls …

☆　☆　☆　☆　☆

Jack stands on CAG's carpet again, surrounded by the three captains of the apocalypse. Boy George, his waterbed and jowls quivering, is downright apoplectic.

Dumb Soldier? Fuck and Shit?

Now you've gone and done it.

Bread and water, admiral's mast,

Red-hot poker up your ass.

CAG, Pro Bono, sits behind his desk and says nothing.

Deputy Deuce Macintosh, in his spot on the couch to Jack's left, seems about to say something when he looks at the door that you don't call a hatch, which opens. In the doorway stands Rear Admiral Zach Taylor, his eyes as wide as the hatch off the hangar bay, and three-toned as a British left-tenant commander's. He sweeps into the room that's also a compartment, and plants his feet on the floor you call a deck.

"This just in," he declares. "Good news. Only moments ago, General Small created a disaster while flying on AWACS in the no-fly zone."

Dumb Air Force Guy

The AWACS crew had decided to let King Kong get "hands on" in this mission. They put him in charge of the unencrypted circuit and let him control the F-15 Beagles. King Kong had never controlled fighters, but he was an old fighter pilot himself and figured he could easily do whatever it was that piss ant AWACS fighter controllers did.

The Beagles flew into the zone. On their radars they saw the French Mirages circling over The Naked Muslim Babe in Al-Have-Another-Look on their radars. They called King Kong and said, "Declare."

King Kong, thinking this was part of an air-to-air exercise everyone had set up so he could play fighter controller, said, "Hostile."

The Beagles didn't know anything about any exercise. All they knew was that they were enforcing a no-fly zone, and if their controller told them a contact was hostile, it was their job to shoot it down.

"Fox Four," the Beagles said, and unleashed a pair of AA-22 Buttshark missiles.

Henri and Pierre were having a jolly old time flying over The Naked Muslim Babe, right up to—but not including—the moment the Buttsharks swam up their tailpipes and went:

Boom! Boom!

★　★　★　★　★

"So we're off the hook about the Dumb Soldiers we didn't shoot down," Zach Taylor says in Pro Bono's office that is also a compartment, and dances around the room with glee. "The Joint Chiefs of Staff are shipping King Kong off to shit-can land, and I'll get my third star."

Pro Bono clears his throat and speaks for the first time in six months. "What about the rest of us?"

Zach Taylor's enthusiasm wanes. "Oh yeah. The rest of you." Zach points at Pro Bono. "You're off the hook for Tailhook. They found some gay Marine infantry major who wasn't even there to take the blame for all that. You've just picked up your first star. You're out of here on the afternoon COD."

"Oh, boy," Pro Bono says, and rushes off to pack his bag.

Zach nods at Deputy Deuce Macintosh. "You're in charge of the air wing now."

Deputy nods back, like none of this is news to him.

"What about me?" Boy George bleats. "Don't I get anything out of this?"

"Yes," Zach says. "Fix Felon wants you as his chief of staff on Second Fleet, his new three-star command."

"Fix Felon likes me?"

"Fuck no," Zach says. "Fix Felon despises you as much as everybody else does. But he needs a Senator Tailhook connection, and tag, you're it."

"She was such a smart girl in high school," Boy George says. He smiles briefly. Then he frowns. He points a tubby finger at Jack, who has crawled into a corner, hoping nobody remembers he's in the compartment. "What about him?" Boy George says. "What about all that 'Dumb Soldier' and 'fuck' and 'shit' on the radio?"

Jack looks at Zach, huddled in the corner, and their eyes meet.

☆ ☆ ☆ ☆ ☆

What does Zach Taylor see in Jack's eyes?

From the couch, Deputy (now CAG) Deuce Macintosh crooks a finger at us. We lean forward, and he whispers in our ears:

"He sees rain smacking against the windscreen on the bridge of the USS *Constellation*, just after The Rocky Horror Recovery. He sees two boys, one big, one fat, saluting him. He wonders if either of them can tell that he's shit his pants."

☆ ☆ ☆ ☆ ☆

Zach Taylor waves the back of his hand at Boy George. "Fuck, I don't give a shit what you do with the dumb son of a bitch. Promote him and give him an Air Medal for all I care."

And that's how Jack gets his Air Medal and his third early promotion. Despite his best efforts to screw his career into the deck, he's still a rising star.

Rise and Shine

"Look what come up with sun," The Tall Thai Girl said as day broke through the curtains on the hotel window. "Make love now," she whispered in his ear.

☆ ☆ ☆ ☆ ☆

Wearing her eggshell-blue sailor dress, she said, "You want me come back?"

Jack, still in bed, mulled it over. "I don't know. We get underway tomorrow afternoon. I'll probably spend the night on the ship."

"Okay," she said, "have nice life," and before Jack could think of anything else to say, she disappeared out the hotel room's door.

Thirty minutes later, Jack woke with a start. He'd taken a bar girl home with him, had sex with her, hadn't paid her, and had left his wallet out where she could get at it. Frantic, he hopped to the wooden desk chair she'd draped his clothes over and checked the pockets of his blue jeans.

The wallet was there, and all his cash and credit cards and his military ID card and his driver's license.

A Crimson Sunbird perched on the tree outside his window and sang for him. Jack showered and dressed. He rooted around in his pants pocket for his room key and felt something odd. Small and hard, with smooth edges here and there. He took it out.

A tiny porcelain Sunbird.

Well, Jack thought. The Tall Thai Girl had been real, and not part of his dream.

★ ★ ★ ★ ★

"You check out this morning, sir?" the bellman asked Jack in the lobby.

"I think I'll stay one more night," Jack said.

Jack had breakfast in the hotel restaurant, and went back to his room for a nap. He got up a few hours before sunset, changed into swim trunks, and strolled down to the beach.

The wrinkled mama-san who walked up and down the beach with a cooler asked Jack if he wanted another bottle of Gatorade.

"Ten's my limit before happy hour," Jack said. "Got to pace myself. Last night of liberty, you know."

"Ha, ha, you funny guy. I not see you no more, then. Have nice life. I ask favor fore you go?"

"Sure."

"You fly-boy, right? You have squadron patch? It for my son. He dream of join U.S. Navy some day."

"Sure," Jack said, thinking that the mama-san's son's father was probably some long forgotten American sailor. He took a squadron patch out of his gym bag. It had his squadron's logo—a cartoon ghost extending two puffy fingers in a peace sign in the center, "Backfire Busters" in bold over the top, and "Peace is our semi-profession" in italics across the bottom.

"He going to love this patch," the mama-san said. "I sew it for him, on the flight jacket he not supposed to have."

Jack chuckled. "It sounds like your son has a bright future ahead of him in the Navy Supply Corps."

Cleaning up in his hotel room, he wished he had The Tall Thai Girl in the shower with him. He got dressed, had a light dinner at the Hotel, and set out on foot to find the bar where he'd met her.

☆　☆　☆　☆　☆

The Thai bartender had a San Miguel opened for Jack by the time he got to his stool. Jack sipped at it and looked around the bar.

"You looking for tall girl with sailor dress?" the barman said.

"Sort of."

"I no see her tonight. Maybe she goes back Bangkok. Big convention little Japanese business fellah start there tomorrow. Tall girl like her very popular with little Japanese fellah. She make enough tip one weekend, take three month off, maybe."

Jack checked out a few other places on his way back to the hotel. Plenty of Thai girls in all of them, but no tall ones wearing an eggshell-blue sailor dress.

☆　☆　☆　☆　☆

"Hope you had nice stay," the bellman said in the morning as Jack checked out.

"I did," Jack said. He handed the bellman what was left of his funny colored Thai money and hoofed it toward fleet landing.

☆　☆　☆　☆　☆

Buzz Rucci, the air wing duty officer, paced up and down the *King's* afterbrow. There's the dip shit, he thought, peering at the ferry approaching the *King's* stern. Leave it to Jack to catch the very last liberty boat back to the ship.

"Jesus," Buzz said as Jack came up the brow. "Could you have cut it any closer? What did you do, forget about this paltry bullshit about getting underway and have a marathon fuck fest with that tall Thai babe?"

Jack winked. "Nah. I was too drunk to get it up."

"Yeah, right," Buzz said. Fucking Jack, he thought. Gets an air medal, gets his third straight early promotion, and bones the best looking hooker in Pattya Beach on top of that. When are things going to go my way? When, when, when, when, when, when, when?

☆　☆　☆　☆　☆

In his stateroom, Jack threw his liberty clothes in a laundry bag. He put the "pull me" chain and the porcelain sunbird in the box where he kept his wedding ring and Carly's SWO pin and Chief Kirk's stadimeter, and locked the box back in the safe on his desk.

Naked, he crawled into his rack. The crisp sheets felt good against his skin.

When Jack woke up again, the *King* was underway, headed for San Diego, where his house and his car and his stereo and the seventh chair waited for him.

ACT III PART II
Long Distance

The Airplanes are Broken

Desperate to catch up with Jack, who is now three years ahead of him in the naval career sweepstakes, Buzz trades his wife's grandparents for a set of shore duty orders to the Bureau of Personnel in Millington, Tennessee. Buzz is a geographic bachelor on this tour. The rest of the Rucci family, which now includes four minor children, two dogs, and a tank full of fish, still resides in Scripps Ranch, a block down from Jack's place.

Don't worry about Buzz, though. He's safe, all by himself in Tennessee. They sell condoms by the case down there.

☆ ☆ ☆ ☆ ☆

Once established at BUPERS, Buzz gets Jack assigned to shore duty back at the E-2 RAG. Not a career enhancing tour for Jack, but Jack's career is already enhanced enough, as far as Buzz is concerned, so fuck him. Besides, staying in San Diego, Jack might find a life again, the dip shit. And if he does, he'll have Buzz to thank for it.

☆ ☆ ☆ ☆ ☆

The fat rent-a-cop at the back gate of Naval Air Station Miramar keeps his seat and salutes the officer's sticker on the windshield of Jack's Trans Am. Jack pulls into his private spot in the Hangar 6 parking lot marked "Assistant Maintenance Officer." The new skipper at the RAG has put Jack unofficially in charge of aircraft maintenance, in a management move to fix the RAG's aircraft, which are still broke-dick from the Goober-Otis-Potato Head administration.

Unlike Potato Head, the present RAG skipper is not a Total Quality kind of guy. He's a total asshole. He wants what he wants, and doesn't care whose life or career he has to total to get it. Captain Robert "Grim" Reaper likes things done the old-fashioned way— the way that will make him look good and pave his way to a set of admiral's stars. Grim Reaper is an E-2 guy, so he has that going against him, as far as making admiral is concerned. But he also has connections, Fix Felonious and otherwise, that improve his odds.

Jack locks the Trans Am and climbs zero ladders to get to his office on the first deck, which in a Navy building is at ground level.

It is Friday morning.

Jack's typing up enlisted performance evaluations on his government IBM clone desktop computer when his boss, the official maintenance officer, walks in the office, slams the door behind him and sits at his desk. Commander "Ape" Appleby buries his face in his hands and makes cry noises. The matted hair on his forearms bristles.

"What didn't Grim like this time, Ape?" Jack says.

"He didn't like the way I wrote up the weekly aircraft summary."

"What did you say on it?"

"I'll show you." Ape puts a latex glove on his right hand, reaches it up his ass and pulls it back out clutching the wadded up weekly maintenance summary.

Jack takes it and flattens it out on his desk with his bare hands. He figures he's developed immunity to hepatitis by this point in his naval career.

"Uh huh," Jack says. "'Zero up airplanes.' I can see how Grim might not like that."

A tear rolls down Ape's cheek. "Three little words," he says.

"The wrong three words, Ape. Tell you something else Grim probably didn't like."

"What's that?"

"You spelled two of the three little words wrong. 'Zeroe up aeroplanes.'"

"Ah!" Ape says. "That's why Grim said he ought to stick a dictionary up my ass while he was at it."

"When are you going to learn, Ape?" Jack taps out a new maintenance message on his computer and prints it out. "Go show him this."

Ape reads it. "Ninety percent aircraft availability pending arrival of spare parts from intermediate maintenance facility."

"Sound right?" Jack says.

"Sort of," Ape says. "Except we'll never get the spare parts we need because they'll get sucked up by the fleet squadrons before we ever see them."

"You know that, Ape, and I know that. Grim knows that, and Grim's bosses and their bosses know that. But they don't want to hear it. So we just tell them the part of the truth they want to hear."

"A half truth?"

"That's right, Ape. And we don't tell them the part they don't want to hear."

"Which is the whole truth?"

"Exactly," Jack says. "And we're not lying, and we're not even misleading anybody—"

"Because they already know the whole truth, they just don't want to hear it."

"Bada-bing, Ape."

Ape, astounded at Jack's acuity, says, "See, it's that kind of logical thinking that explains why you have a career ahead of you and I don't. No wonder you're unofficially in charge of me."

Ape has been passed over for squadron command and is spinning his wheels until he can retire as a commander with twenty years. (Another knucklehead Navy name game. Commanders don't always become commanding officers, and commanding officers aren't always commanders.) Things could be worse for Ape, though. A lot of guys in his position are assigned as safety officers on aircraft carriers or to overseas naval bases as the gay male prostitution officer.

Ape, all excited about this new weekly maintenance message that Grim won't shove up his ass, heads out of the office but stops in the doorway. "Wait."

"What?" Jack says.

"I just thought of what else Grim will ask me about. The skit for his welcome aboard dinner tonight. He told me to tell you to tell the J.O.s to come up with entertainment. Did I remember to tell you? Did you remember to tell the J.O.s?"

"They're up in the ready room right now. The skit will be good, trust me."

"Okay," Ape says. "Then I'm off to see the Reaper."

★ ★ ★ ★ ★

What Jack just told Ape is another half-truth. The J.O.s are in the ready room. That's one of Grim's new non-Quality policies. The J.O.s have to be in the squadron spaces during working hours even if there aren't any planes to fly. And working hours are whatever hours Grim happens to be at work, which is a lot of hours.

Like Buzz, Grim Reaper has a nice home and a nice wife and four nice children and two nice dogs and a nice tank full of fish. Grim is quite fond of his home life, and he'd hate to ruin it by spending any time there. So he spends all his time at Hangar 6 and ruins everybody else's home life instead.

But though the J.O.s are hanging out in the ready room, they are not working on tonight's skit. Nor did Commander Jack Hogan ask or order them to come up with one. You don't send Hawkeye Boys to do a Hawkeye Man's job.

So dubbed by Carly Simon, our late Lady of the Soccer Pitch, Hawkeye Man shuts down his government IBM clone computer.

He closes the office door and locks it. Pressing a secret panel on his desk, he opens a hidden compartment and pulls out: THE MACINTOSH POWERBOOK!

He reverently places it on his desktop, opens it and touches the power button.

An ominous chord sounds.

Hawkeye Man launches the word processing application, and begins to weave a spell of mirth and mayhem.

Jack was willing to play along with Grim Reaper's game by writing the half-truth maintenance message, partly to help out Ape, who had suffered enough, and partly because standing up to Grim, trying to force him to tell the whole truth about the squadron's aircraft, wouldn't have succeeded.

But Jack won't let Grim off Scot-free. He'll have to take a pie in the face, and Hawkeye Man's just the guy to throw it.

✮ ✮ ✮ ✮ ✮

On his way home to change for the dinner, Jack stops at a mall in Mira Mesa, and slips through the hatch of a joke and magic shop.

✮ ✮ ✮ ✮ ✮

Hubbub, hubbub, hubbub …

Everybody's just finished dinner, and they're all shit-faced.

Ape steps up to the podium.

Tap, tap. Phew. "Can everybody hear me okay?"

Thumbs up from all the officers and spouses sitting at tables in the grand reception room of the Half-Ass Hotel in Mission Valley, and the hubbub goes on.

"Welcome, everybody," Ape says from behind the podium. Ape wears a tight fitting blue blazer and even tighter fitting gray slacks that his wife bought him when he was a lieutenant, and a pair of shiny black Corfam Uniform Oxfords he got issued as a freshman you called a plebe at the Naval Academy.

Clink, clink, clink, ahem, et cetera.

"The sooner I can have everyone's attention," Ape tries, "the sooner we can leave and go home."

That works. The noise dies down. Ape continues:

"As you all know, we're here to welcome aboard our new skipper, Captain Robert Reaper, and his lovely wife, Missus ... uh ... Missus Reaper. How about a round of applause for our new skipper and his old missus?"

All hands make the sound of one hand clapping.

"That's enough hoopla over that," Ape says. "Let's have the new skipper get up and say a few words."

GASP!

This is highly irregular. You don't ask the skipper to speak first. The skipper always speaks last. Unless there's no one else to speak or perform any entertainment, in which case the skipper speaks first and last. But that's not supposed to happen. The skipper had ordered Ape to order Jack to order the J.O.s to come up with some entertainment. Which they apparently didn't.

Everybody can tell something is wrong. Ape's wife, sitting at the head table with Grim and Mrs. Grim and the other department heads and their spouses, is so shocked that her tongue drops right out of the ear of the squadron's operations officer, with whom she's been making out in plain sight of everyone.

Grim Reaper: hollow-faced and hollow-eyed; if he were taller, you might mistake him for Fix Felon. Armani and the other quality products and doodads smeared all over him probably cost more than Jack's Trans Am is worth at this point

Grim's chair squeaks as he scoots it back, and he's leaning forward, shifting his weight to stand, when a voice over the Half-Ass Hotel's public announcement system booms:

"NOT SO FAST!"

Comedy Tonight

Jack enters from a side door, wearing a flight suit, and a monk's cowl over his head. He's made his face up to look like the rock star Alice Cooper. In his right hand he holds a papier-mâché scythe. Under his left arm is his forty-pound dictionary from college, and he holds a blue routing folder in his left hand. A giant set of cardboard pilot wings sit above his left chest pocket, and over his right chest pocket is an equally giant nametag that reads "The Grim Skipper."

Ape's wife laughs and runs her hand under the table and up the operations officer's leg. The other wives take that as their cue to go ahead and laugh and run their hands under the table and up somebody's leg too. Some of them actually run their hands up their own husbands' legs. Ape gets back to the head table just in time for Mrs. Reaper to run her hand up his leg. This is turning out to be a fun party after all, he thinks. He just wonders if Mrs. Grim realizes she's running her hand up his leg, and not Grim's, and whether, if she does realize what she's actually doing, Grim doesn't.

Grim realizes he's being put on and sits back down, hoping somebody else's wife will run a hand up his leg. He's the skipper, after all. Why should he miss out on all the festivities?

Jack sets his props around the podium. "Pardon the flight suit. I came here straight from work. I had to leave early."

That gets a laugh from the spouses. The officers laugh less certainly, looking at the head table to see if Grim is laughing.

He is not.

"I had one last item in my inbox," Jack the Reaper says. "I hate to interrupt a social occasion with business, but I'm sure the spouses won't mind. At least this way, everybody got to leave work early, so they could get here in time for the working party."

The spouses roar at that one. The officers roar too, partly because of all those hands running up their shit-faced legs, but mostly because, at the head table, Grim's face has broken out in a verifiable smile, because the safety officer's wife has her hand up his leg.

"I need to do one last review of Ape's weekly maintenance message before we release it to God and everybody. I haven't had a chance to read it yet, but Ape's attempts at composition are usually entertaining."

Titters. Everybody knows that Ape's mentally challenged.

Jack takes the prop message from the folder and rifles through his forty-pound dictionary.

"T-H-E. Okay."

More titters.

"A-I-R-P-L-A-N-E-S. Good, good."

The laugh builds.

"A-R-E. Very good."

Har-har.

"B-R-O-K-E-N."

Jack looks up. "Not good."

Belly laughs.

Jack grabs his scythe and walks over to Ape at the head table. "In some ways," he explains to Ape, "this is a good message. In other ways, this is not a good message. The words are spelled correctly, but ..."

Jack puts the sharp end of the scythe against Ape's neck:

"... they are the wrong words!"

Ho, ho, ho!

"We're going to set a dangerous precedent if we start blurting out the unvarnished truth in official naval message traffic!"

Hee-hee-hee!

"Now," Jack says, "what should the right words be? I know! We'll release two messages. The first one will say, 'Bad news. The airplanes are stolen.'"

Hah, hah, hah!

"An hour later, we'll release another message that says, 'Good news. We found the airplanes ...'"

Jack the Reaper pauses for effect.

"'... but they are broken!'"

Pandemonium. Standing ovation. Joy, rapture, husbands and wives dancing together, having fun-fun-fun, just like a real party that a real squadron might have.

After all the congratulations, Jack sits at the bar, feeling good about himself, and life, and the universe, until ...

Grim Reaper, from across the room, crooks a finger at him. Dipshit Jackie leaves his bar stool and walks over to Grim. Grim puts his arm around Jackie's shoulders and pisses in his ear:

"Come see me in my office first thing Monday morning."

The Last Weekend

Jack didn't have a date that weekend, or anything else to do, so he sat in the seventh chair, listened to music, drank, and dreaded the approach of Monday morning.

Don't get the idea that Jack has been a misogynist this whole time, since we last saw him with The Tall Thai Girl. He's seen plenty of women since then. Well, two. Which was more than plenty, as far as he was concerned.

The first one, she was high class. Loved culture, this one did. Loved Jack's music, loved his "deliciously bohemian" lifestyle. Loved Jack to take her to museums, the opera and her favorite, the theater. Loved to go to the Old Globe in Balboa Park. Had to see the Shakespeare festival, the class act insisted. Jack loved few things more than Shakespeare, and hated fewer things more than watching mediocre actors butcher him.

King Lear, they saw, starring an actor from an old TV cop show. "Blow winds, and crack your cheeks," the TV cop said in Act III.

I can do that at home by myself, Jack thought.

They saw *Coriolanus*, with an actor from an old TV doctor show. Heinous. The production lasted five hours. If Jack wanted to look at something that sounded like the TV doctor's *Coriolanus* all night, he could have stayed married to Liz.

Class Act had just dumped Jack for a high society cocaine dealer when he took up with Lena. Curly brown bangs, Lena had, and a face like the statue of a Greek goddess, and about that expressive too. But Lena had other redeeming virtues, namely the body of a statue of a Greek goddess, especially the first two virtues of the rest of the virtues. Her best virtue, though, was that she wasn't all that virtuous.

Lena was a civilian, worked at the training building. She accidentally ran into Jack every day he went over there to instruct a trainer (Grim hadn't fixed the airplanes, but he'd gotten the flight trainers working). She finally said, "I keep expecting to run into you at the O' Club some Wednesday. I hear you used to go there all the time."

"It's just not like it used to be, I guess," Jack said.

It wasn't the same without Buzz. And there was something about being that close to Carly's old semi-permanent room at the Bachelor Officers' Quarters too. Plus, Wednesday Night Live was pretty dead after Senator Tailhook made them kick out all the professional harlots. Instead of dancers from local strip clubs, they had fitness instructors in leotards putting on aerobic dance demonstrations. Then there were the "lingerie auctions." Talk about players from the farm teams. The lingerie models they trotted out made you think you were watching a 4-H competition.

"What else do you like to do?" Lena said. "You look like you work out. Want to play racquetball after work some time?"

Jack didn't play much racquetball any more. Not the best thing for his aging back and knees, with all that stop and start action. But watching Lena bounce around in a tight T-shirt and a sports bra and shorts might warrant a couple hours soaking in a hot bath later.

"Sure," Jack said. "When do you get off?"

"Every chance I get," Lena said, and winked. "I'm done with work at four. I'll be ready to play by four thirty. See you then, at the courts by the O' Club."

☆ ☆ ☆ ☆ ☆

Lena showed up at four thirty in tennis shoes, shorts, a tight T-shirt, and no sports bra.

Jack let her stay close in the first game, only beating her by two points. He let her win the second game by one point, then mopped the floor with her in the third game, just to let her know she wasn't that good.

"Had enough?" he said.

"Enough racquetball," she said, and pulled off her T-shirt and shorts. She wasn't wearing sports panties either. "Why not take your stuff off and really mop the floor with me?"

Jack stripped and mopped the floor with her. She squeezed his mop, and he mopped the floor with her again. After that, she looked over in a corner of the court and said, "Oh, look, you missed a spot," and Jack mopped the floor with her a third time.

"That was great!" Lena said. "Tell me, how did I compare with The Tall Thai Girl?"

"How do you know about her?"

"From Flip Wilson, of course. Isn't he the best? He knows about everything."

Flip must have heard about the Tall Thai Girl from Buzz. Flip was at the Bureau of Personnel in Tennessee now too, in charge of reserve officer assignments, but he spent a lot of time on temporary assignment in San Diego, partying on government funded per diem. Jack would have to be careful what he told Buzz about from now on.

★ ★ ★ ★ ★

Dip-shit Jackie figured he had to take Lena on a real date after that. He took her to see Bonnie and Stevie in concert at the San Diego State University Outdoor Amphitheater. Stevie had fallen down on stage for the fifth time before Jenny commented, "Do you think he's drunk or something?"

"Or something," Jack said.

As Stevie screamed "Goodnight San Diego," after his last encore, Jenny said, "You think he likes girls?"

"I'd bet money he does," Jack said.

"I'm going to find out," she said, and bounced down the amphitheater stairs, and onto the stage, and smiled at the security guard, and disappeared behind the curtains.

★ ★ ★ ★ ★

A week later, Jack stopped by the O' Club at happy hour for old times' sake. Lena was there, surrounded by a pack of driveling young fighter guys and some driveling old ones too. Flip Wilson was in town and lurked in the background, next to an old Abe Lincoln–looking admiral who was probably Fix Felon. Lena saw Jack walk in and said, "Yoo-hoo!"

"How was Stevie?" Jack said. "He say anything interesting?"

"I couldn't hear too good that night," Lena said. "Bonnie had her legs wrapped around my ears."

★ ★ ★ ★ ★

Jack went back on the woman wagon after that, and spent most weekends alone, drinking, like he did the weekend after The Half-Ass Hotel Skit, wondering how hard Grim Reaper's other shoe would drop come Monday morning.

✩　✩　✩　✩　✩

Yeah, they've definitely added a few rungs to this stairway, Jack thought, as he stepped up the ladder to the second deck of Hangar 6.

Jack had graded the skinny ensign at the duty desk on an NFO tactics trainer the week before. The kid had done okay. Jack had heard him out in the parking lot afterwards, bragging to his classmates how he'd scored an "above average" grade from the mighty Jack Hogan. This impressed his classmates, all of whom considered the mighty Jack Hogan to be an aloof, demanding prick. Which was true. Jack was the senior NFO instructor at the RAG now. Like it or not, he was supposed to be an aloof, demanding prick. These young dip shits might run into something like The Great Big Backfire Raid as soon as they hit the fleet, like Jack had. If they fucked it away, it wouldn't be because the mighty Jack Hogan had been soft on them.

The skinny ensign smiled. "You were really funny Friday night, sir."

"Shut up, Stick Boy," Jack said.

Stick Boy kept smiling. "The skipper's in his office. He said to tell you to come see him first thing you got in."

"Thanks. I'll blow him off right away."

✩　✩　✩　✩　✩

What an awesome guy, Stick Boy thought. Wait till I tell everybody Jack Hogan told me to shut up, and called me Stick Boy, and that line about blowing the skipper off right away.

Man, I want to grow up to be just like him.

✩　✩　✩　✩　✩

Jack skulked over to the coffee mess, and was drawing himself a cup of mud and taking a hard look at those double chocolate donuts when Grim Reaper walked into the ready room and crooked a finger at him.

Grim Realities

Grim Reaper sat behind his mahogany desk. "So. The one and only, world famous, great big bad-ass Jack Hogan."

Grim let the remark hang there. No need for Jack to reply right away. He could sit there and think about things for a while, take a good look around Grim's woodshed while he came up with something stupid to say.

The décor had changed since the Potato Head days. No Elvis, no picture of a football player with sweaty armpits. Nothing in the room that didn't reek of money, power, and influence.

ENSIGN REAPER ESCORTS PRESIDENT NIXON, one photo on the wall you called a bulkhead said.

MY OLD FAMILY FRIEND SENATOR EX-PRISONER OF WAR said another.

The picture of Grim with his antique Porsche collection said YOU THINK I NEED THIS JOB?

And the picture of him and the female star of the movie *Top Gun* said YEAH, I DID HER. WHO ELSE YOU WANT TO KNOW ABOUT?

The nameplate on his desk from Tiffany's or some place back east read ROBERT J. REAPER III. No rank, no "United States Navy."

Grim leaned back in his oversized leather chair, his manicured fingers folded across a flat stomach. His khaki blouse, special ordered from Abbot Military Tailors in Pensacola, held razor creases. Six rows of custom-made UltraThin ribbons sat above his left pocket, and a set of red gold pilot wings rode above them. His salon haircut showed a sixteenth of an inch of skin over the tops of his ears. The brown Florsheim brogan on the foot he had up on his desk blotter sported a shine he must have paid someone to put on it that morning. He smelled faintly of a brand of cologne they didn't sell at the Navy Exchange, and around his neck hung one of those Catholic crucifixes, with the half naked Jewish kid nailed to it. You were seeing more and more of those around the necks of senior naval officers these days.

Across from the massive, polished desk, wearing a faded pair of shipboard khakis that hadn't felt the touch of an iron since he'd left the *Connie*, big bad Jack Hogan sat in a plastic chair designed to fit one of the original *Mercury* astronauts or a circus midget, and tried not to squirm too much.

"I heard you had more balls than brains," Grim said grimly. "You pretty much confirmed that Friday night."

Jack cleared his throat, trying not to cough up his heart and lungs. "Uh, sir, I'd like to—"

Grim leaned forward and slapped his desk. "Gotcha! Relax, asshole, I'm just pulling your chain."

O-kay!

"That was a great skit. Best welcome aboard I ever had. If I live to be a vice-admiral, I'll never forget The Night Jack Hogan Sent Up Grim Reaper. The wives loved it, and all the ensigns got a taste of how much fun naval aviation can be."

"Glad you liked it, skipper." Jack would be even gladder when his heart rate got back below a hundred.

"Here's why I wanted to talk to you, Jack. I have some good news. A buddy of mine at BUPERS called me over the weekend. You used to work for him. Deuce Macintosh."

Deuce Macintosh was finished with his CAG tour already? He sure got that block checked fast. But that was how things went with high rollers like him. "Yes, sir. Good man, Captain Macintosh."

"He thinks highly of you too, Jack. He's head of aviation assignments now. He called me at the golf course over the weekend to tell me you got picked up for command of an E-2 squadron on your first look."

How about that? "Thanks, Skipper. That is good news."

"It didn't hurt you, of course, that Deuce was head of the selection board, or that Fix Felon is head of BUPERS now. It seems Admiral Felon remembers you from your *Connie* days."

"He does? I only spoke with him once, and that was on the phone."

"That must have been enough to impress him," Grim said. "Listen, Jack, I don't want to pull any punches here ..."

Unless Jack screwed things up, Grim told him, he was going places in this man's Navy. Three early promotions, all his ship driver qualifications, early screen for squadron skipper. And his reputation from The Great Big Backfire Raid. Hell, the way some people talked about him at the Pentagon, Jack Hogan had won the Cold War single-handedly. Assuming he did well as a squadron skipper, he might even become the first E-2 Hawkeye NFO to command his own carrier battle group.

Jack was at a loss for words, so he didn't say any.

"But you're going to have to pay some up-front costs for all that," Grim said, taking his Florsheim off his blotter and planting it, with a faint plop, next to the other one on the floor behind his desk. "We had more west coast guys screen for E-2 command than east coast guys this year. One west coast guy will have to move east, and since you're the only single guy in the group ..."

Goodnight, San Diego, hello, Norfolk, Virginia, home of warm beer and cold women; at least that's how San Diego sailors thought of it.

"But there's a silver lining," Grim said.

The world of west coast naval aviation, as they knew it, was about to explode. Senator Tailhook had arranged to have Naval Air Station Miramar, Fightertown USA, home of Top Gun, shut down. "They'll either bulldoze it or give it to the Marines," Grim said. "Same difference."

Carrier aviation was about to undergo a sea change. "F/A-18 Hornets rule," Grim said. "Especially now that Fix Felon has made himself a Hornet pilot, and has Deuce Macintosh flying on his wing." The A-6 Intruder bomber community would disappear almost immediately, to be replaced by Hornets. Half the Navy's F-14 squadrons would go away too, also to be replaced by Hornet squadrons. In the not-too-distant future, Hornets would also replace the S-3 Viking and the EA-6 radar jammer. "It won't be long," Grim said, "before there's no fixed-wing airplanes left on the carrier but single-seat Super Hornets, except the Hawkeye and the two-seat Super Duper Hornet that replaces what's left of the Tomcats, and those will be the only planes that carry NFOs to conduct the mission."

Jack struggled to keep from making the sound of one jaw dropping. "Holy shit, skipper. That's going to put a lot of NFOs out of work."

"Fuck 'em," Grim said. "The world needs overeducated ditch diggers too. Doesn't affect you any. You'll still have a job."

Man. Wow. Looked like being an E-2 NFO wasn't such a bad thing to be after all. You were still at the bottom of the naval aviation heap, prestige-wise, but the heap was a whole lot smaller.

"How soon do I need to put my affairs in order to move east for my command tour?" Jack said.

"It will be more than a year before a slot opens up for you out there, Jack."

Well, that would be okay.

"But you'll need to leave San Diego sooner than that," Grim added.

Because?

"Your buddy Buzz at BUPERS has arranged for you to take a year of study at the Naval War College in Newport, Rhode Island. That'll get you a master's degree, another feather in your record for when you go up for senior promotions and command."

Re-wow. "Sounds fantastic, Skipper. How soon will I have to report to Newport?"

"In two weeks," Grim said, his mouth twisting into something that on a real person might have looked like a smile.

Betty

Not until Jack sticks a "for sale" sign in front of his house does it occur to him that maybe all that "your own carrier battle group" bullshit was a sugar pill. Maybe Grim Reaper's riding him out of town because he wants to make it abundantly clear to everyone that this is what happens when you stand up to Grim Reaper in public. You don't stick around long enough to do it again.

★　★　★　★　★

And how active a part did Buzz play in Jack's pending bi-coastal sex change? Because of his position at BUPERS, Buzz has gotten himself promoted to commander, and screened to be skipper of an F-14 squadron. But he'll still wind up on the east coast, because that's where all the remaining F-14 jobs will be, once NAS Miramar in San Diego shuts down. Buzz has also arranged things so he and Jackie will be squadron skippers in the same air wing, so they'll be in the same competition pool. If Buzz decides he needs to pull a fast one on a fellow skipper to get a top-ranked fitness report from his CAG, it will be to his advantage to have a fellow skipper he already knows how to pull a fast one on.

What's Buzz's ulterior motive for getting Jackie orders to the Naval War College? Most likely he has a genuine affection of a sort for Jack and wants him to take it easy and have a good time for once in his dip-shit life. He also, most certainly, wants Jack to be good and relaxed when he reports for his squadron command tour, so he'll have his guard good and down when Buzz needs to pull a fast one on him. Buzz also, without question, wants to have a free place to crash in case he wants to bounce up to Newport and get drunk, blown, and laid over the weekend.

Funny guy, that Buzz. At times, you might mistake him for a real human being. Then he'll turn around and do something to remind you that he really isn't. Buzz is a Total Quality Piece of Shit. But he's Jack's piece of shit. And Jack got this notion, in his long ago and far away, that if you expect all your friends to be perfect, you'll be a very lonely person.

Which is what makes Buzz perfectly correct in thinking that Jack is a dip shit, and that it's perfectly all right to take advantage of Jack in any way he can. If you can't fuck your buddies, Buzz reasons, what good are they?

★　★　★　★　★

Thursday morning, the day before he needs to leave for the east coast, Jack signs his house over to some Marine major and his wife. The Marine major's wife tells Jack he ought to do something about the crushed up bumper on his Trans Am.

Thursday afternoon, Jack takes the Trans Am for an oil change, then drives down to the Mission Valley shopping mall for some farewell eyeball liberty. Who knows when he'll have a chance to look at that many California girls in one place again?

★　★　★　★　★

His hair was a little long for a Navy guy, Betty thought, but he probably was one, and didn't give a shit how long his hair was. So he must be an officer. Good looking, he was, in a kicked-in-the-face sort of way. Big. Rugged. The kind of guy they'd cast as a detective on a TV show. He'd walked past the cosmetics counter five times, checking her out from the corner of his baby brown eyes.

Make your move, she thought. You got your Dolly Parton thing going. Hair piled high, face made up, boobs stuck out, come-fuck-me pumps on your feet. Hit it, sister!

"Hey, little boy, you lose your mommy or something?"

Jack grinned, maybe blushed a little, in a kicked-in-the-face sort of way. "She said to wait here for her, she'd be right back." He checked his Jap job. "That was only … ten hours ago. I can't imagine what happened to her."

"You need a new watch," Betty said. "You need a new mommy, too. Listen, I just got off work and I'm starved. Why don't you take me to the beach for drinks and dinner?"

"Why don't I?" Jack said. "Let's go!"

"What happened to your bumper?" Betty said in the mall parking lot.

"It's a custom job. Cost me a lot of money."

"Hmm," Betty said.

They ate at a table by a window with a view of the ocean.

"This may sound like a strange question," Jack said, "but do you happen to like horses?"

"Hell, no. They shit all over the place." Betty wiped a flake of snapper almandine from the corner of her mouth. "Pardon my language, but I hate horses. Is that bad?"

"No, it's good," Jack said. "It's very good."

★ ★ ★ ★ ★

"We'll have to do this again," Betty said, as Jack dropped her off at her apartment complex.

"We'll have to do it somewhere else," Jack said. "I'm leaving for the east coast tomorrow."

"For how long?"

"Forever, best I can tell."

Betty punched his arm. "That's not fair. I just met you."

★ ★ ★ ★ ★

Friday morning, Jack packed the seventh chair and his stereo and his records and his gym bag stuffed with books and semi-clean underwear into the back of the Trans Am. He made sure the napkin with Betty's phone number was still in his wallet, and climbed behind the wheel.

The aging Trans Am complained as he punched it south on I-15, then east on I-8. With Dexter Gordon on the stereo and a highway atlas on his lap, Jack started figuring out how to get from San Diego, California, to Charleston, South Carolina.

His Mom

Mom, still in her quilted bathrobe, poured him a cup of coffee. "I hope this is strong enough for you. I can't take it very strong any more."

Jack tried a sip. "Just right, Mom."

Fifteen years since Dad died, six years after Joe's death, two years after her breast cancer had gone, miraculously, into remission, Mom was getting gray and slow.

"What would you like for breakfast, Jackie? Bacon and eggs sound good?"

"Sounds fine, Mom."

Mom pulled the electric skillet from an obscure corner of her pantry. The rest of the world might be confusing, chaotic, but Mom's kitchen was not. Her kitchen was like a ship, a place for everything and everything in its place.

She plugged in the skillet, let it warm up, and laid strips of bacon in it. "I hope you like this. I don't think you've had it before. It's that good honey bacon from Harris Teeter."

The bacon began to sizzle.

"Smells good, Mom." He'd smelled that good Harris Teeter honey bacon a hundred times in the years he'd visited Mom's townhouse in downtown Charleston. Aside from recalling where everything in her kitchen went, Mom's memory wasn't the greatest any more. Images of her earlier life, especially the part before Dad had died, were still clear to her. Things after that, she didn't keep straight so well. Sometimes she remembered Jack's last visit, sometimes she didn't. Which was sort of understandable. Jack didn't visit that often, especially after Joe died, and not for very long when he did. It was like Joe's ghost was there, waiting to pick a fight with him, telling him he should pay more attention to his aging mother. Which was something Jack found difficult—spending time around Mom, watching her fade.

Mom turned the bacon over. "When do you have to report to your new squadron?"

"It's not a squadron, Mom."

"Are they making you go back to a ship? I thought you didn't have to do that anymore."

"They're sending me to the Naval War College. In Newport."

"They have colleges for war?"

"They do. They have several. I'm going to the best one. I'll get a master's degree there."

"That's good," she said. She ran a washrag across the countertop, wiping something Jack could have sworn wasn't there. "What do they teach at this war college?"

"They call it 'national security studies.'"

Mom looked out the kitchen window, then at Jack. "I don't know what that means."

"It's like political science with bombs thrown in."

"Oh." Mom rinsed the washrag, folded it, and put it on the dish rack next to the sink. "That was a joke, wasn't it?"

"Not a very good one I guess."

"It was a good joke," Mom said. "I just didn't get it at first. I still don't understand what you do." She turned the bacon over again. "How long will you be at this war school?"

"A year."

"And then what?"

"I'll go to Norfolk, Virginia."

"And do what?"

"I'll be the executive officer of an aircraft squadron for fifteen months, then I'll be the commanding officer."

"That's where I got confused, when you were trying to explain on the phone. I remember the part where you were going back to flying eventually. That's good, isn't it? At least you won't have to go back out to sea."

"I do have to go back out to sea, Mom. Eventually."

"I thought it was ships that went to sea, not airplanes."

"We take our airplanes to sea on aircraft carriers, Mom. You know, like in World War II movies."

Mom smirked. "Oh, I know what aircraft carriers are. You don't have to explain that to me. But why do you still have to go to sea after all this time?"

"It's the Navy, Mom. That's what we do, go to sea."

"But after a certain amount of time, don't you get too old for all that?"

"What, Mom, you think we're going to let a bunch of kids run around the world in charge of an aircraft carrier all by themselves?"

Mom turned the bacon again. "I guess not. I guess those aircraft carriers are pretty expensive things to let kids run around with, all by themselves."

Mom took a platter from the cupboard, placed a paper towel on top of it, and put the fried bacon on top of that. "How do you want your eggs?"

"Sunny side up."

"When did you start eating eggs sunny side up? You always had them scrambled when you were little."

"Scrambled's fine, then."

"Or I can make an omelet."

"Scrambled's fine, Mom."

Mom smiled. "I'll make them scrambled then. You want salsa in them?"

"Sure."

"How about some cheese? I have some of that good crumbled feta cheese from Harris Teeter."

"Sounds good."

"Peppers and onions?"

"Okay."

"Good. That's how I like my eggs. Peppers, onion, feta, salsa. That's how Joe liked them too."

A sterling endorsement, Jack thought.

Mom set a cutting board, a bowl, and all the ingredients on the counter. "What are you now?" she said.

"You mean how old am I?"

"No, silly, I can keep track of how old you are. I mean what rank are you now? I can remember Army ranks from when your dad was in Korea—I always said it was so funny, how Dad was a second lieutenant first and a first lieutenant second. I finally figured it out, but I have trouble keeping all those Navy ranks straight."

"I'm a commander, Mom. I got promoted while I was out at sea. I called you on the satellite and told you, remember?"

Mom poured the eggs into the mixing bowl and whipped them with a spatula. "That's right, I remember. And what were you before that?"

"A lieutenant commander."

"And what's a lieutenant commander?"

"Like an Army major."

"And what's a commander?"

"A lieutenant colonel."

"And a colonel is?"

"A Navy captain."

"And what's an Army captain?"

"A Navy lieutenant."

Mom diced the onions and peppers. "And what's a general?"

"An admiral."

"Ah." The egg concoction crackled as mom poured it into the hot bacon grease in the skillet. "So you're a commander now because you're going to command something?"

"Not exactly. Some commanders never command anything. And commanders of really big commands are captains or admirals. It's kind of convoluted."

"Sounds like it," Mom said, whipping the concoction in the electric skillet. "The eggs and bacon are about ready. Do you want anything else?"

"No. Eggs and bacon and coffee are just fine."

"How about some orange juice, and some raisin toast with that good Harris Teeter strawberry jam?"

"Sure, Mom …"

Jack ate a mountain of breakfast while Mom nibbled a slice of raisin toast and talked. She was so glad Jack could come for a visit. The house seemed so empty now, with no one to talk to, or cook for, or plan to do things with, or go out the front door with and walk to King Street, or the slave market, or the battery. Oh, well, she had her health, after that scare with the cancer. It looked like lighting all those candles by the altar every week paid off, she guessed. She wouldn't mind so much, living alone now, except she found herself sitting alone in the kitchen a lot, with no radio or television on, imagining what she'd be doing now if the kids were still young, or if Joe were alive, or Dad … Jack didn't smoke any more, did he? No, that's right, he promised not to, after Dad died, she remembered now. God, that was so awful, Dad getting pneumonia, then the doctor finding out he had a spot on his lung, and he wasted away so quick …

She hadn't meant to get so maudlin, she didn't know what got into her just then, she was sorry, sorry, sorry … She just wasn't herself, but she would be soon.

"It's okay, Mom."

Well, Mom said, it was just silly, wasn't it, to waste time crying over things in the past that you can't do anything about now, especially when she should be enjoying the last of Jack's visit? Time to change the subject, wasn't it?

"What about this girl you met in California?" she said.

"I don't know, Mom. We promised to keep in touch. Maybe she'll come out to Newport to visit me. Hard to say how these long-distance things will work out, especially with someone you just met."

"There must be something between you if you just met and she's talking about coming out to visit. It would be so wonderful if you found someone to settle down with, especially after that awful time you went through with that wife Betty of yours."

"Betty's the girl I just met in California, Mom. My wife's name was Liz."

"Oh, that's right. Two Elizabeths. I can't keep them straight. It must be the onset of Alzheimer's," she said, laughing. Or something more than the onset, Jack thought.

Jack put away enough Harris Teeter breakfast to keep Mom happy and pushed himself away from the table. "I need to hit the road, Mom."

She walked him to the door and hugged him. "I love you."

"I love you too, Mom."

★ ★ ★ ★ ★

Jack barely noticed the scenery as he pushed the Trans Am up I-95. How bad would Mom get? If she was slipping into full-bore dementia, what could he do about it? He made okay money now, as a commander, and could cover her home care expenses if it came down to that. But his sisters would have to provide the hands-on moral support while he ran around the world playing action hero with the United States Navy. And if he didn't stay in the Navy, he couldn't afford to help pay Mom's expenses. Overeducated ditch diggers didn't make a whole lot of money.

This sucked. Again.

But as Mom might have said in her more coherent days, he had to do what he had to do.

War Knowledge

Jack found a carriage house to rent up the hill from downtown Newport. He also found the bar scene in downtown Newport a lot more interesting than the curriculum at the Naval War College. The lectures were pedantic. The seminars were neo-conservative group therapy sessions. The reading load was ludicrous. The faculty knew nobody did all the assigned reading, so why did they assign it?

Jack despised the essay tests. By nature he refused to regurgitate what the professors wanted to hear (the dip shit). He flunked the mid-term essay exam.

The question had been, "Why did the Japanese lose the World War II Battle of Leyte Gulf?" The answer was supposed to be 3,000 words long. Jack wrote:

"Because two of their admirals hated each other worse than they hated us."

And nothing else.

That went over like a lead zeppelin with Jack's professor. The professor, a tall, spectacled surface warfare captain killing time in a skate job until he could retire with thirty years, called Jack in for a mid-term conference.

"I know you've already made commander and screened for squadron command," The Tall Surface Captain said. "But that will all change if you flunk out of here."

"Yes, sir."

"You need to take the curriculum seriously."

"I do, sir."

"This mid-term essay of yours indicates that you don't."

"How so, sir? Was there something inaccurate about it?"

The Tall Surface Captain cleared his throat. "Well, uh, no. In fact, it's entirely correct. The Japanese did lose at Leyte Gulf because two of their admirals hated each other worse than they hated us."

"Then what's wrong with it?" Jack asked.

"It's too short."

"How could I have made it longer, sir?"

"You should have included more scholarship to support your conclusion," The Tall Surface Captain said.

"I'll include more scholarship from now on, sir."

"Take notes in class," The Tall Surface Captain said.

"I'll take notes, sir," Jack said.

"Mention the things in your notes on your essays. Copy them verbatim if you like."

"I'll mention the notes, sir."

"Quote Clausewitz, and Sun Tzu, and Alfred Thayer Mahan at every opportunity."

"Any particular quotes I should use, sir?"

The Tall Surface Captain loosened his red striped tie. You wore a jacket and tie at the War College, not a uniform, so no one would feel intellectually bullied by their military seniors, like The Tall Surface Captain was bullying Jack now.

"No. No particular quotes. Just memorize a handful, and use them every time you write something."

"Don't they need to be pertinent to the subject, sir?"

"All quotes by Clausewitz or Mahan or Sun Tsu are pertinent to any subject we ask you to write about."

"Yes, sir. Thank you, sir. Anything else I should do?"

"If you find yourself short of the assigned word count, do what all successful scholars do. Throw in a lot of adverbs and adjectives. Use jargon and buzz phrases. Find creative ways of saying the same thing over and over again."

"Won't that make things prolix?"

"Prolix makes perfect," The Tall Surface Captain beamed. "You can't be too prolix in this business. If you're prolix enough, you can get published in prestigious journals like the *Naval War College Review* and *Naval Institute Proceedings.*"

"Prolix it is then, sir."

"Good," The Tall Surface Captain said, and dismissed Jack, feeling warm and fuzzy that he'd once again set an errant student of the art of war back on the right path.

✯ ✯ ✯ ✯ ✯

Jack and Betty established a weekly long-distance phone thing, during which they discovered they were both childless, both divorced, both at loose ends.

"Except you have a real career and I don't," Betty said. "Selling make-up at J.C. Penney isn't exactly the fast track to becoming Estée Lauder."

Which meant she wasn't exactly tied down, and pulling up roots and becoming a naval officer's camp follower wouldn't be all that difficult for her.

Jack didn't mention the possibility of flunking out of War College, and what that would mean to his career. No need to yet. They were just talking.

As fall term finals and Christmas break approached, Jack asked Betty if she'd like to fly out to Newport for its Winter Festival.

"I have vacation time saved up at Penney's," she said. "Will I need to bring a coat?"

"I won't tell you what to do, California Girl," Jack said. "But you might want to think about why they call it 'Winter Festival.'"

☆　☆　☆　☆　☆

"Hey, sailor!" Betty said as she walked out of the concourse at Providence Airport. You couldn't miss her in a crowd. She still had that Dolly Parton thing going for her. "What do you think of my ski jacket? Isn't it cute? Do you think it will be warm enough for Winter Festival?"

"If you're part Eskimo," Jack said.

☆　☆　☆　☆　☆

Jack put her luggage in the spare bedroom. They walked down to Thames Street, the cobblestone main drag, and strolled by the Cape Cod storefronts decorated for the season.

"Like a Santa Clause town," Betty said.

The sun went down, and the wind whipped up off the bay. Betty's teeth chattered as they ran to James' on Thames, a bar and restaurant where Jack was, uh, known. James, the thirty-something owner, met them at the door. "Who's the beautiful lady, Jackie?"

"I'm his main squeeze," Betty said. "I just flew in from California, and boy are my arms tired."

"Nice to meet you," James said.

"Same here. Just keep that waitress with the boobs out to here and the legs up to there away from Jack and we'll get along fine."

"Will do," James said, and winked at Jack.

He escorted them to the bar on the third floor, where they had a window view of the bay and the holiday lights rigged on the yachts in the harbor.

"Looks downright festive," Jack said.

"Looks downright cold to me," Betty said, drinking her Bailey's and coffee. "Tomorrow, we need to go buy me a winter coat. This ski jacket's doing me about as much good as a hair net."

✯ ✯ ✯ ✯ ✯

Betty slept in the spare bedroom that night.

✯ ✯ ✯ ✯ ✯

The next morning, they walked back down to Thames Street, ate breakfast, and window-shopped. Jack bought Betty a wool overcoat. That night, they went out dancing till eleven.

Back at the carriage house, Betty changed into flannel pajamas, Jack changed into sweats, and they sat in the living room and watched David Letterman. Dave's first guest was boring, and Betty clicked the remote off. "It's freezing down here. Let's go up to your room and get warm."

✯ ✯ ✯ ✯ ✯

A northern cardinal warbled outside the bedroom window as the sun came up. Betty, crawling back into her flannel pajamas, said, "What's the matter, little bird? All your buddies fly south and leave you behind?"

Jack stirred.

"Rise and shine, Popeye," Betty said.

Jack opened one eye. "Do I know you?"

"Yeah. I'm the drunk bimbo you picked up last night."

"Oh," Jack said. "You." He closed his eye and rolled over, turning his back to her.

She shook his shoulder. "Come on, muscles, let's get up and go somewhere."

"Where do you want to go?"

"Someplace warm."

Jack propped his elbows on his pillow and yawned. "We'll have to do some driving, we want to find someplace warm."

"Why don't we go down to South Carolina and see your mom?"

"That's a long drive."

"I'll do the driving."

"Okay, then," Jack said.

☆　☆　☆　☆　☆

"How long will this take?" Betty said as she negotiated the Trans Am through Manhattan.

"Twenty hours. Give or take."

"Why didn't you tell me that when I volunteered to do all the driving?"

"You didn't ask."

"This will cost you."

"Heh, heh," Jack said.

Car Talk

Betty had grown up near Fresno and married two years out of high school to Greg, a rich, divorced farmer. "Not the college type, I wasn't," she said. "And I've always liked older men. Good thing for you, huh?"

"Ouch," Jack said.

The physical abuse wasn't too bad to start with, Betty said. Just pushing and shoving at first. But Greg's drinking got worse and worse, and then he started screwing around on her. She caught on and confronted him, and he knocked her across the room. Marriage counseling, alcohol rehab, none of that made a lasting difference. He finally threw her down the stairs and broke her right arm. Her uncle helped her file for divorce and set her up in an apartment in San Diego, far enough away from Greg to keep her safe. Being rich, Greg hired a kick-ass lawyer, and Betty wound up with next to nothing in the divorce settlement. "Won't let that happen to me again," she said.

☆　☆　☆　☆　☆

"Liz and I argued like cats and dogs on our first date," Jack said as they crossed the North Carolina border. "It was like that the whole time I knew her. I don't know what made me think things would get better after we were married."

"Why did you marry her?"

Jack looked out the passenger window at the dogwood trees lining the highway. "Sex might have been a factor."

Betty laughed. "Sounds like bullshit to me. A guy like you didn't need to get married to have sex."

Jack crossed his arms and pressed his forehead against the window. "She asked me why I'd married her, at the end, and I didn't have a good answer. I still don't. I was pushing thirty. Guess I thought it was time to get married, before I got too set in my ways."

Betty, who was pushing thirty herself now, said, "Hmm. How set in your ways are you now that you're pushing forty?"

Jack thought. "Guess I'm getting a little tired of my ways, to tell you the truth."

★　★　★　★　★

They ran into a thunderstorm at the South Carolina border and pulled off on the shoulder. While rain pounded the windshield, Jack told Betty about his bad grades in War College, how he might flunk out if he hadn't aced the final essay exam, and what that might mean to the rest of his naval career.

"When do you find out how you did?" Betty said.

"We'll get our grades in the mail after Christmas."

Christmas

Eight o'clock Christmas morning, his back killing him from sitting twenty hours in a bucket seat, Jack rang Mom's doorbell. Mom, in her quilted bathrobe, opened the front door. "You must be Betty."

"Last time I checked the name on my driver's license," Betty said. "Nice to meet you, Sue."

"Come in, come in," Mom said, and hugged Betty.

Mom took them to the back of the house, and sat them at the kitchen table. "You two must be starved, after your long drive. How about some breakfast? Eggs and bacon like last time, Jackie?"

Mom took the electric skillet from its special place. Betty got up to help. "No, you sit and relax," Mom said.

"I like to help in the kitchen," Betty said. "I always helped my mom when I was a kid."

"Here's how I beat the eggs," Mom said.

"Here's how my mom cuts the peppers," Betty said.

"Here's how I chop the onions," Mom said.

"Oh, I like the way you do it," Betty said.

Mom and Betty each had a spoonful of scrambled eggs and nibbled on a piece of raisin toast, and watched Jack put away enough good Harris Teeter breakfast to keep a Somali family going for a month.

Beat from the drive, Jack and Betty took a nap in the guest room until noon. Then they got up and dressed, and took mom for a walk downtown to see the Christmas decorations. They ran across a beauty salon on King Street, open on Christmas to cash in on the tourist trade. "Come on, Sue," Betty said. "Let's get you dolled up. Jack, go find a bar, we'll meet you there in a couple hours."

"Roger that," Jack said. "You'll find me in the bar at the Omni Hotel."

Jack was working on his third gin martini when Mom and Betty arrived, acting like they might have had a tipple or two with the ladies at the beauty parlor. The gray was gone from Mom's hair. Betty must have supervised the makeup. Jack hadn't seen Mom wearing makeup, or smiling like she was smiling now, in years.

"What do you think?" Betty said. "Fly her out to Vegas and let

Frank Sinatra get an old blue eyeful of her?"

Mom howled at that one.

They ate a late lunch at the bar, and split a bottle of champagne to celebrate Mom's new look.

Mom tripped and almost fell on the walk home. "Damn, I just have no tolerance for the booze anymore."

Betty took her arm. "We'll get you home, Mom. But you'll have to promise, no more whoring around after we leave."

Mom laughed so hard she almost fell down again, and Betty and Jack both had to take her by an arm to get her back to the house. They hauled Mom up the stairs and put her to bed. "This is the best Christmas ever," she said as they tucked her in.

Jack and Betty walked downtown again, had dinner, and night-clubbed around until ten. Mom was still zonked out in the master bedroom when they got back.

In the guest room bed, Betty said, "I love your Mom."

"Looks like you charmed the pants off her too."

"Speaking of which," Betty said, "you could charm the pants off me if you play your cards right." She ran a hand down his stomach. "Nice abs."

"Don't dwell on them," Jack said. "Keep going."

"Ooh! What's this big thing, Mister?"

"Nothing to be afraid of, little girl. Just old Santa, getting ready to slip up the chimney."

She kissed him. "You're dirty."

"Ho, ho, ho," Jack said.

Outside the window, a cardinal—up late celebrating the holiday, apparently—came to rest on the Myrtle Oak in Mom's small garden, and sang for them.

☆ ☆ ☆ ☆ ☆

Back in Newport, they sat around the living room of the carriage house while Jack sorted through his mail.

Bill. Bill. Ad. Bill. Something from the United States Naval War College.

Jack's fall semester grades. He'd put enough meaningless scholarship into his final essay to get an A on it, which brought his overall grade to a B.

"I didn't flunk out," he said. "Looks like I still have a career."

"Good thing," Betty said, and kissed him. "Somebody has to bring home the Harris Teeter Bacon."

ACT IV
Command and Control

"Catch-69"

Two years later, at 1300 (1 p.m., to you civilian types) on a Wednesday afternoon, Commander Jack Hogan, Master of Arts in National Security Studies and commanding officer of the Carrier Airborne Early Warning Squadron 241 Bear Slayers, stepped out from the main entrance hatch of the oldest E-2 Hawkeye in the United States Navy inventory and onto the flight line. The three next oldest E-2 Hawkeyes in the Navy inventory were parked next to it, and also belonged to Jack's squadron.

The flight line Jack stepped onto was the oldest flight line in the Navy inventory, made of concrete reinforced with steel wire, first poured about the time Dwight David Eisenhower was an army major and last refurbished when he was president of the United States. Twenty feet to Jack's north was the sea wall, and twenty yards to his south was Hangar SP-1, built at the same time the flight line was poured, and home of the Atlantic Fleet's E-2 Hawkeyes.

Jack had to step around several chunks of loose concrete that were too big to step over as he headed toward the hangar. He also had to circle around the air conditioning unit that had fallen from a window on the second deck, and the aluminum picnic table the air conditioning unit had crushed when it had fallen on it.

He also had to hop over a rivulet that had been created by a leak in SP-1's water main. The water main should have been fixed by now. The C.O. of Naval Air Station Norfolk had promised it would be fixed in a week when Jack had complained about it ten months ago.

The smell of raw sewage stung him as he opened the double

swinging door in the rear of the hangar. The single toilet meant to serve all 130 of the squadron's officers and enlisted men was still backed up, even though the C.O. of NAS Norfolk claimed he had copies of the paperwork to prove it had been fixed three months ago.

The squadron's enlisted technicians could have fixed everything wrong with Hangar SP-1 by now. But base regulations prohibited squadrons—"tenant commands"—from doing maintenance on facilities that belonged to the C.O. of NAS Norfolk.

But Skipper Hogan wasn't letting any of that bother him as he climbed over the missing steps on the ladder that led to the second deck of SP-1. He'd just come back from controlling an air combat maneuver exercise between two Air Force F-16 fighter squadrons that had gone well. The notional good guys had won, the notional bad guys had played dead, and everybody had lived to play war another day.

Plus ...

Mrs. Hogan was waiting at home, in their three-story house on Chesapeake Beach, preparing a special first anniversary dinner.

So, all things considered, life didn't suck so bad.

Until ...

Jack got to the second deck.

Big Steve Romanowski, the squadron's command master chief, leaned against the rail of the balcony that overlooked the hangar bay, and the pieces of the ceiling you called an overhead that had broken off and fallen fifty feet to the floor you called a deck, where they had to stay until the C.O. of NAS Norfolk got off his ass and told someone to come around pick them up and take them away. "How's your day going?" Big Steve said.

"Guess I've had worse."

Big Steve gave him a Cheshire grin. "Guess again." He nodded down the passageway at a young Puerto Rican sailor in pressed dungarees standing at parade rest in front of Jack's office door.

"Airman Manriquez? What about him?"

"Let's put it this way. I didn't ask, but he told."

"Oh, not him." Jack sighed, and loosened the chest strap of his parachute harness. "Get him out of sight. Tell him to have a seat in my office till we can sort this shit out. I'll clear out the ready room, you and I will talk in there."

Jack stuck his head in the ready room. "Everybody go home."

"HOORAY!" the officers cried. That Skipper Hogan, he could be a demanding bastard, but every so often, he'd do something to make you think he was a real human being, like order you to go home in the middle of the day in the middle of the week.

★ ★ ★ ★ ★

Jack paced in front of the ready room. "So Manny says this Sailor X is leaving notes on his car windshield and under his door in the barracks saying he's got pictures of Manny playing around with other boys, and he's going to show the pictures to you or me."

Steve sat at the duty desk. "That's about the size of it. You or me, we can burn the pictures, pretend like we never saw them. But if this Sailor X has pictures, he has copies, and they'll turn up somewhere else eventually."

Jack nodded and looked out the window at the flight line, and the airplanes and the bay. If those pictures got into the hands of someone like the C.O. of NAS Norfolk, say, Manny could be out of the Navy with a bad discharge, the rest of his life screwed up, and there wouldn't be anything Jack or Steve could do about it.

"You're sure you're in on this, Steve? We try to sneak this kid out of the Navy with an honorable discharge, and anybody catches on to what we've done, we might pay hell for it."

"I'm in," Steve said. "I might feel different if Manny was a dirtball. But he's a great kid. Always upbeat, even when he's doing shitty jobs like cleaning the backed up head. His chief's put him up for Sailor of the Month three times. The other kids in the squadron like him. Hell, he's everything you want in a young sailor."

Jack grimaced. "Except for one thing."

"Yeah," Steve said. "I'm not even so sure about that. According to his service record, Manny grew up in a Catholic orphanage. I did a little digging, turns out this orphanage got shut down because of some sex abuse scandal."

"So the kid probably took his first pipe from Father O'Toole?" Jack said.

"Something like that," Steve said. "I don't know what I really think, but I never cared for this 'don't ask, don't tell' bullshit. You can join if you're gay, but you can't say you're gay, and if you do anything gay you better not get caught or you'll be screwed forever for being gay even though we said it was okay to be gay. Catch-69. The whole policy sucks from both ends."

Jack walked to the china board in front of the ready room and erased his name from the next day's flight schedule. "All right. I'll call my pal Buzz in the morning and see if I can't pull a Fix Felony for Manny. In the meantime, with this Sailor X stalking him, I don't want to take Manny out to sea on the *Nixon* next week for BFD-EX. Sailor X might be one of our guys."

"I agree, Skipper. We wouldn't want Manny to show up missing for a man overboard muster. I talked to my buddy Master Chief Pikus over at base operations. He says Manny can work for him as long as we need to hide him. Says he can always use a duty driver who isn't pregnant."

★　★　★　★　★

Jack told Betty about the Manriquez incident as soon as he got home, and asked if she thought he was doing the right thing.

"Of course you are. That's why I love you so much. Anybody else would have let that little boy swing in the wind."

"Swing in the wind?" Jack said. "Where did you pick up salty talk like that, little girl?"

"I observed it. I'm a skipper's wife now. I'm picking up on all this Navy talk. It's fun, like a different language, a different world."

"It might be a different world for both of us if this blows up in my face, honey. I can protect Steve, tell the Navy he didn't know anything about it, or that I ordered him to go along with it. But they might nail me to a cross out by the sea wall."

"What could happen?"

"What couldn't? I could get relieved of command. They might spin it like I'm some sort of gay rights sympathizer, or say I'm gay myself."

"I've got a solution for that one," Betty said. She pulled the zipper of his flight suit down to his waist. "Let's break out the video camera and manufacture some evidence to the contrary."

Jack smiled. "Let's just rehearse for now."

JAG

Thursday morning, Jack dialed Buzz's office number down at NAS Oceana, the fighter base in Virginia Beach, and tried to get comfortable in his desk chair. Those late night rehearsals were murder on your back.

"Commander Rucci."

"Is this the Commander Rucci I met at the Oceana Officers' Club last week? Skipper of the VF-22 Fighting Pussies? This is Gwen. Remember me? You said I was a good sport?"

Buzz chuckled. "If you're such a good fucking sport, why are you calling me?"

"I need a favor," Jack said. "I'm trying to pull a Fix Felony."

"You? I've never known you to pull a Fix Felony."

"It's not for me. It's for one of my sailors."

Buzz slapped his forehead. "When are you going to learn, Jack? You don't pull Fix Felonies for sailors. You only pull Fix Felonies for yourself."

"Then let's say it's for me. Will you help?"

"Maybe. What's it about?"

"You still talk to Flip Wilson these days?" Jack said.

"From time to time."

"Then don't ask. I can't tell you."

"Oh," Buzz said. "You sure you want to stick your neck out for a butt bandit, Jack?"

"Just give me a name and a number. One of your BUPERS connections. I'll take it from there."

"Oh, all right," Buzz said. "I'm not supposed to give this kind of information out to mere mortals, but since it's you …"

Jack wrote down the phone number. "What's she like, this JAG officer?"

"Judy Davis? She's, uh, different."

"How different is she?"

"Highly different. Extremely different. Very, very, very different. So, come to think of it, the two of you should get along famously."

★　★　★　★　★

"Lieutenant Davis, JAG Fag Hag, how the hell can I help you?"

Lieutenant Davis the what? "Maybe I dialed the wrong number," Jack said. "Did you say you were the—?"

"That's right, I'm the JAG Fag Hag. I kick little dykes and fairies out of the Navy for a living, and it sucks, and I don't care who knows it or doesn't. Who the hell are you?"

"Commander Jack Hogan, skipper of an E-2 squadron in Norfolk."

"Sorry, Skipper," Judy Davis said. "I was expecting a call from the admiral who's the head of the Judge Advocate General Corps, and

I thought you were him. I put on that act every time I talk to the bastard. I'm trying to get fired from this job."

"That's a good act," Jack said. "You do any other tricks?"

"I used to do a fair impersonation of a real human being."

"Maybe I can help you brush up on it," Jack said, and gave her a rundown on the Manriquez situation.

"Let me get this straight," Judy said. "You have a kid who's about to get outed, and you want to sneak him out of the Navy with a good discharge before he gets kicked out with a bad one?"

"That's about the size of it."

"Hm," Judy said. "You're different."

"So I've been told. But I'm not that different, if that's what you're thinking."

"That wasn't what I was thinking, Skipper. What I was thinking was that you're different enough to confess to a Navy JAG officer that you're aiding and abetting a suspected homosexual."

"I hadn't thought of it that way," Jack said.

"Don't worry about it," Judy said, "because I'm going to help you. That makes us accomplices."

"Shame on us," Jack said.

"This may take some doing though," Judy said. "Getting a homosexual sailor an honorable discharge under 'don't ask, don't tell' is complicated. You can get an honorable discharge if you say you're gay, but not if you do anything gay. If you say you're gay without proof you've done anything gay, you might be lying just to get out of the Navy. But if you prove you're gay, that means you've done something gay, and you can't get out with an honorable discharge. The policy sucks from both ends. Catch-69."

"That's some catch," Jack said, "that Catch-69."

"It's the best catch there is," Judy said. "Tell you what, sir, have your admin chief work up the kid's discharge papers and fax them to me. I'll push his discharge through as quickly as I can, but I might have to sleep with a bull dyke admiral to grease the skids, if you catch my drift."

"I appreciate your help," Jack said, wondering if this Judy Davis person was joking about having to sleep with a bull dyke admiral, and deciding she probably wasn't. But either way, he didn't really need to know.

So he didn't ask.

BFD-EX

Friday morning, Buzz and Jack went to the Big Force Demonstration Exercise planning conference at Second Fleet Headquarters in Norfolk. Buzz had warned their CAG, "Average" Joe Bloe, not to let Jack anywhere near the BFD-EX conference.

"He'll pull a Beadwindow," Buzz told Average Joe, "stand up and say what everybody else is thinking but is afraid to say, or maybe even blurt out the unvarnished truth. I'm telling you, CAG, I know this guy. You can't trust him."

But Average Joe wanted Jack to represent the air wing at the conference. Jack's reputation as a tactician had grown since The Great Big Backfire Raid, and he was a Naval War College graduate. "He knows more about joint force operations than you and me combined," Average Joe told Buzz. "You're so concerned, you go along and make sure he doesn't blurt out any of that truth bullshit."

☆   ☆   ☆   ☆   ☆

Hubbub, hubbub, hubbub …

"If I can have everyone's attention please," said Captain Roy George, Fix Felon's chief of staff. "Does anyone have any pressing questions before we begin the official planning conference business?"

Buzz wilted as Jack stood. "Yes, Chief of Staff. How did the BFD get to be such a big fucking deal?"

Boy George's jowls reddened. "Commander Hogan, will you please—"

"Seriously, sir, we don't do anything in BFD-EX. It's just a waste of tax dollars. Why do we need to waste more tax dollars having a planning conference for it?"

BFD-EX was the long-standing "graduation exercise" that carrier battle groups had to complete before they went on overseas deployment. They called it the Big Fleet Demonstration Exercise until Vice Admiral Fix Felon took over Second Fleet and took charge of BFD-EX, and changed the name to the Big Force Demonstration Exercise. The term "force" announced the BFD-EX was no longer merely a naval exercise, but a "joint force battle experiment," which made it an even bigger fucking deal than it was before.

Except not that much had changed. The Navy was still the only service that contributed any actual forces to BFD-EX. The other services merely provided battle staffs that controlled "notional" forces, under the overall notional command and control of Fix Felon, who was becoming a rather big fucking deal himself.

"Sit down, Commander Hogan," said Boy George, who was running the conference. Fix Felon wasn't there. He was at a ski lodge in Aspen palling around with Senator Ex-Prisoner of War, The Other Senator From Massachusetts, Hugh Hefner, and other military industrial complex luminaries.

"By the end of today's conference," Boy George told the assemblage, "I need all of the joint battle staffs to turn in plans on how they plan to deploy their notional forces, and how they plan to supply them, and arm them and maneuver them."

Jack stood again. "Shouldn't they know what the notional operational objectives are, or what the notional enemy forces are, or where the notional enemy forces are located before they come up with all that notional information, Chief of Staff?"

Boy George fumed. "We won't have a notion about any of that

information until our notional national intelligence analyzes it, or until our notional national command authority tells us what our notional forces will be, or what our notional national objectives will be. Is that clear?"

"Perfectly, sir," Jack said and sat back down.

★　★　★　★

Three weeks of doing nothing into BFD-EX, Jack and Big Steve were sitting in the E-2 squadron ready room on the USS *Richard M. Nixon* when the C-2 Greyhound COD pilots walked in with that day's *Norfolk Virginian-Pilot*. The frontpage headline read:

SECOND FLEET CHIEF OF STAFF ARRESTED IN CONNECTION
WITH HOMOSEXUAL PROSTITUTION RING.

According to the article, the Naval Criminal Investigative Service had arrested Boy George for running a gay male escort service that involved enlisted Marines stationed on amphibious ships in the Norfolk area.

"There's a surprise," Big Steve said.

Jack did a double take. "You're surprised Boy George was running a floating fag whorehouse?"

"I'm surprised NCIS caught him," Steve said. "Those guys couldn't find their ass with a map and a flashlight."

Since Tailhook, the Naval Investigative Service had changed its name to the Naval Criminal Investigative Service. That insured that anyone who put them on a case realized that they would commit more crimes in the course of their investigation than the criminals they were investigating had.

The port-side door to the ready room sprang open and Buzz Rucci skidded in. "Have you heard?"

"Just read about it in the paper," Jack said.

"I don't mean about Boy George. I just came from Average Joe's office. Fix Felon has ordered us to stay out to sea and do nothing for another two weeks."

"Why?" Steve said.

"Because," Buzz said, "Fix Felon's afraid the press will be waiting for us at the pier, which they will be, and afraid they'll ask all of us if we ever suspected Boy George was running a floating fag whorehouse, which they will ask, and afraid we'll say we suspected it all along, which we will say."

Buzz went to the duty desk and called ship-to-shore over the satellite to Flip Wilson, who was drilling with the reserves in D.C., to find out what Flip had heard about the situation from his semi-reliable sources.

Average Joe blew into the ready room from the starboard door. Average Joe, as his call sign implied, was of average height and build, had average features, and average intelligence. Which made him the smartest fighter pilot in the Atlantic Fleet, which was why he was CAG. "Have you heard?" he said.

"About us staying another two weeks?" Jack said.

"No. About The Big Knee Jerk Congressional Hearing. Fix Felon and Senator Ex-Prisoner and the rest of them threw their drinks in a travel cup and jumped on a plane with MUCKETY MUCKS HEADED FOR D.C. smeared all over it. Admiral Lawton is scheduled to meet them in the Capitol building—" average Joe checked his Jap job— "right about now."

"I got Flip on the satellite phone," Buzz said from the ready room desk. "He's in the Capitol, watching the whole show."

☆　☆　☆　☆　☆

The chambers are packed with camera crews from every major news network, including The Playboy Channel and Comedy Central.

Senator Ex-Movie Star's Ex-Husband bangs a gavel. "This committee will come to order. I ask all members to keep the discussion at a civil level. I'll start off the questioning. Admiral Lawton, when exactly did you stop beating your wife?"

Admiral Charles Lawton, Chief of Naval Operations, checks his Jap job. "Exactly ten minutes ago, Senator."

"That answers my question, Admiral. I turn the floor over to Senator Tailhook."

"Thank you, Senator Ex-Husband," Senator Tailhook says. "Admiral Lawton, how many women were involved in this gay male prostitution ring?"

"No females were involved in this gay male prostitution ring that we know of at this time," Admiral Lawton says. "If, at a later time, the Naval Criminal Investigation Service criminally discovers that females were involved with this gay male prostitution ring, we'll discontinue referring to it as a 'gay male prostitution ring' and commence referring to it by whatever cockamamie, politically correct, mumbo jumbo catch phrase my propaganda assistant, the Chief of Naval Information, can come up with."

The Other Senator From Massachusetts runs a long hand over his long face and asks, "Admiral Lawton, who among us doesn't cherish the sanctity of heterosexual marriage? Do you intend to allow these gay male prostitutes to be wed to each other in holy matrimony by Catholic Navy Chaplains?"

"Senator," Admiral Lawton says, "I intend to have the Navy JAG Corps carefully study every aspect of the legality of the Navy Chaplain Corps performing such ceremonies, and the legality of the Navy Supply Corps catering the receptions, and the legality of the Navy Dental Corps cleaning said homosexuals' teeth so they look nice in their wedding pictures, and the legality of the Navy Medical Corps removing whatever inanimate objects said homosexuals get stuck up their butts on their honeymoons—"

"NOT SO FAST, ADMIRAL," Senator Ex-Prisoner of War says. The chamber hushes in awe and reverence, and cameramen from all the networks wake up as Senator Ex-Prisoner leans into his microphone.

"Before we go into the details of who decides what's legal to bless whatever goes up whoever's butt," Senator Ex-Prisoner says, "let's review some basic military discipline issues. Now, what's up with your shirt shit, Admiral? Did your aide wake up on the wrong side of the mirror this morning?"

Admiral Lawton glances down at the front of his dress white blouse. Shit. His shirt shit is all ass-backwards. His ribbons and submariner dolphins are over his right pocket, and his nametag, which reads ADMIRAL BIG SHIT, is over his left. Goddamn aide of his. He'll kill the little bastard.

Senator Ex-Prisoner laughs. "I haven't seen a shittier shirt shit job since I was a plebe at the Naval Academy."

Everybody, including the cameramen, laugh along.

Senator Ex-Husband bangs his gavel. "I think that's all the heavy duty investigating this investigation panel is going to get investigated today. Let's adjourn until tomorrow."

Flip Wilson, talking to Buzz on a cell phone, follows Admiral Lawton down the hill to the Navy compound. As Admiral Lawton walks into the official Chief of Naval Operations residence, Mrs. Lawton starts carping at him about the standard set of things she usually carps at him about.

Flip watches through the window as Admiral Lawton walks to the master bathroom, locks the door, pulls a quart of Drano from under the sink, drinks it, sits on the toilet, and shits himself to death.

☆　☆　☆　☆

The news of The Big Shit's Big Shit took everyone's mind off Boy George and his Band of Brothers for a while. Jack and Buzz and

Big Steve and Average Joe and the rest of them on the *Nixon* got to come home because Fix Felon wasn't in command of Second Fleet anymore. In an unprecedented display of power and influence, Fix Felon leapt over the heads of countless admirals senior to him and became the new Chief of Naval Operations. He gave Mrs. Lawton one day to vacate the Big Shit quarters in the Navy compound, and kicked her unpleasant ass out of there twenty-four hours and two minutes later.

★ ★ ★ ★ ★

The entire known universe speculated on what was beneath the surface of The Big Shit's Big Shit. Sure, getting laughed at in Congress on national television was embarrassing, but it was nothing to shit yourself to death about. Admiral Lawton must have had a mighty big skeleton about to walk out of his closet. He was a big "integrity talker," always going on about "moral sailors" and "core values," so he must have been dipping his hand into the supply corps till, or dipping his wick into that enlisted female driver of his.

Or, as Jack theorized, Admiral Lawton had some connection with Boy George's Marine Corps Culture Club. Once Flip Wilson heard Jack's theory, it spread straight to the Pentagon, and Fix Felon put the kibosh on it right away. He released an All Navy message under his signature that contained three little words: IT NEVER HAPPENED.

So everyone pretended it never happened, even though they knew good and well that it had. Admiral Lawton would have approved, Jack thought. Burying the truth was in keeping with Lawton's cherished Navy Core Values: 1) Deny, 2) Deny, 3) Deny.

★ ★ ★ ★ ★

A week after the *Nixon* came home from BFD-EX, the official message came in stating that Airman Theodore M. Manriquez had been separated from the naval service with an honorable discharge.

Jack fired off an e-mail to Judy Davis thanking her for her help. She sent one back that read:

"It wasn't easy, once the Boy George story came out. Next time, you get to sleep with the bull dyke admiral."

Early Warning

Four weeks later, the *Nixon* left for overseas deployment and spent July and August showing the flag in the Mediterranean. What little flying occurred consisted of routine training operations, which from Jack's perspective was a good thing. The four oldest E-2 Hawkeyes in the Navy were also the four most broke-dick E-2 Hawkeyes in the Navy. They flew, but that was about all they could do. None of the detection and identification radars worked. And early warning aircraft that can't detect or identify bad guys or warn anybody about them aren't worth a bowl of warm chocolate ice cream.

"Just a glitch in the supply system," the CAG maintenance officer told Jack. "Things will be back on track by the time we get to the Gulf."

"They better be, CAGMO," Jack said. "We can't fly Southern Watch with these planes the way they are now."

☆ ☆ ☆ ☆ ☆

Betty had an aunt in Spain. Jack had been so busy as the squadron's XO when they got married they hadn't had time for a proper honeymoon. Jack had told her she could spend as much time in Spain as she liked while the *Nixon* was in the MED as long as she kept track of the family finances and made sure the bills got paid. She met Jack when the ship pulled into Malaga.

Their third morning there, Jack slept in while Betty went out shopping. He got up and dressed around noon and went out on foot to look for her. Where did she say to meet him for lunch? The "El" something. Or was it the "Los" something?

Ten "El" or "Los" somethings later, he found her in a corner booth, sipping a frozen red drink and surrounded by a heap of shopping bags.

He sat across from her. "You leave anything for the rest of the tourists to buy?"

"I got something for you," she said, and took a small box from one of the bags. It was a Swiss chronograph, an Omega, like the one the astronauts wore.

"How much was this?" he said.

"I got a great deal, don't worry about it. You have to spend money to save money, right? Besides, I can't have my handsome skipper husband running around with a cheap piece of Jap crap on his wrist." She unbuckled his old watch and put it in her purse. "Try this on."

The Omega's stainless steel bracelet fit perfectly.

"It's a very prestigious watch," Betty said. "The salesgirl said it's the exact same watch the King of Spain wears."

"The exact same watch, huh? What did you have to do to get it off his wrist?"

"Buy me lunch and take me back to the hotel and I'll show you."

★ ★ ★ ★ ★

Three in the morning, Jack propped himself on his pillow and admired his watch.

"Who bought you the great watch, Commander?" Betty said.

"Some bimbo I met this afternoon at the 'El' something."

"Did you take her back to your hotel room and screw her eyes out?"

"Yes, I did."

"Want to have another go at her before you have to report back to the ship?"

"Yes, I do."

"You sure your back will take it?"

"No, but let's find out."

★ ★ ★ ★ ★

They had a late lunch at an open-air café by the train station, and drank beer in the afternoon sun. At 4:30, they crossed the street. Betty got on board and Jack waved to her as her train pulled away and she headed back to her aunt's. He shouldered his bag and hiked toward fleet landing, which he guessed was two miles away. It turned out to be six miles away.

Jack found another café by the pier and ate dinner, then drank beer until the sun set. He checked the time on his Omega, rubbed his lower back, and left a pile of funny colored money on the table. He walked down the pier and up the brow and through the watertight hatch off the hangar bay and up the stairways you called ladders to his stateroom. He stripped off his civvies and crawled between the sheets.

When he woke up, the *Nixon* was underway, headed for the Suez Canal.

The Airplanes are Broken, Part II

The *Nixon* was making a late-night transit of the Red Sea. Jack sat on the sofa bed of his skipper's stateroom in Sleepy Hollow, forward on the second deck, under the Dirty Shirt, listening to Count Basie on headphones and thinking about Southern Watch, wondering if the spare parts for his radars would materialize in time.

His Omega said one in the morning. He was about to pull the sofa down and turn it into a rack when his door creaked open and Buzz crept in.

"You got problems," Buzz said.

"What kind?"

"The kind that will fuck your career eight ways from Sunday."

"Tell me about it."

Buzz sat in Jack's desk chair. "Average Joe took me along to the admiral's brief this afternoon. CAGMO and the ship's supply officer and the ship's maintenance officer told the admiral and Average Joe that you have four full-mission-capable airplanes."

"Holy shit," Jack said. "I don't have any full-mission capable airplanes."

"It gets worse, Jackie. I schmoozed some of the guys on the staff after the brief broke up, and it turns out they've been telling Average Joe and the admiral you have four full-up airplanes ever since we left Norfolk."

"CAGMO knows better than that," Jack said. "I've been bitching at him all cruise to get my radar boxes fixed."

Buzz snorted. "CAGMO. That bald, pasty-faced bastard. I've known him a long time. He's a bigger piece of shit than I am. Remember? He was my squadron maintenance officer back on our Southern Watch cruise on the *King*. He's the one who let us drill holes in the no-fly zone with broke-dick missiles."

"You were flying around with broke-dick missiles?"

"You didn't know that?"

"No."

"Oh," Buzz said. "I shouldn't have told you, then."

"Did you know about it?"

"Not at the time. Flip Wilson told me about it when I got my secret decoder ring at BUPERS."

"Did your skipper know at the time?"

"He must have," Buzz said. "He was a test pilot and had a master's degree in aerospace engineering. He was too smart about that kind of stuff not to know it."

"How did they get away with it?"

Buzz rolled his eyes. "The same way everybody gets away with everything, Jack. They pencil whipped it. They signed an official paper that said the missiles were fixed, so even thought they weren't fixed, they were—officially."

"A Fix Felony."

"Bada-bing," Buzz said.

Jack stood and leaned against the wall you called a bulkhead. "What happened to all those black boxes I turned into ship's maintenance to get fixed or replaced?"

"I did a little snooping around for you this afternoon. I'll tell you where your boxes are. They're sitting in a storeroom where ship's maintenance put them when you turned them in, and they haven't been touched since."

"Why not?"

"Because the kids who are supposed to fix them don't know how to fix them because they never got trained to fix them."

Jack went to his metal sink and rinsed his face. "There has to be a paper trail. We signed documents when we turned those broke-dick boxes into ship's maintenance."

"Of course you did. And they signed documents that say the broke-dick boxes are fixed."

Jack sat back on his sofa bed. "Why go through all that trouble to gin up a hoax? If they can't fix the broke-dick boxes, why not just have the supply officer ship them back to the States for replacements?"

"When are you going to learn, Jack? If they shipped the boxes back to the States, they'd be admitting they don't know how to fix them. Some rear-echelon mother fucker would start asking questions and find out the ship's technicians never got the training they were supposed to have."

"Ah," Jack said, and rubbed his temples. "And if that gets out, the ship's maintenance officer is in big trouble, and the ship's maintenance officer is—"

"Commander Grandma, a Tailhook poster girl."

Commander Grandma, the matronly Joni Johnson, was part of the Total Quality post-Tailhook initiative to place senior female officers in seagoing positions of responsibility. An ex-enlisted person, Commander Grandma had never been on a ship before. She'd spent twenty-five years pushing paperwork in depot level maintenance facilities, working for high-ranking civil servants.

"And Commander Grandma," Buzz said, "wouldn't know a wrench from a tampon."

"How could she?" Jack said. Like hundreds of other Tailhook poster girls in the Navy, Commander Grandma had been thrust into a job she didn't have the training or experience to handle. "But if somebody blows the whistle and makes her look bad, it will look like somebody wanted her to look bad, and everybody will look bad."

"All the way up the chain of command," Buzz said. "Right up to our beloved battle group commander."

Jack looked at the ceiling you called an overhead. "And thus will end the vainglorious career of one Rear Admiral Winifred 'Bull' Palsy." Bull had been at Tailhook as well, and like so many senior officers, his career was still hanging from the balcony. "This Commander Grandma business would be just what Fix Felon needs to chop Bull off at the fingers."

"And you know Bull Pup will take you down with him if you make waves about this," Buzz said. "He still blames you for The Almost Great Big Train Wreck back on our NORPAC cruise. He almost didn't make admiral over that, and of course he's been on Fix Felon's shit list ever since."

"Oh, well," Jack said, and rubbed his eyes. "Thanks for letting me know about all this. Guess I should have seen it coming myself."

"You don't have to fall on your sword over it," Buzz said. "You've pulled enough Beadwindows, Jack. You blow the whistle on this one and you'll never wash the stink off. Nobody ever said Jack Hogan was in charge of carrying the weight of the whole world on his shoulders."

Jack shrugged. "So I tell my guys to fake it? Fly the no-fly zone with no radars? Let you and the rest of the air wing think we can see the bad guys coming when we can't?"

"Nothing's going to happen, Jack. Bad Guy hasn't flown in the zone for years. The worst-case scenario is we'll bomb some milk truck that's supposed to be a SAM site that's really just a milk truck, just like everybody else who flies in this stupid theater of operations."

"What if something does happen, Buzz? What if one of the guys in your squadron gets shot down because he trusted us—*me*—to cover his six when we knew good and well we couldn't?"

Buzz's turn to shrug. "Breaks of naval air? I don't know. Guess we'll bomb that bridge when we come to it."

"We won't have to," Jack said.

Buzz got up from the desk chair and went to the door.

"Thanks for stopping by, Buzz."

"I was never here," Buzz said.

Jack blinked, and Buzz disappeared.

✯ ✯ ✯ ✯ ✯

Buzz disappeared himself up the stairway you called a ladder to the 03 level and aft to his stateroom, which was just down the hall you called a passageway from Average Joe's cabin.

He'd done the right thing, Buzz figured, as he stripped off his flight suit and crawled into his rack. He'd let Jack in on yet another secret he wasn't supposed to know about. He'd taken his sweet time telling Jack, of course. He'd known about the shenanigans with Jack's radar parts for months. But he'd told Flip Wilson about it, knowing full well Flip Wilson would spread it around the entire known universe. It wasn't his fault that straight-ahead guys like Jack never listened to anything assholes like Flip Wilson had to say.

He hadn't told Jack about Grim Reaper's part in all this either.

Rear Admiral Reaper was the senior E-2 guy in the Navy now and had pulled all the strings that gave Jack the oldest, most broke-dick E-2 Hawkeyes in the Navy, and made sure Commander Grandma got put in charge of maintenance on the *Nixon*, and made sure Commander Grandma's enlisted technicians didn't get the schools they needed to learn how to fix Jack's radars. But even though Buzz knew that to be true, he couldn't prove it in a court martial. So why tell any of that to Jack? That would be like spreading rumors, or repeating anything you heard from Flip Wilson.

Besides, Buzz argued to himself, Jack had pissed Grim Reaper off all by himself with that dumb-ass skit he put on at the Half-Ass Hotel in Mission Valley. Buzz wasn't even in San Diego at the time.

It wasn't his fault Jack was such a dip shit.

Buzz rolled over. His door was locked. His 1MC speaker was disconnected. His phone was off the hook. Life was good.

Buzz closed his eyes and slept the sleep of the innocent.

☆　☆　☆　☆　☆

Down in Sleepy Hollow, Jack tapped out a note to Betty, who checked her e-mail every day on her aunt's computer. What would she think if he turned down promotion to captain and retired at twenty years? They'd have to make a life-style adjustment if he had to go to work as an overeducated ditch digger. No more summers in Spain, no more shopping sprees. He loved her and missed her.

Jack peeled off his flight suit and tossed it over the back of his desk chair. Phew! How many days in a row had he worn the thing? He pulled the patches and insignia off their Velcro and tossed the flight suit into his laundry bag. He pulled a fresh one from his metal closet and dressed it for the next day. Silver commander oak leaves on the shoulders, nametag with NFO wings over the left chest pocket. Over the right chest pocket went the Bear Slayer squadron patch. It showed The Thing from The Fantastic Four reaching up from the

Arctic Circle and grabbing a Soviet TU-95 Bear bomber out of the sky. The Bear Slayers had deployed to Iceland in the early eighties to fill a gap in the North American Defense Early Warning grid, about the same time Jack and Buzz had played war in The Great Big Backfire Raid on the other side of the world.

A small American flag went on the right sleeve. On the left sleeve, Jack attached the CAG 8 patch, which portrayed an old torpedo bomber flying into the side of a Japanese aircraft carrier, which represented all of Ensign George Gay's pals in Torpedo Squadron 8 who died in World War II's Battle of Midway.

Jack slipped on gym shorts and a T-shirt, and took one last look at his e-mail in-box. Betty had written back already.

"I don't care what you do, as long as you do it with me."

Jack shut down the computer, pulled out the sofa and turned it into a bed you called a rack, and rolled into it. His eyelids collided, and he slept a troubled sleep.

The China Shop

At ten hundred the next morning, Jack sat at one end of the long table in the flag conference room. Average Joe sat to his left. Next to Average Joe sat the ship's supply officer, Commander "Natty" Bumpo, resplendent in handmade khakis and a calfskin Navy flight jacket that, as a supply officer, he wasn't supposed to have. To Jack's right sat CAGMO and Commander Grandma.

At the opposite end of the table from Jack sat Rear Admiral Bull Palsy, looking much as Jack remembered him from their *Constellation* days. More vainglorious, certainly. Visibly grayer around the gills. And definitely fatter.

"What in the wide world of mother-fucking sports is going on around here?" Bull roared, and looked at Natty Bumpo.

Natty shrugged his narrow shoulders. "I'm just a paper pusher.

If the paperwork looks right, how would I know anything's wrong?" Natty looked across the table at CAGMO.

Bald, pasty CAGMO mumbled something about training at the enlisted maintenance schools not being what it used to be, and boy, if he were in charge of Navy-wide enlisted maintenance training, things sure would be different. But he wasn't in charge of Navy-wide enlisted maintenance training, was he, so what was a bald, pasty CAGMO like him supposed to do? CAGMO turned to Commander Grandma.

Commander Grandma cried.

Natty Bumpo handed her a tissue from the supply he always kept in the map pocket of the calfskin flight jacket he wasn't supposed to have. Commander Grandma blew her nose and looked at Bull Palsy with moist, rheumatoid eyes. Bull stifled a growl, and looked down the table at Jack.

"I know you from somewhere, don't I?"

"*Constellation*, Admiral."

"That's right," Bull said, his color rising. "You're the asshole who let me walk around the ship all day with my fly open, then tried to blame my engineer the night you almost slammed *Connie* into *Mars*."

"That's not quite how I remember it, sir, but yes, I'm that guy."

Bull lurched forward, like he might leap across the table and punch Jack in the nose, and then sit on him. But before he could do that, a button popped off the belly of his bellbottom shirt and skittered across the table.

CAGMO reached out and grabbed it. "Here you go, Admiral."

"Shove it up your ass, you bald, pasty twerp," Bull said.

"Aye, aye, sir," CAGMO said, and put the button in the breast pocket of his blouse, saving it for later.

Bull, embarrassed about his button popping off, calmed down a bit. "What am I supposed to do? Shine my ass, go out to God and everybody with a message saying my battle group can't support my

E-2 squadron?"

"With all due respect, Admiral," Jack said, "you can either do that or go out and tell God and everybody that your battle group—and the United States Navy—can't perform airborne early warning for Southern Watch, and that Air Force AWACS will have to double up to cover the gap."

Palsy's whole body quivered. Jack thought he might go off on another ballistic tantrum, but he didn't. "All right," Bull said. "Everybody out of here except CAG."

As Jack stood to leave, Average Joe whispered, "Wait for me in my office."

★ ★ ★ ★ ★

Thirty minutes elapsed on Betty's Omega before Average Joe limped into his office and collapsed in his desk chair, looking like he'd just lost three out of three falls to a rhinoceros.

"How'd it go?" Jack said.

Average Joe chuckled feebly. "Bull stretched my asshole some. But I'm used to that. What do I care? I'm a Navy captain and a CAG. That's a lot further than I ever dreamed of going when the Marine drill instructors had me running up and down the sea wall at AOCS. Palsy can't do anything worse to me than that. You, on the other hand—"

Jack made a brave face. "That bad?"

Average Joe gave him a brave face back. "I quote: 'If that square-jawed, big-shouldered bastard ever comes up for major command, I'll personally make sure everybody on the selection board knows what a back-stabbing, disloyal, unpatriotic prick he is.'"

Jack took a deep breath. "Guess I hurt his little feelings, huh?"

Average Joe laughed. "That's my boy, Jackie. Listen, Bull's having his staff gin up a message asking for civilian technicians to fly out here from the States and fix your airplanes before we get to the Gulf.

You and your guys just do the job right in Southern Watch. Don't worry about your career."

"What's to worry about?" Jack said. Fuck my career, he thought. I have Betty now.

☆　☆　☆　☆　☆

The technicians flew aboard *Nixon* just before the ship transited the Strait of Hormuz and fixed Jack's broke-dick radar boxes.

As Buzz predicted, Bad Guy didn't fly in the no-fly zone. The only action occurred when the air wing bombed a milk truck that the intelligence weenies had said was really a SAM site. When the SAM site turned out to just be a milk truck, the intelligence weenies claimed they'd known it all along.

☆　☆　☆　☆　☆

The *Nixon* left the Gulf, and the civilian technicians who'd kept Jack's airplanes working flew home. Left in the clutches of Commander Grandma's untrained technicians, Jack's radars fell apart again.

Vice Admiral Riley O'Really, commander of Sixth Fleet in the Mediterranean, required all units to submit readiness reports as *Nixon* steamed back into his theater of operations on its way home. Jack went to Average Joe's cabin.

"Our radars are broke-dick again. Do I lie or tell the truth?"

Average Joe, who looked ten years older then he had six months earlier, said, "Do what you have to do. You know, though, if you tell the truth, we'll have another ice-cream social with your pal Bull Palsy."

"You think there's any chance we'll go back to the Gulf?"

"No. *Connie's* already on station there. We're going home as scheduled."

"So it really doesn't matter if my airplanes are broke-dick or not," Jack said. "Let me go off somewhere and think."

"Let me know what you decide," Average Joe said and yawned.

★ ★ ★ ★ ★

Jack sat on his sofa that was a rack when you unfolded it and stared at the ceiling you called an overhead, and the floor you called a deck, and the walls you called bulkheads, and his metal sink, and his metal closet, and the door that wasn't a hatch.

Telling the truth again couldn't trash his career any worse than it was already trashed. But what good would it do? He'd already made his point. The Pentagon had launched an investigation into the *Nixon* battle group's supply and maintenance practices. Bull Palsy wouldn't go any further in the Navy. Neither would CAGMO or Natty Bumpo or Commander Grandma. It didn't matter any more that his airplanes were broken. They wouldn't go back into a combat zone this cruise, and the squadron was scheduled to get new airplanes before the next cruise.

Why put everybody else through another ugly scene? Especially Average Joe. He was a good enough guy, for a fighter pilot. Joe had stood up to Bull Palsy when it really mattered, talked him into embarrassing himself and releasing the message that got Jack's radars fixed in time to fly Southern Watch.

Jack called Average Joe shortly after midnight. "I just finished your fitness report," Joe said. "Swing by and sign it."

★ ★ ★ ★ ★

Average Joe had ranked Jack number four of eight squadron skippers—a good enough rating to make captain, but not good enough to ever have command of a ship or an air wing or a shore base. "You understand why I had to do that?" Joe said.

"Sure, CAG." A higher ranking wouldn't have done Jack any good, not after the scene with Bull Palsy. The write-up said nice things about Jack and his squadron. At a glance, Jack saw seven misspelled words in it, but didn't bother to point them out. He signed the fitness report and gave it back to Average Joe.

"What did you decide about your readiness report to Sixth Fleet?" Joe said.

"I just released a message saying we have four full-up airplanes," Jack said.

Joe leaned back in his desk chair. Five years seemed to float off his shoulders. "Thanks," he said. "Thanks for being a good … Thanks for everything, Jack. Go grab yourself some sleep."

☆ ☆ ☆ ☆ ☆

The next morning, Big Steve Romanowski approached Jack in the ready room. "Skipper, I just saw our readiness message that says we have four full-up airplanes. What a crock of bullshit. You didn't sign off on that, did you?"

Jack thought about telling Big Steve what Deuce Macintosh had told him years ago about the right thing and the smart thing and the thing you can live with. But Steve wouldn't have bought any of that.

"I can't explain," he said.

Steve blinked. "You're the boss, Skipper. Just didn't seem like something you'd do."

Steve gave Jack a Colgate smile and walked out of the ready room.

That was the exact moment Jack didn't like being a naval officer any more.

This Is Your Life

Jack came home to find a new addition to the family, a nine-week-old chocolate Labrador retriever. "He's great, baby."

"I'm so glad you like him," Betty said. "I was afraid you wouldn't."

"How could I not like him? I haven't had a dog since I was a kid."

"I know. Your Mom told me all about Miltie. How she followed you all over the woods when you played Daniel Boone or G.I. Joe, and how you and your sisters used to think Miltie and your grandma knew how to talk to each other."

"They did know how to talk to each other," Jack said. "Where did you find this guy?"

"I got him from a breeder in North Carolina. I picked him because he has your hair and your eyes, and he'll grow up to be big and strong just like his daddy. Look at him, staring up at you with those pretty brown eyes of his, sitting at attention like a little field marshal."

"Like a little field marshal," Jack chuckled. "Come here, Rommel." He picked Rommel up and held him against his chest and smiled. Rommel smiled back and licked Jack's face, and peed down the front of Jack's flight suit.

☆　☆　☆　☆　☆

Jack stood the squadron down for a month, which is a Navy way of saying he gave the squadron a month off. At quarters in SP-1, with the Bear Slayers formed up around pieces of the roof you called an overhead littered on the floor you called a deck that the C.O. of NAS Norfolk still hadn't had hauled away, Jack said, "If you don't have anything to do, don't do it here."

Jack took Rommel to the beach every day and taught him to swim and fetch. When they got tired of the beach they played in the yard, and when they got tired of the yard, they played in the house. They learned "sit," "stay," "heel," and "crap outside, dammit."

The week before the squadron went back to work, Jack took Rommel to the vet's for puppy shots. The charge came to $60 and change, and Jack pulled out his MasterCard to cover it. The blonde college girl at the cash register ran the card through the machine.

"I'm sorry," she said. "The system won't take this card."

"It won't? Guess I've had it in my wallet too long, the magnetic strip must be damaged. Try this one." He handed her his Visa.

She tried the Visa and shook her head.

"Let's try American Express," Jack said.

"We don't take American Express."

"I'll pay you in cash, then," Jack said, but his wallet's bill compartment was empty. That was odd. He normally carried $100 in twenties. "This is embarrassing. Let me go find an ATM."

"There's one down the street at the 7-Eleven."

"I'll be right back," Jack said. "Keep my dog as collateral, okay?" He gave the twenty-something college girl a Colgate smile, hoping she'd smile back at him, and not think he was a forty-something deadbeat.

"Whatever," she said and looked away, and pretended to have some files she needed to sort.

At the 7-Eleven, Jack tried to pull a hundred dollars from the checking account. Insufficient funds. Insufficient funds in the savings account too. He had enough change in his pocket to use the pay phone to call home and ask Betty what the hell was going on with the accounts. No answer at home. No answer on Betty's cell phone either.

Across town at the Navy Federal Credit Union branch office, he found out that not only were the savings and checking accounts overdrawn, the MasterCard and Visa were over limit and past due. He drew cash from a money market account Betty didn't have access to, squared the credit card accounts, and drove back to the vet's to get Rommel.

★　★　★　★　★

Betty wasn't home yet. Jack took Rommel to check the mail, something Betty normally did. The power bill and the phone bill were both months past due, and contained shut-off notices. Several other bills, past due as well.

★　★　★　★　★

Jack was on the front porch, drinking a beer, when Betty drove up. "What are you doing?" she said as she got out of her Subaru with a shopping bag.

Jack waved the stack of bills at her. "Tell me what this is all about."

Betty brushed past him and ran inside.

★　★　★　★　★

Betty cried, Rommel ran around the room, Jack raised his voice.

"I just lost track of things while I was in Spain," Betty said. "When I realized how out of control everything was, I was afraid to tell you about it."

"What did you spend all that money on, Betty?"

"I don't remember. Things."

"Twenty thousand bucks worth of 'things' is a lot of things to forget about."

"I was having fun," Betty said. "And I never had control of that much money before. I didn't know what I was doing."

Jack cut up her credit and ATM cards, and took away her checkbook. "You show me all the mail from now on."

Betty went up to the third floor and locked herself in the master bedroom.

Jack took Rommel to the beach. Later, they slept together in the spare bed in the downstairs den.

★　★　★　★　★

Mom called the next week. She had bad news from the doctors. They thought her breast cancer might be back. Not to worry about it, though, Mom would be okay. How were things with Betty and Rommel? Could they all drive down to Charleston sometime soon? The drive wasn't so far, now that they were in Virginia, was it?

"Navy business is picking up, Mom. I have to go down to Florida tomorrow for a couple weeks."

"Do what you have to do," Mom said. "Come visit when you can."

★ ★ ★ ★ ★

Jack left Betty three hundred dollars in cash on the kitchen table. Down in Key West, the Bear Slayers and their new E-2s controlled Buzz's squadron in an air combat play-war exercise against elements of the Air Force's 185th Fighter Wing. At the debrief, everybody claimed victory.

Jack's American Express Card didn't work when he tried to check out at the Key West BOQ. He went to the pay phone in the lobby and called the 1-800 number on the back of the card.

The sign and travel voucher was over balance and past due, as was the Platinum Card account.

"What sign and travel voucher?" Jack said. "What Platinum card. When did I open those?"

The American Express rep told him they'd been opened in November of '96. *While I was at sea on the* Nixon *during BFD-EX,* Jack thought.

"I'll take care of this when I get home," Jack said. He had to drive to the Navy Federal branch in Key West and borrow enough money to pay his bill at the BOQ.

Back at home, Betty wouldn't come out of the master bedroom.

The next Monday, Jack got a call in his office at SP-1 from Discover Card.

"Thanks," he said, "but the last thing I need right now is a new credit card."

"This isn't about a new card," the woman on the other end said. "This is about your current account, the one that's past due."

Betty was locked upstairs (again) when Jack got home that

afternoon. This Discover Card thing was bad. Jack had put Betty's name on his Visa, MasterCard, and American Express accounts. But she'd opened this account—in his name—on her own. And if she'd done that sort of thing once …

Jack and Rommel went down to the den. Jack locked the door and fired up the e-Mac. He found a web site that would download his credit report. Enter this, enter that, sit back and wait while the system pulled down his information.

Name.

Address.

Employer.

Mortgage debt.

Revolving charge debt …

Holy shit.

Two hundred fifty thousand dollars in credit card debt, in Jack's name, spread across fifteen accounts Jack had never known about. All of them opened since he'd married Betty. All maxed out. All past due.

Betty pounded on the door to the den. "What are you doing in there?" Drunk, it sounded like. Rommel went to the door and wagged his tail.

"I'm your wife, goddammit. Tell me what you're doing."

A glass crashed against the door, then a thud as Betty fell to the floor.

Jack got up and opened the door. Betty was a mess. Dressed in Jack's favorite negligee, one breast exposed as she lay on the floor, mascara running down her cheeks.

"You okay?" he said.

"I'm okay," she slurred. "Please don't divorce me, Jack. Please. You're not going to, are you?"

"I don't know what I'm going to do." Jack shut the door and locked it again. He took Rommel out the back patio door and went to the beach for a round of fetch. When they got back, Betty had managed to haul herself back up to the master bedroom.

$$\star \quad \star \quad \star \quad \star \quad \star$$

"It's Buzz. I figured it was best to call you at the office. I hear things aren't going so good at home."

Buzz, having gotten his number one fitness report from Average Joe, was back at BUPERS, and was now Jack's detailer.

"Sounds like Flip Wilson's broadcasting the play-by-play," Jack said.

"More or less. Listen, your change of command is in three weeks. All the other squadron skippers like you who got an also-ran FITREP are getting out of the Navy. But thanks to your early promotions, you have two years to go before you can retire. So I have to fuck you and put you back on ship's company. Sorry, but I don't have a choice. Needs of the Navy, and all that."

Jack sighed and cleared his throat. "Can I stay on the east coast?"

"I'd really like you to go out west. Got a navigator billet on *Connie* I need to fill, and you'd be perfect for it."

Navigator on the *Connie*. Jesus God. "No, Buzz. I need to stay here, to deal with Betty, and my Mom."

"Your Mom?"

"Yeah, her breast cancer's back. She may die."

"Well, that's what mom's do eventually, isn't it?" Buzz said. "Run out of gas and cough out on you?"

Jack counted to ten. "Keep me on the east coast. Pull a Fix Felony for me, or I'll break your legs."

"Okay, okay. I'll pull a Fix Felony for you if I can. But you'll owe me one."

$$\star \quad \star \quad \star \quad \star \quad \star$$

At nineteen hundred—7 p.m.—Jack was still in the office in SP-1 when Average Joe rang. "I got a call from Fix Felon. He asked how things were going on your home front."

Great. If Fix Felon knew about his problems with Betty, Jack was a Navy-wide leper. May as well tell Average Joe the truth.

"Things suck," Jack said.

"You want to turn over command to your XO now?" Joe said. "Take some pressure off yourself, make some room to square your life away?"

That would amount to Jack being relieved of command in disgrace. He'd be the dip shit who'd lost control of his life so bad he had to be shit-canned.

"If it's all the same, CAG, I'd like to take the squadron to Purgatory next week for the air wing weapons detachment and leave halfway through it, as scheduled."

He could hear wind sucking through Average Joe's teeth. The pressure to make Jack disappear must be coming from Fix Felon himself. Get the open sore out of sight.

"All right," Joe finally said. "Just watch out what goes on at home, okay? Your wife's already sent a letter to God and everybody saying you're getting ready to dump her and abandon her, and all kinds of other squirrelly crap about you. You don't sound good, according to what she says."

"You've read it?"

"Yeah, Jackie. I got a copy on my fax machine."

"Has Fix Felon read it?"

"He's the one who faxed it to me."

Purgatory

Jack was putting the finishing touches on his change of command fitness reports in his NAS Purgatory BOQ room when Average Joe knocked on his door and let himself in.

"I know you want to keep things short and sweet when you turn over command tomorrow," Joe said. "Thought I'd give you this privately."

It was a Legion of Merit, a medal normally given to senior captains. Joe must have gone two out of three falls to get Bull Palsy to approve one for Jack.

"Wish things had turned out different for you," Joe said. "Figured this was the least I could do."

"Thanks, CAG."

"I just talked to Buzz at BUPERS," Joe said. "I think he's found a spot for you on the east coast. Operations officer on the *Fillmore*."

☆　☆　☆　☆　☆

Jack was working on the Navy League Senior Enlisted Award write-up for Big Steve when Buzz called.

"It's past noon in Tennessee, Buzz. What are you still doing at work?"

"I fucked up. I did a good job at something by accident, and they made me the head Jesuit."

"The head Jesuit?" Jack the straight man said.

"Yeah. I have to write all the point papers that tell all the detailers it's okay to fuck everybody up the ass. Ends justify means, and all that."

"You're writing point papers, Buzz? Without me there to help you?"

"It's not that hard," Buzz said. "We got all the stuff the real Jesuits wrote to justify the Spanish Inquisition. It's on disk. I just global-replace 'thou' with 'you' and print it out."

"Isn't modern technology wonderful?"

"It's fantastic," Buzz said. "Makes manipulating people so much easier. Speaking of which, thanks for eating this operations officer billet on the *Fillmore* for me. It's not exactly a love boat. The guy in the job right now is a world-class prick, and he's had two years to hard wire everybody else there into the pissed off position. The

admiral's an out-and-out crack head. And the ship's new captain
… Well, remember my squadron skipper who let us fly Southern
Watch with broke-dick missiles?"

"Yeah."

"He took command of the *Fillmore* last month."

★ ★ ★ ★ ★

Jack was still working on Steve's award write-up when the sun
dipped below the mountain range west of the air station. He got up
and looked out the window and glanced at Betty's Omega. Six in
the evening. Yep, fall had come. Jack picked up the phone and called
Mom.

Mom was so glad to hear from him. What was he doing with the
Navy in Nevada? They didn't have ships in the desert, did they? Oh,
just airplanes. Well. That made sense. You could fly over the desert,
but you couldn't sail a ship on one, could you?

"That's right, Mom."

The doctors weren't sounding too optimistic about her cancer.
How soon could Jack and Betty come and visit? She was such a hoot,
that Betty. Mom just loved her. And she loved Jack, of course, as
always.

"We love you too, Mom. We'll get down to Charleston as soon
as we can."

★ ★ ★ ★ ★

The phone rang again just before midnight—three in the morning
east coast time. Jack let it ring thirty-two times before he answered
it. "Betty, I said don't call here."

"Please, Jack." Slurred voice.

"Betty—"

"Please—"

He hung up and took the receiver off the hook. He got a beer from the fridge in the kitchenette, opened it and took a swig. The phone started making eek-eek noise, like in the movie *Psycho* when Tony Perkins hacks Janet Leigh to death in the shower. He pulled the phone cord from the wall jack.

He took another swig of beer, and his stomach turned, and he ran to the bathroom and got there in time to hurl beer through his mouth and nose into the toilet. He kept heaving, even after his stomach was empty. He dropped to his knees and grasped the toilet lid.

He came to an hour later, tits up on the bathroom's tiled deck. The back of his head hurt like hell. He went to the kitchenette and made an icepack for it. Thank God he'd fallen backwards. The troops wouldn't see a big bruise on his forehead when he turned the squadron over at quarters in the morning.

☆ ☆ ☆ ☆ ☆

Goddamn bedroom curtains. You'd think if they went through the trouble to build this nice BOQ in Purgatory, they would have put in curtains thick enough to block the light from the goddamn street lamps in the goddamn parking lot. And made the goddamn windows thick enough so you couldn't hear the goddamn streetlamps hum all goddamn night.

Jack stared at the ceiling tiles until the rising sun washed out the glow of the streetlamps, and their hum was drowned out by the high-pitched whine of a lone F/A-18 Hornet, a mile away on the flight line, its engines spinning up for a morning maintenance turn.

Trick or Treat

Most of a day and the breadth of a continent later, a cab dropped Jack off in front of the house. Betty met him at the front door in the quilted bathrobe Mom had made for her.

"Just in time for trick-or-treaters," she said. "It's Halloween. Let's pretend everything is okay, just for tonight."

She was already drunk, and started dropping candy on the front porch when the first batch of kids came by. "Pick that up, you little shits," she said, hugging the porcelain pumpkin she'd bought to hold all the candy.

"Come on, Betty, let's put you to bed."

"No. I'll do what I want to do. You're divorcing me anyway. I don't have to do what you say."

He managed to coax her inside and up to the living room. She raved, still clutching the porcelain pumpkin.

"Please calm down, Betty. I've just had a long trip, and I'm tired."

"I'm tired too," she said. "I'm tired of not knowing what you're going to do." She threw the pumpkin against the mirror over the fireplace, smashing both the pumpkin and the mirror. Rommel ran downstairs to the den.

Betty picked up a pumpkin shard and held it to her throat. "I have no place to go if you divorce me. I might as well get it over with now."

"Whatever," Jack said.

Betty slashed the pumpkin shard against her left breast and it broke. The pumpkin shard, that is. "Fuck," she said, and threw what was left of the shard at Jack. She lurched to him and tried to hit him in the face.

Jack ducked her punches and ran to the stairs that led to the front door landing. He was halfway down them when Betty flew into his back. He woke up face down on the landing. Betty was curled up next to him, her head jammed into a corner. She came to and screamed. She got up and ran upstairs, and looked at her face in what was left of the living room mirror. "Look what you did to me!"

Jack, who had followed her back up the stairs, said, "I didn't do anything to you, Betty. You did it to yourself."

Betty flew to the kitchen and picked up the phone. "Tell me you won't divorce me, or I'll call the police and tell them you did this."

The left half of her face was turning purple.

"Go ahead," Jack said.

Betty dialed 9-1-1. "Tell me you won't divorce me," she said again. "The police show up, they'll haul you off, and that will be the end of your great fucking Navy career."

"Do what you like," Jack said. "My great fucking Navy career's over anyway."

Somebody answered at 9-1-1, finally. They must have had a big backlog of calls, what with it being Halloween and all.

"I made a mistake," Betty said into the phone. "I meant to dial 4-1-1, information."

She slammed the phone down and stumbled to the couch and passed out. Rommel came up from the den to see what was going on. He and Jack sat on the love seat and watched Betty snore.

At dawn, when Betty hadn't shown any sign of having a concussion, Jack put Rommel in the Trans Am and drove two miles to the BOQ at the Naval Amphibious Base Little Creek. He was in luck. This wasn't a reserve drill weekend. Otherwise, he couldn't have gotten a room, because he was full-time active duty on sea duty orders, and reservists like Flip Wilson got priority over sea duty guys like Jack on drill weekends.

Jack had to sneak Rommel into the BOQ through a back door, because dogs weren't allowed in the BOQ at all, reserve weekend or otherwise.

★ ★ ★ ★ ★

Jack guessed that Walter J. Cowling and his associates must run a successful practice to be able to afford nice office spaces like this: lots of chrome and leather in the waiting area, sun flowing through the skylight, fresh plants all over the place. Magazines on the coffee table like *The New Yorker*, *Harpers*, and *Atlantic Monthly*. Current issues at that.

Jack read a *Harpers* article on Saul Bellow, thinking his choice of Walter J. Cowling had been a good one. "Walter J. Cowling and Associates, LLC, a family law firm," the ad in the yellow pages had said. "Adoption, divorce, child custody, and bankruptcy. Military families our specialty."

And here, emerging from the inner sanctum of Walter J. Cowling and Associates, was Walter J. Cowling himself, his arms spread wide in welcome. "Jack, come, let's talk."

Five hundred dollar shoes, the bottom half of a two thousand dollar suit, the rolled up sleeves of a hundred dollar shirt, galluses instead of a belt, and a twenty-thousand-dollar Rolex Cosmograph on his left wrist. Tall and gaunt, trench-deep lines in his face, curly gray hair, and a moustache. Walter J. Cowling looked like a dressed up version of Kurt Vonnegut, only sadder, especially if you took a good look at his eyes. Maybe he looked so sad because he'd just dropped his last client off in front of *Slaughterhouse Five*.

But Walter J. Cowling wouldn't do that to Jack, would he? Jack's a good guy. Right now, as big and strong as he looks, Jack's like a young sailor, locked alone behind a watertight hatch in a tiny compartment that's his battle station, cut off from communication with the rest of his ship, and who doesn't quite understand what's going on. All he hopes is that somebody comes to get him when the drill is over, or lets him know if the ship is sinking.

ACT V

War is Peace

The Good Ship

Jack ducked his head through the hatch of the operations office of the USS *Millard Fillmore* and went in.

Commander Bill "Reno" Sparks stood up from his desk chair. A tall man, Reno was. Six foot five, maybe. Jack had never met Reno, but he knew about him. Reno was a fighter pilot, and in a world distinguished by its asshole population, Reno was an asshole apart. Everybody speculated that Reno had a set of naval pilot's wings tattooed to his dick. Jack would take everybody's word for it.

"About time you showed up," Reno said. "Where the fuck have you been?" Reno grabbed his ball cap from his desk, his leather flight jacket from the back of his chair, and the life-sized poster of himself standing next to an F-14 Tomcat from the wall. "I had it, you got it. Here's your desk, here's your computer, here's your stateroom key, and here's your pass down. Everything sucks. Everybody sucks. Don't trust anybody except Father Mick, the Catholic chaplain."

Reno stormed past Jack and breezed out the hatch that was a door with a watertight fitting.

Jack put his new stateroom key in his pocket and sat at his new desk. He punched a key that brought his new computer out of the sleep mode. The screen saver appeared, a floating text bar that read, "LIFE IS HARD AND SO'S MY DICK."

A tall lieutenant with glasses, a moustache, and NFO wings on his pressed khaki shirt entered through the hatch, carrying a thick stack of blue routing folders under his right arm. "You must be Commander Hogan," he said, and plopped his pile of paperwork on the metal desk next to Jack's. "Jerry Marx, sir, call sign 'Groucho.' I'm your administrative assistant."

Jack shook Groucho's hand. "Good call sign, Jerry. What do you fly?"

"Tomcats, sir. Enjoying this job, but eager to get back to flying when I'm through here. Hopefully, I'll transition to the Super Duper Hornet."

"You have a good job, Groucho. I served with Buzz Rucci when he was ops-admin officer on the *Connie*."

"So I understand, sir. Captain Rucci called me from BUPERS yesterday."

"Captain Rucci?"

"Yes, sir. He just picked it up. Just screened for CAG too."

Captain and CAG already? Why hadn't he called to tell Jack about it? Maybe he figured Jack had other things on his mind right now. Or maybe he didn't want to rub his success in Jack's face. Nah. Buzz wouldn't be that considerate. He probably just forgot. Or maybe he was trying to distance himself from Jack, now that Buzz was the rising star and Jack was the gaping wound everybody wanted to see disappear.

Jack grinned at Groucho. "So you're in thick with Captain Rucci, huh? Not a bad guy to hitch your wagon to."

"He said I'd enjoy working with you, sir."

"He's a lying piece of shit, Groucho. You'll rue the day I set foot aboard this ship. First thing I want from you, mister, is fifty pushups."

"Rue the day, fifty pushups, aye, sir. It will have to be later though, sir. I have a lot of your paperwork to plow through right now."

"In that case," Jack said, "rue the day on your own time and fit the pushups in when you can."

"Will next month be soon enough, sir?"

"Hey, work your own schedule, kid. Don't expect me to

micromanage around here."

"Roger that, sir. Then by your leave, I need to get a few more things from the ship's secretary's office."

"You better go get them then."

"See you at lunch, sir? The Dirty Shirt? *Fillmore* puts on a good lunch spread in port."

"The supply officer must be making money on the officers' mess fund, then."

"Wouldn't surprise me, sir. See you about noon? That's when the fun people tend to gather. Anything else I can do for you between now and then?"

Jack pointed at his computer screen. "Nothing immediate. But when you get a chance, could you have somebody change this screen saver for me?"

"Oh," Groucho said. "That thing."

That thing floated across the screen again: LIFE IS HARD AND SO'S MY DICK.

"What would you like it changed to, sir?"

"Anything would be an improvement," Jack said.

"I'll have it changed this afternoon, sir," Groucho said, and disappeared.

A fifty-something captain stuck his head in the door. He was balding, had bushy eyebrows, and wore a chaplain's cross on the left collar point of his bellbottom khaki shirt. He made deep sea diving sounds, like he'd just run up a whole bunch of stairs you called ladders. Snot was running down his nose.

"I'm Father Mick," he said. "You must be the new OPSO. Welcome aboard. Will I see you at mass?"

"Not if you blink, Father," Jack said. And even if you don't, he thought.

"Always like to see a lapsed Catholic come back into the fold," Father Mick said.

Jack wondered how Father Mick knew he was a lapsed Catholic. Must have looked in Jack's service record, or something. Who knew?

"Good for your career, these days, being Catholic," Father Mick said. "The captain and XO always come to Sunday mass. Fix Felon's Catholic too, you know."

"I'll have to check my calendar," Jack said.

"See you Sunday, then. I'm off. Have to meet with the altar boys in a couple minutes. Toodles!"

LIFE IS HARD AND SO'S MY DICK floated across Jack's computer screen again.

An ancient looking female lieutenant walked in. "You must be the new OPSO," she said, and took off her *Fillmore* ball cap. "Meg Ryan's the name."

No, she wasn't Meg Ryan the movie star. If you saw that Meg Ryan standing next to this Meg Ryan, you'd know this Meg Ryan from that Meg Ryan right away. "I'm the ship's first lieutenant," this Meg Ryan said. "Boats, anchors, underway replenishments, line handlers, helmsman, all that good bosun mate bullshit, that's me."

Jack waved at Groucho's empty chair. "Nice to meet you, Meg. Have a seat."

"I think I will," she said. "I'm getting too old for this. My flabby old body gets tired of going up and down ladders." She sat. "Welcome aboard the good ship lollipop, New OPSO."

"Call me Jack. It's good to be here."

"You only think that because you just got here. Give it time— about three more minutes—and you'll come around to everybody else's way of thinking. Met anybody else yet?"

"Groucho."

"Good kid," Meg said. "Sharp, fun to be around. Who else?"

"Father Mick."

"Known pedophile. Lucky for me I'm adult female. Otherwise I'd be afraid to go to mass. You met Reno?"

"For about ten seconds. He left me his room key and his screen saver."

"The one about his dick? You're lucky he didn't leave you a picture of his tattoo. Tell you what, New OPSO, your arrival's been the most eagerly anticipated thing on this ship since the coming of the messiah. One thing you got going for you; no matter how big an asshole you turn out to be, there's no way you could turn out to be as big an asshole as Reno was."

Jack laughed.

"I guess you figured I'm no ditz college girl," Meg said. "I'm a mustang, former enlisted. I got close to thirty-five years in now, and I never seen anything like that Reno. They broke it off in the mold when they made that asshole."

"I may not have a prayer of living up to Reno's assholiness," Jack said. "But I'll give it my best shot."

"Don't bother trying. We got plenty of other assholes around here, all we need. You ever met the admiral? Wild Bill Hitchcock?"

"Heard of him. Another fighter guy, right?"

"Another one," Meg said. "Perfect call sign for him, 'Wild Bill.' I was his first lieutenant when he was skipper of the *Jimmy Carter*. The man's an ego with a life support system. And then there's the captain, yet another fighter guy. Miles Benning."

"I flew Southern Watch with him," Jack said.

"Then you know about the broke-dick missiles he let his squadron fly with?"

"I didn't at the time. How did you find out about it?"

"From Flip Wilson," Meg said.

"You know Flip?"

"Who doesn't? He's the Navy's number two source of good dirt, second only to me. You don't have anything nice to say about anybody, come sit by me, that's my motto."

"Then you're not a big Miles Benning fan?"

246 ■ JEFF HUBER

"They're all pieces of work," Meg said. "I seen them come, I seen them go. I guess Benning's no worse than the rest. He's the intellectual type, maybe too intellectual for this business, if you know what I mean. I just talked to him in his in-port cabin about the admiral's barge. Come on, I'll take you over and re-introduce you."

Ship, Captain, Crew

Outside Captain Benning's in-port cabin, Jack and Meg ran into a commander who looked even older than Meg. Five nine, bald, a loose paunch, red jowls; he looked like Santa Claus after two months of chemotherapy.

"This here's our New OPSO, Wattie," Meg said. "Commander Jack Hogan. And this here, New OPSO, is our combat systems officer, Commander Tom Watson."

"Welcome aboard, Jack," Wattie said. "You might have noticed I look older than the Dead Sea Scrolls. Everybody notices that about me right away."

"No, no," Jack said. "You don't look half that old."

"Don't flatter him," Meg said. "I got dead grandparents look younger than Wattie."

"Pay no attention to the old broad behind the curtain," Wattie said.

"Pay no attention to Wattie and me arguing over who looks older," Meg said.

"It's a pot and kettle thing," Wattie said.

"One of our standard routines," Meg said. "One of the crazy things we do to keep our sanity on this loony bin."

"Like I was going to say before Meg changed the subject—"

"That's another crazy thing we do a lot of," Meg said. "Changing the subject. It's the best way we know how to deal with the XO and the captain and the admiral."

"Like I was saying," Wattie said, "my guys fix all the radars and weapons your operators operate with. I'll try not to screw you, but if I do, just screw me back. I'm all broke in after two years of Reno."

A youngish captain wearing pilot wings entered the hallway you called a passageway. "Cheese it," Meg said. "It's the X-yay O-yay. Time to change the subject again."

"You two conspiring to mutiny outside the captain's cabin again?" the XO said.

"No, sir," Wattie said. "Never, sir. And there's no beer hidden in my stateroom either, sir, so you don't need to bother to search for it."

"I wouldn't enter your stateroom in a body-condom, Wattie." The XO turned to Jack. "Jeff Sovine. Call sign 'Red.'"

"Because of his brown hair," Meg said.

"Clever, huh?" XO Sovine said. "So you're the New OPSO? Welcome aboard. Try not to be as big an asshole as Reno was, huh? But don't try too hard. If you're not at least kind of an asshole, then I'll have to turn into a really huge one. Leadership, and all that. Tough job, being an asshole, but somebody has to do it."

"I'll do my best to be an asshole but not too big of an asshole, sir," Jack said.

"That's the team spirit. And oh, be careful around Meg and Wattie. They're troublemakers."

"Troublemakers?" Meg said. "Us?"

"Yeah, you. Is the captain in? I need to talk to him about some legal and discipline issues."

"Going to bust that counterfeit ring they're running down in the photo lab, XO?" Wattie said.

XO Sovine smiled coolly. "Something like that. See you around the campus, New OPSO," he said, and disappeared into Benning's cabin.

"Phew," Meg said. "Guess you hit a nerve with that crack about the counterfeit ring, Wattie."

"Maybe," Wattie said. "Maybe not. Between the supply officer, the chaplain, and the admiral's staff, there's so much Fix Felony going on around this ship a counterfeit ring would be the least of the XO's worries. Besides, fuck him if he can't take a joke."

Meg tugged Jack's sleeve. "XO Sovine, he can take a joke all right. But I tell you what, be careful around him. He can seem like a regular guy, but he's one of them."

"One of them?" Jack said.

"One of them golden boys," Wattie said. "Marked for admiral since he was a plebe at the academy. Connected like you read about. Old skippers. Family. Part of the greater Fix Felon bloodline."

"If you didn't know any better," Meg said, "you'd say the new captain's a little afraid of XO Sovine. Treats him like a son. Wants to make sure his XO has nice things to say about him when he talks to Uncle Admiral and Cousin Congressman."

"Oh," Jack said. "One of them."

They cooled their heels in the passageway, waiting for the XO to get done with Captain Benning. Meg and Wattie did more vaudeville patter, Wattie saying "So Reno just stormed off the ship?"

Meg saying, "Yep. Just handed New OPSO his key and his screen saver and left."

Wattie: "No pass down or anything, huh?"

Meg: "Not a word."

Wattie: "What a fine human being, that Reno. I hope they give him a purple heart for the bruise he got where the door hit him on his way out. Just as well, though, Jack. You didn't really need to have a pass down. The only thing you need to know—"

Meg: "Is who's an asshole, and which assholes hate each other."

Wattie: "Which is easy—"

Meg: "Because they're all assholes—"

Wattie: "And they all hate each other—"

Meg: "Or they're afraid of each other—"

Wattie: "Or both—"

"Or all three," Meg said, and took a breath, and continued. "So, new subject, New OPSO. What sort of planes did you fly?"

"He's an E-2 guy," Wattie said. "Remember? Jack's the one who shot down Commander Grandma on the *Nixon*."

"You're that guy, New OPSO?" Meg said. "Then you're a big hero to us. Every mustang officer in the Navy was hoping somebody would come along and put a bullet in that old horse. Commander Grandma gave mustangs a bad name, Just like Father Mick gives pedophiles a bad name—"

"Or like Reno gives the human race a bad name," Wattie said.

"So like I said, you're a big hero, New OPSO. And that's the last nice thing I'll ever say about you."

"Me too," Wattie said.

"Me three," Meg said, and thought of something else. "Wait."

"What?" Wattie said.

"New subject. I just realized: you're waiting around to see Captain Benning. You normally avoid him like he's got AIDS or something."

"I don't know what he's got," Wattie said. "But why risk getting close enough to him so he can cough on you, that's my motto."

"Then what are you doing here?"

Wattie sagged. "You know how Captain Benning is. Wants to know every little detail about everything, wants to make sure you're doing everything the right way, which is his way, which is the admiral's way, whether it's the right way or not."

"We're talking about Wild Bill's red phone again?" Meg said.

"Bada-bing."

"You'll like the red phone story, New OPSO," Meg said.

☆　☆　☆　☆　☆

A month ago, they're all in this department head meeting and Benning asks how Wild Bill's red phone installation is coming. Wattie asks whatever is Captain Benning talking about. Captain

Benning says he's talking about the special red phone the admiral wants installed in his cabin that will connect him directly to the White House.

Wattie says he never heard of such a thing, but Benning says that oh, yes, the admiral specifically requested a red phone be installed in his cabin, in case he needs to get hold of President Pants right away if something important or embarrassing happens while the *Fillmore* is deployed.

Wattie tries to explain to Benning that piss ant two-star admirals like Wild Bill don't rate having a direct line to President Pants, and that Atlantic Fleet would never allow such a thing to be installed on the *Fillmore*.

But Captain Benning persists. His ship will support its battle group commander in any way the battle group commander wishes to be supported.

Wattie gets frustrated, and blurts out, in front of God and everybody, "Hell, Captain. Nobody wants to talk to Wild Bill, much less the president of the United States."

Benning stops the meeting and asks Wattie to join him in his in-port cabin. Their private conversation ends with Benning saying, "Just, ah, do something that will keep the admiral happy."

☆ ☆ ☆ ☆ ☆

"So I promised him I'd do something," Wattie said. "And he called me this morning and wanted to know what that something's going to be."

"What's it going to be?" Meg said.

"Damned if I know," Wattie said. "I'll think of something." He looked at Jack. "What a pile of happy horseshit, huh?"

"Time to change the subject, Wattie," XO Sovine said, coming out of Benning's cabin. "I'm all done with the captain. He said for the three of you to go right in. See you at lunch?"

"If we manage to get out of the Captain's cabin in time," Meg said.

"That might take some doing," the XO said. "He's watching a TV show on the science channel. Maybe you should put on a belly dancer outfit to get his attention, Meg."

"Please, XO," Wattie said. "Did you have to mention Meg in a belly dancer outfit this close to lunchtime?"

"Sorry, Wattie, I wasn't thinking. Well, welcome again, New OPSO. And like I said, be careful around these two."

XO Sovine disappeared down the hall you called a passageway.

"Shall we go in then?" Jack said.

Wattie stopped him. "One more thing, Jack, before we do. It's very important that you don't call anybody by their real name in front of Captain Benning. You have to remember to call everybody by their ship names. I'm not Wattie, I'm 'Sizz-o,' short for combat systems officer. Meg's not Meg, she's 'First,' short for first lieutenant. And you're not Jack, you're 'New OPSO.' For now. Later, you'll just be 'OPSO,' when you aren't so new."

"Pay attention, Jack," Meg said. "What Wattie said is very important. If the captain hears you calling anybody by their real name, he'll know you know something he doesn't know, because he doesn't know anybody's real name."

"And he'll hate you for knowing something he doesn't know," Wattie said.

"And probably fear you too," Meg said. "Which might be a good thing, if it led him to respecting you as well, but why take chances?"

"Okay, okay," New OPSO said, and he and Sizz-O and First slipped through the door you didn't call a hatch and into the inner sanctum of Captain Miles Janus Benning.

Another Fine Rabbit Hole

Captain Benning sat on a paisley couch, both feet planted on a deck covered with laminate flooring manufactured to look like wood. The deck flooring was laminate because real wood was prohibited on ships by naval regulations because wood burns. Laminate burns too, but it wasn't prohibited by naval regulations, and it looked good. So there it was, on the floor you called a deck of Captain Benning's in-port cabin.

Miles Janus Benning leaned slightly forward, his elbows on his thighs, his hands alternately squeezing a grip exerciser, his eyes riveted on the wide-screen television across from the non-flammable metal and glass coffee table in front of him.

Above the television hung a framed oil portrait of a serious looking man in nineteenth century get-up who Jack guessed had to be Millard Fillmore. The 13th president of the United States, Fillmore had been a one-term wonder who had ridden into office on the coattails of his predecessor and been run out of it by a Democrat. Strange choice of presidents to name a carrier after, Jack thought. Next thing you knew, they'd name a carrier after George Herbert Walker Bush.

On the wide screen television, an atom bomb exploded. Captain Benning said, "Ah!" and looked up, and saw First and Sizz-O and New OPSO standing in his doorway. "First! Sizz-o! Come in, come in, have a seat. I'm watching a science channel special on how they developed the first atomic bombs."

Wattie and Meg took the paisley love seat to Benning's right. Jack sat on the paisley love seat to his left. Nice love seat it was, only slightly less comfortable than sitting on a sharp rock. Benning must have bought the whole suite from a furniture store that had MAKE YOUR SUBORDINATES FEEL UNCOMFORTABLE IN YOUR PRESENCE smeared over the front of it.

Another atom bomb exploded on the television. Benning redoubled his efforts with his grip exerciser. The TV scene cut to a fifties-era scientist wearing birth control glasses, standing in front of a chalkboard. Across the chalkboard, left to right, top to bottom, ran a string of mathematical equations, few of which Jack recognized, but all of which Benning apparently did. Benning took a pen from the breast pocket of his blouse and copied the equations on a note pad on his un-inflammable coffee table. Maybe he planned to build an A-bomb in his garage in his spare time. After he got done reading all the magazines spread across his coffee table.

The New Yorker. Harpers. Proceedings. Joint Force Quarterly. Naval War College Review. Foreign Affairs. Aviation Week. Approach. Test Pilot. Popular Science. Sports Illustrated. Muscle and Fitness. Flex. National Lampoon. The Onion. Mad.

Boys' Life?

Eclectic tastes this guy had, all right.

A third atom bomb exploded on the television. Meg and Wattie looked at the screen, then at Jack, then at each other, and then at the ceiling you called an overhead, as if contemplating the nature of the universe.

Benning kept squeezing the dog shit out of that wrist exerciser of his, and Jack saw now that Benning's forearms looked incredibly muscular, even covered by the long sleeves of his cotton khaki shirt. Benning was muscular all over these days, noticeably so, now that Jack got a good look at him.

Noticeably short too, as always, even while sitting—even shorter than the average fighter pilot. Noticeably balder than the average fighter pilot too, the closer you studied him. A redhead, Benning had taken to doing the Donald Trump comb-over thing.

The moustache was new, tightly clipped and jet-black. Dyed that way maybe?

With Benning bent forward like that, you couldn't help notice he'd put on a bit of a waterbed. Funny how he'd let that happen, what with his apparent passion for all things fit and youthful. In all, Captain Benning looked like an unholy combination of Howdy

Doody, Adolph Hitler, and Zero Mostel. And he'd no doubt put a lot of thought and effort into looking that way.

The horror.

Two more A-bomb explosions lit up the TV screen. Hiroshima evaporated, then Nagasaki, and the credits rolled. Benning dropped his wrist exerciser on the coffee table, clicked the remote off, and turned to First and Sizz-o. "What brings you by?"

"I brought Sizz-o and New OPSO by to say hello," First said.

"I'm glad you came along, First," Benning said. "I was just thinking about the admiral's barge, and that maybe we should—"

"Gee, Captain, I hate to change the subject, but I have to run. I got a doctor's appointment. My woman's problem again. I've shown you all my scars and stretch marks, haven't I? You want to see them again?"

"Ah, no," Benning said. "I mean, ah, yes, you have shown them to me and, ah, no, I don't need to see them again. Go along to your appointment then, First."

"Aye, aye, sir. Sorry to run like this, but it's just as well. Sizz-o has important things to tell you about the admiral's red phone."

"The red phone!" Benning said with gusto as Meg fled the room. "What progress, Sizz-o? What news?"

"Excellent progress, Captain. Excellent news. The Atlantic Fleet communications center tells me we can have the red phone next Wednesday."

"That is excellent news," Benning said. "But is there, ah, any chance they can get it here sooner than next Wednesday? We leave for cruise next Thursday, you know. And Admiral Hitchcock specifically said he wanted a red phone 'ASAP,' and I don't think his idea of 'ASAP' is next Wednesday."

"I'll make another phone call and see what I can do."

"Yes, make another phone call. And tell them that Admiral Hitchcock specifically said 'ASAP.'"

"I'll specifically tell them ASAP, sir."

"Not 'soonest convenience' or 'when they can get around to it.'"

"Absolutely not, sir. As soon as possible."

Benning pursed his cheeks. "Ah, no. Not 'as soon as possible.' That might sound like 'soonest convenience' or 'when they can get around to it.'"

"But isn't 'as soon as possible' the same thing as 'ASAP,' sir?"

"It, ah, sounds different."

"Agreed, sir," Wattie said. "It does sound different. 'ASAP' has fewer syllables."

"Yes, far fewer syllables. And more—"

"Immediate, sir?"

"Yes, more immediate."

"Should I tell them to send the red phone immediately, then?"

"Ah, no. The admiral didn't say 'immediately.' He said 'ASAP.'"

"Then ASAP it is, Captain. Will that be all, sir?"

"Just one other thing," Benning said.

"Yes, sir?"

"The color of this red phone …"

"Yes, sir?"

"Will it be red?"

Wattie hesitated. "I assume so, sir. I mean, what other color would a red phone be?"

Benning rested his chin on his thumb. "One might reasonably assume that a red phone would be red, but it might not be. After all, 'red phone,' that's really just a euphemism, isn't it? Meant to describe the function of the phone, something one uses in emergencies, not necessarily the actual color of the phone."

"Whatever color the red phone turns out to be," Wattie said, "I'm certain it will perform its red phone function just fine."

"That may well be," Benning said. "But Admiral Hitchcock didn't say he wanted a green phone or a black phone or a white phone that performs the function of a red phone. He specifically said that he wanted a 'red phone,' and I'm quite certain he expects it to be red in all aspects."

"I'll specifically tell them we want a red phone that's red, sir."

"Good. But, ah, what if they don't have a red phone that's red? Suppose their red phones only come in green or black or white?"

"That might be a problem, sir."

"Yes, it might be," Benning said.

"Maybe you could explain that to Admiral Hitchcock, sir."

Benning made a low frequency, feral-sounding survival noise, and his shoulders curled forward. "I'm not entirely certain Admiral Hitchcock would understand."

Wattie snapped his fingers. "I know what, Captain. If the red phone isn't red, then we'll paint it red."

Benning rubbed his chin. "That would be a viable option—if the red phone they give us isn't red already."

"All righty, sir. I'll make it happen. Better red than dead!"

"And ASAP," Benning said.

"ASAP aye," Wattie said, and scurried out of the room.

Benning looked over at Jack. "Who are you again?"

"New OPSO," Jack remembered to say.

"Ah, yes, New OPSO. I need to speak with you about a letter I received from a, ah, Missus Hogan."

★ ★ ★ ★ ★

After an hour of reassuring Captain Benning that yes, he had a lawyer and yes, he had things under control, Jack returned to his office, his back killing him from sitting on Benning's granite love seat. On his desk sat a plate wrapped in tin foil with a note on top that said, "eat me."

Jack hit the space bar on his computer keyboard, and his new screen saver appeared, a floating text bar that now read, "ANYTHING

WOULD BE AN IMPROVEMENT."

A Bridge Too Near

It started with a single air raid over Kosovo. General F. Lee Kent, United States Army, Supreme Allied Commander in Europe, ordered the air raid in response to President Pants' desire to do something about all those awful images of refugees on the cable news networks, and his desire to take everyone's minds off his oral office escapades.

The Kosovo War—Operation Allied Force—went down two days before *Fillmore* left Norfolk. Jack had figured that by the time the battle group had crossed the Atlantic, the little war would be over. As *Fillmore* transited the Straits of Gibraltar, it looked like the Air Force had enough of their B-2 Billion bombers and Catch F-22 fighters in theater to get the job done, and that the carrier and its escorts would continue on to the Arabian Gulf and conduct Southern Watch operations as planned. When the Joint Chiefs of Staff committed *Fillmore* to Allied Force, everyone on board figured they'd stick around a few days, long enough to say the Navy was there too, and be on their way.

But days became weeks, and weeks became months. At one point, it looked as if the Navy and the Air Force might bomb the national arsenal dry.

✰ ✰ ✰ ✰ ✰

What was true of *Fillmore*'s cast of characters turned out to be true of the movers and shakers of the Kosovo War as well. Everybody hated everybody else, or was afraid of everybody else, or both; and everybody was an asshole. That was how the good guys felt about each other. The bad guys were just an excuse for the good guys to fight among themselves.

It took Jack three minutes to figure out that F. Lee Kent, who was micromanaging the air show, knew less about air power than Robert E. Lee had. Washington wags critical of Kent said his targeting strategy changed on a weekly basis. From where Jack stood, that analysis was kind. Target changes came in from the CAOC—the Combined Air Operations Command post in Italy—minutes before *Fillmore*'s strike packages took off.

Jack was walking down the blue tile passageway in the flag spaces with the battle group staff operations officer when one of his intelligence officers, a skinny ensign, walked up.

"OPSO," he said, so excited his voice cracked, "I just got a target change from the CAOC." He held up a sheet from a yellow sticky pad on which he'd written the coordinates of the new target.

"What's the new target, Stick Boy?"

"It's at these coordinates," Stick Boy said.

"I don't mean where is it?'" Jack said. "What is it? A bridge? A power plant? A SAM site?"

Stick Boy looked forlornly at the deck. "I forgot to ask."

"Who gave you the new target?" Jack said.

"The CAOC, sir."

Jack rubbed his lower back. "The CAOC is a thing. Who gave you the new target? A Navy guy? An Air Force guy? An admiral? A colonel? A corporal?"

"I forgot to ask," Stick Boy said.

Jack wanted to choke the living shit out of Stick Boy, but the kid was just an ensign, after all. Still, redirecting an air strike on the sole basis of coordinates written on a sticky pad by a Stick Boy was a flat out fucked up way to run a war, in Jack's opinion.

Jack turned to the staff operations officer, Captain "Jerry" Springer, a Tomcat NFO. "Do you want to go to Admiral Hitchcock with this?"

Red-headed Jerry Springer had become Wild Bill's favorite dog to kick. That morning, at the flag brief, Wild Bill had ripped Jerry his nineteenth nervous new asshole in as many days for reasons no one else at the brief could readily comprehend. At Jack's suggestion that they go to Wild Bill and admit that they didn't know who was dictating the *Fillmore* air wing's targets, or what the targets even were, Jerry's nose and upper lip started twitching like a rabbit's.

"No," Jerry said. "We can't question every directive that comes down from high command. Let's just follow orders and redirect the strike."

Jack, Jerry, and Stick Boy went to the ship's intelligence center and plugged the sticky pad coordinates into a computer. The computer pulled up imagery of a target that turned out to be a bridge. Stick Boy ran the coordinates and the imagery up to the flight deck and gave them to the strike lead, who was manning his F/A-18 Hornet.

The twelve-plane strike launched and proceeded to a point fifty miles south of the original target. They acquired the new target on their sensors, released their precision-guided weapons, and destroyed the bridge.

The CAOC had, in fact, intended for them to destroy a bridge. But not the bridge they had just destroyed. Stick Boy, in the heat of the moment, had transposed two digits when he wrote down the coordinates. By coincidence, there was also a bridge at the transposed coordinates.

"Not any more," Wattie chortled when he heard about The Big Bridge Fuck-up.

Wild Bill's reaction to The Big Bridge Fuck-up was somewhat less jovial.

Star Wars

According to Flip Wilson, everybody thought F. Lee Kent was the biggest asshole in the universe. Flip was working in the CAOC as part of the naval reserve planning contingent, and talked to Meg via satellite every day. The scuttlebutt from Flip was that everyone at the CAOC openly referred to Kent as "that fucking lunatic."

Nobody, Flip said, hated Kent more than did his air component commander, Lieutenant General W. Martin Gross, United States Air Force. Warty Marty Gross and his staff worked around the clock to devise master attack plans that would achieve the coalition's strategic objectives. Lamentably, as happens in most modern wars, the second the bombs began to fall on Kosovo, everybody forgot what the strategic objectives were, or that there had ever been any. The real objective became to see which service of which country could drop the most bombs on the most targets without fucking up. Plus, it didn't matter what targets Marty Gross and his air power experts came up with, because whatever targets they came up with, F. Lee Kent changed them for reasons that F. Lee Kent alone understood.

After F. Lee Kent, Warty Marty Gross most hated the coalition's naval component commander, Vice Admiral Riley O'Really, United States Navy. Riley owned most of the cruise missiles in theater, nestled in magazines on his Sixth Fleet destroyers and cruisers and submarines. (The air force had a few cruise missiles too, carried by ancient B-52 bombers, but their cruise missiles sucked, so they didn't really count.)

F. Lee Kent loved cruise missiles. Cruise missiles didn't carry pilots who could get shot down and dragged through the streets of Kosovo. "Cruise missiles," Kent pointed out at every high level command teleconference, "make lousy prisoners of war."

To which Marty Gross always replied, loudly enough for everyone in the teleconference to hear, "Eat shit and die, you knuckle-dragging army fuck."

Which F. Lee Kent pretended not to have heard.

Another thing that made Warty Marty Gross really hate Riley O'Really was that aside from owning all the cruise missiles that didn't suck, Riley was commander of the coalition naval forces.

An impressive armada—almost a hundred ships from a dozen nations—they patrolled the Adriatic to keep Bad Guy's navy, three rusty patrol boats and two rusty diesel submarines, penned up in their homeport.

At what later became known as "The Yalta Teleconference," Jack, who nobody had thought to un-invite, blurted out that using a hundred-ship armada to keep Bad Guy's half-ass fleet in port was like using the Rock of Gibraltar to cork up a pint of flat beer.

From Wild Bill's briefing room on the *Fillmore*, Jack said, "I don't see what the BFD is with Bad Guy's navy in the first place. The whole objective of this war is supposed to be about keeping Bad Guy from killing off his ethnic population, isn't it?"

The admirals and generals consulted with their staffs.

"I believe so," Warty Marty said from the CAOC in Italy.

"So my chief of staff tells me," Riley O'Really said from his flagship anchored off Cannes, France.

"What was that?" F. Lee Kent said from his headquarters in Germany. "Something about an objective?"

"The reason we're fighting this war," Jack said from the *Fillmore* in the Ionian Sea.

In Germany, F. Lee Kent looked at his operations officer, a one-star general. "A reason for fighting this war? Do we need one of those?"

F. Lee Kent's one-star shrugged. "Let me get back to you on that, sir."

"Please do," Kent said, and looked into the camera. "Go on, Commander. Tell me more about this theory of yours about sticking the Rock of Gibraltar up Bad Guy's flat pint of beer."

The whole idea of the war, Jack explained, had been to protect Bad Guy's ethnic population. Bad Guy's navy wouldn't come into play unless all his ethnics jumped into the Adriatic Sea to get away from Bad Guy's army. But even then, Bad Guy probably had enough sense not to sortie his whole half-ass navy to go after them. He'd just let his ethnics tread water till they got tired and drowned, or the sharks got to them.

Wild Bill in the Ionian Sea and Warty Marty in Italy slapped tables over that one.

"He got you there, Riley," Warty Marty said, picking at a wart on his chin. "Hell, if you're so afraid of Bad Guy's half-ass navy, you don't need to keep a Spanish Armadillo in the Adriatic. We'll bomb it to smithereens with air power for you. Take what? Five bombs total?"

Riley smiled politely, showing dimples that might have looked cherubic when he was two months old. "What Commander Hogan fails to point out is that our armada in the Adriatic protects our carrier and cruise missile ships in the Ionian from a credible maritime threat."

Warty Marty farted. "A credible maritime threat? Oh, really, Riley. Quit pulling everybody's pud. Your carriers and cruise missile shooters down in the Ionian are two hundred miles from Bad Guy's navy's port. His rust buckets would never make it down there. Hell, they'd sink before they got ten feet from the pier."

Off the coast of France, Riley O'Really whispered something to his aide, who whispered something back to him. Riley stood. "Something's come up, gentlemen. Vital Sixth Fleet business. You'll have to excuse me."

"You're excused, Riley," Warty Marty said from Italy. "Don't forget to wipe twice."

On the *Fillmore*, Wild Bill guffawed.

In Germany, F. Lee Kent furrowed his uni-brow and said, "I believe that concludes the business at hand for today, gentlemen."

When F. Lee Kent's picture blinked off everybody else's screen, Warty Marty said, "Good. Now we can all go take a healthy shit."

☆ ☆ ☆ ☆ ☆

On the next day's master air-attack plan, F. Lee Kent completely cut out cruise missile and carrier air wing strikes, opting to go with air force bombers alone. Riley O'Really had fallen from grace.

For which Riley blamed Wild Bill.

Date With Destiny

Riley really shouldn't have blamed Wild Bill for his fall from grace. It was really Warty Marty's fault, because Warty Marty was the one who'd been eroding Riley O'Really's reputation from the start of the Kosovo War. Aside from calling Riley's coalition naval force "The Spanish Armadillo," he referred to Riley as "Sir Frances Flake" every chance he got. But Riley hated Wild Bill so much he didn't really have enough enmity to spare for anyone else.

The feud between Riley and Wild Bill went back to an incident from their Naval Academy days. Meg heard about it when she was a chief quartermaster, assigned to the academy to teach basic seamanship to midshipmen. Later, as a newly commissioned mustang ensign, she told the story to Flip Wilson.

Wild Bill was a freshman, a plebe, and Riley was a senior, a first class midshipman. Riley caught Wild Bill coming over the compound wall after curfew. As punishment, Riley made Wild Bill kiss the balls on the statue of Bill the Goat on the academy grounds, and gave his classmates an hour to draw a crowd to watch Wild Bill do it.

Wild Bill fixed Riley's ass for that one.

He enlisted the aid of two of Riley's first class enemies, who got Riley really drunk at a bar in Annapolis and introduced him to Destiny Dupree, a really hot-looking drag club entertainer from Boston.

The next morning, the way Wild Bill told the story, Riley had lamented to his classmates, "There I was in this motel room, sucking this chick's cock, and it dawned on me."

Between the time of Riley's Date With Destiny and the Kosovo war, Wild Bill had only told this story a hundred times—two hundred, max. But then Meg heard it, and she told it to Flip Wilson, and after that, well … Suffice it to say that by the time of the Kosovo War, the story of Riley O'Really's Date With Destiny had really gotten around. Every time Riley heard someone say "there I was" or "it dawned on me," he assumed they were telling the Date with Destiny story.

Which wasn't a bad assumption on his part.

Hence, Riley's really deep hatred of Wild Bill.

Wild Bill was totally pleased that the Date With Destiny story was getting around the Kosovo theater of operations at the same time Warty Marty's cracks about The Spanish Armadillo and Sir Frances Flake were.

But then The Big Bridge Fuck Up happened, for which Wild Bill could be held accountable, and for which Riley O'Really really couldn't.

That knocked Wild Bill right off his horse.

You Rang?

Jack, Wattie, and Jerry Springer stood tall in Wild Bill's inner office. Jerry, nose and lip twitching overtime, didn't know Wattie's dirty little secret about the red phone.

Jack did.

"I bought a red telephone from Sears and put it on his desk," Wattie told Jack the day after they left Norfolk. "I had my guys hard wire it through the satellite to some number in the States nobody will ever answer. Hopefully."

Wild Bill looked like he'd picked the wrong war to stop sniffing glue. Buttons undone on his shirt, stars askew on his collar, his hair jutting in improbable angles. "We just bombed the wrong goddamn bridge, goddammit, but I can't get through on this goddamn phone to explain to President Pants about it."

Jerry Springer got his twitching nose and lip under control enough to say, "Shouldn't we tell Admiral O'Really about it first? He's our immediate superior in the chain of command."

"Fuck Riley," Wild Bill said. "He's a goddamn asshole, and a goddamn black shoe, and a goddamn pole smoker. So shut up, goddammit."

"Yes sir," Jerry stammered.

"And stop that goddamn lip twitch shit before I rip your goddamn face off your goddamn head and shove it up your goddamn ass."

"Yes, sir."

"Goddammit, didn't I just tell you to shut up?"

Jerry nodded feebly, and kept twitching.

Wild Bill paced in erratic circles. "I need to get through to the White House right goddamn now, goddammit, but all this thing does …" He shook a fist at the red phone on his desk. "All this thing does is ring off the goddamn hook at the other goddamn end. I can't even get a goddamn answering machine."

"Maybe there's nobody in," Wattie suggested.

Wild Bill hiccupped. "Nobody's in the goddamn White House in the middle of a goddamn war?"

"I wouldn't know, sir," Wattie said. "I'm not there."

"Of course you're not there, you're here, goddamit, and your goddamn phone doesn't work."

"I'm sure it's just a transient problem with the satellite," Wattie said. "These things happen. It's sure to come back online in a couple hours."

"I don't have a couple goddamn hours," Wild Bill howled. "My goddamn air wing just bombed the wrong goddamn bridge and I need to talk to the goddamn president right goddamn now."

"I don't know what I can do, Admiral. It's probably atmospherics."

"It's probably your broke-dick phone, that's what it's goddamn probably. Did you supervise the installation yourself?"

"I did, sir. Everything checked four-oh when we put it in."

"Well it's not four-goddamn-oh now is it?"

"Like I said, Admiral, I'm sure there's nothing wrong at our end."

"Then you try it, you're so goddamn sure there's nothing wrong with it."

Wattie glanced at Jack, who glanced back at him. Wattie picked up the handset, and hit the speed dial button. "It's ringing, Admiral. That's a good sign."

"No, it's not a goddamn good sign. It was ringing before, wasn't it?"

"I don't know, sir. I wasn't here when you say it was ringing before, but I'll take your word for it."

"Then why are you telling me the goddamn thing is ringing?"

"Because it is ringing, Admiral." Wattie held out the handset. "Don't take my word for it, sir. Listen for yourself."

Wild Bill pushed the handset aside. "Put the goddamn thing on the speaker."

"Put it on the speaker, sir?"

"Isn't that what I just said? Why does everybody repeat every goddamn thing I say around here?"

"Why does everyone repeat everything you say around here? I don't know, sir. I wasn't aware that everyone repeats everything you say around here, but I'll take your word for it."

Jack coughed.

Jerry Springer twitched.

Wild Bill threw his hands in the air. "Just put the goddamn call on the speaker."

"Whatever you say, sir," Wattie said, and he put the goddamn call on the speaker.

✮ ✮ ✮ ✮ ✮

In the wee hours of a summer morning on Rush Street in Chicago, Illinois, a wino shuffled past a ringing pay phone. He looked up and down the street for someone who might be expecting a phone call. He didn't see anybody like that, so he walked over to the phone and picked it up.

"Yeah?"

"This is Rear Admiral Hitchcock, calling from the Ionian Sea for the president."

The wino gave himself a second to absorb all that, and said, "This here's Field Marshall Rufus Johnson, and the president, he say he's in, but he don't want to talk with y'all."

Wild Bill's face melted down the front of his shirt. "Whoever the hell this is, quit jerking my goddamn chain and put me on with the goddamn president."

"Look it here, General, the president says get the fuck off his mother-fucking phone fore he flies out there his self and kicks your mother-fucking ass."

On Rush Street, the wino slammed the phone back on its hook.

On the *Fillmore*, Wild Bill glared at the red phone in astonishment as a dial tone blared from its speaker. He looked at Wattie. "What the hell was that shit?"

Wattie clasped his hands on his belt buckle and stared at his shoes. "Maybe some young White House staffers throwing a party?"

Wild Bill went wild-eyed, pulled the red phone from its wall jack, and threw it at Wattie's head.

The red phone missed Wattie's head by three feet, and missed Jack's head by two feet, and crashed, with a syrupy thwack, into Jerry Springer's quivering face. Jerry hit the carpet like a two-hundred-pound sack of potatoes. His face now immobile, his legs and arms began to twitch. Blood trickled from his mouth and nose.

"Should we call away a medical emergency?" Wattie asked.

"He's fine," Wild Bill said. "Leave him be."

Jerry moaned.

"I thought I told you to shut up," Wild Bill said.

The other phone on Wild Bill's desk rang, the black one. Wild Bill reflexively turned to Jerry Springer. "Aren't you going to get that?"

Jerry moaned again.

Wild Bill shook his head. "Fine. Whatever. I'll get it myself."

He picked up the black phone. "Admiral O'Really? Yes. Oh, really? That is good news. And General Kent says don't worry about The Big Bridge Fuck-up? And we're back on the master attack plan? Cruise missiles and carrier strikes? That's wonderful, Admiral. Thanks for the call."

Wild Bill hung up. He rubbed his hands together, and danced a little jig. "The air force just did us one big fuck-up better. Are you ready for this?"

Jack and Wattie nodded. Jerry Springer twitched.

"Our biggest bestest buddies in the United States Air Force just bombed the Chinese Embassy! Can you believe that? What do you think, they mistook the Chinese Embassy for a milk truck or something?"

Wild Bill danced, pranced, ranted around the room.

Wattie smiled. "Those air force guys are all right."

"You're goddamn right they're all right, the dip shits," Wild Bill said as he almost tripped over the prone form of Jerry Springer. Jerry was still bleeding from his nose and mouth.

Wild Bill nudged Jerry with his toe, and motioned to Jack and Wattie. "Get him a band-aid or something, huh?"

Shock Waves

Jack slept fewer than three hours a night, and that was usually interrupted by phone calls, usually from Captain Benning or XO Sovine, and usually about something that could have waited until morning.

Most of Jack's waking hours were taken up with pointless meetings: pre-planning meetings, planning meetings, post-planning meetings, and so on. The more the plan changed at the last minute, as it had the day of The Big Bridge Fuck-up, the more meetings got piled on in an attempt to plan for the unplanned changes to the plan. At least he got to sit at all those meetings. If he'd had to stand, his back couldn't have taken it. Jack was starting to feel like a very old man.

His workday got even longer when Captain Benning insisted on holding his own private meetings on the bridge so he could tell his department heads his plans on how they should plan at the other planning meetings. Benning quit going to all the other meetings after The Yalta Teleconference, the one where Jack shot his mouth off and all the generals' and admirals' fangs came out. Meg and Wattie determined that Benning had decided it was best for his career to stay out of the bomb pattern.

"He doesn't want to be perceived as taking sides," Wattie said over lunch in the Dirty Shirt.

"Even if he doesn't take sides," Meg said.

"If he's there," Wattie said, "he'll be seen."

"And it will look to somebody that he's on somebody else's side—"

"Either way," Wattie said, "he'll wind up with some admiral or general hating or fearing him or both—"

"Or all of the generals and admirals hating or fearing him or both—"

"Which would screw up his chances of making admiral," Wattie said.

"Unless," Meg said, "by some off-chance any or all of the generals and admirals respect or admire him for taking sides—"

"Which he hasn't really taken—"

"But he doesn't want to take that chance—"

"No," Wattie said. "That would be too much like hoping for an accident to happen."

So Benning banished himself to the bridge and his at-sea cabin, and made his department heads trudge up decks and levels of stairways you called ladders to brief him on the lies they planned to tell at all the other planning meetings.

☆ ☆ ☆ ☆ ☆

"Maybe he's concerned about your health," Meg told Jack on the heterosexual officers' smoking sponson as he kick-started his third Marlborough off his second one. "Wants to make sure you get enough exercise. Sorry I got you smoking again. You quit for what, fifteen years?"

"Nineteen," Jack said, inhaling nicotine like a heroin junkie stabbing a needle in his arm. "But who's counting?"

His trips to the smoking sponson were Jack's only escape, the only place on the ship where a phone wouldn't ring and be for him: in his office, in his stateroom, in the Dirty Shirt, in combat, in air operations, in the intelligence center.

Ring, ring.

"OPSO, it's for you."

"OPSO, we have an unknown surface contact."

"OPSO, we have an unknown air contact."

"OPSO, we have a last minute target change."

"OPSO, we have aircraft coming back with low fuel."

☆ ☆ ☆ ☆ ☆

"OPSO, it's the XO."

"Yes, XO."

"OPSO, I saw one of your enlisted females running around the ship with her sleeves rolled up. You know everybody has to keep their sleeves rolled down in a combat zone."

"I'll find her right away and tell her to roll her sleeves down, XO."

"And I found a black shoe mark on the blue tile in the admiral's blue tile area. Get it wiped up before the admiral sees it."

"I'll wipe it up myself, XO."

★　★　★　★　★

"OPSO, ah, what's going on with the war?"

"I'm not sure right this second, Captain. I'm just leaving to wipe up a black shoe mark in the blue tile area and roll down the sleeves on one of my enlisted females."

"Ah, get back to me ASAP, please. On the war and the sleeves and the shoe mark."

"In that order, sir?"

"Ah, no. Wipe up the shoe mark before the admiral sees it."

"Right away, sir."

"And this female with her sleeves rolled up. Is she, ah, pregnant?"

"Not as far as I know, Captain."

"Well get her sleeves rolled down before she gets that way, and before the admiral sees her."

"Aye, aye, Captain."

"And, ah, don't forget about the war."

"Thanks for reminding me, sir."

★　★　★　★　★

Jack sat in the OPS office at 0430, getting ready for the 0500 pre-pre-pre-planning meeting with Captain Benning on the bridge.

The phone rang.

"Jack?"

"How did you get this number, Betty?"

"Jack, what time is it there?"

"How did you get this number?"

"Rommel misses you, Jack."

"I miss him."

"I miss you too, Jack."

"Have you been drinking?"

"It doesn't have to be like this, Jack."

"I'm in the middle of a war here, Betty."

"When it's over, can we just start again?"

"I have to go."

"I have to talk to you, Jack."

"Have your lawyer call my lawyer."

"I can't live without you, Jack."

"I have to go, Betty."

"Don't you dare hang up on me! I'll call your captain. I'll call your admiral. I'll tell them you got drunk and beat me—"

Jack hung up and dialed Wattie's office. "Wattie, can your guys block incoming calls from my home number?"

"You getting calls from Betty?"

"Just got my first one. Like it to be my last."

"I'll get right on it, pal."

☆　☆　☆　☆　☆

Meg and Wattie knew Jack was going through a divorce, but he hadn't shared too many details. Meg and Wattie had their own war stories.

Wattie was a widower. "I already had my retirement papers in," he said one day at lunch. "Looked forward to spending time with the wife after decades at sea and bam, out of nowhere, she had a stroke and died. At least she didn't suffer. So I pulled my retirement papers and stayed at sea. Guess I'll stay at sea as long as they let me. What I'll do after that, I don't know."

Meg was divorced. Unlike Commander Grandma, Meg had been going to sea since she was a seaman quartermaster. When she took her commission after twenty-five years of enlisted service, she became the first female executive officer of a Navy salvage ship. It was during that tour, while home for a month, that her husband gave her gonorrhea, which turned complicated, and Meg developed cervical cancer. She'd had several surgeries, and was scheduled for another one when *Fillmore* returned from cruise.

"I tell you OPSO," she said, leaning against the rail on the smoking sponson, her cigarette smoke trailing off in the breeze. "I just get up every morning and say, 'what we got going today?' and I go out and do it."

☆ ☆ ☆ ☆ ☆

Groucho carried a thick stack of envelopes into the operations office and dumped them on Jack's desk. "Looks like you won the lottery at mail call, OPSO."

"Mail?" Jack said. "I forgot all about mail. Is this the first mail I've gotten since I've been aboard?"

"I think so, sir. Looks like the Fleet Post Office sent all your mail to the *Connie*, which routed it back to the Fleet Post Office, which finally figured out you hadn't been on the *Connie* in over a decade."

"Doesn't surprise me," Jack said. The Fleet Post Office was run by the Navy Supply Corps.

The first twelve letters were utility bills that hadn't been paid. The thirteenth letter was from one of Walter W. Cowling's associates, telling him Betty's lawyer had filed a complaint because the utility bills hadn't been paid.

The fourteenth letter, a thick one, contained the official temporary support agreement Walter W. Cowling or one of his associates had written and filed with the Virginia Beach Municipal Court. Jack had informally agreed to let Betty stay in the house while he was on cruise. Walter W. Cowling, that sadder-than-Kurt-Vonnegut-looking son of a bitch, had given Betty exclusive possession of all Jack's properties, including the house, the car, and the dog, and made Jack responsible for a $2,000 monthly support payment.

The fifteenth letter was from the Defense Finance Accounting Service. DFAS had received letters from Mrs. Hogan claiming that Commander Hogan had abandoned her, and was now sending all of Commander Hogan's pay and allowances directly to Mrs. Hogan.

The sixteenth letter was from Mom. She was sorry she hadn't been staying in touch, but her cancer was getting worse, and she was on a lot of medicine now. How soon would Jack be back from sea, and when could he and Betty come to Charleston for a visit?

☆　☆　☆　☆　☆

Jack stopped sleeping altogether. He lay on his throbbing back in his stateroom for a few hours each night, waiting for the phone to ring, and listening to sailors waxing and buffing the deck in the passageway outside his door, talking about all the fun things they planned to do when they got home.

Bitter End

Everyone in theater had become disgusted with high command's inability to come up with a coherent strategy when one day, without warning, the little war that wouldn't end, did. Military scholars still argue over why exactly Bad Guy decided to pack it in. Jack guessed that Bad Guy quit fighting because he'd killed as much of his ethnic population as he'd set out to in the first place.

Whatever the real reason for the coalition victory, everybody was perfectly willing to take credit for it. The Air Force took credit for achieving the first "pure air power victory" in the history of armed conflict. The Navy took credit for the first maritime victory ever won without a single naval engagement. The Army took credit for the greatest air and naval victory ever commanded by an Army general. The White House took credit for the greatest military victory achieved under a Democratic administration since Franklin Roosevelt's.

No good guys got killed in combat. Not all that many bad guys died either. In all, Jack reflected, Kosovo was a perfect little war to end the twentieth century with.

Warty Marty Gross went home and told congress that F. Lee Kent was a fucking lunatic and that Riley O'Really was a flake, and retired from active duty.

Riley O'Really retired too. Not because he wanted to, but because Fix Felon told him it was either that or face a court martial, because throughout the war, Riley had used Navy transport aircraft to send Mrs. O'Really on shopping sprees in Spain while he shagged his enlisted female secretary in Cannes, France.

F. Lee Kent retired when President Pants fired him because the Kosovo war had lasted longer than the two weeks Kent had promised it would last.

President Pants was impeached by the House of Representatives but not convicted by the Senate.

Kent, Gross, and O'Really took executive positions with foreign policy think tanks and made big money on the side as military analysts for the cable news networks.

F. Lee Kent, disappointed that the Kosovo War hadn't made him "The MacArthur of the Balkans," hinted at political aspirations.

President Pants, disappointed that he couldn't run for a third term, signed a multi-million dollar book deal.

☆　☆　☆　☆　☆

With Riley O'Really out of the way, Wild Bill wrangled a liberty call for the *Fillmore* in Cannes, France.

The first day at anchor, Jack finally slept.

The second day, Meg and Wattie loaned him some money, and the three of them went sightseeing. They saw Wild Bill walking down the Cote d'Azur with a French babe on his arm.

"That's our Bill," Wattie said. "A harlot in every port."

"I tell you though," Meg said, "the guy's slipping. That broad's almost old enough to be his wife."

The third day, Jack went to some God-awful Navy League function with some of the guys in the air wing. They took a bus to an outdoor restaurant in an outlying hill town and danced with a bunch of French widows. Jack got half looped so he could deal with having his crotch grabbed by old French broads. Then he got tired of having his crotch grabbed and went for a walk.

The town shut down at midnight, and Jack staggered up and down hills for an hour, trying to figure out how to find a cab that would take him to fleet landing. He didn't get back to his stateroom on *Fillmore* till five in the morning.

His phone rang at 0700. Jerry Springer informed him that Admiral Hitchcock required his presence in the flag spaces to begin pre-pre-planning of an air operation against a SAM site in Iraq.

Fillmore steamed to the Gulf at flank speed. The SAM site turned out to be another milk truck. But they bombed it anyway.

And Unto Dust

Jack walked across the flight deck, wearing a protective cranial helmet and a float coat over khakis that stuck to him in the Persian Gulf heat, and stepped aboard a turning UH-53 helicopter. The enlisted crewman pointed to a seat aft of the pilot and copilot. Jack put his gym bag between his feet and clipped the shoulder and lap belts into the single point fitting. The engines spooled up, and the "Desert Duck" lifted off.

Ten minutes later, the Duck slowed and began a visual approach to the small flight deck aft of the superstructure of the missile destroyer *Arleigh Burke*.

"You'll have company on your way to Bahrain, boss," Groucho had told him as he left the office. "Some machinist's mate on the *Burke* managed to kill himself last night. I guess he was working with a lathe, and it came apart, and part of it came through his head."

"Thanks for letting me know," Jack had said.

Back in the air, headed for Bahrain, Jack tried not to dwell on the body bag stowed behind him, but within minutes of leaving the *Burke* he was compiling a mental list of everyone he'd known who had died on active duty.

The first day of The Great Big Backfire Raid cruise, the exhaust from a turning jet blew a kid off the *Ranger's* flight deck. When *Ranger* pulled into the Philippines, divers working on the hull found pieces of the kid's cranial helmet wedged in one of the ship's propellers. Later that same cruise, six sailors died in a main engineering space fire, which had started when someone opened a fuel valve that should have stayed closed. At the end of that cruise, an A-7 pilot who had been one of Buzz and Jack's roommates in AOCS, turned right when he should have turned left, and smashed into the wall of Star Wars Canyon in Oman. There wasn't enough left of him to send home to his parents.

During the summer on the *Nixon*, when Jack had met Betty in Spain, four guys had been in the H-3 helicopter that disappeared over deep water. Four guys were in the S-3 Viking that shot off the catapult, went nose down, and flew to the bottom of the ocean.

And Carly. Who was so smart, the apple of her semi-mom's eye, certain to become the Madame Curie of the Navy, who never had a boyfriend, or ever knew who her real parents are, and who died in her sleep when a supertanker slammed into the side of her ship in the middle of the night, fewer than ten miles from the coast of Virginia.

Dozens more. And none of them had died in combat.

The Desert Duck went feet dry, circled over the military compound in Bahrain and set down on the helo pad. Jack unstrapped, gave his helmet and float coat to the enlisted crewman and got out. An ambulance waited on the taxiway. Two paramedics in blue coveralls wheeled a gurney to the helo, hauled the machinist's mate back to the ambulance and drove away. The helo spun up and lifted off, circled the compound and headed back toward the Gulf.

Jack unzipped his gym bag and rechecked its contents for the twentieth time. Three sets of underwear and socks, two folded sets of khakis, four books, the emergency leave papers that would get him free commercial air passage back to the states, and the American Red Cross Message stating that Betty had died in an automobile accident.

Jack zipped the bag shut and walked across the tarmac to the base operations building, where he hoped to get a ride to Bahrain International Airport.

Voyage Home

Back at the house. No sign of Rommel. Jack drove Betty's Subaru around the neighborhood and walked the beach looking for him, but no joy.

☆ ☆ ☆ ☆ ☆

The police report. Betty had been drinking at a bar at the oceanfront, according to witnesses. She'd taken the Trans Am up

I-264, crashed through the guardrail at the Independence Avenue exit, and piled into a concrete embankment. The nineteen-year-old gas tank had cracked, and the car burst into flames. By the time the cops got there, it was too late to do anything but put out the fire.

☆ ☆ ☆ ☆ ☆

Betty's personal effects. A pair of charred pumps. She must have taken them off, put them on the seat next to her, and they'd been thrown free of the car on impact.

Her engagement and wedding rings, warped from the heat of the fire. She'd picked them out herself, and had been so excited the whole week before they went to pick them up.

"Seven days," she'd said first thing in the morning.

"Four days."

"Two days."

"Zero days."

☆ ☆ ☆ ☆ ☆

His Betty, in a long steel drawer, looking like something somebody had stuck on a barbecue spit then walked away and gotten drunk and forgotten about.

☆ ☆ ☆ ☆ ☆

At home, calling Betty's mom.

"I've been trying to reach her," she said. "Is something wrong?"

☆ ☆ ☆ ☆ ☆

Having Betty's remains cremated. Jack couldn't let her mom see her the way she was.

☆ ☆ ☆ ☆ ☆

Standing in line at Norfolk International with a box under his arm that contained Betty's urn so a big plane with BUMFUCK AIRLINES written all over it could fly her home to her mom. Over at the luggage claim area, people greeted friends and relatives. Jack saw Betty, as she looked in her ski jacket, the day she'd flown in for Winterfest.

"Hey, sailor!"

☆ ☆ ☆ ☆ ☆

The doorbell. Jack's neighbor Dave from across the street. "I saw you were back in town. Look what I found on the beach two weeks ago."

Rommel, out of his mind, he was so happy to see Jack.

☆ ☆ ☆ ☆ ☆

Going down I-85 in Betty's Subaru, headed for Jack's sister Ann's place in Greenville, South Carolina. "You'll be happy there for a while, Rommel. It's in the country, you can run around all you want."

☆ ☆ ☆ ☆ ☆

His sister Ann, sitting at her kitchen table in a quilted bathrobe.

"Are you going to drive to Charleston to see Mom while you're back?"

Jack rubbed his eyes. "Tell you the truth, Ann, I don't think I can take that just now."

"Just as well," Ann said. "Michele's with her. Mom's so doped up now she probably wouldn't even recognize you."

☆ ☆ ☆ ☆ ☆

Back in Virginia Beach, Jack put the Subaru in the garage, locked the house, and took a cab to Norfolk International. He got on a big airplane with CHAPTER 11 BANKRUPTCY smeared all over it and flew to Germany. From there he made connections back to the Persian Gulf.

Welcome Back

Jack stepped off the COD and saw that part of *Fillmore*'s starboard catwalk was curled into the bomb assembly area outboard of the island, a mangle of rusted metal. He had to take the long way to his office.

★ ★ ★ ★ ★

Groucho looked up from his paperwork. "OPSO, Captain Benning said he wanted to see you as soon as you got back onboard."

"Thanks," Jack said. "I'll blow him off right away."

He went to his stateroom and dumped his gym bag on his sofa bed. His desk phone rang. The captain, no doubt: or XO Sovine telling him to call the captain. He'd better answer it.

"Commander Hogan?" A woman's voice, familiar from somewhere.

"Yes."

"*The* Commander Hogan? Protector of young homosexuals and other helpless creatures?"

Jack smiled. "Judy Davis? What prompts the JAG Fag Hag to call all the way out to the USS *Millard Fillmore?*"

"I'm not the JAG Fag Hag any more. I put in for sea duty. I'm the Flag JAG Hag now, working for Admiral Hitchcock."

"You're here on the ship?"

"I am, and I need to talk to you. My stateroom is just down the passageway from yours. Can I come and see you?"

"I just got back on board. Give me five minutes to unpack my bag."

"See you in five," she said.

★ ★ ★ ★ ★

Jack expected Judy Davis to be a pimply, chubby lesbo girl or the biggest, baddest bull dyke to ever drive a motorcycle out of Detroit

City.

Judy Davis was a creature, all right, but not the kind that crawls out of a black lagoon. Take The Tall Thai Girl and make her two inches taller, and lighter skinned, and cut her hair just below ear length, and you have Judy Davis. She could be a pro tennis player, or a fitness model. The kind of gal you might like to take out for a few beers, have fun hanging around with, kind of like being with your best buddy Buzz. Except you wouldn't want to fuck your best buddy Buzz, would you?

The unbidden image of a blackened hot dog encircled by a warped wedding band hits Jack between the eyes, erasing any notion he has of hitting the sack with this Judy Davis creature.

"Judy?" he said. "Come in. Take the desk chair."

He looked around for something to prop the door open. Men and women weren't supposed to be alone together in the same room on a Navy ship with the door shut.

"Kick it shut," Judy said. "We have shit to talk about nobody else needs to hear."

"Okay." Jack shut the door and took a seat on his sofa.

Judy opened her briefcase on the desk and sat in the desk chair facing Jack. "First of all, it's great to meet you. That was wonderful what you did for that sailor of yours. You're the only senior officer I ever dealt with who went to bat for one of those kids."

"I had a lot of help. I always wondered if you were serious about having to sleep with a bull-dyke admiral."

"Don't ask."

"Okay." That answered that.

Judy crossed her legs and folded her hands on her lap. "You look like I imagined you. Like a TV detective. Or the star of some World War II movie."

"You look like the star of that TV show JAG."

Judy smiled. "I went to high school with her. Funny how all this looks so romantic and heroic in books and movies and TV."

"Yeah," Jack said. "Funny how that works."

Judy cleared her throat. "I may as well get to the point. You know about the collision the *Fillmore* had last week with the supply ship *Pluto*?"

"No. I just got back from the States. I take it that's what curled up the starboard catwalk."

"It is. And you also need to know that one of *Fillmore*'s sailors was killed in the collision."

"Shit."

"And as I'm sure you already know whenever an accidental death occurs, the senior officer involved, Admiral Hitchcock in this case, has to convene a safety investigation and JAG investigation."

"Yeah, I learned all that stuff in safety school before I became a squadron skipper. The safety board's all privileged information that can't be used against anybody, and the JAG investigation's a witch hunt."

Judy looked away. "Admiral Hitchcock has directed the JAG board to look into dereliction of duty charges against you."

Jack's heart stopped. "I wasn't even here."

They were doing one of those things, Judy said. What did you call them? When they sent somebody from one ship to another in a chair hung from a rope or something.

A high line rig, Jack explained, sometimes known as a "high chair" drill.

Yes, one of those, Judy said. They were doing one of those and the ships collided and the sailor in the high chair fell into the sea and died.

The *Fillmore* hadn't done one of those high chair things in a long time, Judy said, according to all the records, but they had to do one in order to qualify to win the Battle Efficiency Award, but they should have practiced it first, and Jack, as the operations officer, should have scheduled the practice, but the records showed that he hadn't, and she was sorry, sorry, sorry, but she had to read Jack his Miranda rights.

When she got to the part where Jack had a right to an attorney, Jack asked her if she could represent him, and she said she wanted so much to defend him, and she was sorry, sorry, sorry, but she worked for Admiral Hitchcock, and defending Jack would be a conflict of interest.

"And I shouldn't tell you this," Judy said, "but what you should do is demand an attorney, and demand your right to remain silent until you can get one."

That way, she went on to explain, they couldn't do anything to Jack until the *Fillmore* got home, and he could find a lawyer, and maybe then the whole thing would have blown over and God and everybody would have forgotten about it.

Jack's heart kick-started itself back up. "Sounds like a plan to me," he said.

Judy closed her briefcase and got up. She walked toward the door and stopped. "I just remembered something else," she said. "I heard a story at BUPERS from a couple friends of yours. Aren't you the guy who won the Cold War in The Great Big Backfire Raid?"

Jack smirked. "Lots of guys won the Cold War."

"That's not how I hear it," Judy said. "And only one guy I know of saved the life of Seaman Emanuel Manriquez."

She went out and shut the door behind her.

Who's on First?

Jack went forward to the Dirty Shirt and got a glass of iced tea. It was between meals, and the wardroom was empty except for a couple of warrant officers having coffee and pie at a corner table. They saw Jack walk in and looked the other way. Jack guessed everybody knew about his situation by now, and wanted to stay far enough away that he couldn't cough on them, and give them whatever it was he had, so he took a table at the opposite corner.

Meg walked in, got herself a cup of coffee and a piece of blueberry pie, and sat with Jack. "You want to talk about Betty?"

"No."

"Okay. You want to talk about the other stuff?"

"The collision, and the kid who got killed?"

"Yeah, that."

"What happened?"

"Let me tell you."

★　★　★　★　★

After the mess of everybody but Wild Bill getting shit-canned after the Kosovo War, Fix Felon had told Wild Bill that the Navy would look like a bunch of losers if the carrier that fought it didn't win the Battle Efficiency Award. Twitch-faced Jerry Springer figured out that *Fillmore* had filled all the requirements to win the Battle E except to perform a high line drill.

Meg went to Captain Benning and Wild Bill and told him the ship hadn't done the necessary rehearsal to perform a high line drill, but Wild Bill said, "Just do it" and Captain Benning said, "Just do whatever makes Admiral Hitchcock happy."

Meg would have gone to Jack, but Jack was back in the States dealing with his Betty situation.

★　★　★　★　★

Fillmore pulled alongside the *Pluto*. Rigging the high chair line hadn't gone well, predictably so, as Meg's (First's) bosun mates were out of practice rigging it, not having done a rehearsal.

Wild Bill, watching from the flag bridge in the island (one level below the navigation bridge you also called a pilot house), lost patience and called Captain Benning and demanded to know why things were going so slow, goddammit. Benning, on station in the auxiliary conning station on the starboard wing of the pilothouse, picked up a second phone and called First to find out what the holdup was.

First, on station on the sponson on the first deck, also known as the hangar deck, explained that the rig was fouled, a line was tangled around a pulley you called a winch, but her bosuns were working hard as hell to unframmitz things.

"Let me know, first thing you're ready, First," Benning said over the second phone.

Over the first phone, in Benning's left ear, Wild Bill said, "How soon?"

"First says any second, Admiral," Benning said into the first phone.

"What did you say about a second admiral, Captain?" First said over the second phone.

"Nothing, First," Benning said.

"Are you talking to First?" Wild Bill said over the first phone.

"Just a second, Admiral," Benning said.

"Are you talking to the Admiral?" First said over the second phone.

"Just a second, First," Benning said.

"Goddammit," Wild Bill said. "First you tell me to wait a second, then you're talking to First."

"First is on the second phone, Admiral."

"Tell First to hold on a second and talk to me. I'm the goddamn admiral, goddammit."

"Yes, Admiral. Like I said, First says it will be any second now."

"The sailor's in the high chair, Captain," First said over the second phone.

"First says the sailor's in the high chair, Admiral," Benning said into the first phone.

"Send him across," Wild Bill said.

"Send him across, aye," Benning said.

"Send him across, aye," First said.

The high chair left the sponson and headed for the *Pluto*. First and her bosuns on the first deck and Wild Bill on the flag bridge and Captain Benning in auxiliary conn watched as the sailor swung over the sea turbulence between the two ships.

On the auxiliary conning station on the port side of the *Pluto*, Captain Plato, the *Pluto*'s captain, became concerned as the markers on the phone distance line between the two ships passed through 140 feet, then 120 feet, then 100 feet. At 90 feet, Captain Plato picked up his phone distance line phone and pushed the call button.

The phone distance line phone in *Fillmore*'s auxiliary conning station rang. As its name implied, the phone distance line both marked the distance between the ships and provided a phone connection between their captains. Benning dropped the second phone he'd been talking to First on and picked up the third phone. "Captain Benning."

"Captain Plato on the *Pluto*, Captain Benning. Are you looking at the phone distance line?"

"Who are you talking to now?" Wild Bill said on the first phone.

"Captain Plato on the *Pluto*," Benning said.

"What the hell does he want?" Wild Bill said.

"What the hell do you want?" Benning said over the third phone to Captain Plato.

"Benning, you dip shit," Captain Plato said. "Look down at the phone distance line."

Benning looked down as the deck edge marker on the phone distance line passed sixty feet, and dropped all his phones. "Left three degrees rudder," he screamed.

"Left three degrees rudder, aye," the helmsman said, and turned the rudders left.

The Fillmore's aft quarter slammed into *Pluto's* stern.

"What the hell was that?" Wild Bill screamed into the first phone that Benning was no longer listening to.

Bosun mates on both vessels pulled quick release lines to disconnect the rigs and scrambled to safety.

The sailor in the high chair fell.

Wild Bill looked aft from the flag bridge just in time to see the expression on the kid's face as he hit the water.

"Oh, no," Wild Bill whispered.

The ships' hulls slammed together, and curled up *Fillmore's* starboard catwalk.

★ ★ ★ ★ ★

Meg wiped pie filling off her fingers. "So they rush a bunch of reservists out here to convene a safety board and a JAG board. I tell the head of the safety board that I told Wild Bill and Captain Benning we hadn't done the rehearsal we were supposed to do. Then the head of the JAG board hears that from the head of the safety board."

"That's not supposed to happen," Jack said. "Safety board stuff is supposed to be privileged."

"It is," Meg said, "unless the head of the safety board is Flip Wilson."

"Ah," Jack said.

★ ★ ★ ★ ★

Wild Bill reads reports from both boards, and orders them to take out Meg's remarks. Then Wild Bill has his staff write an executive summary of both reports in which he blames Jack, Meg, and Benning for the collision, and sends it to Vice Admiral Zach Taylor at Naval Air Force Atlantic for further review.

★ ★ ★ ★ ★

"He blamed me for not doing the rehearsal," Meg said, "and you for not scheduling it, and Captain Benning for being the captain."

"Who was the conning officer?" Jack said.

"XO Sovine."

"And he's not in the wringer over this?"

Meg rolled her eyes. "He got off. on a couple of special circumstances."

"Must be some mighty special circumstances, if the conning officer got off scot-free."

"Yeah. Special. Benning fell on the grenade and said that since he actually gave the order to come left, Sovine was no longer the conning officer, which is true, strictly speaking."

"But Sovine should have seen the distance closing before that. What's the other circumstance?"

"Like I told you," Meg said, "Red Sovine is one of them."

"How them is he?"

"He's so them," Meg said, "that he's the father of Fix Felon's three grandchildren."

Jack swirled the ice in his tea glass with his finger. "Fix Felon. Many's the time I've watched the trail of power lead to him. I always wondered what exactly his fix was."

"You didn't know?" Meg said. "He's mafia."

"The whole Navy's a mafia," Jack said.

"I don't mean the Navy mafia. I mean the mafia mafia."

"As in the goombah mafia?"

"Bada-bing," Meg said. "Fix's great grandpa came off the boat from Sicily. Ran booze with Joe Kennedy during prohibition. The Felon family's legit now, of course. Went into oil. *Oil* oil, I mean, petroleum, not olive oil."

The phone on the wall of the Dirty Shirt rang, and a teenage mess crank answered. "OPSO, it's for you. The captain."

"Tell him I just left," Jack said and got up.

"I already had my talk with him," Meg said. "Or I should say, he had his talk with me. I didn't do much talking. What a house of pain."

"Might as well get this over with," Jack said.

"Don't have fun."

"Don't worry. I won't."

House of Pain

Benning was spending more time in his in-port cabin now that the combat and all the meetings were over. The one-way interview lasted an unbearable hour. Benning's usual "ahs," the constant fiddling with his grip exerciser, glances at science programs run by the ship's TV station at his request.

And something else: Benning had a new favorite word, which he used at every opportunity.

"Assumably," according to Benning, Rear Admiral Hitchcock wanted the investigation kicked up to Vice Admiral Taylor at AIRLANT so it would get an impartial review. Assumably, Admiral Taylor would arrive at a fair judgment. Assumably, Jack had little to worry about, because he hadn't been present at the time of the collision.

No mention of Jack's wife, or why he'd gone on emergency leave. Assumably, Benning realized Jack didn't want to talk about any of that. Maybe Benning hadn't remembered why Jack had gone home.

A new program came on the ship's TV station. "Oh," Benning said. "The mission footage from the Kosovo War. The public affairs officer put together a collage of the air wing's bombing tapes."

An oil refinery blew up. A peasant was halfway across a bridge on his bicycle when the bridge blew up. A tank exploded, and a burning soldier climbed out of it.

"We're making copies of this for the Wives Club," Benning said, "so they can show it at the family picnic when we get home."

Jack felt ill. He got up and walked out. Assumably, Benning didn't notice him leave.

★   ★   ★   ★   ★

Back in the OPS office, Jack attacked the mile-high pile of trash that had accumulated in his inbox. Jack signed off on the whole pile without reading any of it. How times had changed. It had all seemed so important, during the Cold War, when Jack was young, and they'd launched off the *Ranger* in the middle of the night to play war with the Evil Empire.

★   ★   ★   ★   ★

Everyone on the *Ranger* could hear the 1MC announcement: "NOW LAUNCH THE ALERT E-2!"

Lieutenant (junior grade) Hogan had jumped from his ready room chair, strapped on his flight gear, and run to the intelligence center. The Backfires were turning up their engines in Kamchatka, the intelligence weenies told him. The admiral walked in and patted him on the back. "Go get 'em, tiger."

Up on the flight deck, enlisted guys with flashlights guided him to the turning Hawkeye and gave him a "carry on, sir," salute. Jack climbed through the main entrance hatch, walked aft to the crew compartment, strapped into his seat, plugged into the intercom, and told the pilots up forward in the cockpit, "I'm here. Let's go."

The pilots taxied to the number one catapult, took tension, and launched into the black nothing to go toe to toe with the Russkies over the Northern Pacific.

On station, three hundred miles down the threat axis, west of *Ranger*, Jack sat in the center seat, Groucho and Stick Boy, a pair of ensigns, sitting on either side of him. The admiral had insisted on using junior crews to execute Jack's plan, wanting to make a point to Admiral Gorschkov that "our greenest guys can beat your best guys."

Jack and Groucho and Stick Boy waited. And waited. Maybe the Backfires weren't coming; maybe the intelligence weenies had been wrong again.

Then a flashing M on the edge of Jack's scope. DOWNBEAT, the Backfires' search radar. Another one. And another, and another. Twenty, thirty of them. The whole regiment. The lines of bearing triangulated six hundred miles from the carrier.

Jack stomped on his microphone switch. "TANGO has Downbeat in Two Seven Juliet. Nickel Five, you're hot."

Buzz, in the back of Nickel Five on the outer fighter station: "Nickel Five is hot for Two Seven Juliet."

Jack: "ALPHA WHISKEY, this is TANGO, first contact, deck sweep, deck sweep."

From the missile cruiser *Bainbridge*: "ALPHA WHISKEY copies, break, ALPHA ROMEO, deck sweep!"

From the *Ranger*: "Deck sweep, wilco, ALPHA ROMEO out."

The whole air wing launched. Buzz, in Nickel Five, was the first Tomcat to light the Backfires up with his missile guidance radar. "Exercise Fox Three," he called over the radio, and the first pretend AIM-54 Phoenix missile didn't really roar off the belly of his jet. Before you knew it, there weren't more Fox Threes in the air than you couldn't shake a stick at, and none of them climbed to 80,000 feet, nor did they descend down to thirty thousand feet, where the Backfires were. None of the Backfires turned into fireballs, and none of the three hundred aircrew manning them scattered in wet, confetti-sized pieces from one end of the Northern Pacific to the other.

Buzz and the rest of the air wing flew through the Backfire formation, popping flares, telling them don't ever try this for real.

Then the medal and the promotion to lieutenant on the fo'c's'le, and the rest of a twenty-year career in the United States Navy.

★ ★ ★ ★ ★

Now, Commander Jack Hogan, United States Navy, sat at a desk, signed paperwork not important enough to read, and played court intrigues with his superiors. He'd done more to serve his country as a little boy, playing soldier in his G.I. Joe uniform, his dad's lieutenant's bars from Korea pinned on his collar.

Jack checked Betty's Omega. Just after midnight. He opened a blank Word document and typed up his request to retire. He printed it, signed it, stuck it in a blue routing folder and slapped it on Groucho's desk. He stared at the folder a few seconds, wondering if he should pick it up and stick it in a drawer and sleep on it a couple nights. After all, he might come through this JAG investigation all right, and still make captain.

The computer called up his screen saver. ANYTHING WOULD BE AN IMPROVEMENT rolled across the monitor.

He rubbed his back, and reached for his forty-pound dictionary on the shelf above his desk and looked up "assumably." Son of a bitch. There was such a word. Not shown as a separate listing. Under "assume." Down at the bottom, under the ninth definition, after "assumable" and before "assumer."

Right where Benning must have found it in his forty-pound dictionary.

I'm getting as crazy as Benning is, Jack thought. As crazy as the rest of them.

He left the blue folder with his retirement letter on Groucho's desk and locked the office door behind him.

Jiggedy Jig

Fillmore pulled into Norfolk. Jack caught a ride home with Groucho, took Betty's Subaru out of the garage, and made it to

Ann's place in Greenville in eight hours. Rommel, in the yard, almost knocked Jack over, he was so happy to see his daddy again.

"Mom's still hanging on," Ann said inside. "I don't know how. I think she's been waiting to see you one last time."

★　★　★　★　★

Four hours later, in Charleston, Jack walked into Mom's hospital room. Mom was asleep, a needle stuck in her arm. Hairless, her skin the color of a Navy ship, she couldn't have weighed seventy pounds. This can't be my mother, Jack thought.

Jack sat in a plastic chair next to her bed for a half hour, and was about to leave when her eyes opened.

"Is that you, Bob?"

Bob was Jack's dad.

"Yes, it's me, Sue. How are you feeling?"

★　★　★　★　★

Back in Greenville, Ann said, "Do you think she'll last much longer?"

Jack shook his head. "I hope not."

★　★　★　★　★

Home in Virginia Beach, Jack and Rommel walked through the house. Jack hadn't noticed what a wreck the place was when he'd come home to take care of Betty. It reeked from Rommel shit in the carpet. The kitchen was a disaster. Litter covered the stairs leading to the third floor. The master bedroom was a dump. The picture window was so filthy you couldn't see the Chesapeake Bay through it.

Rommel jumped on the bed and sniffed at the jumble of unmade sheets and blankets.

"What are you doing, boy?" Jack tossed the bedclothes on a chair, the seventh chair from his marriage to Liz.

Under them was a perfumed envelope from Betty's lavender stationery. On the front of it, in her handwriting, was the single word "Jack." He put the envelope in a drawer of the vanity in the master bathroom.

Jack and Rommel inspected the rest of the place. Leaky roof. Dishwasher busted. Refrigerator busted. Stove busted. Hot water heater busted. The floors needed replacing; the smell of dog crap would never come out of the carpet.

Jack sat at the dining room table and made a list of needed repairs. Rommel sat at his feet. "Looks like we got us one broke-dick house here, boy."

Rommel wagged his tail, wanting Jack to rub his ears, which was all he considered important just then.

✯ ✯ ✯ ✯ ✯

Fillmore went into the shipyard in Portsmouth for a scheduled overhaul. Jack went to work a few hours every day, and spent the rest of his time working on the house. He hadn't swung a hammer in twenty years, but he got the hang of things eventually. His back complained at first about all the manual labor, but in time, it got stronger. XO Sovine made the supply officer give Jack a cell phone, in case some operational emergency came up while the ship was in dry dock. Jack gave it to Rommel to use as a chew toy.

Nothing so far had come of the collision investigation, and Captain Benning still seemed optimistic about his chances of making admiral.

"Stranger things have happened," Meg said.

"And stranger men have made admiral," Wattie added.

✯ ✯ ✯ ✯ ✯

Jack came home from the ship one day to find a message on his answering machine from his sister Michelle. Mom had died.

Jack hadn't expected Mom's funeral to hit him so hard. He thought he'd already written her off, locked her in a compartment next to the compartments where he'd locked everything else away.

He was okay when he got up to speak, but when they wheeled Mom down the aisle, and the church organ boomed, the Mom compartment buckled, and Ann and Michelle had to support him as he walked out of the cathedral.

☆　☆　☆　☆　☆

He got back to the *Fillmore* on a Thursday morning, and went to the XO's office to check in. Red Sovine looking sheepish, maybe feeling guilty, said, "OPSO, you need to be at the AIRLANT building at 0800 tomorrow morning. Mast with Admiral Taylor, you, First, and the captain. Dress blues."

☆　☆　☆　☆　☆

Jack was watching Thursday Night Football with Rommel and drinking a beer when Judy Davis called.

"I can help you tomorrow at Admiral Taylor's if you want," she said. "I'm not on Wild Bill's staff anymore. They fired me after I nailed Father Mick for fooling around with his altar boys."

"Of course they fired you," Jack said, "for something like that."

"You know what's going on with all this nonsense tomorrow morning? Why it's still an issue after all this time?"

"I give up."

"Senator what's her name. From Tailhook."

"What about her?"

"Turns out the kid in the high chair was her nephew," Judy said.

Jack dropped his beer on his toe. "Ouch." Rommel ran over and licked the spilled beer up off the floor.

"Are you okay, Jack?"

"I will be. So what's the rest of the story?"

"From what I hear, Senator Tailhook told Fix Felon she'd block funding for some new aircraft if he didn't court martial somebody over her nephew's death. Felon calmed her down and got her to agree with you and Meg and Benning going to mast with Vice Admiral Taylor."

"Nice of Fix to look out for us."

"You're a lot better off at mast than at a court martial," Judy said. "At mast, Taylor can't convict you of a felony—negligent homicide or something like that. He can just give you an administrative punishment. And mast will be quieter. Nothing in the papers or on the cable news channels."

"I'm sure Fix took that into consideration," Jack said, and walked to the refrigerator for another beer.

"I don't know how much good I can do you if I'm there," Judy said. "Rules of evidence don't apply at mast, and a lawyer can't really do much for you."

"No," Jack said. "Showing up with counsel would likely just piss Zach Taylor off."

"Probably," Judy said. "But as your semi-lawyer, I advise you to say nothing. Whatever happens, just nod, give him a smile job, and walk away."

"Roger that," Jack said.

They Were Expendable

Jack was still buzzed from all the Thursday Night Football beer when he walked into Vice Admiral Taylor's waiting room in the Naval Air Force Atlantic building at O800 sharp. Meg was already there, sitting at a table. "Welcome to death row," she said. "Captain Benning's already in with Admiral Taylor. Grab a chair."

Jack sat across from her. "You know about the dope deal Fix Felon cut with Senator Tailhook?"

"Your buddy Judy called me and told me about it."

"What I can't figure out is why now?"

"I think Fearless Fix was waiting for the planets to align," Meg said. "Your retirement approval came through while you were at your mom's funeral, and the admiral's list came out and Benning's name wasn't on it, so he's dead in the water. Me, hell, I been around so long, they'll never promote me again, and I can retire with thirty-five years in. So the three of us are expendable. We take a slap on the wrist from Admiral Taylor, Senator Tailhook is happy, and Red Sovine and the rest of Fix Felon's universe go on to greater things."

Captain Benning emerged from Vice Admiral Taylor's inner office, walked past Jack and Meg like he didn't see them there, and disappeared out the hallway you called a passageway. A matinee idol–looking commander JAG officer stuck his head out the inner office door you didn't call a hatch. "Commander Hogan? Could you come with me, please?"

☆　☆　☆　☆　☆

Vice Admiral Zach Taylor, as if time had stood still, looking as he had the day *Connie* got underway for NORPAC. He had to be dying his hair now. Maybe got a Botox job too. He sat ramrod straight at the far end of a long table covered with a green cloth.

Ah, that's why they use a long table, Jack thought, sitting at the opposite end of it. So you can't reach across it and strangle the son of a bitch at the other end.

Taylor looked up, his eyes fixed on Jack's left ear. Maybe he was trying to make the JAG, who was standing off to the side, think he was looking Jack in the eyes. Jack thought Zach's eyes looked the way they had in the middle of The Rocky Horror Recovery, fixed on something a thousand yards away.

Zach Taylor, his career stalled out in a three-star billet thanks to having pissed Fix Felon off more than a decade ago, nodded at the collision investigation report by his elbow. It was six hundred pages thick. Zach had read the report thoroughly, several times over, he told Jack.

Yeah, right, Jack thought.

In Zach Taylor's estimation, Jack, as the *Fillmore's* operations officer, had been derelict in his duties for not scheduling the rehearsal of the operation, and for not planning the operation, and for not being present on his ship at the time of the operation, and was singularly responsible for the death of a sailor in the United States Navy.

Zach Taylor, looking as he had the day he'd gone off his rocker and risked collision with *Mars* in the fog, said that he felt compelled to issue Jack a punitive letter of reprimand, and to relieve him of his duties as operations officer of the United States Ship *Millard Fillmore*.

Zach Taylor now, as if a magic spell had worn off, looking like a shrunken old man in the dress blue uniform of a vice admiral in the United States Navy, looking as if he knew full well that this, one of the last official acts of his career, was nothing more than doing a piece of his old enemy Fix Felon's dirty work, told Jack that as per his request, he would be allowed to retire as a full commander, effective immediately, and that he was dismissed.

Jack nodded, gave Zach Taylor a smile job, and left.

☆ ☆ ☆ ☆ ☆

Meg got up. "Looks like I'm next."

"I'll wait for you," Jack said.

Jack sat at the waiting room table, and looked at the service dress blue uniform he'd just been told he was no longer fit to wear. The three stripes and star of a commander of the unrestricted line on the sleeve cuffs. The space where the fourth stripe of a Navy captain might have gone, if things had gone differently.

The ribbons above his left pocket. The one for the Navy

Commendation Medal from The Great Big Backfire Raid. The Meritorious Service Medal the gator had gotten him for NORPAC. The Air Medal Deuce Macintosh had pinned on him after Southern Watch. The Legion of Merit Average Joe had wrangled for him for telling the truth about his broke-dick airplanes.

His gold NFO wings above the ribbons, his gold SWO pin below them.

The first time Betty had seen him in a dress uniform—at their wedding—she'd said, "Nice costume. What's all this business on your chest?"

Mom, at the wedding chapel in Charleston, gave up trying to figure out what it all meant, saying, "Your dad would be so proud."

☆　☆　☆　☆　☆

Meg came out from Zach Taylor's office. "I tell you what, I'm going home and stick a tampon up my ass to stop the bleeding."

When Jack got home, Rommel took him for a long walk.

Falling Action

It was cold in Virginia Beach that winter. Not Newport cold, but cold enough.

Jack seldom left the house. He didn't have a job to go to and was in no hurry to find one. He had his retirement, and he'd inherited more from Mom than he'd expected to. If he kept his lifestyle simple, he'd never have to work for anyone else again.

All that fraudulent debt Betty had run up was still out there. Judy Davis, doing some pro bono work to help him out, had told him the credit card companies could never legally force him to pay it, but his credit rating would probably be wrecked for years to come, and there wasn't much he could do about that. Bill collectors called the house every day, which Jack used as an excuse to stop answering the phone.

He spent a lot of time in bed, down in the den. He slept until bad dreams woke him up, then he lay there for hours, trying to go back to sleep. He'd get thirsty, finally, and get up for a glass of water. Rommel would insist on playing, and Jack took him out in the yard until they both got cold, then they came back in. They sat on the couch and watched TV or listened to the stereo until noon, when it was okay for Jack to start drinking.

Jack didn't eat much. Soup, crackers, cereal. When he wanted a "real" meal, he ordered out for pizza or Chinese.

Lying in bed with his arms crossed over his chest—a habit he'd developed from all his years at sea, counting on his elbows to keep him from being pitched out of his rack—Jack could feel his arms and shoulders shrinking from lack of exercise. That made him think of his Dad, who had shrunk so small from his cancer.

Dad.

Dad taking him to his first baseball game in Saint Louis, taking him to the men's room.

"Hurry up, Jackie. Stan Musial's coming to bat this inning."

"Okay, Daddy. I'll pee real fast."

In the hospital, carrying Dad from his bed to his bathroom so he could pee like a man, and not in a bedpan like a baby.

Dad taking him out to the back yard to teach him how to play football, showing him how to get in a three-point stance, and how to block and tackle. Miltie wanting to play too, jumping between them, knocking them both down. Jack and Dad rolling around in the grass and laughing about it.

Dad sitting in the vet's office, in a plastic chair too small for him, holding Miltie's head up so she could breathe. Dad Crying.

In his stateroom on the *Connie*, thinking how proud of him Dad would have been, after he saved everybody's bacon in The Rocky Horror Recovery.

What would Dad think of him now, lying in bed, drunk, middle aged, bloated, and defeated?

All that time in bed started aggravating Jack's long-suffering back. He'd hurt it during his first squadron tour in San Diego. He had an apartment in Ocean Beach, and every day after work he ran three miles and body surfed for an hour.

The second summer he lived there, an earthquake off Hawaii kicked up the wildest surf off Southern California anyone had seen in decades. The local TV and radio stations warned that surfing was extremely unsafe. Of course, they were talking about board surfing. Body surfing in these conditions was pure insanity.

So Jack had to try it.

The third wave he jumped into was a monster. He rolled to the top of it, kicked his fins, and began gliding down the monster's face.

The monster broke over him and knocked him into a tumble. His arms and legs flailed. The monster collapsed and drove him under the surface. Something in his lower back popped, and his legs went numb. He cried out, pushing out what little air was left in his lungs. Tons of water fell from the dying wave, pushing Jack toward the bottom.

He had no idea how deep he was, or which way was up. The pressure made his ears ring, and the ringing turned into a roar, like a chord played on a cathedral pipe organ. He saw a light in the distance. The light grew brighter.

He opened his eyes. He was on the surface.

He could move his legs, and kicked feebly. His knees struck sand. He crawled on all fours, then stood, then took off his fins, and walked to the shore. He found his T-shirt and towel and jogging shoes where he'd left them. He put them on and walked to his apartment, and took a hot shower, and went to bed.

Jack saw a chiropractor for a year after that, but never mentioned his back problem to a Navy flight surgeon. A Navy flight surgeon might have taken one look at his back and shit-canned his flying career right there on the spot.

☆ ☆ ☆ ☆ ☆

His back ached like hell when he woke up. Rommel stood over him on the bed, licking his face, wanting to go out to pee.

Jack looked around the bed, at all the beer cans and pizza boxes and Chinese food cartons he'd let accumulate on the floor.

"Fuck this," he said.

He dressed and took Rommel outside, and then he started cleaning the house.

Anchors

By spring, Jack had repainted the inside and outside of the house and replaced all the carpet with laminate flooring that looked like wood, and that Rommel could shit on without hurting it.

At Easter, he got a card from Meg Ryan. She and Wattie had gotten married. Wattie had retired, and they'd moved to Key West, where they ran a marina and a computer café. Jack wondered what kind of computer café would go over in Key West, and decided it must be the kind that served alcohol.

By late July, Jack had finished all the major home repairs except for replacing the bathroom doors.

Rommel had a typical dog's love of porcelain-cooled water. When Jack had come home from the Gulf to look after Betty's remains, he found Rommel sized holes in the bathroom doors on all three floors. Rommel must have gone into the bathrooms while Betty was out, and slurp, slurp, slurped, and wagged his big otter tail, he was so happy, and slammed the door shut with it. He'd probably gone to sleep, waiting for Betty to come home and find him trapped, then panicked when Betty hadn't come home from wherever she'd gone to, and clawed and chewed himself out of his self-created prisons.

On a Saturday afternoon in August, Jack was measuring the door on the half-bath off the living room when the phone rang. Expecting a bill collector, Jack was delighted to hear instead:

"Jack. It's Buzz."

"You piece of shit," Jack said. "How have you been?"

"I've been well."

Buzz had just finished up a successful tour as CAG on the *Kitty Hawk*, a west coast carrier, and had been selected for his first star. He was up in D.C. for some military/industrial complex love-in put on by the Naval Institute, and was headed down to Norfolk so Vice Admiral Taylor could officially promote him on Monday morning.

"Zach insisted," Buzz said, "what with having been my skipper on the *Connie*, and commander of the *King* battle group when we did Southern Watch. Wants to pass his first stars on to me. Tradition, and all that."

"Sure," Jack said.

"I'm driving down tomorrow. Thought I'd stop by your place, drink some beer, shoot some shit. If that's okay."

"Why don't you plan on spending the night?"

"I will. Be there about four in the afternoon."

Jack spent Sunday morning straightening up the house. No time to get the bathroom doors fixed, but Buzz would understand. At 1600 on the dot, a maroon Volvo pulled into the driveway, and the doorbell rang.

Jack stuck his head out the kitchen window. "The door's unlocked. Get in here before the beer turns stale."

Buzz walked up the stairs from the foyer to the living room, and saw the hole in the bathroom door. "Is this crapper usable? I been holding a loaf since Richmond, and I need to pinch it off."

"It's perfectly functional," Jack said. "But my dog's around here somewhere. Don't be surprised if you get a four-legged audience."

"Won't bother me," Buzz said. "My dip-shit kids used to walk in on me all the time, hit me up for money while I had my pants down."

Inside the bathroom, Buzz said, "Hand me a beer through the hole in the door, huh?"

Jack stuck a beer through the hole. Buzz was already on the stool with his pants around his ankles. "Don't even think about looking at my dick, homo."

Fucking Buzz: same guy, different color haircut. Same length but grayer than it used to be. Jack got himself a beer and sat at the table with the Sunday paper.

Rommel, who'd been napping down in the den, padded upstairs, skulked over to the bathroom, and stuck his head through the hole in the door.

"Nice to meet you, pal," Buzz said. "Hope you enjoy the show."

Rommel wagged his tail and crawled through the hole.

"Hey, asshole, I'm taking a shit. Do you mind? Get your nose off my balls and get the fuck out of here the same way you came in."

Rommel wriggled back out the hole in the door, and plopped on the floor next to Jack and pouted.

"It's not you, Rommel. He's like that with everybody."

Buzz flushed and came out of the bathroom. "Much better. Now, let's take a look at this dog of yours."

Buzz and Rommel rolled around and wrestled on the laminate floor. "Great dog," Buzz said. "Can I marry him?"

"How would I explain that to Jenny? She'd never forgive me."

"She never forgives anybody," Buzz said. "For anything."

Jack let that one go.

Buzz got two more beers from the fridge, and he and Jack sat around the table catching up on old shipmates. Fix Felon was chairman of the Joint Chiefs of Staff now. Deuce Macintosh had picked up his fourth star, and was on his way to command of Pacific Fleet. Flip Wilson made one-star admiral in the reserves, transferred back to the regular Navy, and was now Chief of Naval Information. Gary Constantine had risen to executive vice president of Northrup

Grumman Corporation. "I ran into him at the shit-bags-of-industry conference I was just at in D.C.," Buzz said.

"Did he ever lose that waterbed of his?"

"Nope. Don't think he ever got laid, either. He did get married, though."

"Good for him," Jack said. "Looks like you're still hitting the gym, Buzz."

"As best I can these days," Buzz said, flexing his arms. "I've put on a few beers, though."

"Haven't we all?"

★ ★ ★ ★ ★

They took Buzz's Volvo to an Italian joint a mile down the road in Chick's Beach, one known for its fine food and fine looking waitresses.

"Will you look at that?" Buzz said as their waitress leaned over to take an order at another table. "That girl has tits all over her chest."

Jack pointed his chin in the direction of the receptionist, a body builder. "She's a cutie, huh?"

Buzz grinned. "She's too young for you."

"They're all too young for me."

"What you need," Buzz said, showing signs of feeling the second bottle of wine, "is somebody like Betty except not all fucked up like Betty."

Or dead like Betty, Jack thought. Buzz, always the sensitive one.

Buzz proposed ordering another bottle of wine. Jack said he had plenty at the house. They might as well go back before driving became an issue. The last thing Buzz needed was a drunk driving bust the night before he became an admiral.

★ ★ ★ ★ ★

Buzz, on the couch, starting to hiccup. "What the hell, you got another bottle? Let's open it."

Buzz was a big strong boy. His appointment with Admiral Taylor wasn't until eleven the next morning. A pot of coffee and some breakfast, he'd be bright eyed and bushy tailed by then. Jack opened the last bottle of merlot, poured for Buzz, and got himself a glass of iced tea. Jack sat on the love seat next to Rommel, who was asleep. "So you pin your star on in the morning and then what?"

Buzz spilled a glop of merlot on his golf shirt, but didn't notice. "Hang out a couple weeks at BUPERS, wait to get assigned a carrier group. I'm hoping for the *Fillmore*."

"Out here on the east coast? You don't want to go back to San Diego? Be with Jenny and the kids?"

"Fuck that," Buzz said. "I just spent two years with Jenny and the kids." He emptied his glass and set it on the coffee table.

"More?" Jack said.

"No. I'm drunk just enough now. Drunk just perfect." Buzz shifted himself, and laid his head on the armrest. "Mind if I stretch out here?"

"Dog lies on it. No reason you shouldn't."

"Thanks for the backhand," Buzz said, and closed his eyes.

Jack checked Betty's Omega. Quarter past midnight. Jack reached to cork the bottle, thinking Buzz was asleep, but Buzz started talking again.

"I hate my kids and the bitch I'm married to, and they hate me worse."

"Yeah?" Jack said.

"The last two years back in San Diego, while I was CAG on the *Kitty Hawk*, were pure, undiluted hell. My kids won't even talk to me. And they're totally fucked up. All four of them are in some kind of therapy program for one thing and another. Jenny sees a shrink. I had to go with her once a week for marriage counseling when I was home. Plus, I got drug along to Mass every Sunday. Christ. What a house of pain that was."

Jack scratched Rommel's ear. Outside the living room window, a cloud cover rolled over the Chesapeake Bay, obscuring the moon. The living room smelled like two grown men had been drinking heavily in it. It was silent. Even the crickets had gone to sleep.

"Here's how bad it was," Buzz said. "When I was home, I went to bed every night bombed out of my skull. That's how much I hated being around her. If she'd known how much I was drinking, she would have bitched at me more, so I hid bottles all over the house and snuck snorts all day."

Buzz didn't need a lecture, but Jack had to say something.

"How much longer can you go on like this?"

Buzz stretched. "I'll be okay, as long as I stay out here, away from her. Them. Knew what I was doing when I married a senator's niece, and then giving her all those kids to keep her happy. Huh. Keep her happy. I knew good and well that wouldn't work, but I went along with it. Totally fuck my career if I divorced her now. And my career's all I have. If I work things right, I'll never have to live with her again."

"Sorry."

"What's to be sorry about?" Buzz said. "I'm an admiral, I'll have my own battle group. I'm a total success. And, hey, I'm in a growth industry. Now that Big Brother and the Holding Company are in power, we'll have a real war finally. They'll have us invading Mars if they find oil on it. I wouldn't want to miss out on any of that."

"Invading Mars, huh?" Jack said. "What are they going to call that one? 'The War on Intergalactic Evil?' "

Buzz belched. "Sounds like a good name to me. Mind if I steal that one from you? I'll suggest it to the Joint Chiefs of Staff when I get back up to Washington."

"Go ahead," Jack said, and pinched the bridge of his nose.

The neighborhood tomcat jumped on the back deck and peered in the window to see if Rommel wanted to come out and chase him. Jack rubbed Rommel's side. "Your buddy's here, boy." Rommel whimpered but didn't wake up. Dreaming of chasing tennis balls on the beach, no doubt.

"Looks like you have it pretty sweet now, Jack. Place looks good, except for that hole in the bathroom door. No wife, no kids. Great dog. Do whatever you want. No more going out to sea. Must have sucked at the end, though, that mast with Zach Taylor."

"Yeah." Jack said.

The tomcat jumped off the deck and disappeared. Rommel woke up, slid off the couch, and went downstairs to the den.

Buzz looked at his watch, a Breitling that Jenny had bought him when he made squadron skipper. "Dog of yours has more sense than we do. You got a real bed I can sleep in?"

"Master bedroom, top floor. All made up for you. Clean sheets and everything. Can you get up the stairs okay?"

"I'll yell if I have any problems."

Buzz made it up the stairs by himself, but it was a close thing.

★   ★   ★   ★   ★

They sat on the back deck, drinking strong coffee and watching the morning mist lift off the bay, Rommel stretched out between them.

Buzz sniffed his coffee. "Just the thing to burn off the alcohol fog before I see Admiral Taylor. Good thing I packed eye drops."

A cardinal flew by. Jack and Rommel saw it. Jack turned to point it out to Buzz, but Buzz was staring at the bay, like he was looking for something out there but didn't know what.

Buzz finished his coffee and looked at his Breitling. "Nine thirty. What is it, forty minutes from here to the AIRLANT building?"

"About that."

"Better get moving then," Buzz said. "Don't want to be late for my date with destiny."

"Don't give Admiral Taylor my regards."

"Don't worry, I won't."

Buzz showered and dressed and came back downstairs in a fresh set of summer khakis, NFO wings and ribbons on his chest, his captain's eagles on his collar. Jack walked him to his car and they shook hands.

"Well, I'm off to the crusades," Buzz said. "Wish me luck."

"So long, Buzz."

Buzz pulled out of the driveway. Jack waved. Buzz waved back through the Volvo's sunroof and drove away.

Jack went up to the master bedroom and pulled the sheets off the bed, and went into the bathroom to get the wet towels. A drawer in the vanity was half open. Buzz must have been looking for toothpaste or something else he'd forgotten to pack. His hands full of sheets and towels, Jack lifted a knee to knock the drawer shut, and saw the lavender envelope he'd put there months earlier. He dropped the sheets and towels and took the envelope from the drawer, and opened it.

Sweetheart,

I know what I did was wrong. I have a problem with money like some people have with drugs. I forged your name on all those credit card applications, and things got out of control. I wanted to tell you so many times, but I was afraid to.

I thought and thought and thought how to make things right, and I could only think of one.

I love you forever,

Betty

★ ★ ★ ★ ★

Jack had gotten in the habit of mowing his neighbors' grass that summer. The lawns were so small in his beach neighborhood it seemed a shame not to take care of everyone at the same time, once he had the lawnmower out and started. Everybody's grass stayed the same length that way. Some of the neighbors started asking if they could pay him for it, and if he could do odd jobs around their houses, what with all his experience from fixing up his own house.

Shortly after Buzz's visit, Jack bought a used pick-up truck and started a one-man landscaping and handyman business.

On the first Sunday in September, when the afternoon football games were over, Jack sat with Rommel on the back deck, listening to jazz float out the window from the speakers in the living room, and watched Buzz Rucci's *Fillmore* battle group transit seaward through the Chesapeake Bay.

As the sun met the horizon, way up to the north as it did that time of year in Virginia, Jack checked the time on his Omega, and thought of Betty.

And the rest of them.

ABOUT THE AUTHOR

Over the course of his 20-year naval career, Jeff Huber commanded an E-2C Hawkeye aircraft squadron and served as operations officer of a carrier air wing and an aircraft carrier. He deployed to both the Atlantic and Pacific Fleet areas of operation, and participated in Operation Southern Watch and the Kosovo Conflict. In all, Jeff sailed aboard ten different aircraft carriers. When stationed ashore—a rare occurrence—Jeff served as a flight and air tactics instructor.

Jeff's satires and analyses of military and foreign policy affairs have appeared in *Proceedings*, *The Navy*, *Aviation Week*, Reuters, Uruknet, and other print and web outlets. Several of his essays have been required student reading at the U.S. Naval War College. He is a contributing editor with ePluribus Media and writes a weekly op-ed column for *Military.com*.

His interests include music, literature, visual arts, sports, animals and home improvement. He is a graduate of Valparaiso University (BA), Ohio University (MFA) and the U.S. Naval War College (MA). He currently lives in Virginia, where he writes, works on his house, and plays with his dogs.

KÜNATI

MADicine
■ Derek Armstrong

What happens when an engineered virus, meant to virally lobotomize psychopathic patients, is let loose on the world? Only Bane and his new partner, Doctor Ada Kenner, can stop this virus of rage.

■ "In his follow-up to the excellent *The Game*.... Armstrong blends comedy, parody, and adventure in genuinely innovative ways." *The Last Troubadour* —*Booklist*

■ "Tongue-in-cheek thriller." *The Game* —*Library Journal*

US\$ 24.95 | Pages 352, cloth hardcover
ISBN 978-1-60164-017-8 | EAN: 9781601640178

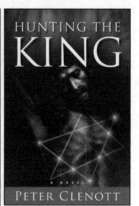

Bathtub Admirals
■ Jeff Huber

Are the armed forces of the world's only superpower really run by self-serving "Bathtub Admirals"? Based on a true story of military incompetence.

■ "Witty, wacky, wildly outrageous...A remarkably accomplished book, striking just the right balance between ridicule and insight." —*Booklist*

US\$ 24.95
Pages 320, cloth hardcover
ISBN 978-1-60164-019-2
EAN 9781601640192

Belly of the Whale
■ Linda Merlino

Terrorized by a gunman, a woman with cancer vows to survive and regains her hope and the will to live.

■ "A riveting story, both powerful and poignant in its telling. Merlino's immense talent shines on every page."
—*Howard Roughan,*
Bestselling Author

US\$ 19.95
Pages 208, cloth hardcover
ISBN 978-1-60164-018-5
EAN 9781601640185

Hunting the King
■ Peter Clenott

An intellectual thriller about the most coveted archeological find of all time: the tomb of Jesus.

■ "Fans of intellectual thrillers and historical fiction will find a worthy new voice in Clenott... Given such an auspicious start, the sequel can't come too soon."
—*ForeWord*

US\$ 24.95
Pages 384, cloth hardcover
ISBN 978-1-60164-148-9
EAN 9781601641489

Callous
■ T K Kenyon

A routine missing person call turns the town of New Canaan, Texas, inside out as claims of Satanism, child abuse and serial killers clash, and a radical church prepares for Armageddon and the Rapture. Part thriller, part crime novel, *Callous* is a dark and funny page-turner.

■ "Kenyon is definitely a keeper." *Rabid*, STARRED REVIEW, —*Booklist*
■ "Impressive." *Rabid*, —*Publishers Weekly*

US$ 24.95 | Pages 384, cloth hardcover
ISBN 978-1-60164-022-2 | EAN: 9781601640222

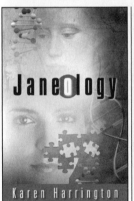

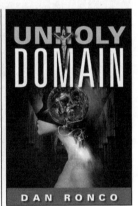

Janeology
■ Karen Harrington

Tom is certain he is living the American dream. Until one day in June, the police tell him the unthinkable—his wife has drowned their toddler son.

■ "Harrington begins with a fascinating premise and develops it fully. Tom and his wife emerge as compelling, complexly developed individuals."
—*Booklist*

US$ 24.95
Pages 256, cloth hardcover
ISBN 978-1-60164-020-8
EAN 9781601640208

Miracle MYX
■ Dave Diotalevi

For an unblinking forty-two hours, Myx's synesthetic brain probes a lot of dirty secrets in Miracle before arriving at the truth.

■ "What a treat to be in the mind of Myx Amens, the clever, capable, twice-dead protagonist who is full of surprises."
—*Robert Fate*, *Academy Award winner*

US$ 24.95
Pages 288, cloth hardcover
ISBN 978-1-60164-155-7
EAN 9781601641557

Unholy Domain
■ Dan Ronco

A fast-paced techno-thriller depicts a world of violent extremes, where religious terrorists and visionaries of technology fight for supreme power.

■ "A solid futuristic thriller."
—*Booklist*
■ "Unholy Domain...top rate adventure, sparkling with ideas."
—*Piers Anthony*

US$ 24.95
Pages 352, cloth hardcover
ISBN 978-1-60164-021-5
EAN 9781601640215

KÜNATI

Provocative. Bold. Controversial.

Kunati hot titles

Available at your favorite bookseller

www.kunati.com

- -

The Last Troubadour
Historical fiction by Derek Armstrong

Against the flames of a rising medieval Inquisition, a heretic, an atheist and a pagan are the last hope to save the holiest Christian relic from a sainted king and crusading pope. Based on true events.

- "... brilliance in which Armstrong blends comedy, parody, and adventure in genuinely innovative ways." *Booklist*

US$ 24.95 | Pages 384, cloth hardcover
ISBN-13: 978-1-60164-010-9
ISBN-10: 1-60164-010-2
EAN: 9781601640109

- -

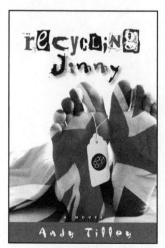

Recycling Jimmy
A cheeky, outrageous novel by Andy Tilley

Two Manchester lads mine a local hospital ward for "clients" as they launch Quitters, their suicide-for-profit venture in this off-the-wall look at death and modern life.

- "Energetic, imaginative, relentlessly and unabashedly vulgar." *Booklist*
- "Darkly comic story unwinds with plenty of surprises." *ForeWord*

US$ 24.95 | Pages 256, cloth hardcover
ISBN-13: 978-1-60164-013-0
ISBN-10: 1-60164-013-7
EAN 9781601640130

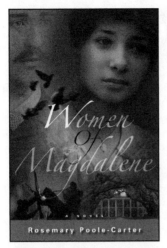

Women Of Magdalene
A hauntingly tragic tale of the old South by Rosemary Poole-Carter

An idealistic young doctor in the post-Civil War South exposes the greed and cruelty at the heart of the Magdalene Ladies' Asylum in this elegant, richly detailed and moving story of love and sacrifice.

■ "A fine mix of thriller, historical fiction, and Southern Gothic." *Booklist*

■ "A brilliant example of the best historical fiction can do." *ForeWord*

US$ 24.95 | Pages 288, cloth hardcover
ISBN-13: 978-1-60164-014-7
ISBN-10: 1-60164-014-5 | EAN: 9781601640147

On Ice
A road story like no other, by Red Evans

The sudden death of a sad old fiddle player brings new happiness and hope to those who loved him in this charming, earthy, hilarious coming-of-age tale.

■ "Evans' humor is broad but infectious ... Evans uses offbeat humor to both entertain and move his readers." *Booklist*

US$ 19.95 | Pages 208, cloth hardcover
ISBN-13: 978-1-60164-015-4
ISBN-10: 1-60164-015-3
EAN: 9781601640154

Truth Or Bare
Offbeat, stylish crime novel by Richard Cahill

The characters throb with vitality, the prose sizzles in this darkly comic page-turner set in the sleazy world of murderous sex workers, the justice system, and the rich who will stop at nothing to get what they want.

■ "Cahill has introduced an enticing character ... Let's hope this debut novel isn't the last we hear from him." *Booklist*

US$ 24.95 | Pages 304, cloth hardcover
ISBN-13: 978-1-60164-016-1
ISBN-10: 1-60164-016-1
EAN: 9781601640161

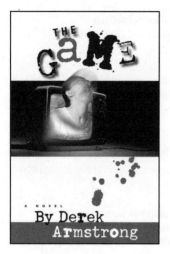

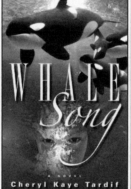

The Secret Ever Keeps
A novel by Art Tirrell

An aging Godfather-like billionaire tycoon regrets a decades-long life of "shady dealings" and seeks reconciliation with a granddaughter who doesn't even know he exists. A sweeping adventure across decades—from Prohibition to today—exploring themes of guilt, greed and forgiveness.

■ "Riveting ... Rhapsodic ... Accomplished." *ForeWord*

US$ 24.95
Pages 352, cloth hardcover
ISBN 978-1-60164-004-8
EAN 9781601640048
LCCN 2006930185

Toonamint of Champions
A wickedly allegorical comedy by Todd Sentell

Todd Sentell pulls out all the stops in his hilarious spoof of the manners and mores of America's most prestigious golf club. A cast of unforgettable characters, speaking a language only a true son of the South could pull off, reveal that behind the gates of fancy private golf clubs lurk some mighty influential freaks.

■ "Bubbly imagination and wacky humor." *ForeWord*

US$ 19.95
Pages 192, cloth hardcover
ISBN 978-1-60164-005-5
EAN 9781601640055
LCCN 2006930186

Mothering Mother
A daughter's humorous and heartbreaking memoir.
Carol D. O'Dell

Mothering Mother is an authentic, "in-the-room" view of a daughter's struggle to care for a dying parent. It will touch you and never leave you.

■ "Beautiful, told with humor... and much love." *Booklist*

■ "I not only loved it, I lived it. I laughed, I smiled and shuddered reading this book." Judith H. Wright, author of over 20 books.

US$ 19.95
Pages 208, cloth hardcover
ISBN 978-1-60164-003-1
EAN 9781601640031
LCCN 2006930184

Rabid
A novel by T K Kenyon

A sexy, savvy, darkly funny tale of ambition, scandal, forbidden love and murder. Nothing is sacred. The graduate student, her professor, his wife, her priest: four brilliantly realized characters spin out of control in a world where science and religion are in constant conflict.

■ "Kenyon is definitely a keeper." STARRED REVIEW, *Booklist*

US$ 26.95 | Pages 480, cloth hardcover
ISBN 978-1-60164-002-4 | EAN: 9781601640024
LCCN 2006930189